ELAINE TAYLOR

FINAL BETRAYAL

A 25-inch television was centered on the middle shelf; a boom box with CD player and dual tape deck to the left. Below were a VCR and a collection of porn films. Atop the VCR was an empty cardboard tape jacket. Catherine pushed the eject button. A tape slid from the VCR. No markings on the label.

She slid it back into the player and powered up the TV and the VCR. She held her breath and pressed *PLAY*. Screen fuzz was replaced by the image of a naked man and a naked woman, missionary position in a four-poster bed. She could see only body parts—the man's legs and buttocks, the woman's knees pulled wide, her hands stroking his back. No faces. But, it was Catherine's bedroom—Catherine's bed. She didn't have to read the credits to know the identity of the stars.

Fear fed anger. She shoved the tape into her briefcase, locked up, and vacated the premises.

FINAL BETRAYAL

ELAINE TAYLOR

ibooks

DISTRIBUTED BY PUBLISHERS GROUP WEST

A Publication of ibooks, inc.

Distributed by:
Publishers Group West
1700 Fourth Street, Berkeley, CA 94710
www.pgw.com

ibooks, Inc.
24 West 25th Street
New York, NY 10010

ISBN 1-59687-155-5
First ibooks, inc. printing November 2005
10 9 8 7 6 5 4 3 2 1

Printed in the U.S.A.

Acknowledgments

Learning to write fiction requires the guidance of drama gurus and the support of loyal beta-readers. For their assistance, I owe much to many people.

The extraordinary James N. Frey, author of the *How to Write A Damn Good Novel* series, has been my mentor and friend for more than a decade, reading my early twaddle, banging me over the head, and screaming, "Conflict! Every scene has to have conflict!" until my characters began to figure it out for themselves. I would not be a writer of suspense had it not been for Jim's tireless teaching.

Three other writer-teachers also provided immeasurable assistance to my progress: best-selling author Elizabeth George, who passed on some of her genius for "characters with attitude" and "going where it makes you uncomfortable" at her Mystery Writing Intensive; Robert Crais, whose taut thrillers are sublime examples of the "pacing" lecture he delivered at The Book Passage Mystery Writers' Conference; and, Hollywood "Story Seminar" instructor Robert McKee, who consistently lives up to his reputation as a "legend" among writing instructors.

Berkeley book-doc Barbara McHugh, The B Group writers (including Cara Black, author of the Aimee Leduc series), my agent, Elizabeth Pomada, and my editor, Marianne Paul provided invaluable commentary and support. And then there are the "early readers," whom I should pay to destroy the first drafts to which they were subjected: Judy and Jim Paire, Jackie Autry, Donnatella Sigmund, Denise Kemp, Shannon Vowell, Kasey Sixt, and Pauline Chabot.

To Russell Leiman, the friend and lover who warms my heart and makes me laugh—long may it last. And most of all to Chris Jorgensen, whose lifetime of support, critical commentary, and unflagging belief in me opened the doors to places I never thought I would go.

To Chrissie, the most remarkable woman I know.

Prologue: Monday Night

Second muzzle flash. Quick snap and burn in his abdomen—no more than a bee sting, really—and, bah-de-bing, Stephen Forsster conceded the situation had headed south faster than the Dow Jones on Black Monday; but he never for an instant considered he might actually die.

Two minutes before, he'd been settled against the driver's door, wedged between the steering wheel and seat back, right knee cocked across the soft curve of the leather console. His big black Mercedes lounged on a bluff high above the Pacific Ocean. Milky stretches of beach fanned out far below. Moonlight surfed the troughs and peaks of frothy waves. Breakers crashed on sand and drowned the buzz of traffic on the Coast Highway that snaked the hilltop a hundred yards above.

"Come on, ace," Stephen cajoled in the direction of the shadowed profile. "You already raked in your dividends. Now that it's my turn to do a little profit-taking, you're soiling your Depends like some Joe-lite who yanks his buck-fifty out of the market every time the NAS-DAQ drops six points."

His agitated companion flicked him a quick glare, shoved open the car door, and lunged out, retreating down the gravel path, pale trench coat flapping.

Fishy-smelling salt air whistled through the sunroof, feathering Stephen's hair. He sighed and reclined his head against the car window, disgustedly reaffirming his belief that "people" were the one investment that invariably paid a lousy return.

In the bright moonlight, a flash of khaki crossed his peripheral vision; a face appeared above the open sunroof.

"Ahhh... a change of heart? Or did you come back to suck my dick?" Stephen asked with a slow-growing smirk. He lifted the end of his tie and flopped it over his shoulder.

"Suck this, asshole." A pale sleeve blurred upward and a gun barrel reflected moonglow.

"Hey!" Stephen jerked forward, banging his ribs on the steering wheel, palms outstretched protectively.

The blast punched his chest and cut off his words. Stink of cordite filled the car.

He slowly dropped his chin. Studied the dark flecks that speckled his monogrammed cuffs... the inky stain that crawled across pale blue Egyptian cotton. He slow-motion pressed his hand against the fabric. Warm blood tickled and webbed the backs of his fingers.

Stephen looked up to the fingertip hooked around the trigger—anticipated another blast; but the world downshifted to freeze-frame while his mind hurtled forward like an out-of-synch movie where the actor's words are heard before his lips have formed them.

Confusion creased his brow. He wanted to say, "This was a very expensive shirt."

The muzzle flashed again.

Bee sting. No actual pain, but... perhaps it was time to send out a mayday?

He closed his eyes and forced his mind to calm. He couldn't be dying. He didn't hurt anywhere and there weren't any tunnels of bright white light luring him to the "other side." Wasn't that the way it was supposed to happen? Here in California, at least? A wry grin tugged his lips.

He opened his eyes. The gun and the khaki coat were gone.

Thank God. Now he'd be all right. He was too hot—too *cool*,—to die. Another twitch at the corners of his mouth. Yeah, man, the world needed him... and he just needed to wait. Give that gun-toting maniac time to reach the highway. Then he could safely book on home.

Mellow out, he silently instructed as he hummed a few bars of "The Real Slim Shady" and reconfirmed his future existence with a mental rundown of tomorrow's calendar. His investment firm was IPO'ing a hot biotech company in the morning and he had to be at the office before the opening bell. And that new blonde receptionist in the law office downstairs—she was on his calendar for a late lunch. He planned to fuck her after the market closed.

He smiled weakly. Yeah, he would come out of this just fine. Just like he always did.

But man, was he whacked. His eyes gazed upward, dazzled by the silvery moonbeams that stretched to embrace him. He focused his attention on that foxy little receptionist, certain a fantasy would give him a lift.

She always wore those form-fitting sweaters that emphasized her young, firm breasts. He pondered the size and tint of her nipples, wondered how they would taste, tried to imagine them rigid against the fur of his chest. Expected to feel the image stir his ever-primed penis. Was surprised that it didn't. Instead, he felt heavy. Lethargic. Like when he'd sat weighted down in those steaming Calistoga mud baths Lili used to drag him to when they were first married.

Vague movement caught his attention. Something thumped his brow. The back of his head smacked the window and he tasted warm, coppery blood.

Okay. That's it. Time to go. Get home before the kids go to bed. He wanted to ask Jared about his soccer tryout... hear Stephie play that new piece on her cello. Mozart? He thought it was.

He tried to reach for the key in the ignition. Too tired. Bummer. Wished he had some blow. Give him the jolt he needed. But he didn't do drugs anymore. Not for two years. No uppers in the console—not even a cigarette. He'd given up most of his vices for Lili.

Uh-oh. Lili. She had some fundraiser thing tonight and he'd promised to be home for dinner with the kids.

He tried to check his watch, but his arm hung limp. Disconnected.

Now he *was* getting worried. He started to call for help, but then hesitated. What if he really *was* badly hurt? What if he had to go to the hospital? Lili would find that stuff in his briefcase. Shit. That would be the end. She would leave him—would take their children... and fifty percent of his net worth. Panic burbled. He couldn't let that happen.

He couldn't let Lili find out about those other women. She'd never understand they were just... a hobby. Especially since some of them were her friends. And that sex therapist. The one Lili insisted he see. Oh yeah, he saw her all right. Wrote a check to her every week, but instead of curing him of his all-consuming fixation, she'd spent the last three sessions sucking his balls while he spanked her bare ass with a metal ruler because she was a bad girl.

The irony made him chuckle. But Lili wouldn't see the humor.

His thoughts began to slow. Like the pulse that thumped in his ears.

Have to get home. Pretend nothing happened. Don't upset the kids.

He stared up at the full moon. It smiled. Like Lili when she was happy. It moved against him... leaned to caress him... kissed his lips with Lili's warm, soft mouth. He sighed. Closed his eyes. Contented.

It would be all right. Lili would forgive him.

Chapter One: Tuesday

The cell phone blurped out the first five notes of "*Home, Home on the Range...*" Catherine adjusted the mouthpiece of her headset in preparation for the auto-answer feature that would open the line after the second ring.

She quickly cornered through the amber traffic light and crunched the brake to prevent her big Rover from doing a Jurassic-style munch of the diminutive BMW tail inches from her front bumper guard, while she simultaneously grabbed for her suede satchel as it slid to the edge of the passenger seat and regurgitated a four-inch stack of contracts onto the floorboard. The FedEx containing the two cutout photos of Stephen Forsster—stretched atop an unidentifiable female, wearing nothing but his wedding ring and a light sheen of perspiration—plopped unceremoniously onto the heap. She sighed, shook her head in resignation, and mouthed the words, "*...where the deer and the antelope play...*" in time with the second ring of the cell. Seven A.M. Lazy fog swirled among the glare of brake lights strung over the crest of Folsom Street and bathed San Francisco in a subtle veil of *eau de fish-brine.*

She announced, "Catherine Calabretta," when the answer-light clicked from red to green.

"James Richardson Harris just phoned to complain that he's been unable to check his account balances this morning."

Catherine recognized—was in fact expecting—the aristocratic enunciation of Z. Winfield Edwardes.

"'James Richardson Harris.' Whew," Catherine whistled softly. "Y'all all go by three names up there in New Hampshire? Does anybody ever call him 'Jimmy Dick' for short?" She paused a beat. "Nah. Prob'ly not."

"How much longer?" he asked tightly. Catherine heard a soft clink in the background and imagined him raising a delicate porcelain teacup to his lips, little finger crooked in a style he would find natural.

"I talked to my vp of security administration five minutes ago," she said. "They're restoring from archived files and targeting to have your systems back online before noon, your time."

"Noon?" He sounded both alarmed and indignant. "And what, in the meantime, am I supposed to tell Mr. Harris—and the rest of the bank's clients, for that matter?"

Catherine yanked a sharp left onto Third Street the FedEx envelope slid and clunked against the passenger door, tipping out one of the photos of Stephen, alabaster butt aglow in sharp contrast to the mat of dark hair on his back and legs.

"Tell them you did a system upgrade last night and there was some kind of hardware glitch—you've got all your best techs working on it, et cetera, et cetera. Ten to one, they'll shrug, brush imaginary lint off their brocade smoking jackets, and summon their respective butlers to put a flame to their hand-rolled Cuban cigars."

The telephone line was silent except for the cross-country static.

"I can't lie to James Harris. We've been friends since first grade at Country Day."

"Okay, then. Tell him a cracker who calls himself Robin Hood hacked through your flimsy-ass firewall like a herd of Black Angus through a lace curtain. That he electronically redistributed eight hundred and forty million dollars from corporate ledgers into personal checking accounts, churning your data like a roto-tiller preps a field for the spring plant."

A moment of electrified silence. "Why would anyone do this to us?"

"Same reason any hacker does," She said. to prove he can."

He sounded forlorn. "My ancestors founded this bank on this very site in 1799. It's withstood acts of man and acts of God, but now a computer is going to bring it all to an end."

Catherine resisted the impulse to tell him to suck it up and instead said, "First of all, this is an act of man, and not a computer rebelliously taking your general ledger into its own hands—so to speak. Secondly, you've got the best techies in the business putting your shop back in order. By this time next week, none of your clients will even remember there was an outage."

"This isn't a mere outage." His baritone voice took on a perceptible screech. "And I can't deceive the bank's customers. The very foundation of this enterprise is 'rectitude, veneration, and tradition',—everyone in town understands that. The words are carved in the marble arch above the main entry. They've been there for one hundred and thirty-seven years."

"Wow." Catherine inched forward, fifteen idling cars between her and the entrance to the Moscone Convention Center garage. "The town where I grew up? In East Texas? People couldn't even define those words... and a lot of 'em still can't count that high."

"Those are tenets to live by, Ms. Calabretta, not mere words my great grandfather learned at Harvard business school," he said, voice restored to stoic baritone.

Catherine rolled her eyes skyward. Obviously her sense of reverence fell short of his expectations.

"Well, I never went to business school, Mr. Edwardes. I developed my 'tenets' at my grandmama's knee when she recounted her tactic for feeding her five little kids during the Great Depression. Said she stopped shooing the white-tailed deer out of her cornfield and instead fattened them and lured them to a salt lick she set up eighty yards from a deer blind. Stood guard all night every night to keep poachers away, and by day she sold hunting rights to your *compadres* from the white-glove crowd... what was left of 'em. Two dollars a deer and five dollars for any buck with a rack bigger than eight points. Know what she called her entrepreneurial enterprise?"

He responded with silence.

"The Buck Stops Here."

More silence followed by, "Is your penchant for fabrication as ingrained as your penchant for folklore?"

"True story except for the name, of course; but it kinda works, don't you think?"

He didn't miss a beat. "Your company did a security analysis of our systems last fall. Why didn't you warn us about our vulnerability?"

"Page one," she replied cryptically. "Computer Network Security Assessment for Edwardes Bank of New England. Completed November fourteenth and presented to EBNE on November sixteenth. Two months and nineteen days ago. I suggest you re-read the sections on password authentication and intrusion detection."

"I'll check with Robert," he replied stiffly, referring to his CIO. "I haven't seen the report."

"Yeah, well, Bobby-boy's bowels were in quite an uproar when he 911'd us at two A.M. this morning, left coast time. I suspect he may have taken that report to the outhouse to backfill his t.p. supply."

Silence. "You have such a way with the English language, Ms. Calabretta."

"I'm even snappier with ones and zeros," she said, wondering if binary code had yet been developed back when Z. Winfield was per-ambulating the Harvard quad.

"Should I assume there will be many zeros in the fee you charge for this debacle?"

"We'd have a hard time staying in business on the deluge of love you're sending our way, Mr. E. I'll update you every hour until you're back online," she said and disconnected after his prim, "Goodbye."

Catherine rolled down the Moscone ramp and braked adjacent to the sign that read, *WELCOME! Y2K Pacific Rim Technology Conference VIPs—Valet Parking*, cut the engine of her Rover, and abruptly silenced Willie Nelson's lament about Georgia-on-his-mind. Tires squealed and echoed in the recesses of the parking structure as she scooped up and stuffed contracts and the FedEx containing the naked Stephen Forsster pictures back into the satchel. In the elevator, she inspected her reflection in the chrome doors—moved to the left six inches to dispel the funhouse effect that added two sizes to the width of her womanly hips—smoothed her shoulder-length auburn hair, and straightened red cashmere blazer over ebony silk dress. A quick turn of calves confirmed there were no runs in her black stockings and that her shoes were actual mates.

Humph. No matter that the personal image consultant said she looked sophisticated enough to be the chairman of Chase Manhattan, Catherine felt like a Piney Bluff hog caller who'd undergone a Neiman Marcus makeover. Others might be fooled by the spit-shine, but Catherine knew the truth: just because you hosed the pig shit off your boots that didn't mean you were no longer a hog caller.

One elevator flight up, she flashed her exhibitor's badge at the uniformed security guard and walked through the wide metal doors of Moscone Convention Center, into the world of the Y2K Pacific Rim Technology Conference. The clanging and hammering of crews creating booths out of portable components and the smell of new carpet, printer's ink, and wooden packing crates refocused Catherine's attention on the events that lay ahead.

She felt the thrill of being here—the overwhelming pride, and the remnants of disbelief that she had germinated ETC, Emerging Technology Consultants, from her passion for her work. She'd certainly never intended—or wanted—to be a CEO with an expectant board of directors and a multimillion dollar monthly payroll to meet. But she'd discovered a natural talent for computers back in the mid-eighties when eight megs of RAM was considered an impressive system, and subsequently, while working as a programmer at Boeing in Washington some fifteen years prior, she had stumbled into the information security arena before it was recognized as a "business opportunity." Now, doubts of her ability to nurture ETC—her fear of failing the 320 employees who looked to her for leadership and, more importantly, the bimonthly paychecks that put tofu on their dinner tables and stock options into their kids' college funds—frequently caused her to bolt upright in the middle of the night, heart pounding and mind racing. But on occasions such as this, walking into the West Coast's premier tech conference, she was painfully proud that she had created an elite consulting company that was acknowledged alongside the Microsofts, the Intels, and the Ciscos of the computer industry.

She looked toward the east, as the event map directed, to locate the ETC booth. Her gaze was snagged by ten-foot-tall silk replicas of the two-week-old *BusinessWeek* cover that featured her face beside the headline, "Guardian of Privacy."

"Oh, yuck!" Embarrassment crawled onto her cheeks and slowed her step. This wasn't what she'd been expecting—it was so different than the tiny little proofs the ad agency had circulated for sign-off. These things—her face!—Were so *biiiig*. Humongous. Looming over the convention floor. A covert glance at other companies' displays in their various phases of completion confirmed Catherine's first impression: Among the tastefully eye-catching branding images, ETC's campaign screamed, "Look at Catherine! Isn't she special!"

Catherine picked up her pace, careening around hammer-wielding set-up crews, slick-haired sales reps, and white-socked technology geeks, reaching the ETC booth just as the third banner inched past half-mast on its way up the display pole.

"Y'all stop right there," Catherine called to the ponytailed waif of a man who was balanced on a ten-foot ladder, intent on raising the furl of silk. "Take it down."

From his perch, he glanced over his shoulder and smiled recognition. "Hey, Catherine."

"How's it going..." What was this kid's name? He was the crew chief in charge of convention installations for the ad agency that did all of ETC's promo. Ray. That was it. "Ray, I've got a problem with the display."

He glanced at the crinkled, drooping banner. "Oh, don't worry. It's not finished. Wrinkles will be gone—it'll be straight and smooth and waft beautifully when I've secured it."

Catherine dropped her suede satchel and her laptop in a heap at her feet, and pulled her cell phone free. "No, that's not it." She heard her partner, Sam Princeton, call her name as he sauntered toward the booth carrying a steaming styrofoam cup. She greeted Sam while she punched numbers on the phone pad.

"What's the problem?" Sam asked, arms crossed over a pink Oxford button-down. Khaki Dockers were pressed-and-creased. Thin, carrot-colored hair was streaked with comb tracks like a freshly furrowed field.

"I don't like it." She nodded toward the banners and pressed the phone against her ear. "It's not what I expected. I can't believe I let them talk me into this campaign," she said, referring to the creative team who had sold the idea. "'...Capitalize on the *BusinessWeek* exposure'...'build brand recognition'...'generate additional revenues to increase pre-IPO value'...," she mimicked as the phone rang in her ear. "See what happens when you let a bunch of Madison Avenue tadpoles mess with your mission?"

"Which mission would that be?" Sam needled as he sipped cautiously.

She eyed him for a moment before she responded. "Contrary to your opinion, Sam, I'm not out to convince the world that I'm the only lightbulb in Vegas." She hung up and punched a different number into the cell.

"Bet you would have liked it fine if they'd put you astride a silver stallion, waving a ten-gallon hat."

Sam had become increasingly hostile since the electric company meltdown eighteen months earlier when ETC employed their digital immune system software to identify and remove a network virus that had shut down a power grid which had supplied energy to one million Bay-area residents. The publicity generated by the incident catapulted Catherine from obscure computer geek running an anonymous little consulting firm, to "the name that is synonymous with computer security." She hated the attention; Sam coveted it.

Ray, the crew chief, had come down from his high-ladder job. Phone still pressed to her ear, Catherine addressed Ray and ignored Sam.

"I thought I signed off on little bitty posters," she held her thumb and forefinger two inches apart, "maybe something you'd stick to the wall back there." She pointed.

Just then, Catherine's assistant, Aida Ortega, said, "Hello?" into the phone. Catherine stuffed a fingertip into her right ear.

"I'm at the convention center and I hate this display. It's gotta go— and it's gotta go fast." She quickly rattled off instructions for Aida to roust an ETC team to pick up previously used displays from a warehouse and rush them to the convention center for immediate installation.

The blue-tee-shirted installation crew stared in disbelief, silently polling each other before looking to Sam for intervention.

"The show opens in less than three hours, Catherine. You can't be serious."

"I'm about as serious as a rattlesnake chomped on your butt."

Ray was a statue, his eyes masking the emotions he felt probably should remain unexpressed in the presence of a large-revenue client.

Sam clenched his lips into a tight line. "Why don't we get another opinion before we start demolishing a very expensive display?" As he finished the sentence, his gaze shifted over Catherine's shoulder and he deadpanned, "Oh, hurray. The Mod Squad's here."

Catherine turned to the threesome: Joel Hodges, ETC's vp of security architecture, prissy, five-ten frame impeccably attired in monochromatic taupe shirt-and-suit, laptop shoulder strap producing a leftward list, flaxen-streaked light-brown hair carefully gelled to look slightly mussed; Linda Gordie, vp security administration, spiky platinum bangs framing sky-blue eyes and rosy cheeks, A marathon runner's body decked in straight-legged jeans and a sweatshirt with a rendering of Dirty Harry and his .357, framed on top by the words, "Tell me a blonde joke," and on the bottom, "Make my day," cell phone pressed to her ear, and Wilson Ramsey, ex-juvie hall resident, firewall guru-in-training, ubiquitous black shades obscuring stoic golden eyes, shaved scalp the color of liquid chocolate, onyx cashmere turtleneck tucked into pleated onyx pants. A buff six-five with the rhythm of a Ninja.

Catherine greeted her handpicked team, three of the nation's best techies.

Joel pointed to the semi-installed *BusinessWeek* banners. "Are we supposed to genuflect... or just kiss your ring?"

Catherine eyed Ray. "Take them down," she said before flicking a dispassionate gaze at Sam. She turned back to the trio. "What's happening on the Robin Hood hack?"

Linda Gordie folded her cell phone and responded. "The systems have been restored from back-ups. The first test was good. They should be online within the hour."

"Yes!" Catherine pumped her fist into the air.

"Exciting news?" The question floated across the ETC crew, delivered by a nasal, unfamiliar voice.

Catherine swiveled to identify the speaker, a pudgy, baby-faced twenty-something sporting a UCLA sweatshirt over rumpled Levi's; but the thing that put Catherine on full alert was the woman beside him, who was already snapping photos with an autowind Pentax. Catherine was alarmed that the man might have overheard her reference to Robin Hood.

He stuck out his hand. "Jerry Woodstock. *InfoTech* magazine." He thumbed toward his companion. "Melinda Allan, photographer on assignment with me." His gaze swept Catherine. "I've been following you." His voice was high-pitched, like Ross Perot.

"Not my favorite way to start a conversation," Catherine responded as she shook his hand. Palm cool; grasp perfunctory.

"You're on my interview schedule this morning. I wrote about you after you spoke at the senate hearings on Internet privacy four weeks ago." Thick glasses shrunk his eyes to buckshot.

"Yeah, who woulda guessed that defending everyone else's privacy would render my own as scarce as armadillos on a twelve-lane highway. Let me introduce you to some of our key folks."

She started with the techies—Joel, Linda, and Wilson—who were moving away to check out the computer system demo.

"And my partner, Sam Princeton." She fraternally laid her hand on Sam's shoulder. "He's ETC's CFO and CAO—oversees finance and admin. Wharton MBA. Owns half the company. Invaluable to our day-to-day operation."

"Actually I own 39 percent," Sam corrected as he shook Woodstock's hand. "Catherine has forty-seven—"

Catherine interrupted, curtailing Sam's penchant for coma-inducing minutiae, anxious to phone Z. Winfield Edwardes at EBNE with the good news about the restoration of his computer system. "Maybe y'all would like to spend a little time with Sam—learn more about ETC... our long-range plans... give me time to tie up a few loose ends." She glanced covertly at Sam. He looked pleased at the opportunity to share the limelight.

Jerry Woodstock opened a notebook, scribbled in green ink, and barely glanced at Sam. "With all due respect, MBAs are retro; tech gurus are the gods of the new millennium. Frankly, Sam, I doubt you could say anything that would impress my circulation department."

Sam stiffened and the color on his cheeks blossomed like a three-second time-lapse video of a peach going from pre-pubescent to overly ripe.

"Whoa, Sam!" Catherine responded, an element of warning in her tone. "I think we have before us the valedictorian of the Howard Stern School of Tact and Sensitivity."

"Nothing personal," Woodstock shrugged. "Our readers just don't read articles about... you know—bean-counter stuff. No offense."

"No problem," Sam responded tightly. "I already have a full schedule this morning... what with pencils to sharpen... paperclips to count... I'll leave you to your audience with Catherine the Great."

Sam stomped down the aisle toward the back of the cavernous convention center.

"Is one of us gonna need stitches after this interview?" Catherine asked.

Wiry curls brushed Woodstock's forehead as he glanced after Sam. "He's awfully testy. Word on the street is there's tension in the part-nership."

"Well, hell yes, there's tension. Did you ever string a barbed-wire fence, Jer?"

"Can't say that I have."

"Without tension, your fence posts fall down." She winked at him. "Besides, I bet you can be a little testy first thing in the morning. Before you've downed a double espresso, and taken a big ole crap..."

"There's also speculation that one of the reasons you're so zealous about Internet privacy is that you yourself have something to hide," Woodstock goaded as his photographer recorded reactions.

Catherine's thoughts leapt involuntarily to the naked Stephen-Forsster photos in her satchel, but she responded, "Back in the 1840s and '50's, the California high desert was strewn with the bleached-out bones of prospectors who wagered their lives on speculation." She looped her hand around Woodstock's arm and led him away. "Allow me to escort you to the press lounge where we can rustle up that espresso... find you a clean toilet. Get your attitude whipped into shape." Over her shoulder she said to her crew, "Y'all keep this herd out of the farmer's corn fields. I'll be back as soon as I can."

For over an hour, Catherine perched on a corner of the press room conference table, legs dangling in mid-air while she fielded questions from the various reporters and journalists queued up to interview her. And all the while, she silently maligned Sam for being so... so boring. It would have been the perfect partnership if he could be here in the press room preening for the media while she went about something—anything!—more productive.

When she saw Aida, her assistant, slip through the door displaying a folded note, Catherine waved her forward, interrupted a Sacramento *Bee* reporter, and read the cryptic, "back online without a hitch at 8:49 PST." She recognized Linda Gordie's scrawl, and she knew Z. Winfield Edwardes was probably faint with relief back there in frosty New Hampshire.

She took advantage of the interruption to terminate her session with the media hounds by enthusiastically inviting them to the conference keynote address she was scheduled to deliver in an hour. She slid down from the conference table perch, feeling as if the wood had stamped its imprint on her backside.

"How'd it go?" Aida asked when they were clear of media ears.

"Not a very cyber-savvy group—some of them probably think they can pick up a high-speed modem at Nordstrom. So instead of asking tech questions, they ask about my marriages—both of which were as

10

steamy as a two-year-old cowpie—and my teenage daughter, who claims she's fled all the way to Paris to get away from her domineering mother and the endless stream of questions about why she isn't studying computers." They navigated the main corridor between the numerous technology displays. "When are those brilliant men and women of journalism going to accept that my life is about as exciting as a fishing trip with the game warden. It ain't a headliner news story. Hallelujah and thank the gods."

They turned the corner toward the ETC booth. Catherine sighed with relief. The company logo flew in purples and greens above the brightly lit enclosure. Computer cases were closed; the staff wore an air of satisfaction. All was well in conventionland.

"Did someone set up my laptop?" Catherine asked Aida.

"Wilson was testing the projection system five minutes ago. Want to see what *The Chronicle* has to say about you this morning? You're on the front page."

Aida held out a newspaper folded in quarters. Catherine scoffed and waved it away.

"Fiction is for weekends in front of a fire. Do you have my satchel?"

Aida removed it from a locked cabinet and handed it to Catherine as she offered the paper once more. "This article seems pretty accurate."

"Here are the contracts I reviewed last night," Catherine pulled the stack from the satchel and handed them to Aida. "I modified the limitation of liabilities clauses in three of them and the third-party software warranties in another. Call up Bleedum, Screwum, and Reprise and tell them I'm deducting two grand off their most recent invoice, and that I expect to be added to their payroll if I have to continue functioning as my own legal counsel."

Catherine buckled the satchel and spun the combination lock, safeguarding the Stephen Forsster FedEx envelope that remained inside. At her office, later in the afternoon, she would check the mailroom's FedEx log to see who had signed out the label that was glued to the blue-and-orange package. She wanted to disprove Stephen's absurd notion that someone from ETC had been in possession of these *flagrante delicto* snapshots; that an ETC employee—namely Catherine—had sent them to Stephen as a subtle threat of blackmail. She would squelch his paranoia by discovering who from ETC had overnighted *something* to Stephen—marketing materials, product announcements—whatever; then he could figure out who—undoubtedly someone at his own company—had replaced those materials with the incriminating photos.

Catherine handed Aida the satchel with a "Would you keep this safe?" and brushed aside thoughts of Stephen Forsster with a mental "Later." She checked her watch and headed toward the conference auditorium.

The event crew clucked and fussed at the front of the room *Do you have everything you need? Is the podium where you want it?* Catherine reassured them and sent them on their way. Wilson Ramsey, not a speck of lint to despoil the blackness of his attire, greeted her at the dais. Convention attendees jockeyed for position among the two thousand chairs.

"This coyote ready to howl?" Catherine asked as she pressed the page-down key and watched images flick across the huge screen to her right.

"More like Pavarotti singing *Nessun dorma*," Wilson responded as he finished looping and stowing excess cable inside the podium.

At four minutes after ten, Catherine welcomed a packed house to the Sixth Annual Pacific Rim Tech Conference. As the assemblage settled and finally quieted, Catherine began.

"I'm going to talk about Internet privacy this morning, as I'm sure you're all anticipating, but first let's play a little word-association game. I'm going to list off some descriptors that we sometimes use to refer to various people and I'd like you to visualize a person who fits each characterization." She smiled out at the audience.

"Here we go." Catherine paused, and then slowly ticked off, "Tattooed Hell's Angel biker. Nationally renowned cardiac surgeon. Mensa member. Welfare mother. Poet."

"If you were going to choose one of those people to fall in love with, which would you choose?"

A pause. "Or how about this group: Philanthropist. Used car salesman. Recovering alcoholic. Chemical engineer who holds more than one hundred U.S. patents. Gourmet chef."

She gave them a moment to consider and then continued. "These two groups of characterizations actually 'define,' if you will, two individuals who I personally know. The first is Dr. Rose Merrill, formerly known as "Rosebud," who, at age fourteen tattooed, a Rebel flag on her ass, withdrew all the funds from her college-tuition savings account, bought herself a brand-spanking-new Harley Davidson, and convinced her boyfriend, Chainsaw, to acquire a forged driver's license in her name. At fifteen, she gave birth to a premature baby boy, Sartre, who had a heart malformation of some kind—Dr. Rose could give you the exact medical terminology. At sixteen, she was a welfare mother struggling to save her baby's life. She had a very high IQ, but no talents, no skills, no education... and she was not successful in that most important of missions. Sartre died when he was thirteen months old." Catherine continued somberly. "Rosebud pulled herself through her grief and reinvented her life.

"Second group of descriptors fit Rick Joshua, who had the great fortune of selling a seven-year-old Toyota to my friend Doreen Snyder Joshua. Rick was a has-been chemical engineer who prided himself in being a part-time used car salesman and a full-time alcoholic. When my red-haired, leggy friend Doreen visited the car lot where Rick worked twelve years ago, he had more on his mind than a sales commission. He asked her out; she thought he was cute. But on their second date, after Rick downed five Jack Daniels straight-up, he laughed and told her, 'if alcohol is a crutch, Jack Daniels is a wheelchair,' yuck-yuck-yuck..." Catherine waited for the laughter to die. "Doreen took his keys. While she drove him home, she told him about her husband and five-year-old son who had been killed by a drunk driver three years before... and she told Rick it had been fun but she wasn't going to see him any more."

Catherine pressed a key on the laptop and smiled as she said, "All y'all brainy computer geeks have already guessed how that story trotted along to its happy ending.

"So why am I beginning a techno-presentation with this little human-side exercise?" She scanned solemn faces. "To remind us all that people are complex. We're all very complex. And no matter how astute we consider ourselves to be at developing 'first impressions,' it takes a really long time to get to know someone."

She glanced at notes illuminated by the podium lamp. "Details. Descriptors. Incidents reported out of context... do not a human being make."

"With today's easy access to very personal data, we're living as if there were a 24/7 web cam broadcasting the details of our lives, real-time, up close and personal, onto the Internet... but we don't even realize its lens is aimed in our direction.

"What can we, in the industry, do to advocate and staunchly protect the privacy of each and every individual?"

She spent the next twenty minutes talking about data encryption, intrusion prevention and detection, and other computer security strategies, and then segued back to personal privacy with, "Who is examining the digital 'you'?"

The audience sat motionless as Catherine continued. "I'm not talking about the things that we've *accepted* are no longer private domain: The D you pulled in Psych 101. The Visa bill you don't pay on time. Or even the sealed court files from your own personal summer of love when you and a friend got busted for smoking half a joint. In this day and age, we all expect those invasions into what we used to refer to as 'our private lives'. But how about this: If I access the digital data that exists about you, I can learn your favorite food, the books you read, whether or not you have a penchant for pornographic movies. I'll know if you like to go to Vegas and hit the slots; if you get along with your colleagues at work or if they find you an abrasive jerk; that you and your spouse have sought marriage counseling; that your teenage son has a substance-abuse problem. I'll know you're cheating on your mate and I'll know with whom. Your contraceptive of choice. Whether you're heterosexual or homosexual... or flexible in your preference. If you fight constipation or incontinence. That you've had your breasts augmented..."

Several people squirmed in their chairs.

"...that you have problems getting an erection. That you take anti-depressants and that you're driving on a suspended license."

Catherine shifted into a more conversational tone. "Last year, I applied for health insurance with a new carrier. You know how you have to fill out those questionnaires and disclose your medical history? Everything from gas pains to heart attacks? Well, I honestly and legitimately forgot to list the exploratory knee surgery I had eleven years ago. Forgot about it completely... until the new policy came back with a rider exempting coverage for knee injuries because of a 'pre-existing condition'." She silently scanned the audience. "Eleven years ago. In a different state. With a doctor whom I visited only for that injury and have never visited since."

Catherine toggled a key on the laptop and moved to the next slide. "Every time you make a charge on a credit card. Every phone number you dial. Every prescription you have filled—someone knows about them. Every time you swipe your employer's electronic access badge, drive through a Fastrak lane on the Golden Gate Bridge, withdraw a few greenbacks from an automated teller machine, step through the doors of a retail store—someone knows where you are... where you've been.

"And what about cyberspace fingerprints? How many 'cookies' have been surreptitiously deposited into your Web browser? How many e-marketers know where you go on the Net—what you read? What you buy—what you don't buy? With whom you communicate and what you say to each other." She raised a finger in caution. "Virtually every email you send or receive is archived in an ISP's data warehouse.

"Who has access to all this information? And what do they do with it?" She paused to let it sink in before she continued. "And this is only Y2K. How much privacy do you think you'll have left by 2010? 2012?

Movement at the left of the auditorium momentarily distracted Catherine. She flicked her eyes in the direction of the mini-cam news cameras just as two of them swiveled their aim toward the man who'd stepped inside the doublewide metal doors and settled against the wall. Catherine didn't recognize him as a scion of technology, but who could tell these days; he did look like an aging computer nerd—plaid green coat open over tan polyester shirt that covered a basketball belly. He raised a Coke can to his lips and squinted past the glare of the photographers' lights, making eye contact with Catherine from across the thirty feet that separated them. She turned her attention back to the audience.

"I'm gonna close this gig with a very profound quote from—of all people—Monica Lewinsky." Catherine smiled at the audience's amused response. "The quote is," she pressed the page-down key and read the words as they flashed on the screen. "'This is so *wrong*.'"

"When Monica said those words, she wasn't referring to the international humiliation heaped on her because of her Rubensesque figure and her big hair; or the fact she turned her girlish fantasy of consorting-with-the-king into a reality. No. While we all watched in bemusement, yucking it up about cigars and thongs, our duly elected officials ransacked Lewinsky's digital records, including her credit card statements, so they could learn and then publicly broadcast her list of personal book purchases. And then, my friends, my neighbors and my fellow human beings—*please* pay close attention to this. Government-sanctioned marauders performed the ultimate invasion of privacy: they secured unimpeded access to Monica Lewinsky's private thoughts. Please tolerate my repetition here because this is important. Her *private... thoughts...* as recorded on—but never mailed, emailed, or in any other fashion distributed from—her personal computer."

A camera flash caught Catherine's peripheral vision and she glanced at the man who had the attention of the news cameras. A reporter shoved a microphone under his chin; he shook his head once and brushed the mic away. The movement parted his jacket; a gun was holstered against his ribs. Catherine's heart skipped a beat. She truly hoped he was a cop and not some gunslinger out to make headlines for himself.

"Whatever you may think of Ms. Lewinsky or our former president, I implore you not to let this extreme and ultimate violation of private domain go unnoticed." Catherine powered off her laptop and continued. "As human beings, we're not all beautiful. We're not all smart, funny, or even interesting. But we are all, each and every one of us, complex; it takes more than a pile of digital droppings to define us."

"Think about that the next time, you design software or hardware." She smiled. "And the next time you vote."

She took a deep breath, thanked the audience for their time and invited them to visit the technology booths on the trade show floor.

The audience applauded. Aida, along with a surge of the curious, arrived at the stage as Catherine descended the steps.

Above the swell of miscellaneous conversations, Aida said, "Catherine, this is Tim Nyland." She indicated the pudgy, bright-faced man who slumped beside her. "He's a seventh grade computer instructor from Bakersfield, California, and these are some of his students. They asked if you would be willing to autograph their copies of *Business-Week*."

Catherine smiled at the half-dozen self-conscious thirteen-year-olds. "You guys haven't mistaken me for Britney Spears?" she asked and accepted a magazine and a felt-tip pen from a ponytailed girl.

"She is way uncool," the girl quipped, exposing parallel rows of plastic-fenced teeth. The girl turned her back so Catherine could use it as a writing table. Catherine scrawled her name beside "Guardian of Privacy." One of the teenagers raised a disposable camera and snapped a picture. Four other replicated the process as Catherine signed and bantered with them, trying to remember what she and Chloe had talked about when her daughter was a young teen.

As Catherine signed the fifth student's *BusinessWeek*, the gun-toting man squeezed through the crowd, trailing an entourage of mini-cam operators and reporters with microphones at the ready. He apologized for the interruption, flipped open a leather case to expose a gold shield, and introduced himself as Inspector Harry Hiller, SFPD, Homicide Department.

Catherine blew on wet ink and asked, "Are you here to learn something new about the criminal mind, Inspector?" In the recent past, more than one officer of the law had sought Catherine's input on issues involving white-collar crime.

"There isn't anything new. After twenty-four years in the murder business, everything boils down to love, power, or money... and one or more dead bodies."

"These kids are on a field trip, Inspector Hiller. I doubt your lecture was featured on their permission slips." Catherine smiled to the group and pointed to the last boy who stood blushing at the side. "Next?"

"I forgot my magazine," he stammered and flushed red, shyly holding up the day's newspaper, the one Aida had tried to show Catherine prior to her speech. Catherine recognized the top of her hair and her forehead on the quartered page.

"Sorry to intrude on your educational session," the cop continued, "but I'd like to ask you a few questions."

Catherine raised her eyebrows at the boy. "This is an opportunity of a lifetime to tell a policeman to get in line," she smiled and held out her hand for the newspaper. The boy turned and offered his back. She flapped the newspaper open, aiming the pen at the bottom of the photo. Her gaze was snagged by a black-and-white photo of Stephen Forsster above the headline, "Investment Banker Murdered."

Catherine froze. Her knees jellied and warmth drained from her face. The felt-tip pen slid from her fist and bounced off the toe of her shoe as emotions roiled and her mind churned at a hundred million instructions per second. Stephen couldn't be dead. She'd seen him just yesterday.

Tears stung and bile rose as newsprint phrases leapt and blurred—*body discovered late last night... shot three times... large caliber weapon...*

Murdered? Sometime after she was with him?

And now there was a homicide cop who wanted to ask her "a few questions."

"Anybody see my pen?" Catherine asked and bought a few seconds as she dipped her face downward, ostensibly watching the boy who dived to the carpet in search of the felt-tip.

No one knew about her relationship with Stephen—and it would be better if no one did. They had been alone yesterday. At his isolated beach property. And she was fairly certain no one had seen her storm down the trail to Sloat Street where she'd flagged a taxi for the trip back to her office. Stephen had been very much alive when she left him; but he had that gun...

Shit. She needed time to collect herself—time to think. Figure things out—maybe talk to a lawyer. No matter that she wanted to curl in a fetal position and weep for Stephen, her gut told her she'd find herself strung from somebody's lasso, dancing a mid-air ballet if she were honest with this homicide cop.

The boy handed her the felt-tip and she forced a smile, pointing at the photo of herself. "Really bad hair day," she grimaced and scrawled her name across the page. She capped the pen and handed it back to one of the teens. They thanked her and turned to push through the throng. Catherine faced Inspector Hiller and said as pertly as she could, "The future of the world, Inspector. Doesn't it do your heart good to see those fresh-faced little nerds idolizing a forty-one-year-old ex-hacker like me instead of clamoring on the other side of a police barricade at 'N-Sync's hotel?"

A microphone appeared in front of the inspector's face. "Are you here to question Ms. Calabretta about Stephen Forsster's murder?" a wing-haired blonde asked in a voice shrill with anticipation of a major news flash.

"I'm here to ask for a date. Back off and give me some space."

Hiller led Catherine to a curtained wall a few feet beyond the stage. The contingent of cameramen and media stars watched from a distance, straining forward like jackals eagerly witnessing the final death throes of their next meal.

"Cops and innocent people," the inspector shook his head in disgust. "The press' favorite targets."

"I've noticed," Catherine said, emboldened by his reference to "innocent people."

"Stephen Forsster was murdered last night. We're questioning everyone who knew him."

Catherine scrunched her brows in a questioning look, but said nothing.

"We found your business card in his briefcase," he explained. "Looks fresh. Unsoiled. As if you'd given it to him recently."

Catherine didn't remember ever giving Stephen her card, but supposed she might have done so early in their relationship. "I give out about five hundred cards a month, Inspector. It's the business equivalent of dogs meeting and sniffing each other's private parts."

"I'm really sorry to inconvenience you—I know you're a busy woman. And important." Inspector Hiller shrugged it off. "I just have a few questions. Shouldn't take more than fifteen or twenty minutes." He looked over his shoulder toward the hovering reporters.

The group had doubled in size. Aida was on stage packing up Catherine's laptop and notes. She glanced surreptitiously toward Catherine.

"Where would you like to do this, Ms. Calabretta? I mean, we've already gathered quite a following." He emphasized his words with a nod toward the crowd. "I'd be glad to go to your office downtown... or we can go to my office—it's only three blocks away."

Catherine did not want to talk to this man; but more importantly, she did not want to bring more attention to herself by her refusal.

"I don't mean to appear uncooperative, Inspector, but I have a convention to run; and I seem to recall that under the law, I don't actually have to talk to you at all."

"That's absolutely accurate." He held up both hands in surrender. Catherine tensed as several camera flashes recorded the moment. "You can send me away. You can stop talking to me at any time." He turned his palms upward. *Flash. Flash.* "Knowing how you are about your personal life, I thought you would prefer I talk to you directly rather than question other people about your relationship with Mr. Forsster."

"That sounds ominous." Heart racing, she said the words with a calm smile.

"No, no, I don't mean it to be. That's why I came to you first. I've read about you; I know you value your privacy. I'd rather not involve your employees. Your friends." He shrugged and looked apologetic. "I'm not playing hardball, but your name is the next one I have to clear off my list."

"I should probably check with my attorney," Catherine said.

Hiller reached for his back pocket. "Want to use my cell phone?" The ensuing flashes rivaled a small-town Fourth of July celebration.

"That's all right," Catherine held out her hand. More strobes.

Acid kindled Catherine's stomach as she considered her options. The convention center was a media strip-show, and she didn't want to trundle this issue to her office where employees would exchange glances and the rumor mill would kick into fifth gear.

"Fifteen, twenty minutes at most and we'll be done," Hiller said. "You can get on with running your convention." He thumbed over his shoulder. "Impressive exhibits, by the way. I've got a virus on my PC—you think I could find some software that would clean it up for me?"

"I'll refer you to someone who can help," she said. "I'll meet you at your office in ten minutes, Inspector."

"Parking's impossible for a civilian," Hiller replied. "My car is right outside. Why don't we ride over together?"

As he drove, Hiller chatted inanely about his exasperation with modern technology, from his answering machine to his microwave oven to his PC. "And DVD!" he said. "Why the heck do we need DVD?"

When they arrived at the station, he fumbled around until he located a place where they could talk: a small, windowless room that reeked of used ashtrays and dirty sweat socks.

"Not your big corporate office," he apologized, "but at least no one can eavesdrop on us."

She stepped hesitantly into the room.

"Be right back—just have to get the file. Refresh my memory." The door closed silently behind him.

Catherine skirted the scarred wooden table with the two beat-up chairs shoved under, facing each other. Jesus. What was going on here? She wanted to sit down, put her head on the table, and weep for Stephen. How could he be dead? Murdered. His family must be devastated. Losing a father... a husband. How could–

But this wasn't the time to get emotional. She forced the thoughts away. In a moment, Inspector Hiller would be back, asking questions she didn't want to answer. In his mind, the truth would hang her. She had to stall. Should she insist on an attorney? She wished she'd read the newspaper article–wished she knew more of the details outlined there.

Stop. Think, she silently instructed.

Her business card in Stephen's briefcase. That's what Inspector Hiller claimed had lead him to her. He didn't seem to be the sharpest tooth on the saw, but maybe he'd gotten an advanced degree at the Colombo School of Interview Techniques. In any event, she trusted him about as far as she could see up an alligator's butt at midnight; but she hadn't killed Stephen, so there could be no actual evidence to incriminate her.

But then she thought about the gun and her heart rate spiked again before logic prevailed.

Settle down, she silently coached. If Stephen had been killed with his own gun and if her fingerprints were still on it, Inspector Hiller wouldn't have come to her with some phony business card story. Because of ETC's work, Catherine held government security clearances, which meant her fingerprints were on file with the FBI. It would be easy enough for Hiller to ID her; and he would have flat-out arrested her. Until she heard otherwise, she would assume the gun was lost. The obvious logic of it calmed her.

The door opened and Inspector Hiller slid through carrying a gray file folder and a tape recorder with a black electrical cord looping toward the floor. A uniformed officer–a pumped, friendly blonde with a fraulein-style braid–sauntered into the room and extended her hand.

"I'm Officer Cadell," she said in a friendly Carolina drawl. "I'm gonna sit in and make sure the SFPD is appropriately respectful to members of the opposite sex." She grinned knowingly.

"I grew up in Texas, Officer Cadell," Catherine said, her hand in the pudgy vise of the woman's grip. "You can rest assured I've milked more than one rattlesnake and stamped out a few prairie fires."

ELAINE TAYLOR

Officer Cadell's hand back-swiped the air. "Standard operating procedure," she brushed it off. "Not meant to infer you can't take care of yourself. Can I offer you some coffee? A soda pop?"

Catherine declined and returned her attention to the black cord Inspector Hiller stretched to an outlet on the opposite wall. Hiller hadn't said anything about taping their conversation. She began to reconsider; he seemed to read her thoughts.

"Don't be concerned about this recorder, Ms. Calabretta. You're the victim of departmental policy. We're required to tape all conversations." He shook his head sadly. "Dishonest cops ruin it for the rest of us."

Inspector Hiller removed his green plaid sports coat exposing the tan polyester shirt, short sleeves emphasizing the paleness of his freckled arms, protruding belly challenging the grasp of the button-holes, Marlboros and Rolaids putting edges on the worn breast pocket. His shoulder holster was empty. The knot of his yellow and brown patterned tie had been dragged to the right exposing flesh that looked like a freshly plucked chicken. He settled one hip onto the small tabletop and held out his right hand toward a chair, inviting Catherine to take a seat.

"Ready?" Hiller extracted a small, mangled spiral notebook from his hip pocket and pressed a button on the recorder.

Catherine dropped onto a rickety wooden chair. When the "record" light glowed red, she said, "I want to start by stating that I'm speaking voluntarily; and that I may choose to terminate this meeting at any time."

"First, I need to identify the participants," he interrupted. He tediously recorded the names of those present at the interview. Officer Cadell lounged in the corner, picking loose skin from her cuticles.

"I really appreciate your cooperation, Ms. Calabretta," Inspector Hiller responded. "So let me confirm for the record that you are not under arrest and, as you've already stated, you're free to stop this conversation at any time..." He shrugged casually and continued, "...answer—not answer... get up and leave the room... whatever you choose. I assume you're clear on that."

He waited silently until she said, "Yes."

"Would you like to call your attorney before we start?"

Catherine hesitated. "Why don't you throw out the first pitch, Inspector, and we'll see how the umpire calls it."

22

"My preferred style, too," he responded, "but you never know. These days, I ask somebody the time, they want to call a lawyer before they lift their wrist." He turned his palms upward and looked forlorn.

"It's a wise man who doesn't squat on his spurs." She flashed a lips-only smile.

Hiller nodded and cleared his throat. "Now when we find the perp and go to trial, if you were called in—like as a witness or something—you know that whatever you say here would be a part of the permanent case file and could come up in court? You understand that?"

Catherine eyed him thoughtfully. "Why, Inspector Hiller, I think you just Mirandized me."

"Just...'managing expectations'." He looked impressed with himself. "Isn't that what you business people say?"

"You'd get along real well with my CFO," she responded with the surreal feeling they were on a movie set, conjuring up hokey characters, each for the benefit of the other.

He asked Catherine to state her name, address, and place of employment.

She complied.

"What's the business of ETC?" he asked.

"Our specialty is computer systems security. Kinda like keeping horse thieves out of the corporate data corral."

Hiller wrote painstakingly on his notepad with a chewed-on yellow Bic. "You own this company, ETC?"

"No point building someone else's herd."

"That means you're president?"

"No. My partner, Sam Princeton, is president. I'm CEO."

"Did your company have business dealings with Mr. Forsster's company?"

"What company is that, Inspector?"

"Uh..." He flipped through pages. "San Francisco Financial Services."

"Doesn't flip on any lightbulbs."

"Did you personally do business with Mr. Forsster?"

"No."

He looked up from the notebook. "What was the exact nature of your relationship with the deceased, Ms. Calabretta?"

"Whoa, now, Inspector. I never said I knew a Mr. Forsster."

"He had your business card. In his briefcase. Can I assume you at least met him?"

She leaned forward and rested her forearms on the gouged tabletop. "Like you, Inspector, I meet a lot of folks. It's just part of doing business."

"Does that mean Mr. Forsster was a..." he slow-motion shrugged, "...prospective client?"

"Every corporation that owns a computer is a prospective client."

"I get it. That's like a cop saying that every person we meet is a potential victim or a potential suspect. When was the last time you saw Mr. Forsster?"

Catherine phrased her words carefully. "I would want to check my Palm Pilot before I answer that question, Inspector."

"So, it was a meeting? With Mr. Forsster?"

She shrugged and looked helpless. "Don't have my Palm Pilot."

He grinned and pointed a finger at her. "I know you computer types are very meticulous."

She returned his smile. "If I tell you it's Christmas, Inspector, you can feel confident hanging your stocking."

Hiller flipped through the pages of the file folder. "You're recently divorced?"

She cocked her head. "Have you researched my personal life?"

"You're big news right now. There's a lot to read about you. What business is your ex-husband in?"

Catherine readjusted herself on the unyielding wooden chair. "He cashes his alimony checks."

"He doesn't work?"

She rose and paced in the tiny space, wishing there were a window to open. "He's a psychologist. I think he has a small private practice."

"How long were—"

A knock at the door stopped him. He exchanged glances with Officer Cadell, and then nodded yes. The officer rolled her eyes and left the room. Hiller looked at Catherine as she resettled on the rigid chair.

"How long were you involved with the deceased?"

"You're putting elastic in my words, Inspector. I never said I was involved with him."

Hiller stared blankly at her before he said, "So that means I can't hang my stocking?" He guffawed at his own joke, shook his head, and flipped through the file again. "Sorry. I'm just..." He read something from the pages. "What kind of car do you drive?"

Catherine hesitated, surprised at Hiller's change of direction. Stephen had never been in her car; the question seemed innocuous enough. "A Range Rover."

"What kind of video camera do you own?"

She frowned. "I don't..." She'd had a video camera when Chloe was younger, but she thought Nicolas had ended up with it when they divided their community property. "I don't own one."

Someone tapped on the door and Hiller opened it. Office Cadell handed Hiller a ten-by-twelve-inch manila envelope, smiled briefly at Catherine, and resumed her place in the corner. Hiller peeked inside the envelope and laid it carefully in the center of the table, loose flap sticking up. Catherine returned to her seat. She sensed a new tension in the room. It quickened her pulse.

Hiller turned his chair backwards and straddled it.

"Do you ever wear latex gloves?"

She thought about the gloves she wore when she installed computer components or changed the toner cartridge in her printer. "What does that have to do with—"

"How many raincoats do you own?"

She pursed her lips. "I own two."

"I know these interviews are tedious," he said and rubbed his eyes as if to demonstrate he, too, was bored. "We just ask a bunch of meaningless stuff to confirm the truthfulness of the person we're interviewing."

Catherine pulled her pager from her belt and checked the time. "This is about as much fun as a hoe-down in the middle of harvest season, Inspector, but can we head this horse to the barn? I do have a convention to run."

The tape recorder rasped as the reels turned.

"No problem." Hiller moved the envelope toward him. "Did you have a disagreement with Mr. Forsster when you were together at his beach property yesterday afternoon?"

Catherine's jaw released and her heart pounded her ribs. How did he know she'd been at the beach with Stephen? He couldn't have guessed that. He *had* been playing her. All along, he'd been a cat toying a trapped bird. Something was terribly wrong here. She looked at the red record light and tried to say, "Stop," but her vocal chords seized. Like in a dream when she tried to scream but couldn't.

Hiller rose. "The M.E. estimates time of death to have been between three and seven P.M."

Between three and seven? But the newspaper said... How had she gotten the impression he was killed much later? She had been with Stephen from four until approximately five o'clock. Her mind whirled.

The Inspector picked up the envelope and toyed with the flap. "Do you know where Mr. Forsster was killed, Ms. Calabretta—where his body was found?"

Her pulse reverberated in her ears. She intuitively knew what he was going to say.

"Stop," she croaked.

"His body was found in his car, which was parked on a dead-end trail overlooking the Pacific Ocean. On a wilderness property owned by his family."

In his car. Still parked at the beach property. Exactly where she had left him at five P.M.

"Did you ever go to such a place with Mr. Forsster?" Hiller asked, his question cutting into her thoughts.

"Stop, Inspector." Her voice was hoarse. She rose on unsteady legs. "I'm going to leave, now."

Silently, Hiller pulled a page from the manila envelope and dropped it onto the table. Catherine's gaze followed. Her breath caught. She was staring at a full-color photograph of herself striding up the beach, face creased with irritation, wind flapping her blue raincoat. Stephen followed behind, reaching his hand toward her arm. In black marker, someone had scrawled across the top, *Feb 3*. Yesterday's date.

Catherine's heart pounded so hard her vision began to blur. They had been alone on that beach; but Stephen had voiced suspicions that his wife had hired a detective. Was that who photographed them? And what about the FedEx with the ETC label? Was she, in fact, the woman in the cutouts with Stephen? No. Not possible... They'd never been... together... anywhere except her own apartment. Her own bedroom.

"Did you kill him because of the video?"

Video? Acid curdled her stomach. She stared at the photo, her mind racing with all that had been asked, all she had responded. Her pulse rattled her voice, but she thought it important to say for the record, "I didn't kill him."

"Oh, yes. You did."

Catherine slowly shook her head, fighting terror, trying to piece it all together, but her heart hammered so hard she could barely breathe; black spots swam in her vision.

"Ms. Calabretta?"

Inspector Hiller waited until she met his gaze.

"You're under arrest for the murder of Stephen Forsster."

They took her picture, took her fingerprints. They took her shoes, her stockings, and her belt. She fought to keep her dignity.

At first, she was numb with disbelief—disbelief that Stephen was dead and that someone thought she had killed him; disbelief at what was unfolding before her. Like last year when that Muni bus ran up on the sidewalk and took out the advertising kiosk six feet away from where she was waiting for a cab. Unbelievable.

Then she was angry. Angry at herself for letting Hiller patronize her. Trick her into complacency.

They handcuffed her with a white plastic band that resembled an extra-large garbage bag tie. They led her to a room with a pay phone and left her unattended.

She called Beverly Rathman, her divorce attorney, but Beverly was in court. Her secretary said ever so politely she would track down Beverly as soon as possible. "You go find her right now!" Catherine hissed. She didn't want to involve anyone else.

Wilson Ramsey, ETC's firewall guru extraordinaire, had once told Catherine, "White chicks can't imagine being arrested." Catherine now believed that a serious understatement.

Two dark-haired, dark-skinned, brown-uniformed matrons came for her. They looked like Siamese twins who had been detached at birth. Stout. Like a boulder cleaved in two, with stumpy legs stuffed under each half. Sandwiched between them, they guided Catherine through a maze of concrete hallways—first right, then left—stopping for bars to slide open, waiting for gates to clang closed, each area redolent with a different combination of body odors and industrial antiseptics.

"You get a VIP cell," one of them said. Her singsong voice was cheerful, her accent Samoan. Or some other type of islander. Catherine had an absurd flash of the women on their day off, lounging in halter-tops and hula skirts. That convinced her she was losing it.

They delivered Catherine to a private cell with two unoccupied cots crammed between mint-green cinderblock walls. The temperature suggested the room could be used as an auxiliary morgue freezer when the big one was full. The ceramic toilet—shiny white, no lid, no seat—reeked of disinfectant. Until that moment, Catherine had never considered Lysol a perk.

One of the matrons banged the door closed and gave a brief smile and a fleeting wave of pudgy brown fingers through the small square of bars that functioned as a window; then the two shuffled off down the corridor.

The space was tiny. Walls pressed inward. Catherine clenched her hands and squinched her eyes closed, battling the urge to scream. To cry. To pound the door and shriek, "Let me out!" until her fists were bruised and her vocal chords raw.

She stood that way for an indeterminate time. Until her heartbeat smoothed out and her breath slowed. Then she began to pace, toes aching with the chill that permeated the prison-issue socks that had replaced her shoes.

Think, she chided herself. Line up the data in little rows and examine it like an engineer looking for a flaw in the logic of an algorithm. Instead, her thoughts tumbled. Finally, in the solitude of the cell, she allowed herself to think about Stephen.

How could he be dead?

Catherine lifted the cheap roll of toilet paper off the concrete floor and sank onto a rigid cot. She sobbed quietly, scratchy tissue soaking up tears. She grieved for Stephen—for the short life violently extinguished, for the widow who would probably learn things about her husband she would never understand, and for his children. The son and the daughter who would grow to maturity absent the love and active participation of their father. She couldn't imagine what it must be like in their upended world.

Who had done this—killed this man and destroyed his family?

Stephen had said on more than one occasion his wife would kill him if she found out he was "placing trades from multiple accounts." At the time, he'd grinned at the cleverness of his euphemism; but yesterday, when he called Catherine about the FedExed photos, he was agitated. Genuinely worried. He insisted they meet so he could show Catherine the package. Against her wishes, he drove to his family's wilderness beach property, zigging erratically through traffic, pounding his horn and racing through stoplights. When he parked his Mercedes on the gravel trail high above the Pacific, his anger dissipated and he turned glum. He admitted his wife had been "acting suspicious." That lead to rants about how much he loved his family and how he would kill himself before he would lose his wife and children.

Catherine was bemused. "This is high drama, honey, considering you've mounted more fillies than a two-hundred year old saddle—even though you've said at least a dozen times that your wife would be less than delighted with your extracurricular activities."

He responded by lunging across the console, flipping open the glovebox, and groping for a gun Catherine could see snuggled in the back. She frantically shoved his hand away and snatched up the pistol as her heart percussed in her chest.

"Jesus, Stephen!"

He leaned his back against the driver's door, cocked his leg over the center console, and casually draped his arm over the steering wheel. "Go ahead, Catherine. I'd rather have a bullet between my eyes than have my wife open an envelope containing those pictures."

Catherine checked the safety of the Colt .45, ejected a fully loaded magazine, and tossed it into the glovebox. She took the gun, grabbed her belongings and the FedEx envelope, and leapt from the car with an adrenaline-fueled slam of the door. She stalked down the gravel trail toward the exit from his property, leaning into the wind, barely hearing Stephen's angry accusations over the surf that crashed far below. Just before she arrived at the wrought-iron gate, she flung the gun into dense brush, ignoring Stephen's screeching protest.

Had he found it? Somehow managed to dig it out of the under-growth in spite of the deepening twilight? Had he been shot with his own gun?

Catherine's heart banged against her chest. Were her fingerprints on the murder weapon?

She didn't know if Hiller now had the .45, but if he did, it would be difficult to convince a jury that she hadn't pulled the trigger.

She stopped mid-thought. She had heard of some kind of test—paraffin testing, maybe?—to determine if one had recently fired a gun. The police hadn't done any such test. Hope burbled. She would ask Beverly, her attorney, to insist they perform that test. She knew it would be negative.

Confidence began to return. Since she *hadn't* killed Stephen there must be a way to confirm her innocence. She considered what she could present as an alibi for the time between three and seven—the window during which the medical examiner said the murder had occurred. After she'd exited Stephen's property, she'd hiked down the trail to the Great Highway and the additional quarter mile to Sloat Street where she'd flagged a cab and gone directly downtown to her office garage to pick up her car. The automated exit system would have logged her departure time—probably around 5:30. That could do it!

She slumped to the crusty edge of the cot. Wrong. The garage log—the taxi from the beach—would work in her favor only if the medical examiner adjusted the time of death much later in the evening. She sighed and rubbed her forehead. Her mind continued to track possibilities, pulling them like threads from a ball of twine, following each until it led to the conclusion everyone else would reach: She had been at the right place at the right time to have murdered Stephen Forsster.

Rubber soles squeaked on tile and keys jangled in the hallway. One of the Samoans pressed her face against the small square of bars in the middle of the cell door.

"Your attorney's here," she singsonged.

The door swung open and Catherine followed her to a room like the one where Hiller had questioned her—except this one had a small, eye-level window in the door. A minute later, Beverly Rathman's straight-nosed profile appeared in the rectangle of glass. The attorney spoke to someone outside Catherine's line of vision, then nodded twice, setting in motion a strand of shoulder-length black hair that floated free from her ballerina's bun.

Beverly, who had handled Catherine's divorce from Nicolas two years before, squeezed into the small room and greeted Catherine with motherly concern. Catherine felt like weeping with gratitude that Beverly was there.

"I've taken the liberty of contacting Jordan Lawrence," Beverly launched immediately into the business at hand. "He's got the best criminal defense record in the state. We were both tied up in court until fifteen minutes ago. Jordan is with Inspector Hiller and Peter Hansell, the D.A., right now. I just left them. Lawrence is negotiating your release, but I have to tell you, Catherine, it's not going well."

As if on cue, Lawrence entered the small room and Beverly quickly introduced them. Catherine thought that, stripped of his smoky cashmere suit, hand-tailored white shirt, and gold Piaget watch, he could be mistaken for a balding lumberjack. Except his nails were buffed and the hand that shook hers was soft as rose petals.

"They're not cutting us any slack," he said through thin, pursed lips, annoyance etched on his brow. "I've got five minutes with you, so let me do this fast. You want the good news first?"

Catherine swallowed hard. "Bad news."

"Hiller won't release you. He can hold you for twenty-four hours while Hansell dicks around deciding whether or not to charge you."

"Wait a minute. What does that mean—'whether or not to charge me'?"

"They're being very tight lipped, but it usually means the case is weak and totally circumstantial. Hiller hasn't convinced Peter to file. I reminded Peter the press will be all over this one. Your name is very media-worthy right now. I suggested to Peter that, if he files on you, this would rapidly become a high-visibility debacle reflecting solely on the incompetence of his office."

"You mean..." Catherine's brow scrunched with confusion. "You mean they may be holding me when even *they* know I didn't kill Stephen?"

He held up both hands to caution her. "Don't get ahead of it. They've got something—enough to make Hiller bold. But it's a good sign they're fighting each other."

Catherine changed tacks and asked if the media had already learned of her arrest, futilely hoping to escape this predicament without public vilification. Without a pillaging of her past.

"We missed the noon broadcast; but I expect you'll make the five and the six o'clock news. Whether or not Peter lets you go, the media will lock onto this."

"But—"

"Hiller has convinced Hansell he'll have a tighter case by morning."

"What's he going to do—plant seeds and hot-house them overnight?" Catherine asked, fear and anger rising in her chest.

"Don't talk to the cops. Don't answer any questions—don't even confirm your name." Lawrence said. "I've already warned Peter—and Hiller—about questioning you again. I expect they'll leave you alone.

They've agreed to keep you in a VIP cell. You'll be safe there,–away from the general population."

One of the Samoans pounded the door and called, "Time to go."

Panic burbled in Catherine's throat. "What about that test? The one that shows whether or not someone fired a gun? Can you make them do that test?"

Lawrence shook his head no. "It's been too long since the shooting." He rested his big hands on her shoulders. "Let me worry about your defense. You just relax. I'm in charge of your problems now."

His eyes had the fire of a television evangelist who asks God to take away all your cares... and offers to relieve you of your social security check. And, like a rapt television audience, Catherine was awash with the need to turn her future over to this man who had an understanding of this world of criminalistics—a world she couldn't even fathom, but her intuition screamed to stay alert, to not be taken in by the lure of releasing the helm to someone else.

"We hope to have you out by morning." Beverly nodded her moral support.

A guard tapped Catherine's arm. "Call my office," she urgently instructed Beverly. "Ask Wilson to take care of my dog."

"Anything else?"

"I had plans for the evening," she said, her heart sinking to a new low. "What's the proper etiquette when you can't get out of jail in time to keep your dinner date?"

In her cell, Catherine sat on the bunk, knees pulled to her chest, arms wrapped tight around them. She rocked back and forth and tried to figure out how bad this was going to get. She wanted to trust that Jordan Lawrence could get her out of this predicament. She wanted to wash it all away and go back to yesterday, to the life that had been controlled and predictable. Until Stephen was killed. She closed her eyes and let her mind wander to things she hadn't previously allowed it to review.

What if Chloe, her nineteen-year-old daughter who was at university in Paris, heard about this? Chloe knew nothing about Stephen Forsster. If the press learned of her arrest, they would declare open season on Catherine's personal life, exploiting and twisting and exaggerating the most insignificant statements or actions to create circulation-enhancing headlines.

And what about her staff? Did Joel and Linda and Wilson—and the rest of her employees—know why she hadn't shown up at the ETC trade show booth? Did Sam Princeton know his business partner was being held on suspicion of murdering her married lover? That would play really well with Sam, father of four, devout Presbyterian who had probably lost his virginity to his wife. *After* they'd said, "I do." Catherine suspected lingerie ads were about-as-far-as-we-need-to-go erotica to Sam.

Would ETC clients read about her arrest over their morning granolas and cappuccinos? Embarrassment flamed her cheeks and she fought futile tears. Even when it was proved that she had nothing to do with Stephen's murder, people would still link her to him. The, "other woman." A mere blip on the screen of his infidelities, but she would forever be the poster girl for his unfaithfulness.

Stephen's unfaithfulness.

Catherine thought again about Lili Forsster. She'd never met the woman. Stephen rarely mentioned her, but Catherine knew he loved her. And he loved his children. In more ways than one, this was going to be hard on his family. Not just losing the husband and father, but also discovering his philandering. They would have to think of him differently, now. They would have so many questions. And no answers. He wouldn't be there to disclaim—to explain or to make amends. To reaffirm their importance in his life.

"Stephen, you shit," Catherine murmured.

She scooted backward across the thin mattress and propped herself against the cold concrete wall. She finally allowed herself to think about George Hallison, the dinner date she wouldn't be able to keep.

They'd met only six weeks ago and had become lovers. Had he heard the news? Her shoulders drooped further and she suppressed the urge to cry. Sitting in his hot tub on Sunday night, after a day on the bridle trails that crisscrossed his two-hundred-acre Napa Valley vineyard, she had alluded to the fact that since her divorce two years ago, she'd had one minor fling. She hadn't told him it had been a sex-only relationship with a married man. She hadn't really considered it any of his business. But, now he would certainly find out. Would he rush to judgment? Think differently of her?

George Hallison. Hal, she called him. The image that leapt to mind was from Saturday morning, how he'd easily hefted the saddle onto his own horse, observing with a fleeting smile as the ranch manager catered to Catherine's equestrian needs. Rugged and tanned, he looked as though he worked the vineyards himself; but Catherine knew he didn't. He was a quiet man. Cautious reserve bridled every conversation, every sharing of history. Catherine had learned from her friend who'd introduced them that he was still grieving the death of his wife of twenty-six years.

Catherine had been with Hal only four times, including the past weekend that they'd spent at his ranch. He seemed to really enjoy her company, as she did his, but there was an emotional distance in him. A guardedness. Like a firewall set up to keep casual explorers at bay.

That was all right with Catherine, because she'd felt her own heart involuntarily opening in a way that alarmed her. She was at once exhilarated and terrified by the experience. What if she really fell in love with him? What if he didn't feel the same? She'd wrestled with the possibilities. After two failed marriages and the thing with Stephen, her psyche was working to convince her that a computer nerd like herself should abandon all romantic fantasies of happily ever after.

Especially now. Hal didn't seem the type to exchange jailhouse love letters with a woman who was imprisoned—falsely or otherwise—for murder.

One of the caretakers interrupted Catherine's thoughts with a plastic bowl of lukewarm something. Dinty Moore beef stew? At first, Catherine pushed it aside but then decided nourishment was necessary.

As she picked at the food, she mulled unanswerable questions.

Photos of Stephen in an ETC FedEx envelope. How was that possible? Photos that were cropped in a manner that reminded Catherine of the magazine montages Chloe had cut and pasted when she was a little girl. Edges rounded. The woman's head severed by someone's careful scissors. Identifying details clipped away. Why?

What else? Slightly blurred, grainy quality, she recalled. Stephen deduced they'd been extracted from a video clip rather than shot with a still camera. Catherine didn't know enough about photography to agree or disagree with his assessment. But he'd also said he thought Catherine was the woman in the photo. Couldn't be.

They'd had sex only at her apartment. If she were the woman in the cutouts, that would mean the photos had been taken in her own bedroom. Not possible. But then she remembered Inspector Hiller's question about a video camera. What the hell was that about?

Catherine rubbed her temples to relieve the pounding. Too many questions. No answers.

Suddenly she remembered Stephen had been on his cell phone when she climbed into his car yesterday. What was it he'd said about a meeting? Something like, "I'll see you in an hour. I'm headed that way now."

That was it! She was certain—and she was excited. She had to tell Jordan Lawrence to get Stephen's cell phone records. She pounded the cell door and called through the tiny barred square until the matron appeared.

"I need to call my attorney. Right now. Please."

The matron grinned and whacked the metal door with something hard. "Bag it, Cinderella. No more fox-trotting with Prince Charming until tomorrow."

Chapter Two: Wednesday

Unseen clock hands marked sluggish hours as the jailhouse grew still and quiet. Mind numbed by an exhaustive and fruitless review of possibilities—questions, attempts to second-guess Inspector Hiller, and the criminal justice system—Catherine's thoughts turned to Stephen. How could he be dead—his life ended for all time? Sadness weighted her heart as she involuntarily imagined him lying on a slab of stainless steel. Lifeless.

It was unnerving. She preferred to remember him the way he had been on the day they met, almost a year and a half ago.

It had been late August, one week before her fortieth birthday. She received a call from Laura Tyler Jackson, owner of the ad agency that handled the ETC account. Laura and Catherine were more than just business associates. Over the past few years, they had bellied up to a few bars and groused about the social challenges of career-focused single women.

"I've got a very special birthday present for you," Laura had said in her voicemail message, "so bring along your spirit of adventure. I'll see you at one-thirty."

Catherine was to meet Laura at an old Victorian mansion, recently converted to a chi-chi, south-of-Market French restaurant. As usual, Laura was late. A few unhurried diners were visible through the wide archway of the main seating area, beyond which, Catherine knew from a previous visit, other rooms had been fashioned into smaller dining rooms. Vacant tables had been reset with snowy linens, sparkling crystal, gleaming silver. Lamps were turned low; vanilla candlelight flickered. Sting crooned a sultry song through speakers she could not see.

As she waited at the antique writing desk, she spied a tall, rotund man—white-coated, large chef's hat tilted precariously over pony-tailed, sandy curls—in a rear corner, adjacent to a kitchen door. His back was to her and he was talking, with much hand waving, to someone who was obscured from Catherine's vision.

The missing maitre 'd? As she speculated, the wildly gesticulating chef burst out laughing and collapsed against the wall, revealing his audience.

He was tall and trim and he leaned casually against a kitchen door jamb, grinning at the chef, navy suit jacket unbuttoned and draped back by hands shoved casually into pants pockets, Mid-thirties? Wavy, dark brown hair, longish over the tops of his ears. Fashionable wire-rim glasses perched on small, straight nose. Lips full and pale against the heavy shadow of the beard he'd shaved earlier in the day. A conspicuous dimple dented his chin.

His gaze shifted as if he felt Catherine's inspection. He smiled and raised his eyebrows questioningly. Seductively? She quickly dropped her gaze and fidgeted with her handbag.

The host, a tuxedoed young man, stepped to the desk, took Catherine's raincoat, and hung it in an heirloom armoire as Laura arrived in a whoosh of swirling rain cape. "Darling, you look wonderful!" She stage-whispered, "The make-over is fabulous. You're a new woman!"

Catherine blushed, self-conscious that she'd succumbed to Joel's badgering her to engage a "personal image consultant" ...uncomfort-able with her pleasure at the results.

The host picked up two menus and they followed him through the main dining room, into a library. Mahogany bookshelves filled with leather-bound volumes lined two walls; double French doors over-looked a small, private garden lush with foxglove, snapdragons, and irises. A wood-burning fire blazed in a mammoth fireplace.

Four tables were vacant; two businessmen who talked over empty coffee cups occupied another.

The host offered drinks and Laura insisted on martinis: "Stoli Cristal, very dry, up with a twist." Catherine settled into a tapestried, wingback chair as Laura twittered gaily about birthdays being a time to renew, a time for exciting adventures. Then cocktails arrived with a flourish.

Martini in hand, Laura toasted. "You look spectacular—better than at any time since I've known you. Welcome to your prime."

They drank; Laura chattered. Their two businessmen shuffled through their departure; a crew of busboys quickly and quietly removed all signs of prior occupancy. The waiter replaced the women's empty martini glasses with fresh ones.

"Now's the time to do things you wish you'd already done—live with abandon before it's too late."

"Like what? Toss my undies into the drawer unfolded?"

"Have a fling. Have a wonderful affair to celebrate your womanhood. Your sexuality."

A *deja vu* conversation. When they first met a couple of years ago at a Women At The Top business conference, Laura talked about sex so much Catherine thought she was obsessed.

"On the scorecard of intimate relationships," Catherine said, "if it weren't for handicap points, I'd have no points at all. Besides which, I don't think 'sex' lives up to its ad campaign."

"That's because you squandered a critical decade in wedded bliss with Mr. Asexual. You've had a year to regroup. It's time for you to get back in the saddle. So to speak." She winked at Catherine. "You need a boy-toy."

"I'll pick one up next time I'm at the pet store." Catherine turned toward the door of their tiny, private dining room. "But right now, I need to sponge up some of this alcohol. Where's our waiter?"

"I'll find him on my way to the ladies room." Laura fumbled in her handbag, removed a purple bow—the stick-on kind—and laid it on the linen tablecloth. "This goes on your birthday present," she said as she pushed back her chair and picked up her handbag. "Don't go away."

"No problem. Now that I've got this new image to maintain, I can't be seen leaving on my hands and knees," she said to Laura's departing back.

Catherine lifted the purple bow, contemplated it with curiosity, shrugged, and put it back on the table. She idly raised her martini glass, surprised to find it empty. No wonder she was hearing the trumpet of pink elephants.

A waiter appeared with two fresh martinis. Catherine ignored the drink and asked for bread—something to absorb the alcohol.

"Happy birthday, Catherine."

She looked up to see the man who'd been talking to the chef. He smiled at her. She flushed... wondered how he knew her name.

"I'm Stephen Forsster," he said and handed her a lavender envelope. "I'm your birthday present." He settled into Laura's chair and picked up the purple bow, peeled off the backing and stuck it to his lapel.

Catherine stared at him with apprehension.

He lifted Laura's fresh martini and said, "Cheers."

"That drink is taken." Catherine noted that "is" came out with a slight slur.

He smiled and sipped. "I think it's all in there." He nodded toward the card she held in her hand.

Catherine watched him with a growing sense of dismay. She slipped a finger into the folds of the envelope flap, pulled out the card and read:

Dear Catherine,

For this, your most significant of birthdays, I've selected a very special gift. Stephen is a fantasy fuck. He'll introduce you to a world you've not yet experienced... but always imagined.

Embarrassment heated her throat. How could Laura know what Catherine had imagined? In her peripheral vision Catherine noted that her "birthday present" was relaxed, watching her thoughtfully. She continued to read.

I didn't get him from Tiffany's or Gump's, so you can't return him or exchange him. You'll just have to take him home and enjoy him. (I promise you'll thank me for this!)

Happy Birthday, sweetie!

Love, Laura.

Anger and indignation flared Catherine's cheeks. She felt betrayed. She had confided in Laura—trusted Laura with her rawest confessions about failures with members of the opposite sex... and this was how Laura, who had a knack for eliciting more intimate information than she ever shared, had used that knowledge?

She glared at Stephen Forsster. "If I were looking for a mercy fuck, I'd take out an ad in a personals column."

"And no doubt that's what you'd get—a desperate, artless mercy fuck. I, on the other hand, tend to think of myself as a sexual connoisseur."

"Did Laura tell you she feels sorry for me?"

"She didn't tell me anything except that I would enjoy your company."

Catherine crossed her arms over her chest and nurtured a glare—preferable to the irrational tears that threatened.

"And she thought you might enjoy mine." He casually picked up the menu and began to peruse. "Apparently, she was wrong."

"Don't take this personally, but..." Why the hell was she trying to protect his feelings; it was personal. Very personal. She stood and clutched the chair back. "Tell Laura..." she stopped again. She didn't know what to tell Laura.

"Tell her yourself." He laid down the menu and eyed her.

Vodka had pickled her nervous system; she was afraid to release the chair.

He smiled and shrugged. "Okay, so you're not sexually attracted to me," he flicked his fingers across the menu. "Can we at least have lunch?" He raised his eyebrows questioningly, as he'd done when she'd first seen him.

"Did Laura pay for that, too?"

"You think Laura offered financial incentives?" He grinned quizzically. "To the contrary. This celebration is on me."

"Excuse me?" Had she misread the card?

He held out his hand toward the chair. "Please. Be my guest." His eyes were playful and full of innuendo. "For lunch."

The waiter appeared and smiled uncertainly. "Ready to order?"

Stephen watched. Catherine debated whether to ask the waiter to call a taxi, or to make her way to the host stand and take a chance that the maitre 'd would still be there.

"Give us a minute," Stephen said. "But bring some bread right away. We're both famished." Stephen rose and shrugged out of his jacket, exposing a pale blue shirt with white collar and monogrammed French cuffs secured with simple gold links. "It would be my pleasure if you would join me for lunch, Catherine," he said and held his hand toward the seat she'd vacated.

Catherine stood her ground, clinging unsteadily to the proffered chair.

Forsster shrugged, resettled in his own chair, and picked up the menu again. "I recommend the bouillabaisse. The only person who makes it better than Maxim is my wife."

41

Catherine's eyes widened. "Your wife?" She sank to the edge of the cushy seat. "You're married? I thought you were some kind of... of male prostitute."

"I've been called worse," he grinned devilishly. "I'm in the brokerage business."

She stared, incredulous, certain the vodka had caused her to misunderstand all that had transpired.

"And I'm very interested in you and your company. That recent Systems House article left no doubt that ETC is ahead of the market on data security and Internet privacy issues. Are you going to take the company—"

"Wait a minute," she said and held up her hand. "What's going on here?"

"As I understand it, we're both hungry; I've suggested we have lunch. I generally find dining more pleasurable when the participants converse about a topic of common interest. It so happens I deal with a lot of technology companies."

"But I..."

He waved her off. "Forget the sex thing. Bad idea. Let's just talk business."

She drooped against her chair back and observed him. The waiter came again. Stephen ordered for both of them—looked to Catherine for approval. She shrugged. Whatever.

He asked questions about a software product ETC had recently taken to market; she answered haltingly. He'd recently read an article about state-of-the-art strategies for securing corporate data and asked her opinion.

"Maybe it's because of the Y2K emphasis, but companies are just beginning to understand that 'corporate data' is their biggest asset," Stephen said. "For years, there have been inventory management systems and all kinds of checks and balances to make sure no one absconds with a company's ballpoint pens or their copy machines, but no one was looking at what walked out on little floppy disks."

"Exactly!" Catherine launched into some of her own pet theories. She relaxed. Was relieved to be back on familiar turf.

Stephen drank vodka; Catherine drank water and ate bread. Stephen described a new security product that had just come out of one of Silicon Valley's hottest software houses. When he outlined how it created a security architecture for multiple networking protocols, it became apparent to Catherine that he was not only extremely intelligent, but also well informed.

Still confused by the enigma he—and the situation—presented, she studied him as he switched subjects and animatedly described a recent sailing trip.

His eyes were blue and danced with energy and playfulness as he spoke. His voice was velvety. It sounded trained. Like a radio announcer. Or an actor. And she was fascinated by his pouty mouth. She toyed with Laura's birthday card where it lay on the lavender envelope. She lifted the front and glimpsed the message.

...fantasy fuck... take him home and enjoy him...

Stephen covered her hand with his own. She jerked away as if a spider had just crawled onto the white cloth.

"You're obviously not a sailor." His smile was boyish.

"I get seasick." She cleared her throat and sat silently while the waiter delivered plates of steaming food. When he had gone, she held up the card. "How did this come about?"

"I had a drink with Laura a couple of weeks ago." Nonchalant. "She saw the Systems House issue in my briefcase—your picture on the cover, and mentioned she knew you. She hatched this plan to introduce us."

"Why?" Catherine blew steam from a fish-laden fork.

"Because she knows I enjoy making love to intelligent, sexy women," he answered. Casual. He speared a prawn.

Color rose up Catherine's throat. Irritation bloomed anew. Sexy woman? Yeah, right. Was he making fun of her? Fork on plate, arms crossed over chest, she said, "My bullshit detector just shattered like a thermometer dropped in boiling water."

"Oh, I suspect you carry a spare in your handbag."

"I can't imagine why Laura would do this. Don't take it personally, but I could never be attracted to a man like you."

"Who are you kidding," he said between bites. "I'm the perfect man for you."

"Is it your arrogance or your deceptive nature that's supposed to beguile me?"

"How about that I'm equally proficient with my penis and my brain,—and I can give you exactly what you want with no extraneous complications."

"You presume to know what I want?" She raised her eyebrows haughtily.

"I know more about you than you can possibly imagine."

She gritted her teeth. "I hate when people talk about me. Especially when they're betraying a confidence."

"You're the only one who's betrayed anything. What I know about you, you've told me yourself."

"Then you know virtually nothing." Arms tightened protectively over her chest.

"Wrong. You've given me a complete autobiography."

She glared silently, wondering what she'd said that he'd found so revealing.

"Shall I tell you what I know about you, Catherine?" He angled his chair, pulled it closer. "You're a very sensual woman." He slowly trailed a fingertip from her shoulder around the crook of her elbow, across her forearm and the back of her hand. Propped his left elbow on the table, cupped his chin in palm, studying her. "But it's possible you've never had an orgasm that wasn't self-induced."

"You audacious asshole," she hissed, cheeks aflame.

"It's not your fault." He shrugged. "Your lovers—how many have you had?–Two? Three?–were men who believe the only requirements for good sex are a stiff dick and an artificially lubricated cunt. And you feel inadequate for not having inspired them to greater passion."

"You... are full of shit."

"Maybe. But, I'm not terrified. Like you are." He sipped his martini.

"You're not going to dare me into screwing you."

"What a pity. For both of us."

"Do you try to fuck every woman you meet?"

"Not every woman turns me on."

"Why doesn't your wife divorce you?"

"Because she loves me. And because I'm an excellent husband and father. My family always comes first."

"No pun intended?"

"Say that with a smile and I might begin to suspect you have a sense of humor."

"What kind of woman would fall for your line of crap?"

"A smart woman who always reads the fine print on the contract before she drives a new car off the lot." His gaze pinioned her. "Full warranty. No balloon payments at the end of the lease." He touched her cheek. He drew a finger lightly over her jawbone, down to the hollow of her throat. "Of the two genders, women have the superior ability to experience sexual pleasure." He leaned forward and his fingertips trailed up her skirt, teasing her thigh. His touch singed. "But, as they'll tell you at the track, without the right jockey even a Triple Crown winner is nothing but a nice-looking horse."

Catherine's jaw went slack. Sexual heat—and panic—rippled her spine.

"If you decide to let me make love to you, Catherine, I will explore you." Electric caress punctuated his words. "And I will discover anything and everything that inflames you beyond your wildest imagination."

Goosebumps prickled her skin. No man had touched her like that. Ever.

She squeezed her arms tight to her chest; looked at him with what she hoped was disdain. "The decision is already made. I'm not going to sleep with you."

"Well, that's true. With me, you would not sleep." He leaned back in his chair and studied her. "But actually, that's just as well. You're not the type of woman I usually get involved with."

"That's surprising, considering I have tits and a twat."

"You're divorced. You could be dangerous. You're probably one of those clingy women who want 'love'—or at least the pretense of it—with their sex."

"I don't believe in love."

He leaned in until his face was inches from hers. He smelled of starch and light citrus. "How about a warm, soft mouth on your rigid clit—do you believe in that?"

Catherine froze as heat enveloped her. Stephen's hand scalded her knee.

"A wet tongue in the hollow of your throat..." Fingertips traveled slowly under her skirt, scorching a trail like an out-of-control prairie fire. "Your back arched... your nipples raw with arousal." Hand traveled the curve of her stockinged hip, smoothed its way back to her knee. "Do you believe in that?"

She swallowed hard. Wanted to tell him to stop.

He kissed her palm, tonguing it lightly. Teasing. "It's very stimulating... fantasizing what I'll do to you..." He closed his eyes.

Her imagination flared. "...What you'll do to me."

He guided her hand slowly under the napkin that draped his lap, sliding her fingers up the length of his sizeable erection.

Catherine closed her eyes and a small moan escaped her throat.

"You're feisty. I like that." His hand on top of hers sustained pressure. "You're extraordinarily responsive. When I stroke your thighs, your nipples stiffen. And that rosy flush on your throat isn't embarrassment. Tell me, Catherine, are your panties wet?"

She sat. Motionless. Terrified to move. Terrified to stay.

"What the fuck, Catherine. Give it a test run."

She shoved back her chair, jerked to her feet. Rattled glasses and silverware. Snatched her purse off table. Her chest stung from lack of oxygen.

"I can't," she rasped. Close to tears.

He rose and slowly reached for her hand, as though she might bolt if he moved too fast.

"I'm not after your soul," he said. He kissed her palm, all the while studying her as though reading gauges on a delicate instrument. "I'll be the most caring... sensitive... exciting lover you'll ever have—I promise." Eyes and mouth curved to a benignly mischievous smile. "And the most fun."

He had lived up to his promise.

On the musty jailhouse cot, Catherine sighed and covered her face with both hands. He'd not only been fun and exciting; he'd been a Ph. D. in sex education.

But now he was dead. And the sound of clinking in the hallway outside her cell brought home the fact that her innocuous little sexual adventure could cost her dearly.

As keys scrapped the lock, Catherine dropped her feet to the floor, finger-combed her hair—wished she had a toothbrush—and greeted the pale, thin matron who opened the door.

"This way," the woman said without preamble. She led Catherine through a maze of fluorescent-lit, interconnected hallways to a door where Beverly Rathman handed Catherine her shoes.

"You're free," Beverly said. "Jordan's waiting at the car."

Elation and disbelief rivaled fear for top billing as Catherine followed Beverly down a noisy, crowded corridor into a brightly lit garage area where Jordan Lawrence greeted her.

"They didn't file charges?" she asked, still afraid to feel relief.

"No charges," he said as he cupped her elbow and guided her into the spacious backseat of a stretch Lincoln. Car doors slammed and echoed; Catherine pressed into the bend of the seat, luxuriating in the scent and feel of the buttery leather, contrasted with her last hours on the unforgiving jail mattress.

Jordan Lawrence continued. "They finally admitted the evidence isn't strong enough." His smile was laced with triumph. "Your name looms large on the media's radar screen right now; the D.A doesn't want to be routed in the press for bungling this case."

A metal garage door slowly trundled toward the ceiling and the vehicle edged forward into an alley behind the police station. Lawrence handed her a large brown envelope marked with the SFPD logo. It contained her watch, pager, and other belongings.

"Did they arrest someone else?"

Lawrence shuffled the yellow pages of a legal pad, distracted as he responded. "They're following some leads."

Now she understood why she was afraid to feel relief.

The limo turned the corner and a throng of reporters converged, screaming questions and jamming microphones toward the blackout windows. Catherine grimaced and shrank from the glass. The irony of her situation was not lost on her. One day she was touted guardian of personal privacy; the next, her image was just another heap of deconstructed data elements—praiseworthy traits jettisoned, salacious tidbits plumped up like a calf at auction time. All to feed the voracious media machine.

Lawrence noticed her dismay. "By tomorrow you'll be old news," he said. "A non-event."

He asked for her address and she gave him the number on Union Street. He pressed a button on an intercom and repeated the address to his driver. "We'll drop you off."

"We're not going to your office? To discuss next steps? Go over the evidence Hiller claims to have?" She wanted to get this cleared up once and for all.

"I've got to be in court in half an hour. Different case," he said as he closed his notebook and slid it into an oxblood leather briefcase.

Catherine felt betrayed. And distressed. "I could be facing a murder charge, Jordan. What does it take to get a space on your dance card?"

Catherine glanced back and forth between the two attorneys. Beverly Rathman silently picked invisible lint from her skirt.

"My job doesn't officially begin until you're charged."

"I'm hoping to get ahead of the curve and *avoid* being charged."

"If Hiller thought you were good for this, you'd be in arraignment right now."

"Then why do I feel like a peahen pecking corn in the shadow of a circling hawk?"

"We can meet tomorrow morning," Lawrence acquiesced. "I'll have my investigator join us; we can start building your alibi–in case you need one."

Catherine wasn't placated. "What about the evidence? Who took that picture at the beach? What else does Hiller have?"

"We don't get that information unless they file."

"Did they find the... the murder weapon?" She hoped like hell they'd found it and that it wasn't the gun from Stephen's glovebox.

He eyed her silently. "Don't know," he shrugged. "They searched your apartment."

Catherine slumped and rubbed her forehead with her fingertips, anticipating the chaos they'd likely left behind.

"Would they have found anything I should know about?"

"Diamond-studded whips... how-to guides for sacrificing virgins... an electric cattle prod or two," she deadpanned.

"They will have left a copy of the warrant at the search site. Bring it with you when you come to my office tomorrow." Lawrence checked his watch and glanced out the window as the limo turned right off Van Ness, onto Union Street. "Let's discuss how you're going to use the media. They could be your greatest asset right now."

"If I wanted to perform in front of cameras, I would have been an actor, not a hacker." At the traffic light, Catherine watched tourists board the Hyde Street cable car.

"You should express indignation–outrage at this debacle. That will improve your public image."

"Yeah, it did wonders for O.J."

The limousine clanked across the Hyde Street tracks and slowed through the traffic that snarled her block. Before the driver could pull to the curb, another clamoring group surrounded them. A Channel 3 satellite van was parked just ahead. Yellow flashers discoed with the blue and red lights of a police cruiser. One uniformed officer directed traffic around the congestion; another wrote citations. Reporters jostled for position, working their microphones as if they were geiger counters in search of gold.

The chauffeur opened the passenger door and Jordan Lawrence said to Catherine, "Give me a minute," as he stepped between two blue uniforms.

Catherine grabbed at his coat flaps, but the soft wool slid through her fingers.

"Hey!" She started out behind him; the onslaught of camera flashes made her back-pedal. She flopped onto the leather seat, huffed and crossed her arms tightly over her chest. *Okay*, she admonished herself, *assume a zen-like composure. Then confront the cameras.*

Beverly Rathman, who had been silent for the entire ride, said dryly, "Jordan is possibly the best defense attorney in the country, but he considers every case a marketing opportunity for his firm."

Catherine gritted her teeth and listened to his words above the purr of the Lincoln's engine.

"...Ms. Calabretta is appalled to have been questioned and detained for a crime, which even the District Attorney knows she did not commit. In their desperation to find a scapegoat..."

Forget zen; she bridled at his speaking on her behalf. She shoved the door open with the toe of her shoe. "May I borrow these?" she asked as she snatched Beverly's sunglasses off the seat and shoved them over her eyes. By the time her foot hit the pavement, Jerry Woodstock, the pushy *InfoTech* magazine reporter who'd interviewed her yesterday at the convention center, was in her face.

"Is it true, Catherine, that you and Forsster supplied undocumented Korean children—eight- and ten year-olds—to influential politicians for the purpose of sexual activity?" His eyes were microscopic hazel dots behind wireless Coke-bottle lenses. Corkscrew curls hung in disarray.

Catherine shoved by him and grinned over her shoulder. "I thought alien abduction was the big thing in your line of work."

Car engines revved; police whistles trilled. Catherine pushed toward the lobby door of her building, but didn't get far. Five reporters and a couple of TV crews closed the path in front of her. Lawrence's bulky chauffeur stepped ahead and smoothly blocked through the crowd. Catherine admired his style—very agile for a guy whose belt pretty much hit her at eye-level and whose shoulder measurements exceeded the width of her peripheral vision. Catherine put her palm against the starched back of his white shirt to encourage him to keep moving. Lawrence closed in protectively behind.

"According to his psychiatrist's records..." Jerry Woodstock called above the din in a voice that sounded like a Chihuahua on helium, "...Stephen Forsster was a sex addict."

Catherine wheeled, ducking under Jordan Lawrence's arm at the same time she ripped the sunglasses off her nose, coming face-to-face with the reporter. "Medical records are confidential," she snarled.

"Only if you don't have the right contacts, he said. Although I must admit, I haven't yet found much of interest about you, Catherine. Where are your secrets hidden...?" He leered conspiratorially.

Catherine punched her index finger toward the UCSB logo on his gray sweatshirt. "I'll find your source—"

"Yeah, right," he cut her off. "There's a whole world of leaky databases out there. Haven't you been reading your own interviews?"

Catherine did an about-face; the chauffeur/bodyguard followed suit and they inched toward the door of her building. Woodstock again edged out the din of reporters vying for attention.

"Forsster was known to have a well-developed black book. A lot of women will be looking to replace him. What about you Catherine? Got any prospects lined up?"

"What are you fishing for, Woodstock? *InfoTech* isn't going to publish crap like this," she hurled, still pressing toward the door.

"Didn't I mention I'm a freelancer?" he shot back. "I've already written headlines for three rags that are salivating for the details of this story. So, what do you think, Catherine? Should I advise the general public to buy stock in an adult toy company?"

Catherine wheeled and ran smack into Jordan Lawrence, who grabbed both her arms and tried to manhandle her toward the front door. She fought Lawrence while she shouted at Woodstock, "Stephen Forsster was a husband and a father. He was a philanthropist. He sponsored a kid's soccer team and his family is a major financial supporter of a rehab center for teenagers. I'm sure you could find lots of good things to write about him." She whacked Lawrence's muscular arm and shrieked through clenched teeth, "Let go of me, dammit." He freed her so quickly she almost lost her balance. She indignantly straightened her skirt as she continued. "Think about this Jerry: The Forsster children must be reeling from the loss of their father and no doubt they'll hear through friends what the newspapers print about him. Would it be a career-limiting move to describe him as something besides a zipless fuck?"

"Hey. You and your paramour conceived this story, Catherine. I'm just the humble reporter who's documenting it."

"Wrong!" Catherine shouted as muscular arms lifted her feet off the sidewalk and floated her toward the apartment building. "You're a mouse turd on the birthday cake of life!" She kicked and fought to get free until her feet scuffed the lobby floor. She glared at the chauffeur as he planted her on the tiles. "That'll look great on the ten o'clock news," she said and turned to Mrs. Dorsett, the building manager, who stood dumbfounded beside the concierge desk. "I don't have my key," Catherine said. The woman nodded silently and slipped into the manager's office.

"Where is it you conceal the fuse to that emotional fireworks display of yours?" Jordan Lawrence asked dryly.

"In my don't-dick-with-me closet," Catherine responded as she drummed fingers on the reception desk and craned to watch for Mrs. Dorsett. Eucalyptus branches in the fresh flower arrangement cast a medicinal smell across the open area.

"Imagine, if you will, that little clip being played by the prosecution just after I've addressed the jury with, 'Look at this woman's face and try to imagine her killing a living human being.'"

"How bad could it be?" Catherine shrugged him off as adrenaline dissipated, leaving exhaustion in its wake. "I didn't deck anybody. I didn't even say the F-word."

"That's true. And there's no prior of your having skewered your enemy's skull and left it to decompose at the gates of your draw-bridge," Lawrence said as Mrs. Dorsett returned and held the key solemnly for Catherine.

Catherine murmured her thanks and said, "I'm not a barbarian," to Lawrence as she headed for the elevator. "I would never pollute the environment in such a disgusting manner."

"The police were here yesterday," Mrs. Dorsett called. "I phoned your office when they showed up with that search warrant. I didn't know you'd been arrested. That black guy came to get your dog. He almost got himself arrested...."

"Unplug your phone," Lawrence said to her departing back. "You've just amphetamined the media frenzy... and you'll be getting crank calls by now. Don't make any comments about this case until you talk to me."

Catherine nodded as the elevator doors closed. She would gladly avoid the media. In fact, she planned to climb into a hot bath and ignore the entire world.

Catherine turned the key and stepped into the eerie silence of her seventh-floor apartment. The cluttered, hushed hallway smelled foul—like sweat. She immediately spied the eight-by-fourteen-inch pages of the search warrant lying on the hall table. She skirted bedding and a jumble of bath towels past a picture hanging askew to the Post-it note stuck on the entry hall mirror. She read: *Garbo is with Wilson. Call as soon as you get this. Joel.*

Relief surged. Since Chloe's departure for the Sorbonne in Paris a year and a half before, Garbo, Catherine's three-year-old Weimaraner, had filled in as surrogate child. Wilson Ramsey was well established as Garbo's "primary care giver" when Catherine was on the road. The dog was in good hands.

A quick scan of all rooms confirmed that Hiller's minions had invaded her sanctuary and pawed through her personal belongings. In the bedroom, mounds of lingerie, sweaters, T-shirts, and miscellaneous clothing on hangers lay piled on the floor. Peach sheets were tumbled into the corner and the king-size mattress hung crooked on the box springs. Catherine ground her jaw, ripped off the red cashmere blazer, marched into the bathroom, and, abandoning thoughts of a luxurious soak, turned on the shower jets full force, anxious to scrub away the jail cell experience. As she stuffed the jacket into the dry-cleaning bag, the phone rang. She picked up the bedroom extension.

"Yes?"

"Ms. Calabretta? This is John Samuels with *Enquirer* magazine. Is it true about Mr. Forsster?"

Catherine slammed down the phone and stared at it. It rang immediately. She yanked the plug from the wall and followed the ringing to the other three extensions, pulling plugs as she went. Back in the bedroom, she hurled her shoes against the wall, clawed the back buttons of her dress, and was just about to yank it over her head when she thought of the FedEx photos... and the possibility,–remote as it might be,–that they'd been shot in her own bedroom. She let the silk resettle on her hips as she carefully scanned the walls, up high, close to the ceiling. Above the closet door was a four-inch, freshly plastered, ragged splotch encompassed by a squiggly blue pencil line. It took only a moment to realize a smoke alarm had hung there when Catherine left her apartment yesterday morning. Where the hell was it now?

She dashed to the kitchen, found a flashlight and a step stool, and examined the wall. The new plaster was dry. Inside the closet, on the backside of the patch, a blue-lined, gaping hole blotched the otherwise unblemished surface. Directly beneath, white powder silted the hardwood floor. On the backside of the light socket, she found a newly carved inch-wide gap, also outlined in blue.

She slumped onto the edge of the bed and stared at the plaster patch as the shower hissed and steam rolled out of the bathroom. Where was the smoke alarm—the one that had been installed some... what? Six? Eight months ago?

If the cops had removed it, they certainly wouldn't have bothered to plaster over the hole. She snatched up the search warrant from where she'd tossed it on the mattress and, at the end of the legalese, found a list of items the cops had searched for, including "video camera" and "video location." She peered at the spot again. While she was out preaching about electronic invasions of privacy, had someone perpetrated the most basic of low-tech invasions on her planting a camera in her own bedroom? And then removing it before the police searched her apartment?

She rocked forward, cradling head in forearms as if bracing for a crash. After an indeterminate amount of time with unanswered questions swirling through her mind, she trundled to the shower. Hot spray scoured away jail-cell memories. Afterward, she pawed through the clothes pile on the bedroom floor until she found a sweat suit. Damp hair finger-combed, she skulked across the hall to the room that served as her home office.

Shades were pulled high on the two walls of windows. Coit Tower glared white to the east. Alcatraz, to the north, felt like a personal taunt. Layers of file folders, pens, paper clips, and business cards were strewn across the rug. The careless destruction tightened her jaw. She straightened the dartboard that hung lopsided on the far wall, found a cell phone, and dialed Mrs. Dorsett downstairs. The answering machine picked up and Catherine left a message that she wanted to ask some questions about the smoke alarm. Then she dialed Joel

Hodges at his ETC office. While the phone rang, she located a cache of darts and tossed off three quick bull's-eyes.

"Were you *really* banging Stephen Forsster?" Joel whispered conspiratorially as soon as he heard her voice.

"How are things?" she responded, ignoring his penchant for collecting—and dispensing—, gossip.

"Oh honey, let me tell you, Mercury is truly retrograde. My astrologer warned me to stay in bed today. We closed the Pac Rim Conference booth early because people only wanted to ask about you and your... um... situation. Sam's in such a snit you'd think he had an extra-sharp, number-two pencil lodged up his butt. Reporters harassed us until we had building security turn off elevator access to our floor. Employees are asking indiscreet questions. We've lost tons of man-hours on the BankNet project because no one can focus on their work—it's just a mess." Joel finally ran out of breath.

"You're a VP," she responded, hammering another dart to the center of the cork circle. "Assume a leadership role."

"Don't start on me," he sniped. "I didn't create this disaster."

She sighed and replaced the two unthrown darts in their slot on her desk. She changed the subject because she knew he was right. "How's Garbo," she asked, rhetorically.

"Oh, sweetie, I should have asked how you are. Garbo is fine. You know Wilson always takes really good care of her. I think he loves that dog as much as he loves his own mama. But where are you? You must have gotten my note—are you at home? We heard on the radio a little while ago that they were releasing you and not charging you with any crime. I should think not!" He paused and Catherine could almost hear his brain calculating. "Of course, I was absolutely floored to learn—in the newspapers, no less—that you were doing Stephen Forsster."

"What's the client reaction?"

"Oh, do we ever have a lot of curious people out there. Everyone here is getting these hi-how-are-you-and-by-the-way-is-it-true-about-your-boss?phone inquiries. People who wouldn't return our calls for days are suddenly very anxious to reach out and touch someone. We don't quite know what to tell them..."

"Suggest they toss their own soiled laundry into the ole Whirlpool and leave mine to me."

"That's rather a pompous attitude for someone whose sexual indiscretions are currently front-page copy," he gibed.

"Are you and Sam covering my meetings?"

"We cancelled or rearranged all your appointments for the next three days." He sounded miffed. "We didn't know how long you might be... incommunicado."

"Thanks. I should be there in a few hours. After I take care of some things here."

"Honey, don't worry about the office for one little second. We'll keep everything going. You just take care of yourself. I'm sure you need to decompress. A night in jail must have been just dreadful— very stressful. Are you taking vitamin C?" His pause was too short to expect an answer. "It must be very upsetting that your lover has been killed. And what about George Hallison? I can't imagine what he must be..."

"Where's Wilson?" Catherine interrupted. She had casually mentioned to Joel last week that she'd met—and was spending time with—George Hallison. Joel had immediately started reciting an article he'd read about Hallison and his winery, but Catherine stopped him. She wanted to get to know the man on his own terms, unencumbered by the gossip-column-style details Joel tended to spew from his repertoire.

"He's here. Debugging some problems with the BankNet firewall."

"I'd like to get Garbo as soon as possible."

"I'll send him along. And, by the way, Linda got your Rover out of valet at the convention center. It's in your garage."

Catherine's voice almost broke as she said, "My ace team. What would I do without you?"

"We love you too, honey. And I'm sure Garbo misses her mommy. You two can comfort each other."

She told him she had unplugged her phone and gave him the number of the cell phone she was using.

After she hung up, she trailed her fingertips over her computer keyboard and felt comforted by the familiarity. She glanced at the back of the CPU tower and checked the cable connections. At least the cops hadn't mucked with her hardware. She booted the system and logged on. From the audit program she could tell the cops had looked at her personal financial records, a few memos and her email.

The telephone answering software showed the system had logged thirty-seven incoming phone calls since Monday night. All but five were marked "Number Blocked" or "Number Unknown." Three were from Johnny White. She didn't know anyone by that name. She sighed and started to press the "erase all" button, but decided she'd better wade through the messages.

There were a lot of hang-ups and numerous calls from reporters who left callback numbers and messages imploring that she call them first.

Yeah, right.

But then "Johnny White," who immediately began denigrating her as a Jezebel who would bring God's wrath to all humankind, distracted her. When he began predicting earthquakes and famine, she pressed erase. After a dozen more messages from reporters, the famine-guy was back. She erased again and a new voice croaked: "Hey, guardian of privacy, this is your angel of salvation."

The voice sounded choked, as though someone had a boot stomped on the caller's throat. Catherine couldn't decide if the voice was male or female, but she didn't really care. She rolled her eyes and slid the mouse toward the erase icon, but stopped as the caller continued.

"Hiller thinks you're good for Forsster. He found a beige scarf like the one you're wearing in the picture."

Yeah, yeah, Catherine thought; there must be ten thousand pashmina wraps just like it in San Francisco. The "like the one you're wearing in the picture" caused a nanosecond's pause; but then Catherine assumed info about the photo had been published in some news account and the caller had learned of it that way. Another crank. She reached for the erase icon but once again was stopped by the words.

"He also found a silver card case. Etched on top with the Eiffel Tower; your business cards inside."

The Eiffel Tower card case? Chloe had given it to Catherine for Christmas two years ago. It was missing—she'd looked for it several times in the past few weeks. Her heart pounded. Had she lost it in Stephen's car? That didn't make sense; except for Monday evening, she hadn't been in Stephen's car for three months. She focused on the rest of the message.

"And he's got a latex glove with your prints on the inside, black particles on the outside. They're testing for gunshot residue."

Catherine's mind raced. She sometimes wore latex gloves when she changed printer cartridges, but was certain she hadn't been carrying one on Monday. Who was this on her voicemail? How could this person know so much about a police investigation? Catherine checked the caller ID screen as she listened.

"I have more." Breath wheezed audibly through the machine; Catherine's heart pounded harder. "But not until we meet. In person."

The tape went silent except for the caller's labored exhalations.

"Listen carefully," the voice rasped. "Do not tell anyone I called. I am your angel of salvation—but only if you are mine. Call me at exactly four o'clock." The voice scraped out a San Francisco phone number and the line went dead.

Catherine stared at the words "Number Blocked" on the caller ID screen, her pulse pounding frantically in her ears. That couldn't be a crank call.

She shoved back her chair and raced to the coat closet where she always hung the pale pashmina scarf on the hanger with her blue raincoat. She pawed through the garments on hangers and the ones on the floor. No beige scarf. Even more surprisingly, no blue coat.

She ran into the bedroom, again raking through the clothes heaped there. To the living room, where books lay in a jumble on the white carpet. She searched under taupe sofa cushions that had been thrown randomly around the room; under the windowseat pillows that were tossed in a pile. She went through each room—each closet—several times. She even went down to the garage and looked in her Rover.

Back in her apartment, she grabbed up the pages of the search warrant. Attached was a handwritten list of items the police had removed from the premises: mostly clothing, including the suit and blouse she'd been wearing when she met Stephen on Monday and three pairs of shoes. She checked and re-checked the inventory. The beige scarf and the blue raincoat were not listed. And they weren't in her apartment.

Catherine greeted Wilson Ramsey at her front door, and then bent to Garbo, laughing and cooing unabashedly as seventy pounds of wagging, mewling Weimaraner almost took her off her feet. Wilson hummed—self-consciously, Catherine thought. It wasn't every day he witnessed his boss playing kissie-face with a dog. Garbo aborted her greeting, sprinted down the hallway, and disappeared into the kitchen.

"Making sure her food bowl is safe," Catherine said with a grin.

Wilson responded with a slight curl of his mouth and a glow of humor in his golden eyes.

Catherine thanked him for rescuing her dog. "The building manager said you almost got arrested."

"Cops," he said, as if that explained everything. He glanced uncomfortably at the piles of bedding and towels in the hall floor. "Need help?"

"As a matter of fact I do," Catherine said, and he followed her into the office, ducking his shaved head under the arched doorframe, shrugging off his full-length leather coat.

Reflected sunlight glittered off the tiny gold hoop in his right earlobe. His pale eyes took in the mess strewn on the office floor.

"I need a cross-reference on this phone number." Catherine handed him the yellow Post-it on which she'd written the number of the raspy-voiced man who claimed to be her angel of salvation.

"Biz? Or res?"

"I don't know. I rang it, but there's no answer. Find out whatever you can about whomever is attached to it."

Wilson furrowed his brow. "How will I know if I'm onto the right 411?"

"There may be some connection to the police department."

"Messin' with the man," Wilson murmured. "What do you want to know?"

"Everything you can tell me. And I need it..."

Catherine's cell phone rang and she reached across her desk to pick it up.

"...by 3:30. Hello?"

"I'm parked down the street from your building," Joel's voice came through the phone. "There's a Channel 7 news van with three media types out front. What do you want me to do?"

"Pick 'em off one at a time and try not to get blood on the sidewalk."

"I'll take out the cameramen first, so they don't Rodney King me," Joel responded and the line went dead.

Catherine clicked off the phone as Wilson asked, "Joel?"

"Yeah."

"I'm on it."

Wilson disappeared down the hall and Catherine heard her front door open and close. A couple minutes later, as Catherine was restacking office supplies in the appropriate drawer, Garbo raced in carrying a ragged yellow tennis ball clenched in her mouth, her short, stubby tail wagging ecstatically.

"You could sniff the king of diamonds out of a deck of cards," Catherine cooed as she bent to scratch the Weimaraner's silky gray ears. The front door clicked open and Garbo dropped the ball, bared her teeth, and lunged down the hall.

"Don't woof at me, sweetcakes," Joel's words wafted up the hallway. "I know you're just a big old lap dog." Catherine smiled; Garbo whined happily.

Catherine and Garbo had recently begun visiting Joel's house on weekends because Garbo's antics were the only thing that brought a smile to chubby-cheeked Tatiana, Joel's four-year-old niece. Tati's mother, Joel's only sister, had died five months earlier after a long, HIV-related illness. Garbo seemed to read the little girl's moods. She dropped a ball at Tati's tiny feet if she seemed inclined to play; curled protectively beside the beatific child when she napped, as if wicking off the sorrow that enshrouded her. Garbo's interaction with Tati had reinforced Joel's affection for the dog.

"Aida sent your bag," Joel called.

The satchel with the FedEx. Thank goodness it hadn't been here for the police to find.

"Let's get you a cookie to help you recover from your recent watch-doggie trauma," Joel said to Garbo; and to Catherine as he passed the office door, "What a disaster. Is your housekeeper coming?" He dropped the soft-sided valise just inside the office door.

"I left a message," she responded and retrieved the satchel. The scent of cigarette smoke pricked Catherine's nostrils as she quickly opened the combination lock and slipped the blue and orange FedEx from the bag into a desk drawer. "Where's Wilson?" she called as she heard Joel rummaging in the box of dog biscuits.

"I was about to ask you the same thing. He said you have some hot project—something about getting information on a phone number. What gives?"

"Let's run that one under the 'don't ask–don't tell' policy."

"Well, aren't we just as cagey as the fricking Pentagon." He entered the office brandishing what appeared to be a thread-wrapped cigar.

59

His gray flannel suit coat clutched tight to his body and a billow of smoke preceded him. He raised his eyebrows, haughtily. "I guess I'll have to wait to read about it in the headlines, along with all the other intimate details of your life."

Catherine eyed the smoking mini-baton. "Are you preparing to burn me until I confess?"

"White sage smudge stick. I'm purging bad energies from your space." He waved it around the room as he continued. "You think you're a real mystery woman, but I know exactly when you got involved with your infamous love jones. Stand still so I can cleanse your aura."

He coiled the plume in her direction as she swatted him away.

"'Love jones'? Oh, yeah. That is soooo me," she said drolly.

"It was last year right after that Systems House interview. Remember when I told you you looked like my third grade teacher, Sister Mary Joseph, without her wimple?"

How could she forget? After years of Joel badgering her with "you need to Cleopatra yourself, kitten," which she interpreted as smearing some dark stuff around her eyes, she finally "got it" when her photo appeared on the front page of Systems House adjacent to a shot of Carly Fiorini from Hewlett Packard. Carly looked sophisticated, stylish, and powerful. Catherine looked like a female version of Bill Gates fighting off a bad bout of pneumonia. Even to her untrained eye, it was embarrassing. After a mental wrangling with one side of her ego urging her to "be your natural self" and the other side arguing "even the Range Rover gets waxed and detailed more often than you do," she hired a personal image consultant and was shocked by the simplicity of the transformation. A two-hundred-dollar cut-and-color job, some trendier duds, ten minutes in front of the make-up mirror each morning, and, for the first time in her life, Catherine felt feminine. Pretty—on the surface at least—because she knew that deep inside she was still an awkward, self-conscious redneck from Cow Patty, Texas.

"Remember?" Joel continued. "When you re-engineered yourself to look like a breed that purrs rather than one that woofs?"

She crossed her arms and glared at him. "How generous of you to omit me from the oinking and mooing categories."

Joel waggled his index finger at her and directed the smudge stick smoke into the hall. "That was around the time you stopped looking as if you were about to fling yourself off a very tall bridge—got some natural color in your cheeks and a sparkle in your lovely green eyes and you looked as though you were doing each and every one of the things your shit-heel ex-husband would disapprove of. If it wasn't because of Forsster, then it was some other man."

"I should be flattered you didn't suggest it was a team of plow mules."

"Don't sound so defensive. Personally, I'd be delighted to hear the body count was higher. Speaking of which..." He clamped his front teeth around his index finger and looked anxious.

Catherine dropped her chin and glared through her eyebrows.

"I'm an itty bitty bit confused about the thing between your current *amour* and the late, great Stephen Forsster—assuming of course, George Hallison still gets the nod in your heartthrob department."

It wouldn't have surprised Catherine if Joel asked about the connection between her friend Laura Tyler Jackson and both these men who'd inhabited Catherine's bed, because it had been preying on her own mind that Laura had been responsible for Catherine meeting each of them. But George and Stephen involved in some coincidental manner?

"Forsster and Hallison in a relationship? If this is some kind of drag queen fantasy, it falls in the 'more than I want to know about you' category."

"Oh, my God, you *don't* know." His eyes held drama—no humor.

Catherine studied him quietly. "Cut to the chase, Joel," she said with a sense of dread. Joel was obsessed with the local social scene. He knew all the players. If he thought George and Stephen were connected in some way, Catherine's intuition told her he wouldn't be wrong.

"George Hallison used to be president of San Francisco Financial Services. He worked for Judd Delaney—the founder. But when the old man died, his grandson—same grandson being one Stephen Forsster—" Joel said, hands splayed dramatically, herbal smoke wafting toward the ceiling "wanted to run the firm, so he convinced the board of directors to oust Hallison."

Catherine sank to her chair, a sick feeling lodging in the pit of her stomach. She turned her back on Joel and stared unseeing at Coit Tower.

Like herself, George Hallison was a very private person. He dispensed the details of his past sparingly. On their second date, he talked briefly about his wife of twenty-six years, who had died two years previously from ovarian cancer, and about his 'corporate career', which had ended at about the same time.

When Catherine inquired, he explained that for the last fifteen years of his corporate life, he had run a family business. He gave her a wry smile. "Unfortunately," he'd said, "it wasn't my family—and it wasn't my business. When the old man died, the grandson made it his mission to take the helm. When Jennifer got sick... I chose to focus on helping her heal instead of fighting political battles. I resigned."

"Are you sorry?" Catherine had asked.

"I'm proud of the business I built." He shrugged. "Now I have a different career. I enjoy the physical labor of running the vineyards... the winery." His expression turned morose. "Under junior's two-year reign, the company's stock price has dropped eighteen percent." He looked wistful. "I couldn't save Jennifer, but I'm glad I had those last months with her."

"Honey, how could you not know?" Joel asked gently.

Catherine lowered her head into both palms. She thought about George Hallison. How he slept curled tight against her in his king size bed—how good and how natural it felt to be with him. Yes, she was terrified by the unfamiliar emotions she was feeling for this man; but she had been hopeful that she might get past them to... To what?

For the first time it occurred to her there had been no phone message from Hal. Had he left one at her office? She ran her hand through her hair; tried to put herself in Hal's place, tried to imagine what it must feel like to learn—in the newspapers, no less—that your new lover was previously sleeping with your nemesis.

Joel rummaged through the clutter on the desk, located a brass pencil cup, and ground the smudge stick against the side until the smoke died. "The morning paper says Hallison has been called back to run SFFS. Apparently..."

"I don't want to hear anymore." She held up both hands like a traffic cop taking on hostile commuters. "I can't think about this now." She couldn't allow her attention to be redirected or her energy to be sapped by the dejection that threatened. "You don't mend the fences when it's plowing season." She picked up a stack of folders from the mess on the floor and shoved them haplessly into a drawer.

"Well excuse me for mentioning it, but you look as if you were standing in the middle of the field when the John Deere came through."

"I held the dance, and now I've paid the band. Let's just refocus on the job to be done."

"Which is...?"

"Research."

"Well, I'm the research queen." Joel flashed a fake smile. "So who's Wilson checking out?"

"I told you..."

"I collect secrets, I don't dispense them," he snipped. "And I'm just about maxed out with your tight-lipped, clenched-rectum attitude."

She slumped in her chair. "Okay, Wyatt Earp. Listen up." She speed-dialed her voicemail and pressed play. "I am your angel of salvation," rasped through the speakerphone.

Joel looked surprised, then scoffed. "A drag queen with laryngitis." But by the time the message ended, Joel's brow was furrowed with concern.

"Oh, sweetie, do you think he knows what he's talking about?"

"The pashmina scarf is missing."

"Houston, I think we have a problem. I'll go back to the office right now and help Wilson do the digging." He started for the door and then turned. "You can't go meet this guy by yourself—he sounds like someone who participated in Jimmy Hoffa's *bon voyage* party. I'll send Wilson—"

"I don't want Wilson to go. He needs to finish the test work on BankNet." She looked at Joel. "Lone Ranger. No Tonto."

Joel planted both hands on his hips and narrowed his eyes. He sauntered back toward Catherine, maintaining a steely gaze. "Gonna do it all on your own, huh? Just close out everyone. When are you gonna figure out that *life* is a team sport?"

"I'm not closing..."

"Push us away like you always do. You know, Catherine, you and I have been friends—close friends, I thought—for nine years. I can make jokes about it, but the truth is, it's really very hurtful to learn in the newspapers—along with everyone else—that you, my good friend, have been involved in a year-long affair, but you didn't trust me enough to tell me about it."

"Joel, you know..."

"Yes, Catherine, I know how you are about your privacy. You use it as an excuse to keep us all at bay. To let no one in."

She spoke quietly. "You get hurt when you let people in."

"Is that why you chose to have sex with a man who was emotionally unavailable?"

"Whoa. That's so low a snake couldn't get under it if he'd been smushed flat by a tow truck."

"Don't try to hide behind that Texas cow-patty bullshit. It doesn't fool me like it fools everyone else. Here you are, embroiled in a situation that could very well destroy your life—and a whole lot of other people's too—yet you still want to keep those of us who love you—those of us who care—you want to keep us at arm's length. Use us like waiters and hairdressers, let us perform whatever service you need from us, but not let us close enough to smell your fear, to see you bleed. Do you know how much it would mean to Wilson to be able to repay you just a little for the opportunities you've opened to him?"

"He doesn't need to repay me," she said quietly, gaze averted to the blue sky outside the window.

"Yes, Catherine, *he* does. You may not think you need anything from him, but he sure as hell needs to give something back to you. We all need to give something to you, Catherine, because we're your friends, not just your loyal servants." He dropped his hands to his side and his gray eyes were full of hurt. "I just wonder if you'll ever let any of us get that close to you."

He turned and marched down the hall. She heard the door slam.

Catherine swiveled her chair and stared out the window. Ferryboats churned white wakes as they cruised near Alcatraz. She heard the muted bell of the cable car as it climbed the Hyde Street hill.

She was just trying to insulate Joel, not drag any of them into this two-hole shithouse she'd trapped herself in. Did he really misunderstand her motive? This business of friendship confused her. And made her anxious. Nicolas, who had peppered their marriage with his unending psychobabble, used to claim it was because she hadn't been allowed to socialize with other kids when she was a child. No one came to play at her house; she wasn't allowed, "to waste time pretending to be a socialite." But, unlike Nicolas, Catherine refused to blame her deficiencies on some long-ago unhappiness. She simply needed to get better at this nurturing business. And Nicolas had, in fact, been helpful in that regard.

"When you hurt a friend," she said to the ever-attentive Garbo, "whether it's intentional or not, you feel just as bad." Nicolas had said that, and Catherine knew it was true.

"The phone number. It belongs to a jane," Wilson's voice came through the cell phone's speaker as he updated Catherine on his "angel of salvation" research.

"Name is O'Malley. Maureen," Wilson said. "Got two email files on the way to you. First one's short. Four pages. It's the 911."

Shorthand, Catherine knew, for "important".

"Second is everything else. We found a lot."

Garbo turned three circles and settled at Catherine's feet. Catherine toggled to her email screen as Wilson continued.

"The big stuff came from the media. January seventeenth Last year. She was front-page news."

Catherine opened the email file and read the headline. *"Homicide inspector Critically Wounded."*

Homicide Inspector? Was the "jane" a colleague of Hiller's?

"Good work, Wilson. Let me review this and I'll get back to you if I have questions."

"I'm hangin' here."

She hesitated. "Is Joel there?" She had rehearsed an apology.

"Went out for a sandwich. Told me to call."

"Okay. Thanks for your help." She clicked off the phone and turned to the screen, leaning to scratch Garbo's ears.

> *Police inspector Maureen O'Malley was critically injured in a late-night shoot-out when she accosted three men alleged to be suspects in a murder case. O'Malley and her partner, Inspector Harry Hiller...*

"Hiller's *partner?*" she whispered in disbelief.

Garbo raised her head. Catherine absentmindedly stroked the dog. She read the balance of the account and learned that O'Malley had been alone in an alley, waiting for back up, when the shooting occurred. Other details were sketchy, but concluded with:

> *O'Malley, a 19-year veteran of the San Francisco Police Department, is in critical condition at St. Francis Hospital, with multiple gunshot wounds to the back and shoulders.*

Catherine continued to study the email files until she dialed O'Malley's number, as instructed, at exactly 4:00.

"Jesus told me you would come," the voice rasped.

"Was that in a face-to-face conversation," Catherine asked dryly, "or do you communicate through visions?" Then she remembered the woman was in a wheelchair for life, felt guilty for her casual callousness, and started to apologize; but O'Malley rolled over her.

"Fuck you. Write this down, bimbo." She gave an address in the Sunset District that was a half dozen blocks from the ocean. "Be here at five o' clock. And try real hard to make sure you're not followed."

Even in the dusky fog, it was apparent the working class residents of O'Malley's neighborhood had little time for—or perhaps little interest in—gardening, painting, or even basic window washing.

A paperboy peddled toward the two-story, two-flat structure that was also Catherine's destination. He flipped a rolled-up newspaper in the general vicinity of the house and rapidly pumped down the sidewalk.

"Ya little fuck!"

Catherine paused, fingers wrapped around door handle, Rover door half open. The screech had a banshee quality and seemed to be originating from the shadows of the porch that was protected by a silver wrought-iron gate.

"I've told you a thousand times to put the fucking newspaper inside the fucking gate, you little Chink fuck!"

Catherine slammed her car door and crossed the pavement, eyeing the wheelchair-bound gnome who banged her palms against the back side of the gate, metal bars rattling against metal lock.

"You know what they say, Inspector O'Malley: You catch more flies with honey than with vinegar."

"If I wanted to catch flies, I'd plop down a big ole pile of fresh dog shit." The woman stared with a surly expression. "You're running for what—Miss fucking Congeniality?" She sounded like Wolfman Jack in desperate need of a nicotine patch.

Catherine tried to reconcile the information Wilson had compiled with the concave-chested, chalky-skinned woman with long, gray-streaked, fly-away hair.

Gold medal swimmer, 1976 Olympics. B.A. in Sociology, Ohio State University, 1977. Lieutenant, Senior Grade, U.S. Navy—honorably discharged, 1981. First in her class at the Police Academy; first female motorcycle cop in California. Weightlifting champion, Police Athletic Competition, Women's Division, 1987–1994. Mezzo-soprano, soloist, Grace Cathedral Choir.

"You don't believe kindness helps you get what you want, Inspector?"

"It's 'former Inspector'," she corrected. "Connections get you what you want." Her tone was bitter. She pointed a ragged-nailed finger at the rubber-banded *Chronicle* on the spiky lawn.

Catherine picked up the newspaper and slid it between the rusting bars. The woman shoved wheels and rolled backward through the opening, one of two doors that stood side-by-side on the tiny concrete apron. O'Malley reached toward a button on the wall; the gate lock buzzed and released.

Catherine stepped tentatively through the opening and followed the wheelchair down a dim hallway. The place smelled like spaghetti sauce and hospital disinfectant.

O'Malley rolled to a shelf that held a small boom box. She cranked the volume until Mexican music reverberated off the walls.

The space was configured as an all-in-one: traditional family room to the left, separated from the kitchen/eating area to the right by a hip-high, yellow formica-topped counter. A musty, blue plaid sofa and a scarred, unpainted pine coffee table shared the center of the small living space; a matching end table was bare except for the yellow shine of an economy-size Juicy Fruit package. Curtains with the brown geometric designs of the '70s closed out fog and dusk; fluorescent tubes cast heavy shadows and leeched life from colors.

Maureen O'Malley rolled between the tables and repositioned the dingy, Navajo blanket that wrapped her legs and covered the bottom half of her olive sweatshirt. Catherine stood at the edge of the room, arms crossed over her chest. "How do you know what they found at the crime scene?" she shouted over the music.

"I still have contacts."

Catherine read her lips as much as heard the words. "Sounds like a conflict of interest. Can we kill the mariachis?" she asked and marched to the radio, twisting the dial.

"Now you've got an audience," O'Malley said.

Catherine looked around the room. No one else was present.

O'Malley nodded upward and rolled her eyes to the ceiling. "The cunt that lives upstairs—she listens to everything. Keeps me incarcerated—against my will." She screamed the last words and the sound made Catherine's throat hurt. "You want her to hear us discuss your legal problems that's okay by me."

Catherine twisted the dial until Mexican trumpets were loud, but not deafening.

O'Malley sat perfectly still and stared at Catherine with hostile blue eyes; she looked like a House of Wax mannequin who might—or might not—come to life.

Catherine crossed the dingy carpet and stopped near O'Malley. "Do your contacts know you're passing information to a former suspect?"

"None of your fucking business."

Catherine folded her arms over her chest. "You said in your message that you're my angel of salvation, but only if I am yours. What does that mean?"

Maureen picked up the Juicy Fruit package, removed three sticks of gum, unwrapped them, and wadded them into her mouth. She smashed the gum wrappers into a tight ball and tossed them over her shoulder; they hit the wall and rolled under the sofa. She chewed like a baseball pitcher. "You didn't kill Forsster." She stated it with certainty.

"You're not going to win any blue ribbons with that kind of no-alarm chili," Catherine said, further convinced of the uselessness of this meeting.

"You've been framed. Big time. There's enough evidence to lock you on Mars."

"My attorney says they don't have a case—that they would have charged me and kept me in jail if they did."

"You're too high visibility for the D.A. to go circumstantial. He wants Hiller to wrap up a few details before he files." O'Malley chewed contemplatively. "Hiller's like a hawk on a field mouse. I guarantee he'll nail you."

Catherine stuck out her chin defiantly, but her heart rate increased. "He's got nothing to nail me with. I didn't do it."

"You're right. You didn't."

She studied O'Malley. "If Hiller can't figure that out, why are you so certain?"

"The evidence is too clean—too convincing. You're too smart to leave a trail like that."

She didn't know how O'Malley had come to that conclusion, but she let it pass. "Then Hiller will figure it out, too."

O'Malley gave a short, barking laugh. "Hiller's two years away from retirement and embittered as hell about rich people buying their way out of justice. He'll go for you like white on rice."

"All he has is a photo of me on the beach with Stephen." Catherine paced. "The scarf, if he actually has it, doesn't mean anything." She paused. "You said you have other things."

"We deal first."

Catherine re-crossed her arms and stared silently at O'Malley.

Maureen gave the gum one last chew, pulled it from her mouth, and stuck it to the bottom edge of the coffee table where it hung like a large, ugly mole. She reached into the side pocket of her wheelchair and pulled out a gun.

"Wait…" Catherine locked on O'Malley's steely gaze, her heart pumping harder, feeling as if she were trapped in some Wild West time machine. Two crazy people—two guns—in three days.

O'Malley steadied the weapon with both hands, right index finger poised against the trigger; she aimed it at Catherine's chest and cocked it.

Catherine's heartbeat lunged into her throat and her eyes bugged; she rocked back a quarter inch.

With a fluid, practiced motion, O'Malley swiveled the gun 180 degrees, dropped her lower jaw, and put the barrel between her teeth; she never lost eye contact with Catherine.

"What the…" Catherine reached out her right hand as she started forward.

O'Malley pulled the trigger. Catherine froze as the gun clicked on an empty chamber. Even above the Mexican singer, she heard it. Once. Twice. Three times. Through it all, O'Malley sat unblinking, unflinching.

"What the hell are you doing!" Catherine yelled, her heart pounding so hard her whole body trembled. She rushed O'Malley, snatched the gun from her hands, and quickly opened the cylinder. No bullets.

"Holy shit! You are fucking crazy!" Catherine stomped around the kitchen, looking for a towel to wipe down the gun.

"You should meet my brother," O'Malley said calmly. "He says the same thing. Except not the 'holy shit' part."

Catherine marched back and forth, working off the adrenaline rush, polishing her prints from the revolver with a damp cloth, never taking her eyes off O'Malley. "Did that little demo have a purpose, or are you preparing an insanity plea?"

She picked up the package of gum. "I want a box of rounds. Thirty-eight caliber. Nothing special. You deliver and I'll work for you. I'll use my knowledge and my contacts to help you beat Hiller. And you'd better believe, without me, he'll fry your ass."

Catherine laid the gun on the yellow countertop and stared at her. "Rounds? You want bullets."

O'Malley watched silently.

"You're going to kill yourself."

She pulled three fresh sticks from the package and unwrapped them.

"I'm not in the business of helping people shake hands with the hereafter."

O'Malley shrugged. "Your life for mine. Make your choice."

Catherine snatched up her handbag. "You want to drill skylights in your brain cavity, go buy your own goddamned bullets."

"Can't get out."

"Of what? Your own way?"

"The house."

"A big-time detective who can't find her way out her own front door? Yeah, sure I need you for Hiller. You'll be about as helpful as a screen door on a submarine," Catherine rumbled.

"Look around you, bimbo." O'Malley stuffed the gum into her mouth and chewed while she talked. "My brother has rigged this house—my house—" she thumped her chest, "like a jail."

"Let your fingers do the walking. Try mail order."

"My brother cancelled my credit cards."

"Ever hear of COD?"

"Ever hear of a court order restricting deliveries except those received by—" she tilted her head toward the ceiling and yelled in her throaty rasp, "the fucking cunt upstairs who monitors my every inhalation—my every fart."

"Ask the paperboy, call Waiters on Wheels." Catherine threw up her hands. "How hard can this be in a country where any nine-year-old can buy a gun and ammo?"

"Waiters on Wheels... Ummm." O'Malley chewed and wadded the wrappers. "Hadn't thought of that one." She banked the yellow wad off the corner of the coffee table. It hit the arm of the sofa and rolled to the middle of the floor.

"You really want to die? Hang yourself from a light fixture. Slit your wrists with a kitchen knife. I'm not believing a hotshot homicide detective can't get creative with a suicide attempt."

"Has to be more than an attempt. Watch this." She rolled across the room and turned down the radio until the sound receded completely. She awkwardly positioned the wheelchair so she was facing Catherine. She inhaled deeply, expanding her chest against the olive sweatshirt, and held her breath like a little kid throwing a tantrum.

Catherine watched, waiting to see what O'Malley was up to. After a full minute, Catherine held out both hands in impatient appeal. "You can't kill yourself by holding your breath."

O'Malley put one finger to her lips, quieting Catherine. She glanced at her watch, and then silently raised her left hand. Fingers splayed, she began to count down from five. Her face was turning red. At the count of one, O'Malley pointed to a non-descript white plastic box that sat at the other end of the shelf from the radio. It looked like the baby-monitor speaker Joel put in Tati's bedroom so he could hear her when she cried in the night.

Sure enough, the box crackled and a strident voice pierced the room. "Maureen? What are you doing, Maureen?"

O'Malley released her breath and gasped three times before she answered. "I'm reminding myself how much my brother loves me. Go back to your soaps, cuntface."

"Don't make me come down there, Maureen. I'll tell your brother—"

O'Malley cranked the radio dial. Twangy guitars drowned out the voice.

"House arrest," she said above the blare of the radio. She wrestled up her sweatshirt and exposed a wide black strap that wrapped her ribs. *Med-Alert* was stenciled in large red letters around a caduceus. "It's connected to a computer that sends out an alarm if my heart rhythm changes substantially." She held Catherine's gaze. "I have to make sure when I do it that there's no chance for resuscitation."

Catherine studied O'Malley. The woman's fiddle was clearly missing a few strings. Sitting there with Mexican trumpets blaring, soliciting suicide assistance from a total stranger like it was an everyday negotiation. "I'm not gonna Kevorkian you," Catherine said. "Get somebody else."

"Look, you dumb fucking cunt," O'Malley choked. "You think you're not a court of last resort?" She wheeled across the small space and jerked to a stop at Catherine's knees. "I've exercised my other options. I tried to starve myself while I was still in the hospital—they just shoved feeding tubes into my stomach until they convinced me I couldn't win. The first day I was home, I smashed the TV screen and slit my wrists with the glass—waited until the fucking day nurse left, but the alert system kicked in and summoned the fire department and the fuckers got here before I could bleed out. The judge, the one whose cock my brother is undoubtedly sucking, told me if I try this one more time, he'll put me in a loony bin—and, in fact, the only reason he hasn't done so already is because he's known me for twenty years and now he feels sorry for me." Spittle sprayed upward then dropped to her lap; her screech was demonic. "The only fucking thing worse than this fucking wheelchair and every fucking asshole in the world feeling sorry for me is the threat of being locked up in the fucking loony bin! I'm not gonna fucking let them do that to me!"

She wheeled the chair into a sharp left turn and circled the room. "No one has the right to make me live this way! It's my fucking life," she stopped and beat her chest with her left fist, "and I don't want it anymore." She bowed her head and turned her chair to the wall.

Catherine sank to the edge of the faded sofa. For the first time, she noticed a dark stain that ringed the worn, beige carpet. She tried to imagine what it would be like if her own life were so drastically altered. She knew O'Malley was long-divorced and that she had no children. This most difficult game of her life was apparently one of solitaire. Catherine didn't know this woman, but she felt an overwhelming sadness for the situation Maureen found herself in.

"Why don't you get help? Talk to someone."

"Fuck help. A court-appointed psychiatrist comes here twice a week. He hasn't done a fucking thing to *help* me get up and walk away from this goddamned chair."

Catherine moved to the window and parted the musty curtains. Smoke shimmied from a chimney two houses away; a streetlight blinked on, creating a rosy pool against the inky sky. Across the chain-link fence, a neighbor was spotlighted at her kitchen window, arms and shoulders rotating as if she were washing dishes. Or peeling potatoes.

"I'm sorry for the bad things in your life," Catherine said. "But I can't help you."

"That's your fucking choice." O'Malley turned, tight-jawed, and wheeled toward the kitchen. "I'll find someone who will and you can memorize my obituary while you're passing time on death row."

Catherine pivoted, picked up her handbag from the sofa, and started down the short hallway. Police department contacts or not, she was ready to put some pasture between herself and this wild-eyed mare. Just as she reached for the doorknob, Maureen's voice stopped her.

"Hiller thinks you killed Forsster because of the videotape."

Catherine turned back, apprehension filling her voice. "What videotape?" The search warrant indicated the police were looking for video equipment and a video location.

"The fuck film."

She walked back into the room and stared at O'Malley.

"You and Forsster. Fucking. Recorded for all posterity."

Heat climbed Catherine's cheeks and acid backed up in her stomach. This was the confirmation she'd dreaded. "We never taped..."

"Somebody did. In your very own bedroom, from a location above the closet on the wall opposite your four-poster bed."

Catherine sank into a kitchen chair. How did O'Malley know she had a four-poster bed? "Did you see it? What makes you so sure it was me?"

Maureen filled a tea kettle with water. "The search confirmed the location." Her face contorted into a lascivious sneer. "From what I hear, your gynecologist coulda confirmed your identity without ever seeing your face." She put the kettle on the electric burner.

"Where did Hiller find the tape?"

"Forsster's car."

"But..." Catherine scrubbed her forehead with her fingertips.

"I figure you've got a couple of days—a week if your luck runs better than Evil Kneivel's—until Hiller rolls you up."

"This can't be happening." Panic pressed through her veins.

"You'd better find out who popped a cap on Forsster before Hiller takes you permanently off the streets." She took two brown mugs from a bottom cupboard. "You know that picture of you on the beach with Forsster? They don't know who took it." She dropped teabags into the cups. "It appeared at the station—no one knows how it got there. It's marked with a date, but there's no one to corroborate it."

"Then they can't—"

"If there's gunpowder on that latex glove, you're in deeper. A couple more pieces fall in place and you're dead meat."

The kettle whistled and O'Malley rolled to the stove.

"Why would anyone tell you this?"

The bitterness returned to O'Malley's tone. "Because they owe me." She poured steaming water into the teacups. "I've seen your prize stud-fuck in action. He caught our attention in a stake-out three years ago." O'Malley put the kettle back on the burner. She shoved a steaming teacup toward Catherine and blew vapor off the top of her own. Rancor colored her words. "Forsster was a devoted family man, just like the media is portraying him, but he was also a risk junkie. He dealt street drugs to his yuppie friends—packed his own nose pretty regularly. And he liked to fuck other men's wives in very public places."

"You saw him doing that?" She felt color rise.

"So many times I could pick his dick out of a line-up."

"So you have ideas about who might have killed him?"

O'Malley looked contemplative. "If you include cuckolded husbands, it's gonna be a really long list."

Catherine paced, feeling trapped. The things Maureen told her tied to Hiller's questions about gloves and video cameras.

Maureen interrupted her thoughts. "You're not like Forsster's other women. He mostly fucked socialites. Rich housewives whose only schedule conflicts were tennis lessons and manicure appointments." She squinted through the steam of her cup. "Why did you get involved with him?"

Catherine shrugged it off. "My manicurist went on vacation."

"Yeah right. And next you're going to tell me you moonlight as a dancer at the Beaver Club?"

"I just..."

Catherine rose and walked to the window again, parting the curtains and staring into the night. The woman was no longer at her kitchen sink; her window was dark. Somewhere on the other side of the fence, a dog barked and a trash can rattled. She knew exactly why she'd padlocked her heart and opened herself to an emotionless sexual relationship. And the memory still had the power to flame her cheeks and pierce her heart.

"Catherine, dear," Nicolas had said one night a year before Catherine left him, "you have to understand that our love is mature now. It's no longer a frivolous, sexual love." He reclined on a pile of pillows propped against the headboard, lamplight pooling on his freshly pressed, blue-striped pajama shirt and the copy of *Psychology Today* on his lap. She stood in a white satin nightgown, towel-dried hair redolent of jasmine blossoms, frothy toothbrush in hand, staring at him from the bathroom door. The scene was as crisp in her mind as if it were being staged at that very moment in Maureen O'Malley's living room.

Nicolas removed his reading glasses and lowered them to the magazine. "And quite frankly, dear, you should face the fact that you're no longer eighteen. Gravity and childbirth have worked against you. This nymphet behavior is unbecoming in a woman your age."

He gave her his kindest, fatherly-psychiatrist, you've-forced-me-to-state-the-ugly-facts-of-this-unfortunate-situation expression as she put the toothbrush in her mouth, backed into the bathroom and closed the door.

"I didn't mean to hurt your feelings, dear," he called from the bed. "But you keep trying so hard... and you must understand that women your age are simply not sexually desirable..."

His voice trailed off. Catherine felt as though she had walked haplessly into an out-of-the-park baseball bat swing.

She spat toothpaste into the sink and ripped the silky nightgown over her head. She refused to look in the mirror as she grabbed a baggy tee shirt off the wall hook and pulled it over her head, refusing to look at the naked body her husband apparently found repugnant. What was so wrong with her that Nicolas—who understood so much about people... about relationships... about sexuality—that her own husband found her loathsome? She must truly be inadequate in some way she didn't understand. She covered herself with a shapeless, flannel robe and dropped onto the toilet lid. Hung her head and sobbed.

When she finally turned off the light and quietly opened the bathroom door, Nicolas' bedside lamp was dark and he was curled on his side, snoring loudly.

Standing in O'Malley's living room, Catherine pushed away the memory and stared defiantly at her inquisitor. O'Malley sat like a crouched cat watching a bird hop closer.

"Because he was safe," she confessed. "I got involved with Stephen because he was safe."

"Maybe he didn't infect you with HIV," O'Malley's full-blown cynicism was back, "but if you don't find out who killed him, you'll have to choose between electric chair... and lethal injection. How fucking safe is that?"

The two women stared silently at each other.

"Call up your high-priced attorney," O'Malley said, "and tell him you've got a big problem. He's got a hot-shit private investigator, Bobby Windsong, who does work for him. Hire Bobby. And tell him I'll help with the case." She pointed a stiff finger at Catherine. "But don't tell anyone about our deal."

Catherine picked up her purse. "We don't have a deal."

Through the slammed door, she heard Maureen O'Malley screeching, "You'll be back! Jesus told me you would come."

"Definitely an inside job, lady," the locksmith said, pointing at the corner window in Catherine's home office. The man wiped his hands on his dark blue jumpsuit and began clanking tools into a metal box.

Catherine wrapped her arms around her chest and tried to stop shivering. She felt like a hunted animal—one that hasn't yet identified the hunter.

"Fixed it so's the window appeared to be locked, but what he did was he removed the guts. See here?" He held up the defective part for her to see. "Once he did that, he could come in or out that fire escape anytime he wanted to."

Her hands trembled uncontrollably as she wrote a check. Garbo shadowed her when she walked the man to the door.

"You need another set," he said as he handed over keys to her new locks, "you just call up and tell me."

She thanked him and closed the door. She turned the shiny new bolt and began to hyperventilate. She tried to walk off the stress, pacing up and down in the hallway. Garbo lay at the edge of the living room rug, chin to paws, eyes following anxiously.

She glanced at the dog. "You warned me, didn't you Garbo?"

The dog cocked her head and perked her ears as Catherine tried to remember the first time she and Garbo had returned to the apartment. Garbo had growled and went into a rigid stance, hackles rising along her back. They had both been spooked, Catherine remembered. She had gone through the apartment, heart pounding in her throat, checking closets and behind doors until Garbo decided it was a game. It must have been the third or fourth time it happened that Catherine's adrenaline rush changed to a bolt of irritation.

"Stop that!" she'd yelled at the dog. "Stop sending out those false alarms." After that, Garbo would begin the growling, then shrink into a guilty look. Catherine tried to remember how many times Garbo had done that—how many times this unnamed intruder had been in her apartment.

Catherine skulked into the bedroom and stared up at the spot where the camera must have been. The white plaster looked like exposed bone. She went into the office and removed the FedEx from her safe.

She studied the cutout photos. She stared at the spot where the smoke detector had hung and decided it was the right angle.

She scrutinized the other walls. Felt eyes watching and shuddered uncontrollably. She grabbed a suitcase from the closet and slammed in clothes and toiletries.

Even with new locks—with phantom camera equipment removed— she could not stay in the apartment tonight. Maybe not ever again.

She packed dog food and milk bones and leashed Garbo. She double checked all the locks and left the lights ablaze. She fled to her Rover and drove Lombard Street toward the Presidio until she found a motel that allowed dogs in the room.

She invited the surprised Garbo onto the bed and curled tightly around her, watching neon blink rainbows against the closed curtains.

Chapter Three: Thursday

"This wasn't what I had in mind, Catherine, when I suggested we exploit the media's interest in you." Sam Princeton's voice was a combination of sarcasm and concern as he stepped into the light shaft that sliced the dark hallway outside Catherine's office door.

Sam put his steaming Tully's coffee cup on the rosewood conference table and dropped his briefcase onto the seat of a plum silk chair. He pushed tortoiseshell glasses up the bridge of his patrician nose before he handed Catherine the morning *Chronicle*. "Perhaps in the future, we could devise a strategy that would be less... detrimental to ETC."

Catherine glimpsed *Privacy Advocate Publicly Accused*, folded the words in on themselves, and dropped the newspaper into the wastebasket beside her desk. She glanced at her watch. 6:40. Still a night sky out her floor-to-ceiling windows, distant Golden Gate Bridge aglow with the morning commute.

Sam's inquiry, "How are you holding up," sounded perfunctory.

Catherine breezed over it with, "Any negative reaction from clients?" She crossed the oatmeal carpet to the dartboard nestled between rosewood bookshelves. She whiffed Sam's herbal hair tonic and his Kona vanilla roast. Sam leaned over the wastebasket and retrieved his newspaper. The motion parted his khaki topcoat and revealed a brown wool suit. His neck was chafed under the white button-down shirt with its crisply knotted tan tie.

Sam's cheeks flushed rosy under his thin, carrot-colored hair. "Several clients have made less-than-discreet inquiries. Two business development meetings were cancelled by prospects."

Catherine tossed off two quick bull's-eyes. "Sounds like business as usual," she said, feeling a pulse of relief that the news wasn't worse.

Sam's face mottled. "Shame and embarrassment aren't 'usual' in ETC's corporate culture."

Catherine eyed him quietly before she asked, "What's the agenda here? Are we gonna work together to quell this stampede... get the cowpokes back to driving the herd down the trail? Or are you looking to conduct a sunrise prayer meetin' and a public hanging?"

"From the time the police took you away from the convention center, the media has been relentless." Sam removed his glasses and polished the lenses with a white handkerchief. Catherine could tell he was ramping up to deliver some sermon he'd been stewing on since her arrest. "No doubt they'll be back for round three today. I'm really curious what you're going to tell them."

"Screw the media." She hurled a dart in her best imitation of a major league pitcher, burying the tip in the board's tiny center circle. "They're like Julia Child whisking egg whites to a froth. They just want to see how much volume they can create by whipping air into the story."

He dropped his lanky frame onto the edge of the beige silk sofa, gingerly sipping his coffee from the grande-sized paper cup. "Consider that it might be to ETC's advantage for you to whitewash your antipathy for the press—just for a few days."

Catherine leaned her butt against the conference table. "Let's talk about clean-up and damage-control with the staff."

"Clean-up happens at the end of the storm. According to media accounts, the cops aren't through with you." He pushed his glasses up the bridge of his nose with a manicured index finger. "You have a different impression?"

She hedged. "I have a meeting with my attorney at nine o'clock to wrap up loose ends. I expect to be back to ridin' and ropin' before noon." She planned to hire Jordan Lawrence's P.I. to investigate Stephen's murder. That should quickly get the cops off her butt. Plus she expected the P.I. to finger the scumbag who'd planted a video camera in her bedroom and to retrieve any unauthorized home movies in which she might have starred.

"Have you considered what you'll do if this isn't... the end of it?"

"Oh, Sam, let's just brand this herd one rump at a time."

Sam sighed through a clenched jaw. "Shelving, if we could for a moment Catherine, your homespun aphorisms, I hope your primary objective will be to save ETC. That's certainly mine."

"Of course ETC is my priority." She eyed him thoughtfully. "You've got a plan."

"Just a suggestion. I have, after all, spent a good deal of time strategizing how we can survive this debacle." He put his cup on the glass coffee table and entwined his hands in his lap.

"If you continue to be linked to a murder investigation, it may be prudent for you to distance yourself from ETC. Because at this point, ETC and Catherine Calabretta are one and the same... which means ETC could be taken down by a scandal in your private life."

"Hoisting a white flag is not a talent I've honed," she said, but internal conflict bloomed into an ache between her brows. Would it be better for ETC if she... what? Stepped aside? The idea was too absurd to contemplate.

Sam shrugged. "It's your business, Catherine. If you've got a better idea, I'll be glad to help you implement it."

She was surprised he backed off so easily, considering he owned thirty-nine percent of the company.

He continued. "I'm just trying to put myself in the client's position— or even the employees'."

"I've been doing the same thing, Sam. Obsessively." She swallowed hard, voicing her gravest fear. She sank to the opposite end of the silk sofa. "You really think it's that bad?"

He held his palms up in surrender. "I think we're navigating an unfamiliar mine field and we have to be willing to think outside the box."

She pursed her lips and rubbed her forehead with her index finger. "Okay. If it looks like this investigation is going to continue, I'll take a sabbatical."

He crossed his arms over his starched white shirt and contemplated her silently.

"That would create distance." She heard the defensiveness in her own voice. "Then I wouldn't be associated with ETC."

"I know you're trying to come up with a solution, but a sabbatical isn't a separation. You give all your techies a sabbatical every three years—that's just time off."

"I'll take mine unpaid," she said indignantly.

When Sam's stoic expression didn't waver, Catherine said, "I'm not going to *resign*."

"There is another option."

"What? A swan dive off the Golden Gate Bridge?"

"It's a strategy similar to the one used by public officials when they take office. It removes any appearance of a conflict of interest. I could temporarily assume stewardship of the company—you would need to relinquish your stock to me, just on paper, and when your... situation, is cleared up, we transfer everything back to you."

"A paper transfer?" She eyed Sam uncomfortably, not wanting to appear unwilling to consider his solution. "I guess I missed that class at Cowlick U." She was confident in the arena of firewalls and network protocols and parallel sysplex; but finance—and this separation of church and state—was foreign territory.

"I'm not an attorney, but I know the guy who handled it for Gray Davis and for Ronald Reagan. I could have him draw up the papers and then we'd both have the answers to your questions."

"Hmm." Until that moment, she hadn't realized her heart could get heavier. "I'll think about it."

"Well," Sam said with a look of encouragement. "Don't put much attention on it for now. Hopefully this will all blow over and we won't have to think worst case scenario."

"I'll take that as a show of support, Sam," Catherine said as her phone rang. "I'm really sorry for..." She wasn't quite sure what to apologize for. She walked to her desk and distractedly lifted the receiver after the second ring.

Sam gave her a thumbs up. He picked up his coat, briefcase, and newspaper and left her office.

Catherine blew air through tight lips.

Before she had a chance to say hello, she heard, "I can't believe what I just read in the *New York Times*."

Although the voice was an octave higher than usual, Catherine immediately recognized Laura Tyler Jackson.

Catherine had tried to reach Laura at her ad agency yesterday, but learned she was on a business trip to New York. This morning, Catherine had left an urgent message.

"You know how I love being front-page news," Catherine quipped.

"I tried to reach you at home last night, but you didn't answer. I'm so upset about Stephen's death—I heard about it yesterday. But I'm dumbfounded about this thing in the newspaper. They think you're linked in some way? What the hell is going on, Catherine?"

Catherine explained about the arrest and the release.

"But you told me three months ago you weren't seeing him any-more." Laura's voice conveyed bewilderment. Betrayal.

"I wasn't seeing him—well except when he called on Monday. He..." Catherine didn't want to tell Laura about the photo cutouts that had been delivered to Stephen in the ETC FedEx. "He had an urgent matter to discuss."

There was a moment of quiet, and then Laura's words were slowed by confusion. "You were with him the day he was killed? That creeps me out."

Catherine gave minimal details about the trip to the beach—about the photo that documented it. She didn't mention the porn video that allegedly existed.

"You were there—at the place where he was killed?" Laura's voice was soft with disbelief. "Who took the picture?"

"I'm looking forward to learning the answer to that myself," Catherine said. "I know this whole thing is very weird, but that's not why I called. I need your help. I need you to tell me everything you know about Stephen's private life—about his business life."

"I can't believe he's dead." Laura's voice broke.

"Laura, listen to me." Catherine wondered if she would be able to get Laura refocused on the questions she needed her friend to answer. "You've known Stephen a long time."

"Not that long," Laura protested.

"Well, you certainly knew him better than I did. I need you to tell me about him. Everything you know. When are you coming back from New York?"

"Wait a minute," Laura sounded panicked. "You can't connect me with Stephen—or this murder. I can't have Ben thinking—"

"I'm not going to 'connect' you," Catherine interrupted, annoyance rising. "And you *did* know Stephen. Are you going to pretend other-wise?"

"Ben's re-election campaign is about to begin, Catherine." Laura's voice took on a note of escalating hysteria. "The media would love to link me to something tawdry, make headlines out of me. They already follow us like—"

"Okay, okay! Ease up on the reins."

Since Laura began dating Senator Ben Admire last summer, she had buried her party-girl image and donned the white-bread mantle of a politician's wife—a role Catherine knew Laura perceived herself to be auditioning for. Now she was almost prim, with her spare time invested in "causes" and political pseudo-debates, instead of the sexual escapades with which she'd previously amused herself. Laura strove to be viewed as a semi-conservative, serious-minded business woman. It was clear to Catherine her friend wanted to be the woman on the podium, standing ever-so-slightly behind the powerful widowed Senator from California.

"Did you tell anyone I introduced you?" Laura asked, still panicked.

"No."

"Please, Catherine," she implored. "Don't involve me in this. Just yesterday Ben said he thought the press liked me, that I could be a real asset, plus, of course, the fact that he loves me. This is a make-or-break-time for our relationship, Catherine. I can't—"

"Geez, Laura," Catherine cut her off. "I get it!"

"All right, all right." Laura inhaled deeply. "All right. Sorry if I'm overreacting."

Catherine heard her friend sigh with relief. "I also need to ask about George Hallison."

"Do they think he's involved in Stephen's death?" Laura sounded surprised.

"How could you introduce me to George when you had to have known about the bad blood between him and Stephen?"

"Oh, that." She sounded contrite. "I bet he wasn't happy to hear you had an affair with Stephen."

"I haven't had the opportunity to chat with him about it yet... what with jail and all." Catherine's sarcasm turned to exasperation. "Why didn't you tell me about the connection between George and Stephen? *Before* you introduced us?"

"I considered telling you... but I knew you wouldn't meet him if I did. And remember, he asked to meet you—because of that Senate hearing thing you were doing. Plus, he's always been a large contributor to Ben's campaigns, so... I didn't want to disappoint him. And besides, I thought you would like each other."

"You didn't think it might come up that his nemesis had deposited DNA samples on my silk sheets?"

"You'd already stopped seeing Stephen." She blew it off. "Besides, I didn't think you even knew where Stephen worked. You were always so adamant about not knowing anything personal about him."

"Oh. Now I see how this minor little oversight was actually my fault."

"Hold on." Laura covered the phone; muffled voices traveled through the line.

"I have to go," Laura said. "We're doing a big presentation to Johnson and Johnson this morning and my people are waiting for me. I'll try to call you tonight. I'll help you as best I can, but I have to be careful."

With that, the line went dead. Catherine stared at the receiver in her hand, irritated with her friend. She hadn't learned anything new about Stephen, but she had been reminded that it was George Hallison who initiated the introduction to Catherine. The coincidence was odd. Okay. It was more than odd. And it connected uncomfortably with questions she'd avoided mulling.

If someone really *had* followed Stephen—taken pictures, set up a secret video camera in Catherine's own bedroom—who had done it and what would they gain? Certainly Stephen's wife, Lili, was the most obvious suspect; but it could also have been a wronged husband. Or perhaps a business adversary? Someone who perceived he had something to gain by blackmailing Stephen Forsster?

Catherine battled her own logic—tried to keep it from going where it insisted on going. She had spent intimate hours... days... with George Hallison. Her gut told her he couldn't possibly be involved in this. But her brain insisted on a lengthier debate.

Catherine sat on a brown linen sofa in Jordan Lawrence's thirty-eighth-floor Transamerica office suite, disconcerted by the inward-leaning walls of this world-famous Pyramid building.

The defense attorney lounged in an antique leather side chair. Catherine inhaled the scent of lemon furniture polish and expensive cigars.

"I talked to the D.A. this morning," Lawrence said. "He wouldn't commit, but he alluded to the fact that Inspector Hiller thinks he can make you for Forsster's murder."

Catherine tried to maintain her composure, but her heartbeat ratcheted up several notches. "I didn't kill Stephen. And I'm convinced Inspector Hiller can't find his butt with both hands and a flashlight, so I'd like to hire your private investigator, Bobby Windsong, to help lead the big duck to the right pond."

He gave her a polished smile. "Ms. Calabretta, our job is to defend you against any charges that are forthcoming, not to conduct a police investigation. This isn't Perry Mason."

She returned the cool smile. "So you're saying your guy isn't as good as I was led to believe?"

His eyes measured her; then he shrugged. "He'll be here any minute. We'll ask him. In the interim, let's talk about your whereabouts on the day Mr. Forsster was killed."

Catherine briefly recited things she'd already considered. During the time in question, she hadn't talked to anyone, visited any retail establishments, or used her credit cards. She'd already checked her phone records and email account to see if she'd left timestamps that would exonerate her and found none.

She told Lawrence that when she left the beach on Monday, she'd flagged a taxi at Sloat Boulevard. She had considered trying to track down the driver... but that would only confirm her presence at the murder scene rather than support claims of innocence.

Lawrence scrawled notes on the leather-bound legal pad that lay across his lap.

"Let me be very clear: I'm not planning to lie here like road kill waiting for Hiller to pick my bones."

A male voice through the intercom interrupted with a, "Mr. Lawrence?" Jordan pressed a button on the phone bank on the table at his right. "Yes, Emory?"

"Judge Lerner is on the line for you. He said I should interrupt."

"I'm on my way." Lawrence closed his portfolio and laid it on a low, glass-top table as he rose from the antique chair. "I'm chief counsel on the Yurgarian defense. The case is out to jury," he explained. "I have to be available any time the judge requests. Please excuse me while I take this call." He left the room and closed the door.

Yurgarian? Catherine shuddered. She'd read about the case online. Stanislav Yurgarian, an infamous San Jose porn king, was accused of killing his wife and two school-aged daughters—stabbed them and sawed off their feet after a family wedding where the three were allegedly caught folk dancing in the kitchen with a cook and a waiter.

To suddenly realize she was inextricably linked to Yurgarian because of their mutual need for Lawrence's services made Catherine want to wretch. She rose and paced the Persian carpet.

The office door clicked softly and Lawrence strode in, followed by a tall, lanky man with a shock of unkempt sandy hair that lay across his head like dune grass permanently bent by the wind. Knobby shoulders poked his blue windowpane plaid sport coat as if he hadn't bothered to remove the hanger.

"Sorry for the interruption," Lawrence said. "This is Bobby Windsong." And to the man, "Ms. Calabretta was just telling me that she thinks we should look for Forsster's 'real killer'."

Catherine thought there was hidden meaning in the look that passed between the two men as she shook Windsong's dry, limp hand and studied his hooded eyes. Irritation clogged her veins.

"Hmmm," Windsong murmured unenthusiastically as he ambled to the cushioned window seat and lounged in splotchy sunshine, framed from behind by white puffy clouds that drifted over the Bay Bridge. He crossed one leg over the other; pale, bony shins glowed between the cuffs of his baggy brown cords and his tired navy socks. Light streaming in behind him made it impossible for Catherine to see his eyes.

Lawrence picked up his portfolio and resettled in the leather chair. Catherine perched on the sofa.

"Where were you at the time Forsster was shot?" Windsong asked.

"At the beach with my dog. I—"

"Mr. Lawrence?" the intercom interrupted again. "Judge Lerner's clerk."

"Excuse me," Lawrence rose and strode to his desk, speaking into the phone as a scrubbed and polished young man slipped quietly into the room and began gathering files.

Catherine blew exasperation through tight lips.

"Fine. I'm on my way." Lawrence hung up the phone and turned back to Catherine, explaining that he had to be in San Jose in less than an hour. "The jury is in."

The young man, presumably the assistant, removed a navy suit coat from a cedar-lined closet.

"Bobby will talk with you further to develop a plan," Lawrence said as he shrugged into the jacket and popped his cuffs. "I'll phone from the car to finalize the details." He took the attaché case his assistant handed him.

"Is the make-up bag in here?"

His assistant nodded yes.

Lawrence answered Catherine's unspoken question. "Can't have the defense attorney looking haggard on television." He gave her a conspiratorial wink and nodded toward the young man. "Emory has the Request for Services Agreement for your signature. You can leave a retainer with him," he said and he exited, Emory trailing like ripples behind a canoe.

Catherine stared as the door closed on her high-priced, media-hungry criminal defense attorney. "'Leave a retainer,' my ass," she thought.

She glanced at Bobby Windsong. His quick grin was the color of weak tea.

"Just you and me. Let's cut to the chase," he said fraternally. "Why'd you kill Forsster?"

She tucked her chin and glared. "You always assume your client is guilty?"

His shoulder twitched in a microscopic shrug as he hung a fresh cigarette off his lower lip. "It's not unusual. I see it a lot in my line of work." Windsong one-handedly rasped flame from a match that protruded from a closed matchbook like a finger caught in a door.

Catherine crossed her arms over her chest and peered into his hooded eyes.

He sucked on the cigarette and blew smoke in a steady vertical stream, proclaiming his self-imposed immunity from California non-smoking laws. "I worked a case last year where a woman beat her old man to death with a cast-iron skillet because he couldn't get it up one night."

"I see you get right into the psychological complexities of your cases," she drawled.

He flicked ash onto a porcelain plate and his eyes narrowed self-importantly. "Intuition is key in my business."

Catherine picked up her handbag from the sofa and turned to face him. Despite the fact O'Malley thought this clown was "a hot shit investigator," Catherine knew she wouldn't trust him to hunt down the fleas on Garbo's ass—if Garbo ever *had* fleas on her ass.

"And your intuition tells you I'm guilty."

He sat perfectly still, watching her movements like a lizard watching a fly. "Hey, I don't *care...* I do the job either way." He smoked.

"Even when my life *isn't* at stake, Mr. Windsong, if there's one thing I can't abide," Catherine said as she turned and headed for the door, "it's someone who doesn't care."

"Were you followed?" Maureen O'Malley buzzed the gate; Catherine walked into the dim hallway. The place smelled like bed sheets that were long overdue for washing.

"I don't think so. But your caretaker really checked me out when I came up the walk."

"Don't drop in on me anymore. Only come when I'm expecting you." Her Wolfman Jack rasp was tired and barely audible above the Mexican announcer who competed from the radio speaker. O'Malley's eyes were shielded by heavy lids; she looked as if she were about to doze. She wheeled to the radio and cranked the volume. The sound of mandolins, trumpets, and Spanish lyrics reverberated off the walls.

Catherine moved close in order to be heard. "I thought in your ongoing dialogue with Jesus, He might have mentioned I was on my way."

"Fuck you, bitch. I don't believe in God. I don't believe in heaven or in hell—except the one I'm living in—but Jesus spoke to me."

"Hey. Where I grew up, that was as common as river baptisms and speaking in tongues."

"In a dream. On Sunday night. Jesus—He looked just like the picture that hung in my catechism class—He pointed his hand at a woman who was standing by a lake, staring into the water. He said, 'Maureen, this is your angel.' The woman turned and looked at me, and it was you. Your face was so clear I coulda had a composite artist do a sketch. Then, two days later, you're front-page news, my former partner's trying to nail your fucking ass for Forsster, and I'm a believer. You are my angel of salvation." Her eyes had taken on a livelier spark. "And you're fucking lucky I'm yours."

Catherine paced in the small living room, impatient with the woman's delusions of angels. "I've just taken a leave of absence from my business," she said, mentally skimming the anguish of having called ETC's employees into the big conference room to personally announce she would be taking some time away from ETC until her "personal situation" was resolved. Bile backed up in her throat. She was ashamed for disappointing the people she cared about and terrified of doing irreparable damage to ETC. But after the Windsong/Lawrence debacle, she knew she couldn't place her fate in anyone else's hands. She'd decided to devote her full attention to finding Stephen's killer. She had to clear her name and get Hiller off her back.

"I've got two people to help with the investigation, as needed, of course."

"Good. Did you hire Bobby Windsong?"

The radio station switched to a staccato of Spanish phrases, with Catherine recognizing only "Mattress Town" somewhere in the middle of the auditory assault. She marched to the radio and twisted the volume knob, feeling instantaneous relief as the decibels fell away from her eardrums.

O'Malley pointed a tired finger toward the ceiling. "You want Judas to hear every word we say?"

"I don't care. I can't stand that noise," Catherine responded.

"Okay." O'Malley shrugged and rolled the chair backward, knocking into the corner of the unstained pine coffee table. "I'm sure she can use Hiller's snitch money."

Catherine clenched her jaw and twisted the tuner dial until she found "An American in Paris" on a classical station. She raised the volume to create a sound barrier.

O'Malley rolled her eyes. "So. You hired Bobby Windsong?"

"Windsong's a strutting example of the old axiom, 'It's better to be silent and thought a fool than to open your mouth and remove all doubt'."

"Uh, huh." O'Malley looked cynical.

"If Windsong's so hot, then I'd say anyone could be a detective."

"Right. So who, then?"

"No one you've worked with before."

O'Malley held up her palms as if to say, *I'm dealing with an idiot.* "You gonna tell me who'll be running this fucking op?"

"I will."

"You? Ha! What they say about attorneys applies double here. 'He who represents himself has a fool for a client.' Who are your help-mates? Batman and Robin?"

Catherine crossed her arms over her chest. "People I know. People I trust."

"Any other qualifications?" she sneered.

"They're good with computers. And they care a great deal about the outcome."

O'Malley rolled into the kitchen. "Call up San Q," she rasped, "and tell 'em to buy some new syringes. You're in line for lethal injection."

"Listen, buttercup. I clawed my way out of Hog Waller, Texas, which is so far out of the mainstream, they don't get Monday Night Football until Thursday morning. I've got a whole wagonload of experience adapting to quick changes in the weather and I know how to navigate my horse around leg-laming gopher holes." Catherine crossed her arms over her chest and held O'Malley's gaze. "With your help, I can do this."

"Are you telling me we have a deal?" Maureen filled a tea kettle.

"I can pay you. Anything you want. Well, almost anything."

O'Malley slammed the kettle on the countertop and glared at Catherine. "You dumb cunt. Have you been listening to me?"

Catherine leaned straight-armed on the counter and glared at O'Malley. "Don't call me a dumb cunt ever again—and no, I won't help you paint your brains on the ceiling."

She raised wiry eyebrows. "Think of it as giving me the ability to make my own choice."

"I'll do this investigation without you before I'll help you pull the trigger."

"Then get the fuck out of my face."

"Please," Catherine said. "You know I'm innocent. I need your help."

"And I need yours."

O'Malley put the tea kettle on the electric burner and twisted a dial; she snatched a box of Lipton teabags from the cabinet and dropped them in her lap. She turned to Catherine and studied her thoughtfully.

"I'm expecting a delivery. Stashed in the garbage can on the concrete pad at the side of my house," she said and a pointing finger accompanied her instructions to, "Go get the can."

"A delivery? In the trash can?" Catherine stared skeptically. "You're right. Maybe I don't need your help."

"Name a better fucking place that's safe from the warden."

Catherine considered picking up her handbag and simply walking out. O'Malley seemed to read her thoughts.

"I can't fucking help you if you're going to question everything I say."

Catherine pursed her lips, and then went to do O'Malley's bidding. When Catherine dragged the gray plastic container up the steps to the open sliding glass door, O'Malley instructed, "Bring it over here."

"You're kidding," Catherine said, but, when O'Malley didn't respond, she hauled the can to the center of the kitchen.

Maureen removed the black lid and Catherine smelled molded lemons and rotting food. "Take this bag out and open it." She pointed as the tea kettle whistled.

Catherine hefted the white plastic onto the floor and untwisted the tie; Maureen poured steaming water into two mugs.

"Does this have anything to do with—"

"Dig down to the bottom. I'm looking for a wad of paper."

"Promise me no one's wiped their ass on it," Catherine quipped dryly. She walked into the family room, picked up yesterday's newspaper, spread sections onto the floor, and dumped out days-old banana peels, rancid plastic food containers, soiled adult diapers, disposable plastic syringes, and the wrappings and remains of other and sundry medical supplies. Catherine remembered Nicolas, her highly paranoid ex-husband, saying you can tell a lot about someone from their trash. She realized she was learning things about Maureen O'Malley that she didn't want to know.

"You weren't aware of the video camera in your bedroom?" O'Malley asked as she peered at the pile of trash.

"Do I strike you as someone with porn star aspirations?"

"Not here," O'Malley perused the heap with a bored expression. "Move it over and take out the next one." She dunked her tea bag as Catherine gritted her teeth in quiet exasperation; her gut told her to go with it. She opened another plastic sack.

"For the sake of argument, let's say there was a camera, but you didn't know about it. Who had access to put it there? And why would they want to?"

"I've asked myself those very questions non-stop for the past thirty-six hours and I don't have any answers."

"Of course you don't, girl detective. That's one of the things you have to find out. Did Forsster have a key to your apartment?"

"No." She emptied the bag onto the previous pile.

"Never borrowed one, had some excuse to have it—even for a short time?"

"Never." She grimaced at the smelly mound. "You should recycle."

"I won't be here long enough to piss off the planet. Move those boxes," O'Malley pointed. "Somebody went to a lot of trouble to take pictures of you."

Catherine didn't need O'Malley to help her figure that out, but she let O'Malley continue without response.

"And don't assume the person who wired your bedroom is the same one who took the beach photo—or the person who killed Forsster for that matter. Never assume anything. That's rule number one. Rule number two is, don't believe anything anyone tells you. Verify your facts six different ways from fuck, and still doubt what you think you know. Take out that last bag."

Catherine spread more newspapers and dug into the bottom of the can.

"Who was being watched? You or Forsster?" O'Malley asked.

"I assume Stephen was the target, since he's the one who was killed."

"A reasonable, although not necessarily accurate, assumption. And it is, after all, an *assumption*. There." The finger pointed again. "Hand me that."

Catherine picked up a crumpled brown wrapper between thumb and forefinger. It looked like the wax-coated paper used by butchers. Maureen ignored a smear of goo and peeled back the sheet to expose a wad of white paper.

"Who benefits from Forsster's death?" She dropped the brown piece to the floor and laid the ball in her lap, then wiped her hands on the Navajo blanket that covered her atrophied legs. She rolled to the low counter, tracking wheels through the edge of the foul refuse. She began unfolding the corners of the ball. "Nobody kills without a reason, no matter how logical or how fantastical the reason may be. Check family members first, with the spouse being the primary suspect."

So far, O'Malley had offered up no esoteric investigative techniques, nothing that wasn't generically known by the television generation. Catherine considered again that she was wasting her time. She eyed the pages that were taking shape in O'Malley's hands and decided if they weren't relevant to her situation, she would terminate this association. "What do you have there?"

"The starting point of your investigation."

"Is this the delivery you were expecting?" Catherine asked skeptically. "In your trash can?"

"You think I shoulda had stolen case files messengered over from the station? Maybe asked Hiller to drop them off on his coffee break?"

She raised her eyes and turned snarly. "I wanna fucking die, not do jail time for tampering with a police investigation."

O'Malley laid the pages on the counter and ironed the wad flat with both palms. She squinted at the top page. "You're off the hook on the glove." She tapped the page with a yellowed fingernail. "Your fingerprints were inside, but there was no gunpowder residue."

"What is that—the lab report?"

Catherine scuttled over to see for herself, but Maureen yanked up the stack and stabbed her index finger toward the pile of trash. "Clean up your mess!" Catherine raised her eyebrows and maintained an eye-to-eye standoff before she moved back toward the smelly pile.

"I'll tell you when it's your fucking turn." O'Malley returned the papers to the countertop. She folded the top page and put it aside.

"Tell me what happened on Monday. When you were with Forsster at the beach."

Catherine hesitated, but only briefly. As she talked, she shoveled garbage into plastic bags and O'Malley studied the pages one at a time. Catherine told her story, including the bit about the gun from the glove compartment, honest in every detail, leaving nothing out. O'Malley interrupted occasionally for clarification, but all the while she examined the pages, back and forth, from one to the other. Catherine washed her hands and concluded her narrative simultaneously. O'Malley restacked the papers and held them out to Catherine.

"Here you go, girl detective. What have we got?"

Catherine walked to the kitchen counter and straddled a chair. The music changed to a pounding Strauss waltz. Catherine's jaw dropped as she stared at the photo of herself striding down the beach with Stephen following behind. It was the photo Hiller had shown her.

"How did you get this?" she asked.

She slid the page aside to look at the second one. Her eyes were drawn to Rorschach splotches of red. It took her a moment to realize she was seeing blood splatters and pools with Stephen Forsster's empty gaze at the center of the frame. Oh, God. Stephen. Dead.

Catherine swallowed hard as her mouth filled with saliva; cold sweat beads stippled her forehead. She clenched her jaw to suppress a heave and vaguely heard the chair hit the floor as she staggered across the kitchen and barfed into the sink.

After a moment, she turned on the tap, trembling as she splashed cold water on her face. When her stomach calmed, she ripped off a paper towel and dried her hands, blotted her cheeks and chin. She crossed to the bar, turned the photos face down, and stared at O'Malley.

"Who's passing you information about Stephen's murder?"

O'Malley's eyes were indifferent. "Bobby Windsong's viewed at least a hundred dead bodies in his career. Live and in person. Wet and fragrant. I bet he never once tossed his cookies."

Catherine righted her chair and sank onto it. She took a deep breath and steeled herself. She turned the photos over and spread them on the counter.

"What am I looking for?" she asked.

O'Malley drained her teacup and pointed to the photos of Stephen as she talked. The first was a close-up. Catherine noted how he reclined against the driver's door, his head tilted back, resting comfortably on the window, his left arm casually draping the steering wheel, the same way he had posed when he suggested she shoot him with the gun she'd removed from his glovebox. But this time, his eyes were rolled back in his head, his mouth hung open, and his shirt was soaked with blood.

Catherine forced distance between her emotions and O'Malley's words.

"The victim was shot with a large caliber gun. Three entry points. Head shot came last, probably thirty to sixty seconds after the first chest wound."

"How can you tell?" Catherine hadn't even noticed the bullet hole in Stephen's forehead.

"Because it didn't geyser the way head wounds usually do. The chest wounds..."

The blood on his chest looked like one big blob until O'Malley pointed out the two red-camouflaged holes in Stephen's shirt.

"...drained off the pressure in his upper body. No powder tattooing, so the shooter was at least five or six feet away. The perp just stood there biding his time... watching to make sure Forsster died."

Catherine shivered with the callousness of O'Malley's conjecture.

O'Malley aimed her finger at the other photo, which had been shot through the open passenger door from some ten feet away. Catherine could see Stephen's... Her stomach queased as she corrected herself: She could see *the victim's* body, as well as the full length of the Mercedes and the pampas grass growing on the dune behind it.

"What does this tell you?" O'Malley asked.

Catherine picked up the print and examined it closely.

"The car door was closed when he was shot. See the blood spatters on the inside of the door?" She pointed to the stains. "The gun was probably fired through the open sunroof."

"Good. What else."

Catherine studied the position of the body, with the knee cocked over the car's leather console. "The victim is relaxed." She swallowed hard. "He knew his killer."

She pointed to what she recognized as a white towel and a CD case that lay on the passenger-side floor mat, and to the glovebox door, which hung open. She looked up at O'Malley. "Did the cops find a gun clip in the glovebox?"

O'Malley shook her head no. Catherine felt some relief: If they'd found the clip, her fingerprints would have likely been on it, but where was it? Had Stephen retrieved his gun, loaded it, and then been shot with it?

"The killer was looking for something." She squinted at the steering wheel column. "Wait. There are no car keys." She looked at O'Malley. "Did they find them at the scene?"

O'Malley shrugged.

Catherine returned to the photo. "He's still wearing his Rolex so this wasn't a robbery gone bad."

"Dick 101," O'Malley said sarcastically. "Come up with something that any third grader couldn't figure out, or you oughta just fucking wait on the courthouse steps for Hiller to lock you up."

"Have you considered removing that sour persimmon you've got stuck up your ass?"

O'Malley studied her blandly. "My body's so numb I could have a whole tree rooted in there and I wouldn't know it."

"Sorry," Catherine murmured and flushed at her faux pas. She returned her attention to the photos and scrutinized them until her temples started to hammer. Just as she was about to give up, something caught her attention. "Hold on. I think I've got something."

She dashed to her car and returned with her tool case, flipped open the top, and pulled out the magnification work glasses she wore when replacing computer chips or motherboards. She switched on the headband light that always made her think of the seven dwarfs hi-ho-ing their way into the mines, then focused on the Xeroxed photo.

"He was killed by a woman. One he'd previously had sex with," she said, her look of conviction meeting O'Malley's rolled-eyed skepticism.

Catherine picked up a small screwdriver from the case and used it as a pointer. "Look at his tie. Look at the pattern of blood spatters."

O'Malley squinted. "There aren't any," she said.

"Right. I bet there are some on the backside. His tie was rearranged after he was shot."

"And that proves he was killed by a woman he'd screwed?"

"See the position Stephen's sitting in? Well, he had this ritual—I've seen him do it a dozen times. He was very fond of..." Catherine felt her cheeks begin to color. "He liked oral sex. But rather than ask for it directly, he would sit like this," she used the tip of the screwdriver to follow the angle of Stephen's thigh down to his ankle, "relaxed against the seat or chair, left arm casually back, and he would lift his tie with his right fingers and say something like, 'can I interest you in a lollipop, little girl?'—or something equally dumb and euphemistic. And then he would lay his tie back over his shoulder, like he was getting it out of the way. He was very paranoid about leaving signs that might clue his wife to his infidelity. Anyway, if he got a positive response, he would begin to unzip his fly—or he might just grin and point to his crotch."

"Mr. Seduction," O'Malley croaked.

"You know men. They like to think they're being cute. Anyway, the point is, if you look at this photo, look at this unmistakable line," she marked just below the knot of the tie, "where there's some blood splatter, then it's perfectly clean—except for this spot on the end that looks like bleed-through."

"Go on," O'Malley said, curiosity shadowing her skepticism.

"Okay. His tie was over his shoulder when he was shot," Catherine was getting excited now, "because he'd just tried his little blow-job ritual on whomever shot him."

"I'm still not there yet," O'Malley said.

"She shoots him and realizes his tie is still back. She had to know the cops would take pictures of the crime scene and if someone who knew Stephen, like she apparently did, saw him like that with his tie over his shoulder, they might put together the blow-job thing and start looking for women with whom he'd been involved."

"Coulda been a man. What if Forsster had just asked some guy to suck his dick?"

"He was homophobic. He wouldn't have done that."

"Maybe he did it as a joke."

"Hmmm." Catherine pondered that possibility.

O'Malley narrowed her eyes and stared at the photo. "Not too shabby, girl detective. But remember what I told you about 'never assume'?"

Catherine nodded and Maureen continued.

"So, how about this scenario: Forsster's in the car with some guy's wife. The guy sees what's going on, pulls his wife out of the car, plugs Forsster, and decides to do a little rearranging. Maybe even zips his dick back in his pants."

"Stephen's too relaxed."

O'Malley nodded. "Maybe." She continued to nod. "It's a good theory. But I'm warning you about quick conclusions. They'll trip you up and lead you way the fuck away from where you need to be." O'Malley pulled over the first photo—the one of Catherine and Stephen on the beach. "How about this one?"

"Do you know how the police got it?"

"It arrived at the station in a plain brown envelope, lots of finger-prints on the outside. None on the inside. None on the photo."

"So, it seems conclusive that someone hired a detective to follow us—I mean, if there actually was a camera hidden in my bedroom. And someone sent pictures to Stephen at his office. They must have been watching when he picked me up on Monday and followed his car to the beach."

"I don't think it's a P.I.," O'Malley rasped, "I think it's an amateur." She held up the photo. "Look at this picture as if you didn't know anything about it—who these people were or where it was taken. Would it convince a wife that her husband was having an affair? Because that's what most P.I.s are hired to do in cases like this."

Catherine studied the shot. "We both have our clothes on... there's nothing incriminating here."

"Right. How about convincing the police they're at the scene where the murder took place?"

"You can't see the Mercedes," Catherine said, getting excited. "And this beach could be anywhere. There aren't any identifying landmarks that would tell you it's the place where Stephen's body was found."

Now she understood why Hiller's case was weak. She was elated and sure she would soon be exonerated.

"The photo is shot tight," O'Malley said, "with nothing but these two fully clothed people marching down a beach. Even a junior investigator would do better than this."

"How about the gun. You can see the butt of the gun in my hand." Catherine held out the photo and O'Malley took it.

She shrugged. "You got *maybe* a gun. *Maybe* someone was killed with it. *Maybe* on this beach. Maybe on the same day." She dropped the photo on the countertop. "Not much of a fucking case. Until Hiller finds the photographer. And the murder weapon with your prints on it."

Catherine ran her hands through her hair, elation sinking once again to anxiety.

"And he fucking will."

"I didn't kill him." Catherine said the words quietly.

"Tell it to your priest," O'Malley said, "because nobody else gives a shit." She crossed her arms over her chest and stared into the distance. She pursed her lips and looked at Catherine. "Are you beginning to see how much you need me?"

Catherine treated that as another rhetorical question.

O'Malley sipped hot tea. "I've got fifteen minutes until the fucking physical therapist starts banging down my door. I want you out of here in five." She clunked the mug onto the countertop. "I'm going to tell you how to start your investigation."

"I've already started," Catherine interjected. She told O'Malley that Wilson Ramsey, one of Catherine's most trusted employees, was at City Hall doing research on the Forsster family. "Checking court records, property ownership, lawsuits—anything he can find." And that she had asked Joel Hodges, another key employee and a close friend, to visit Over the Counter, a popular bar patronized by stockbrokers and others in Stephen's profession. "I know Stephen went there often," Catherine said. "I sent Joel because I'm sure people would recognize me. Joel will be less conspicuous and hopefully learn more than I could."

"Ooooh, very impressive," O'Malley said with a roll of her eyes. "So you've decided you don't need my services?"

"Of course I need your services; I just can't agree to your terms."

"Oh, that. You will. Eventually." O'Malley smiled, cat-like. "Remember, I got the divine word, delivered in a dream by the Man Himself. You're my angel of salvation, Catherine Calabretta. Jesus promised it. And I think you're too smart to fuck with Jesus."

Joel Hodges loved being a vice president at ETC. He was thrilled that because he'd helped nail some high-visibility hackers, he was virtually canonized in Silicon Valley. But he lived for the day he could retire and spend all his time watching soaps and reading gossip columns.

John, his domestic partner of fourteen years, often said, "Too bad you can't do hair. You'd be ecstatic in a Maiden Lane salon, listening to rich bitches diss each other all day."

Joel pushed through the crowd at Over the Counter and perched on the only empty barstool. He ordered a '99 Sauvignon Blanc and scanned the room. Mostly male. Young Turks with monogrammed shirts and hundred-dollar haircuts framing their ski- and golf-tanned faces. This was Forsster's former watering hole. His crowd.

It didn't take long for Joel to realize the foursome—three men and a woman—who stood at a bar-height cocktail table directly behind him were talking about their fallen comrade.

"I'm not buying the Calabretta angle," the tenor voice came from over Joel's right shoulder. "Odds are it was a pissed-off husband."

"My money's on Rina Gold," a deeper male voice said with certainty. "I heard she was one burned babe when Steve-o told her he wasn't going to leave his wife to marry her."

Hmmm. Rina Gold? Joel was intrigued. She was a regular in the society columns, always photographed with different dignitaries, heads of state, crown princes...

Ice rattled in a glass and Joel strained to hear the only woman in the group.

"I can't believe you guys are betting about a dead man who's not even in the ground yet. How irreverent."

"Let me tell you irreverent," a different male voice picked up the lead. "Remember that NASD inquiry last year when Forsster's client," the man's voice lowered to a whisper and Joel couldn't hear the name, "dropped a bundle on those questionable United Wholesalers transactions, and then Forsster allegedly propositioned the guy's wife? I heard that when the firm was sanctioned and fined, Forsster complained how unfair it was because the client got fucked, the firm got fucked—everybody got fucked but him because the wife turned him down cold." The man guffawed. "Now, *that's* irreverent!"

Joel made a mental note to scour NASD databases to flesh out this Forsster misdeed as the woman responded, "Over the top. I'm outta here."

Joel glanced over his shoulder. The three men watched the woman's back as she slowly pushed through the packed room. One said, "Niiiice," and formed his lips into a silent whistle.

Joel rolled his eyes. This group was mentally time-trapped in the moment when they discovered they were growing pubic hair.

Someone jostled Joel's elbow and said in a gauzy voice, "Are you a stockbroker?" The woman's mouth was so close, breath tickled Joel's ear. Like a mosquito buzzing. He resisted the urge to swat; and sat perfectly still, hoping to avoid this annoying interruption.

"I bet the son-of-a-bitch died with a hard-on," one of the suits said and they all laughed.

"If they bury him face up, they'll have to put him under Coit Tower." They dissolved into manly giggles.

Joel glanced at the wispy blonde sitting on the barstool next to him. Water-blue eyes... probably an Aquarius. She wore a tacky pink Nicole Miller dress that Joel recognized from the spring collection two years earlier. She gave him an inviting smile.

"I'm meeting someone," he said. This distraction was bothersome, but Joel took it as validation that he'd slipped into a convincing James Bond personae.

"Look at Buzz Benson and his mighty hoard of sycophants," the conversation continued behind Joel. "Now there's a guy who seriously thought Forsster was doing his wife. I saw him square off on Forsster in the men's room just last week. Heard him say something about '...Angelina again.' I think Benson would have gone after Steve-o if the two of us hadn't walked in."

A glass thunked the table behind Joel; the blonde brushed his arm.

"Well, she's obviously not here yet, so maybe you should talk to me until she gets here. My name is Nikki." She had a Marilyn Monroe smile and her perfume smelled of field flowers.

The men summoned the bartender and interrupted their conversation to exchange money for fresh booze. Joel turned full on to this nuisance woman and gave her a kindly look. "You are really cute, honey," he cooed, "but I don't think you're my type."

She responded with a head-ducking smile. "You'll never know if you don't talk to me."

Her voice was a petulant Melanie Griffith. Her pout was insistently seductive, but Joel suspected she'd sparred with rejection before. He sighed—hated to do it, but she wasn't going to make this easy for either of them.

"You know, sweetie, you remind me of Starlet, my late Aunt Sheila's Yorkshire terrier," he said in a honey-sweet voice. "Whenever Aunt Sheila had a gentleman caller, she had to lock that cute little pooch in the kitchen, because if she didn't, next thing you knew, there was Starlet with her legs locked around the visitor's shin, hunching his sock for all she was worth."

It took a second, but Joel finally saw frostbite set in around the woman's blue eyes. She flounced off her stool, insulted his ancestry, and dove off through the boisterous crowd. Joel shook his head in sad victory just in time for the boys to pick up their change and their fresh drinks and resume their gossip.

"Did you hear Benson's already approached some of Forsster's high-net-worth clients?"

Joel angled so he could see the group in his peripheral vision. They were facing the back wall, staring toward five men who sat at a beer bottle–littered table. A crew cut, thirty-something, twenty-four-hour Nautilus type raised a Budweiser to his lips.

"You know he's an ex-Marine," one of the men said. "Aren't Marines trained to kill?"

"Man, I'm telling you, Rina did it."

There was a moment of conversationless ice rattling before one man changed their direction. "You playing Pebble Beach this weekend?"

Joel pulled out his PDA, made a few quick notes, and tuned out the group as they pursued their new topic. He was excited that his first espionage job was going so well.

He picked up his wine glass, left a tip on the bar, and circled the room, moving slowly among the clientele. Virtually everyone was talking about the late, great Stephen Forsster. Joel listened for any significant snippets, but heard nothing worth dawdling over. He angled beside Buzz Benson's table, hoping to eavesdrop on their conversation, but their words were swallowed by the noise.

He returned to the bar and squeezed into the narrow space where the waitresses ordered drinks, surreptitiously sliding a twenty-dollar bill toward the bartender with a, "I need some information." He tried to be discreet, but he had to yell above the din of the crowd.

The bartender leaned in and took the bill. "About what?"

"One of your clients." Joel tried to look trustworthy, efficient. Important.

The bartender shrugged. "This is only my third day on the job," he said as he tapped the twenty into his shirt pocket. "The previous bartender said if I ever needed to know anything about anyone that I should check with a barfly who's here every day and knows everything that ever has or ever will happen in this bar." He quickly scanned the room. "Her name is Nikki." He pointed. "She's the blonde over there."

Catherine fumbled her keys when she handed them to the valet in the parking garage in the basement of the Bank of America building. Her stomach was flip-flopping like a tennis shoe in a clothes dryer. She was on the way to see George Hallison.

Word was out that Hallison had resumed his former position as CEO of San Francisco Financial Services—at least on a temporary basis. Catherine had called SFFS and, through Hallison's executive assistant, requested a meeting. She was confirmed for 2:00.

In the elevator, she considered the two scenarios she imagined possible. One: Hallison was somehow enmeshed in the recent surveillance, and potentially in the murder of Stephen Forsster; or, two, their having met, she and Hal, and becoming romantically involved was a cosmic farce worthy of a Mozart opera. In either case, one of them was fated for disenchantment: Catherine herself if Hallison turned out to be the bad guy; or Hallison, if he was innocent of any wrongdoing, but couldn't get past the fact that his new love interest had previously done the horizontal cha-cha with his arch enemy. She sighed. No matter which way it played out, she could snuff the candle on this fledgling romance.

Don't knot your rope before the jury's in, she silently reprimanded herself. Give the man the benefit of the doubt. Hadn't he told her on Sunday, when he kissed her goodbye beside her open car door, that she was a special woman who made him feel happy and hopeful for the first time in three years? She was still that same person. Nothing had changed. Well, not much.

But forget romance; she was here to ask Hal, as Stephen's former boss, for information that could help Catherine identify Stephen's killer. Hallison should be able to name Stephen's business enemies.

Elevator doors opened at the forty-ninth floor; Catherine checked in with the receptionist and waited in a black lacquered oriental chair until Betsy Tanner, a gray-haired woman who looked sophisticated enough to be a member of the White House staff, escorted her down thickly carpeted hallways. When Ms. Tanner opened a wide mahogany door and stepped aside, Catherine hesitated, heart pounding and mouth dry. Then she squared her shoulders and brushed past. The door clicked closed.

George Hallison stood on the other side of a vast expanse of red-hued oriental carpets and dark wood floors, staring out a floor-to-ceiling window. A collection of tan sofas and rust leather wingback chairs separated them; his imposing desk was to Catherine's right. When he turned to face her, he was backlit by the bright blue February sky. Catherine squinted into the muted sunshine and noted the brown leather braces that cleaved the broad shoulders of his starched white shirt; but she couldn't see his eyes, the expression on his face.

For all her silent rehearsals, the only words that came were, "I didn't kill him."

Hallison stood motionless, his six-two frame obscuring wispy clouds. "But you did fuck him."

The words gut-punched her. Indignation, despair, and guilt jousted in her brain; she bit back a glib retort. "And that would be a crime under what penal code?" she asked quietly. She needed to see his eyes, read the emotions there. She moved to navigate the furniture between them, but he spoke and the ice in his voice stopped her.

"This is quite a plot you and Stephen conceived." He shoved his hands into the pockets of his gray flannel slacks and turned back to the world outside. Sunlight glinted the silver of his temples. "Attempting to destroy the business—that doesn't surprise me. But why the seduction?" He stalked away from the window toward the broad, ornate desk.

Catherine breathed in the scent of his citrusy aftershave: it brought a fleeting memory of his hot bare skin burnishing hers. Her brow crinkled in confusion. "Hal, I don't..."

"Don't call me Hal." He held up his hand and once again stopped her forward momentum. "That presumes an entirely different relationship."

Embarrassment and a deep sense of loss suffused Catherine's cheeks and threatened to flow in the form of tears. But she stiffened her spine and fought to steady her voice as she spoke. "Fine. We'll skip the ice cream social and get down to business."

"Ah, yes. Business." He lowered himself into the leather executive chair and steepled his fingers. "And what is your business, Ms. Calabretta? Blackmail?"

"Blackmail?" She was confused. Incredulous. And she hated that he addressed her so formally.

"Do you prefer the term 'hostage'?" Muscles tightened and ridged the clean line of his jaw. "As in, 'you're holding this institution hostage'?"

"Could we rewind and start from the top, because I'm not following the plot line of this conversation."

"Drop the charade. Stephen said he would destroy SFFS before he would let me retake the helm—that if I ever tried, I would find myself navigating 'landmines and booby traps'." His expression was simultaneously wry and angry. "Who could have guessed he would engage *BusinessWeek's* "Guardian of Privacy" to be my seductress—"

"You think Stephen 'engaged'—"

"*As well as*," his voice boomed over hers. Then he finished the sentence with a soft-spoken flourish: "the architect of this company's demise."

"I'm about as confused as a goat on astroturf," she said, attempting to lift the tension.

He held out his hand palm up, as if introducing a guest, and swiveled to face one of two computer monitors that sat on a side extension.

Emotions entangled Catherine's thought processes but she directed her gaze to the computer screen. Golden letters in the middle of a bright blue field. She leaned in and read. It was a quote attributed to *Aesop*:

"*The haft of the arrow had been feathered with one of the eagle's own plumes. We often give our enemies the means of our own destruction.*"

At the bottom, it read: *You're not authorized to be here. One more keystroke and the entire SFFS computer system goes up in smoke... bites the dust... fries itself crispy... ETC, ETC, ETC.*

Catherine turned her gaze to Hallison. His brown eyes studied her thoughtfully.

"This is the landmine? Stephen planted a virus?" she asked.

"Oh, I suspect he had some assistance. Someone who has an intimate understanding of systems security." He formed his finger and thumb into a gun and aimed it at her.

"You're suggesting..." She glanced again at the screen and made the leap he'd apparently made. "You think the 'ETC' refers to me? To my company? You think I mined your computer system?"

"It wouldn't be much of a coup for Stephen if he couldn't rub my nose in it."

Anger shook her words. "Are you not aware that I've built an international reputation by protecting companies from exactly this type of sabotage?"

"Stephen always believed in hiring the best."

She crossed her arms over her chest. "Funny. All that time we spent naked last weekend, I never noticed your inclination to go off half-cocked."

His jaw worked again. "Don't feel alone in your poor observation skills. I didn't realize I was getting sloppy seconds."

Catherine's mouth dropped. "You condescending... hypocritical... chauvinistic... asswipe."

He held her angry gaze. She fought the compulsion to pack up her tent and get the hell out of Dodge. She couldn't do that... because she needed information. That's what she'd come for. And now she understood Hallison's willingness to meet.

"Did you invite me here to rectify your computer problems?"

"Who better than you?"

"Congratulations. You finally got something right. Who better than me." She leaned straight-armed on the desk. "And here's the deal. I want information. I need to learn everything I can about Stephen Forsster. He made lots of enemies. I bet you know who they are."

His expression turned cautious.

"That's the ransom. I'll clean up your system in exchange for information." She removed her cell phone from her handbag and dialed Joel's pager number. "But if I think you're not forthcoming with everything I need," she said through clenched teeth, "I'll fry your little piss-ant mainframe so completely it'll melt through the floor of your computer room—and the floor below, and the one below that until it craters in the basement of this fifty-two story building." Her voice and her hands shook with anger. She flipped the phone shut and studied the expression on his face. He looked as if he believed she could—and would—do as she threatened. She shook her head in disgust and turned her back on him.

She wanted to scream, she wanted to cry. She wanted to rewind to last Sunday and edit this nightmare out of her life.

She stomped across the thick rug to a wingback chair, dropped stiffly to the leather cushion, and stared out at the blue sky, waiting for Joel to return her page. Nausea pressed against her stomach; she ignored it and shifted her mind to neutral—into logic mode.

George Hallison's reaction, his accusation that Stephen and Catherine had actually plotted against *him*, made Catherine think Hallison hadn't been the requestor—or the recipient—of the home movie allegedly filmed in her bedroom. His anger was too palpable, his pride too offended. His attitude was a twenty-one-gun salute to the fragile male ego. As her friend Laura was fond of saying, a man wants his lover to be sexually adept, but doesn't want her to have experience with any other man. The virgin/slut phenomenon. And the good old double standard.

Catherine tapped her foot and waited for the cell phone to ring.

Hallison interrupted her thoughts. "There were many women on Forsster's extracurricular calendar. He was never going to leave his wife to be with you."

"Good, Lord. I should hope not!" Catherine almost laughed aloud. "Is that what cocked your pistol? You think I was in love with Stephen Forsster?"

He looked surprised. And defensive as he crossed his arms over his chest. "It's well documented you were involved with him."

"Whoa, big guy. 'Involved' is a pretty powerful word."

Catherine strutted across the carpet and leaned over his desk. She gave him a slow wink, made her voice suggestive. "You know, Hal, we're not all swans who, for better or worse, mate for life; so let me introduce you to a philosophy contemporary women occasionally employ. Sometimes it's pleasant to invite a neighborhood stray to sit on the back porch and watch the moon rise with you, but then you send him home to mama when it's time for his kibble and his flea dip."

His eyes narrowed.

Catherine drawled. "If that attitude offends your sensibilities, then you'll want to go back to the herd and rope yourself a different mare."

Her phone rang. She crossed to his office door with a hip-swinging saunter and said over her shoulder as she flipped open the phone, "I'll wait in the lobby until my crew arrives."

Catherine led Joel and Wilson to a private conference room and outlined the situation with the computer system.

"You mean," Joel huffed indignantly, "that buffoon is accusing *you* of mining their system? How asinine. Who does he—"

"Joel." She cut him off. "I'm here because I need information Hallison can provide. The trade-off is that you look at his system... and he talks to me about Stephen."

"Well, I think you should just—"

"Joel." Her tone was firm. Decisive.

He crossed his arms over his navy suit coat and glared at her; then he rolled his eyes and said, "Fine. What do you want us to do?"

"Fix it so it runs like God on a three-year-old thoroughbred."

They laid out a strategy for locating and disarming the implanted virus. Then they called in the SFFS people. George Hallison entered first, trailed by Wayne Johnston, SFFS's Chief Information Officer, who gave off the superior air of a self-impressed Harvard MBA. Three senior technicians—the crew that was responsible for computer systems security—completed the group. Catherine thought the techs dressed more like stockbrokers than computer nerds. She wondered if they were competent or just looked good, a quality that seemed to be of inordinate importance in some image-conscious financial services firms.

Hallison sat at one end of the long conference table; Joel stood at the other and took the lead.

"We're probably looking for a logic bomb," Joel said. He ticked off the things he would require, including documentation on SFFS's security architecture, answers to any questions he considered pertinent—like Stephen Forsster's social security number, his date of birth, children's names—and unlimited access to their security engineers and their computer system.

"And last, but not least," Joel said, "Wilson and I work alone. We'll set up in your data center and I want everyone else out of the area and out of the way."

"Absolutely not." Wayne Johnston half rose, his bulky, ex-jock form towering over Catherine. "That's unreasonable and you know it."

"You can't steal second base if you keep one foot on first," Catherine responded stoically.

She knew Joel worked alone. Virtually always. Even a born-again hacker had to occasionally cross the line between legal and illegal access of systems; use procedures he wouldn't want anyone to witness.

"I defer to the opinion of my CIO," Hallison said and stood, shoving his leather chair backwards. He glared coldly at Catherine. "Our deal's off." He started for the door.

"Your choice," she said as she reached for her handbag. "Joel Hodges is the premier security architect in the nation," she continued, "but if you want to try to find someone else to do this job—someone who'll mess around in areas they don't understand, probably end up compromising the integrity of your data, while contaminating your applications and bring your company to its knees in a matter of nanoseconds—that's your option. As a consulting firm, ETC only advises—we don't make mission critical business decisions for the client."

Hallison studied Catherine impassively, then turned to Wayne Johnston. "Do you know the professional reputation of this man?" he asked. He nodded toward Joel.

"Yes," Johnston answered hesitantly. His neck twitched under the starched blue shirt.

"And?"

"Well. Yes. He's the best." His face clouded into protest. "But if they're the ones who mined us in the first place..." He clearly didn't like being in a position of diminished power.

"Then that should work to our advantage: they'll know exactly how to un-mine us."

"I have to go on record—"

"Do you have a better solution?"

"Yeah. Make him do it with us watching his every move." Johnston was indignant.

"I'm a solo act," Joel said. "I don't do audience participation." He picked up his briefcase and moved toward the exit.

Hallison glared at Catherine and spoke through gritted teeth. "I don't respond well when someone grabs me by the balls."

"Isn't it surprising how much we have in common," she replied.

Hallison stepped in front of Joel. "You'd better not fuck this up," he said and turned and walked out of the conference room, saying over his shoulder to Wayne Johnston, "Give him whatever he demands."

"'Fuck it up'?" Joel said, his face contorted with amused derision. He pointed to Catherine. "Honey, before you spend anymore time with that man, you'd better make sure his rabies shots are updated."

Wayne Johnston barreled out of George Hallison's office, jaw set, eyes fiery. Catherine wasn't surprised; while she paced in the waiting area, she'd heard angry voices. When Betsy Tanner gave her the go-ahead, Catherine stepped into the office, closed the door, and crossed the expanse of dark hardwood floor to where Hallison had enthroned himself in a rust leather wingback chair, legs crossed and hands dangling casually from the upholstered arms.

"You should have fucked my CIO," he said. "Apparently he's feeling left out."

"Look. You've already made the point that you think I'm a two-bit slut who's seen more pricks than a secondhand dartboard," Catherine said, "and since I have no intention of trying to justify my actions—especially now that I realize you're more close-minded than a white supremacist—why don't we call time out on the pissing contest and just conclude our business." As she delivered her monologue, Catherine settled on the tan sofa, coffee table separating them like the proverbial line in the sand.

"My son called from Boston this morning," he responded. "He was having trouble connecting the dots on the my-dad's-new-lover-is-accused-of-killing-my-dad's-nemesis-who-was-also-her-lover soap opera in which I now find myself starring."

Anger and adrenaline leaked from Catherine's veins; she felt emotionally drained. "I didn't kill Stephen," she said in a quiet, resigned voice.

"Too bad. Think of all the people—SFFS shareholders, wronged husbands—who would have been grateful to you."

"You didn't include yourself on that list."

Hallison's blue eyes were glacial. "What do you want to know?"

Catherine closed her eyes and remembered standing in his kitchen last weekend, Hal slowly unbuttoning her dress, letting it slide to a silky jumble around her feet. His mouth hungry on hers as his fingertips brushed her bare skin. The heat of it.... Her heart ached to think it would never happen again. She opened her eyes and held his gaze. "When we were together, I felt a special... connection to you."

"Don't go there, Catherine." His voice softened but his eyes were veiled. If there was any future for them, he was making clear it wouldn't begin today.

"Fine." She opened her notebook and pulled out a pen. "Let's start with Stephen's business enemies," she said crisply.

They talked for twenty minutes, and although Hallison clipped out concise answers to Catherine's questions, his demeanor relaxed. She filled three pages with names of people who might have had a beef with Stephen. Unhappy clients. Jealous competitors. Disgruntled employees. But nothing stood out. Catherine didn't know if any of it would be of use; was daunted by the idea of checking out all those possibilities.

"Was he ever threatened? By a client? By a shareholder? Anyone you heard about?"

"Someone angry enough to kill him? That's more likely to be personal than business-related. It was widely rumored he had a whole line-up of bimbos he serviced on a regular basis. I'd look first to their resentful husbands."

She didn't take the "bimbos" bait. "Anyone specific leap to mind?" she asked dryly.

"No."

She tried different angles, but the volley of questions was returned with answers that didn't offer much hope. Finally, she closed her notebook and said, "I'd like to talk to Stephen's assistant."

"That would be Mary Louise Harrington. She's in Fiji—on her honeymoon."

Catherine perused the room, studied the ornate desk against the back wall. "This was Stephen's office?"

"It's the office of the CEO." Hallison's voice tightened again. "Stephen occupied it for a period of time."

"Did the police search it?"

"More like a pillage. They took out boxes of stuff and left a God-awful mess."

No point revisiting sullied ground, Catherine decided. She sighed with frustration. She wasn't making much progress.

"Where does Mary Louise sit?"

He motioned with his head. "Right outside. Across from Betsy."

"Did the police take things from her office, too?"

"I'm not sure. Betsy would know."

Catherine rose. "May I take a look?"

He pursed his lips. "I don't think that's a good idea."

She grinned. "Afraid I'll purloin a letter opener?"

He rubbed his index finger across his forehead and contemplated her.

"You can strip-search me on my way out," she taunted with a smile.

"I'd have more fun buying a new letter opener," he said as he headed for the office door.

Catherine glared and stuck out her tongue at his departing back; but she followed him into a side office where he flipped on fluorescent lights.

The nameplate on the desk read "Mary Louise Harrington." If the police had searched it, someone must have reorganized it after they departed. Knickknacks covered the bookshelves, the desktop, and the credenza. Old Beanie babies. Coffee mugs with colorful logos. A menagerie of shiny glass animals. Bright, frilly picture frames in various shapes and sizes. Catherine wondered where the woman did her work. She skirted the desk and opened the two large file drawers. One contained a stash of packaged foods—canned tuna, crackers, cup-of-noodles, protein bars. The other, office paraphernalia—folders, boxes of pens. In a desk drawer, Catherine found empty hanging files.

"Did the police remove files from this drawer?" she asked.

Hallison summoned Betsy Tanner, to whom he repeated the question. Betsy confirmed they had.

"Where are the rest of her files?" Catherine asked. "I mean, one tiny drawer? There must be more."

"There's a store room where she archives the inactive ones."

"Let's take a look," Catherine said.

The room was two doors away. Betsy disappeared into her office and met them with a ring of keys. She unlocked the door; the light was already on. The room was crammed with file cabinets and shelves stacked with supplies. A copy machine and a shredder hugged the back wall.

"This is hers," Betsy said, pointing to a four-drawer wood unit.

Catherine pulled a handle, but the drawer didn't budge.

"Mary Louise and Mr. Forsster are the only ones with keys," Betsy said.

Catherine's pulse quickened. "It hasn't been opened since Stephen's death?"

Betsy shook her head no.

"Okay, thanks," Catherine said, and waited until the woman took the hint and exited. Catherine pushed the door closed and examined the cabinet's brass lock. She scoured supply shelves until she found a box of paperclips. She removed two, straightened the first curve of each, and returned to the lock. She worked the metal prongs in the tiny opening.

"You didn't learn that in Girl Scouts."

"Sure I did. Survival Skills badge."

She'd never told anyone about the times her raging mother had locked her, for hours, in the blackness of her bedroom closet, or in the dank, bare-earth root cellar under their farmhouse kitchen. When Catherine was about ten, rebellion overrode terror. She learned to "pick" her way out of the darkness so she could curl up in her room, reading and dreaming about the world beyond Springtime, Texas, ears alert for her mother's old Buick rattling down the gravel road that fronted their acreage. When the warning came, she would swiftly scuttle back to her prison, secure the lock, and obediently wait to be released.

That was a different lifetime. Now, she worked the clips until the first drawer slid open. It was crammed tight with hanging files stuffed with manila folders.

"May I?" Catherine asked.

"No."

Hallison removed a folder, paged through it, then handed it to Catherine. He pulled out the next one and repeated the routine. Catherine reviewed each as he finished. She occasionally asked him a question about a note or a document she found. Half of it was SFFS business; half related to Stephen's personal property or personal holdings. It took an hour to go through all four drawers. Catherine found nothing of interest until she started replacing the folders in the last drawer. She noticed a sliver of white lying on the bottom, previously concealed by the crush of files. She separated the hanging racks and removed a fat envelope. It was sealed.

She angled it to the light, ripped off the end, and removed a multipage document. It was a printed form entitled *Background Check*. "Jeremiah J. Benson" was listed under *Applicant*.

"Is this Buzz Benson?" Catherine angled the page toward Hallison. She recognized the name from the list of competitors/enemies he had recited. Hal stared at the form with a puzzled expression.

He took the pages from her hand and flipped through them. She moved so she could read over his shoulder. Proximity emphasized the citrusy scent of his aftershave, his body heat.

The pages contained sections labeled *NASD Licensing, Industry Record, Criminal Check, Educational Review, Financial Report,* and *Personal Information*. The report was dated January 27. Ten days ago.

"Why would Stephen run a background check on Buzz Benson?" Catherine asked.

"As an SEC-regulated company, we're required to do a background check on everyone we hire. This is the standard report form from the agency that handles the investigations for us."

"Benson works here? I thought you said he was Stephen's biggest competitor."

Hallison reached for a phone that hung on the wall beside the door. He dialed, silently reading the phone number from the logo on the form. He asked to speak to Trevor McMillan; then he asked Trevor about the background check on Buzz Benson. He had to assure Mr. McMillan there was no problem with the information provided, and then asked if the request had come from Linda Djesik in Human Resources.

"I see," he said. After a few more exchanges, he hung up the phone and turned to Catherine. "Stephen requested this investigation. Personally. He told Trevor it was highly confidential because Buzz worked for a competitor and was afraid it would get back to his employer that he was thinking of changing jobs."

Catherine crinkled her brow. "My bullshit detector just went to code red."

"If Benson finds out SFFS did an unauthorized background check, he could sue. The SEC could sanction the firm..." He clamped his jaw and looked perturbed.

Catherine gently took the pages from Hallison as he stood chewing over his dilemma. She moved to the back of the crowded room and dropped the pages into the top tray of the copier. When she pressed start, she turned to watch Hallison. The clatter of the machine shook him from his reverie and he crossed the space in two strides. Catherine stretched her arms and covered the machine with her body. "Ready for the stripsearch?" she asked.

"You're not leaving with that document."

"You started this meeting by accusing me of blackmail. I'd prefer that not become a self-fulfilling prophecy."

His eyes narrowed into a hostile squint. "Are you threatening to go to Benson?"

The machine went silent. Keeping her eyes on Hallison, Catherine groped behind her back, cautiously removing the original. She handed it to him then folded the warm copy into thirds.

"I'm just letting you know I plan to mow down any and all briars that sprout between me and my search for Stephen's murderer."

On her way out of SFFS's offices Catherine asked Betsy Tanner about Stephen's calendar and his cell phone records. According to Betsy, Stephen kept an online schedule of appointments, which she wouldn't be able to access until the computer system was up. She thought he also had a small black diary that he kept in his briefcase which she presumed would have been in his car at the time of his death. Inspector Hiller had taken the cell phone records found in Mary Louise's desk. When Catherine asked Betsy to request a duplicate from the service provider, she said she would "check with Mr. Hallison."

At 3:45, Catherine turned the key in the new lock on her apartment door, expecting to hear Garbo coming to protective attention; instead there was silence. She frowned, pulse rate ramping up. It was much too early for the walker to have taken Garbo for her 4:30 run.

Catherine stepped inside, senses attuned, and closed the door without even a click. She waited. No foreign smells, no unusual noises. Nothing.

At the end of the Oriental runner, she peeked inside the basket that stored unread magazines... and Garbo's leash. Magazines were there; the leash was gone. She breathed audibly. Donny, the walker, must have come early; no stranger would be brave enough—or stupid enough—to try to enter the apartment when Garbo was "on duty."

Catherine checked the fire escape window and confirmed it was as secure as when the locksmith departed the evening before.

In her bedroom, she automatically scanned the perimeter of the ceiling, searching for telltale signs of another video camera as she grabbed sweats from a drawer in preparation for her next task: She was going to the beach property to look for Stephen's gun.

Maureen O'Malley had said the D.A. specifically challenged Hiller to find the murder weapon. It was possible Catherine's freedom hinged on whether or not Stephen had been killed with his own gun. She hoped he had not. It would give her a great sense of relief if, instead, the gun were still buried where she'd tossed it into the brambles on his property. She had to find out.

Lafayette Park, where Garbo had her afternoon run, was only a quick detour. Catherine immediately spotted Donny, Garbo's walker, in his standard black running shorts, A's baseball cap, and baby blue sweatshirt imprinted with Man's Best Friend in black across the chest. A pack of seven dogs chased a yellow tennis ball toward a stand of pines. Catherine squeezed the Rover into a parking space across from Danielle Steele's mansion and strode briskly up the walkway, breathing in the smell of freshly mown grass.

At a break in the ball-chasing action, Garbo spied her mistress and crossed the distance in four loping strides, mewling ecstatically, wagging and rubbing against Catherine's legs, almost taking her off her feet.

Catherine greeted Donny with a smile and the obligatory polite exchange, and then asked, "Have you seen anyone going in or out of my apartment? Someone you didn't expect to see?"

It was apparent to Catherine that someone knew Donny's schedule with Garbo. No one could have entered her apartment and installed a video camera—or removed the locking mechanism from the fire escape window—while Garbo was there. Someone had watched Garbo's comings and goings almost as intimately as they had watched Catherine.

Donny's hazel eyes widened with alarm; he blushed as if he were responsible for the unauthorized entry. "I saw the stove guy."

With further questioning, Catherine learned Donny had seen the man twice: the first time, some months ago; the second, just last week. On each occasion, the man had been coming out of Catherine's apartment, locking the door, when Donny brought Garbo home from her walk. The man had explained that he was, "repairing Mrs. Calab-retta's stove."

Donny couldn't describe the man except to say he had been wearing brown overalls and a baseball cap over curly black hair. "I was too busy holding Garbo back. She was really upset that a stranger was at her door."

Donny blew a whistle to summon his charges. The dogs, including Garbo, fanned out in a semicircle around him, dropping to their haunches like a covey of first-graders gathered at their teacher's feet, waiting for a story.

Catherine asked other questions, but learned nothing more.

She clipped the leash to Garbo's collar and asked, "If you remember anything else, would you please let me know? It could be important." She led Garbo down the hill, in the direction of the Rover.

Donny called after Catherine: "He knew Garbo's name."

Catherine stopped; turned back to face him.

"When she was barking at him the guy said something like, 'Get back, Garbo!' Or maybe it was 'Get away, Garbo.' Whatever." He shrugged. "It must be a command she's familiar with, because she backed right up and sat right down and stopped barking."

A chill prickled Catherine's spine. "Did he say, 'Stand down, Garbo!?'" Catherine asked and immediately felt the resistance go out of Garbo's leash as the dog backed up six inches and lowered her haunches to the grass, panting contentedly in the afternoon sun.

Donny gestured as if a lightbulb had just gone on in his brain. "Musta been it."

Catherine shivered as if the temperature had just plunged twenty degrees. The watcher had apparently been close enough to hear Catherine issue commands to her dog.

As she headed the Range Rover west, Catherine dialed Wilson's cell phone. He had spent several hours at city offices that morning, doing research on the Forsster family. She wanted to know if he had learned anything about the beach property.

When Wilson answered, she first asked about progress on the SFFS computer virus.

"Too early to tell," was his cryptic reply.

They talked generically about his research; then she asked about the beach property–ownership records and limitations on public access.

"Is it completely private and off limits? Or are there allowances for beachfront ingress or egress?" She didn't tell him she was headed there now—that she was concerned about being busted for trespassing on private property. If possible, she wanted to avoid landing in jail again if some cop ventured by to do one more looksee at the murder scene while she was digging around for Stephen's gun.

"Nothing about public access," he responded, "but some interesting 411." In his clipped sentences, Wilson laid out what he'd learned. Judd Delaney, Stephen's grandfather, had been obsessive about the ecological importance of leaving the coastline property undeveloped. Although he willed the property to Stephen, his only grandson, he specified that if Stephen pre-deceased George Hallison, the loyal, longtime CEO of the investment firm Delaney had founded, the property would transfer to Hallison. Delaney also stipulated that any custodian who made even the slightest "improvements" in the property would forfeit all rights and the land would pass to a Sierra Club conservatorship.

Catherine was shocked. George Hallison now owned the beachfront property? Whoa. The dude sure was racking up some hefty death benefits.

As she navigated the traffic back-up on the Great Highway, Catherine did another mental sort of everything she knew about Stephen, about the murder, trying to parse the possibilities. She still couldn't see Hallison as the primary suspect, but no way could she drop his name off the list.

Just after Sloat Boulevard, Catherine turned onto the gravel trail that curved through a forest of scrub trees. The wrought-iron gate that accessed the Forsster property—or, more accurately, the Hallison property—was a quartermile away. In the flat light of deepening dusk, she rounded the last bend and jerked the steering wheel to avoid smacking a rusted grocery cart that was nudged in against a wiry tree trunk. The cart was piled with black garbage bags. Faded bungie cords crisscrossed the top. She remembered seeing an identical cart in about the same spot on Monday night when Stephen drove to the gate. Had it been there all this time?

Catherine knew homeless men were encamped up and down the beach among the sheltering vegetation. Stephen had complained that they kept prying open his gate, destroying the electronics of the locking system. She'd also heard stories about muggings and fatal knife fights. Was it possible that some anonymous vagrant was responsible for Stephen's death?

Garbo pranced excitedly in the back seat, sniffing ocean air through the two-inch opening at the top of the rear passenger window as the Rover's headlights flashed on a yellow banner stretched from one side of the black gate to the other. A length of chain hung from a crossbar with a shiny padlock dangling limply from the end like the victim of a hanging. Catherine rolled down her window and punched the keypad, entering the code she had watched Stephen key in: 0402. Probably his birthday.

Brisk sea air shirred through her window; the gate ratcheted open two feet and stuck.

Catherine pocketed a flashlight and an old pair of gardening gloves she'd grabbed from a kitchen drawer. When she opened the door, Garbo leapt from the car and immediately put nose-to-ground, sniffing her way toward the gate.

Catherine scanned the sky. It would be completely dark within a half hour. She flicked on the flashlight and swept the bushes that crowded the edge of the gravel road. No signs of occupancy; no homesteader charging out to shoo her off his stake. Perhaps the grocery cart had been abandoned.

She fruitlessly attuned her ears for rustling in the bushes, but a dozen bison could have stampeded by and not been heard above the roar of the surf that pounded the beach below.

Catherine ripped loose the yellow *Police Line DO NOT CROSS* tape and left it flapping wildly in the cold wind. She slid through the opening and started down the trail. Garbo raced ahead.

To her left, towering dunes angled away from the twenty-by-forty patch of knee-high scrub that was her destination. That was where she'd tossed the gun when she exited the property—with Stephen scampering to catch up, yelling at her to stop—on the night he was killed. The sky had been the same as now: pale gray deepening to black. It wouldn't have been impossible for him to retrieve the gun from where she'd flung it, but he would've needed a flashlight... and patience. She thought there was a good chance the gun was still buried in the weeds.

She stuffed her blowing locks under a toboggan cap and pulled on the gardening gloves.

Garbo was captivated by a flattened burger box. "Stay here," Catherine commanded.

She aimed the powerful beam of the flashlight along the base of the bushes that lined the rutted trail. Faded potato chip bag. Half a dozen shriveled cigarette butts, burned all the way to the filter. One clear beer bottle, two brown. Nothing that looked like the glint of gunmetal.

She did a slow sweep of the landscape to reassure herself she was alone, then picked through the knot of roots, up the slope to the backside of the overgrown plot. Scrappy vegetation smelled of juniper; stiff branches jabbed her shins and tore at her socks.

Bending at the waist, she parted bristly foliage with a gloved hand, peering at the sand-drifted roots. Finding nothing of merit, she negotiated her sneakers between another clump of roots and replicated the process.

She worked the plot systematically, finding used condoms, disintegrating paper cups, the tattered remains of a yellow wool scarf. But, no gun. Occasionally, she would straighten, uncrinkle her tortured spine, and take a moment to pinpoint her snooping dog; then she would sweep the area again, making certain she was still alone, before bending back to her task.

By the time she was down to the last five square feet, the sky had long been black, her back ached, and her optimism had evaporated. She stretched and looked for Garbo, she couldn't locate her.

Catherine fished a dog whistle from her coat pocket, but the pounding surf swallowed the trill. She was antsy about how much time she'd been on this property so she decided to quickly finish her search before setting out after the dog.

Her light glinted on a sliver of dull gray something exposed in the sand at her feet. Her heart skittered as she squatted between the gnarled branches and reached to dig the item free.

As gloved fingers brushed unidentified metal, a bright flash illuminated the surrounding bushes. Her heart shifted into overdrive. She lunged upright, feet tangled in a knot of roots, arms flailing like a tightrope walker struggling to avoid a fall.

"Nice maneuver," Hiller shouted above the surf. "Learn it in ballet class?"

He stepped between two bright beams twenty feet away and seven feet apart, which pinned her in a blinding glare. Apparently there were two cops backing him up. Catherine was relieved he wasn't alone.

She masked her fear. "I do declare, Inspector Hiller. I think you've been following me."

"Hey! I get an anonymous tip that my favorite suspect is returning to the scene of the crime, I gotta check it out. You got treasure buried in those bushes, Ms. Calabretta?"

She hadn't yet identified the sand-covered object, but knew it wasn't the .45. "One man's treasure is another man's..." she began as she bent toward the ground.

"Freeze!" Hiller commanded. "Put your hands above your head. Keep them where we can see them."

"You must have gotten those lines from *Dragnet* in 1950," Catherine said, but she straightened and raised palms into sight. "You oughta watch *NYPD Blue*," she continued as a silhouetted figure jogged toward her. Hiller and the other cop remaining stationary. "Let Sipowicz update your lexicon."

A uniformed officer picked his way up the slope to where Catherine stood. He bent and pressed through the bushes at her feet, freeing the gray metal from its grave. He looked up at Catherine, and then checked the ground again before he made his way back to the trail, displaying a twisted metal container.

"Be careful with that," Catherine called as she fought her way out of the tangle of brush. "It's my favorite coffee pot." A broken branch jabbed through her sweat pants.

Metal thunked and bounced once on the gravel trail as Hiller tossed the relic aside.

"Save your comedy routine for Jay Leno."

"I need to call my dog," Catherine said, fearing the confrontation that would occur if the very-protective Garbo perceived Catherine was "under attack."

"This is private property. Did you happen to notice the padlocked gate?"

"The chain was cut when I got here. Plus I have the security code." She glanced over her shoulder hands still in the air. "I have to call my dog," she said with more urgency.

"Take her in for trespassing," Hiller ordered.

"You might want to check your facts, first," she snapped, trying to keep fear out of her voice. She did not want to go to jail again. "This property now belongs to George Hallison—county records will verify that. I met with him earlier this afternoon and he gave me permission to be here." Not exactly true, but she figured 50 percent was close enough.

"Practicing for a perjury charge, Ms. Calabretta?"

"You can't arrest me if Mr. Hallison doesn't press charges."

"You're wrong there. I may not be able to file on you... but I can arrest you."

"That's about as reckless as a calf kicking at yellow jackets, Inspector." Surging anger was evident in her tone. "You'll make Jordan Lawrence's day if you haul me in on one more trumped up charge." She squinted in the direction of the light-bearers. "You gonna drag your partners into your scam?"

"You're giving me a blister on my balls."

"I can demonstrate I know the code for the gate."

"And I can sing all twelve verses of 'The Star Spangled Banner.'" His voice muffled when he instructed the officer, "Call George Hallison. Ask him—"

Catherine heard Garbo's pounding feet, heard her throaty growl and the first vicious bark. Catherine whirled; a spotlight picked up the charging animal, closing fast from eighty feet.

"Shoot!"

"Noooo!"

"Shoot the dog!"

A shot rang out. Gravel rained on the trail. Catherine instinctively stepped between Garbo and the light source, pitching the charcoal-colored animal into darkness. "Garbo! Stand down!" she screamed, and flung her pointed index finger straight down by her side.

Another shot.

"Stand down, Garbo!"

Garbo skidded, crashed against Catherine's shins, taking them both off their feet. The dog yelped and growled as she struggled to untangle from Catherine's legs.

Catherine grabbed for the choke chain, trying to get her arms around the animal's neck.

"Garbo! Stand down!"

She didn't know if the Weimaraner had been hit by gunshot or simply blinded by the spotlight.

The dog struggled until she was on her feet; Catherine scrambled to her knees, gravel puncturing her shins, arms clutching the quivering canine tight against her own heaving chest, hands already exploring for injuries.

"Sit! Now!"

Garbo hesitated, sank to her haunches, but strained against Catherine's grasp and growled low in her chest, lip curled, inch-long incisors catching the glare.

Another gunshot exploded. Catherine ducked as gravel spewed and pelted the top of her head. Garbo yelped and tried to back away.

"You motherfucker!" Catherine screamed, adrenaline-fueled tears crystallizing on her cheeks.

Hiller was backlit by one spotlight, gun braced and aimed in their direction.

"Got things under control, Ms. Calabretta?" he asked calmly.

She spoke through clenched teeth. "If you hurt my dog, Inspector, the combined efforts of all the gods on Mount Olympus will not be enough to save you from my vengeance."

They had conferred quietly. Radios squawked. One cop jogged back toward the gate. Catherine calmed and examined Garbo, finding only raw scrapes on her hindquarters. In less than five minutes, they let her go without explanation.

Hiller disappeared; the officers stood at attention as Catherine put Garbo in the Rover. They waited for her to drive away.

As she reached the Great Highway she realized the grocery cart— the one loaded with garbage bags—was gone. It had been nowhere along the trail. She wondered who had moved it. Hiller? The owner of those bagged possessions? And what about Stephen's gun? Before Hiller arrived, she had inspected virtually every bush on the east side of the hill. The gun was not there.

Catherine's cell phone rang insistently inside her purse. She quickly pulled to the shoulder of the highway.

"I've left four messages," Joel said. "Where the piffle have you been?"

"Walking my dog," she quipped. "Are you still camped out at SFFS?"

"Just vacated the premises."

"Tell me their computer is humming along happier than a brand new Frigidaire."

"What else would you expect from a world-class security expert? We'll give you the details when we see you. How about we meet at Lil's?"

"I want to take Garbo home. Read her a bedtime story... tuck her in."

"If anybody in the world would actually do that, you would. See you in an hour."

"Make it thirty minutes. Nietzsche puts her to sleep fast."

Liverpool Lil's was packed; Joel and Wilson were seated at a table in the back corner.

Joel was effusive; he couldn't stop chattering. Wilson even grinned a couple of times as Joel regaled Catherine with tales of how they had conquered the SFFS security issues.

"I mean, Forsster really had them going. There was nothing. Watch my lips: NOTHING in the system. No viruses—no mines. No logic bombs of any kind. He just bluffed them. Of course, they were very, very smart to not take a chance. Their security is awful—a nine-year-old script kiddie could take down their entire architecture. You should send in the business development team. Their CIO would be an easy sell right now."

"What did you tell them?" Catherine asked.

"We told them we fixed their problem and that if they wanted more information, they'd have to talk to you. We only fix it—you report on it."

Catherine smiled, probably, she realized, for the first time in three days.

They data-dumped more details of the SFFS project in between instructions to their waitress. Then Catherine said, "It seems like forever ago, but I'm anxious for a download on your day's research."

Wilson said he'd sent all his City Hall findings to her email address; Joel couldn't wait to tell her about his visit to Over the Counter. His coup was the part about having to convert an enemy, "Nikki the blonde," into a bosom buddy.

"How does that work?" Wilson asked. "I mean. She's got a bosom. You what? Just envy it?"

Joel rolled his eyes and theatrically turned to Catherine, giving his back to Wilson.

"I followed that bimbo around the bar for forty-five minutes. I tried everything. Confessed I was gay—told her I was having one of those days when my hormones just hate me, suggested we exchange make-up tips... she ignored me."

"A talent many of us are trying to perfect," Wilson murmured.

"Finally I told her I was a single parent and showed her a picture of Tati. She got curious about that and of course she had to ask questions, so she finally thawed. Now, we're best buds. And let me tell you: that sex-kitten is a fricking goldmine of gossip."

He regaled them until Catherine finally asked if he'd learned anything of actual value.

"You *know* I did, sweetcheeks!" Joel parroted the tale of Rina Gold's determination to lure Stephen away from his wife—"which Nikki confirmed," and reprised the Buzz Benson saga Catherine had heard from George Hallison three hours before.

Joel's stories helped Catherine solidify, in her own mind, the potential suspects she would target first. Buzz Benson, business enemy number one. Rina Gold, jilted lover? And then, of course, there was still George Hallison to consider....

On the way home, Catherine dialed into voicemail. Twelve messages. She pressed play and zipped through the first eight crank calls—a category into which she lumped media requests for interviews. As she wheeled into her garage, she recognized the nasal voice of caller number nine.

"Catherine dear, I know you're a little busy right now, but my alimony is late." Nicolas's voice grated like a rusted saw on a metal pipe, his topic as predictable as maggots on a cadaver. But she knew this was a phony complaint: money was auto-transferred from her account to his on the first of every month.

"And you know what they say: One can't live as cheaply as two..."

"Get a job!" Catherine yelled as she pulled into her garage. "You'll have less time to shop."

"...So please make sure I get my money on time each month."

She turned off the ignition and put her head in her hands as his tone shifted.

"I didn't realize you had a boyfriend." The tease sounded like a seven-year-old making fun of his teenage sister. "It's tragic that he got killed. And by the way, I don't believe for a minute that you killed him, but I'm glad to see you've gotten on with your life since our divorce. That's healthy. And dear, if you need someone to talk to, you know you can always call on me."

Ah-ha. The real purpose of his call: to rub it in. She headed for the elevator.

In a perverse way, it was comforting that Nicolas remained absorbed in his own greed. At least one thing in her life was consistent. She pushed out of the elevator.

Twenty feet away, she spotted a purple and orange FedEx package on the hemp mat in front of her door. Her heart pinged erratically in her chest. It hadn't been there when she dropped off Garbo two hours earlier.

She took a Kleenex from her purse and used it to pick up the package by the edges. In her office, she examined the envelope. She knew instinctively the label would show this package was sent from ETC's corporate account. No disappointment there.

She opened her office safe and removed the FedEx Stephen had received at SFFS–the one that had precipitated his request to meet. Catherine compared the bill numbers on the two labels. They were exactly the same except for the last digit:–a "3" on his; a "4" on hers.

She pulled on latex gloves and gingerly examined the package. There was a rectangular object inside. A small book? A videotape.

"Oh, no," she whispered aloud.

Her hands trembled as she pulled the zip tab and extracted the cassette, heart pounding with dread. She looked for a note. Nothing. Was this a copy of the tape Hiller claimed to have found in Stephen's car? The tape that had convinced him Catherine was the murderer?

She took the tape to the living room and slid it into the VCR. Remote in hand, she dropped to the edge of the sofa and pressed play. She ignored the tennis ball Garbo dropped at her feet.

White fuzz faked to black screen, then a wide-angle view of an empty four-poster bed appeared, peach satin duvet plumped neatly in place and reading lamps atop nightstands on either side. Cherry armoire against the left wall. Five-by-seven photo of Chloe on the nightstand at the right.

Catherine's bedroom.

There was no movement on the screen. No sound until she heard a loud knocking followed by the muffled thud of steps treading carpet. A door banged closed. There was one, perhaps two, aborted and unrecognizable words; then the faint sound of scuffling. Still no movement on the screen.

The sound sharpened and Catherine recognized Stephen's voice off-stage. Gruff. Forceful.

"Don't ever stand me up again."

"Check your six-shooter and your bad attitude at the dance hall door, big guy, because—" She followed him into the camera's sights; but he wheeled on her. She yelped as he maneuvered her against the wall, pinning her. She was full-face to the camera; he was angled away. Ivory shirt, navy slacks, dark curly hair thinning ever-so-slightly at the crown. The camera caught him mostly from the back, but his actions were unmistakable.

His mouth explored hers until she moaned.

Catherine watched the screen and her face flamed with embarrassment. She knew when this was filmed. It was the first time Stephen had played the game he called "submission fantasy." He theorized that all strong, decisive women fantasize about submitting to a sexually aggressive lover. At the time, she hadn't bothered to decide whether or not she agreed; she wasn't about to abridge his fertile imagination.

Catherine put the remote on the rosewood coffee table and cradled her forehead in her hands. Closed her eyes. Theirs had been a completely private affair. Because she felt safe, with no emotional attachment, she had abandoned her inhibitions. All her self-conscious feelings of inadequacy. She had opened herself to sexual adventure with him.

Who had desecrated these most intimate moments? Who had recorded them? Who, other than the filmmaker, had now witnessed their interaction?

Another moan, then, "Stephen—"

"No talking!"

She returned her gaze to the screen. Appalled. Riveted.

Stephen grasped her wrists, moving her hands until they were squeezed between the wall and the small of her back, jutting her breasts against his chest. He released her left wrist and the camera recorded the coldness in his voice. "Don't move your hands," he ordered.

He unbuttoned the top button of her green wool dress, pulled the collar aside and nibbled her left ear. He spoke quietly, but his words were discernible.

"I wanted to fuck you yesterday but you weren't here when you said you would be."

With his back to the camera, Catherine imagined his tongue tickling her jawbone, the hollow of her throat as he worked his way toward her breasts.

She moaned.

"Don't make a sound," he commanded.

He unhooked another button and whispered, "I wanted to undress you... bit by bit... until you were naked and completely at my mercy."

Her eyes were closed. Head back. Lips parted. Breath audible.

His teeth nipped the flesh of her cleavage. He released her other wrist and yanked her dress and bra straps down around her shoulders, pinning her arms.

"Don't move," he repeated.

His lips brushed her ear and his fingertips squeezed nipples through white lace.

"My cock was hard, Cat. I wanted to feel it sliding in and out of your wet cunt."

He wedged his knee between her legs, straining the fabric of the tight skirt, pressing against her pelvis. "I wanted to fuck you. Over and over." His fingers played the wool skirt up over her hips, exposing garterbelt and stockings. He rubbed his hands over her ass, jammed her against his erection.

"Oh, Stephen," she groaned.

"Quiet," he snarled. He continued to grind his pelvis against her as he spoke.

"I wanted to suck your clit and feel you come in my mouth."

Her breath was fast and jagged, her excitement unmistakable to the invasive microphone.

The pressure of his knee against the insides of her thighs pushed her legs farther apart.

"I wanted you to ride my hard cock until I exploded inside you."

He slowly knelt at her feet and gentled her panties over the garterbelt. Down her calves. Silk taut against ankles as his mouth teased the insides of her thighs. She trembled, her inhalations raspy. Shallow.

"Please..."

"Don't talk!"

As she watched the video she could almost feel his hot breath.

He parted tender flesh and his tongue caressed. She went rigid. Reached out for him. He sprang to his feet, grabbed her wrists, and wrenched them firmly behind her back.

"I told you not to move!" he snapped.

"I have to move," she pleaded.

His mouth bruised hers.

She moaned.

He released her wrists and pointed his finger at the tip of her nose. "Don't move and don't make a sound," he instructed coldly.

His fingernails scratched across her rigid nipples, finger pads inched lightly down her torso. Again, he knelt, grasped her hips and buried his mouth between her legs. Tongue teased.

She whimpered as he took her to the edge of orgasm and held her there. Just as she was about to peak, he stopped.

She opened her eyes and stared down at him in disbelief.

"Bad time to close the candy store," she said.

He lifted his wristwatch and pressed the sides of the dial between thumb and finger. "Four minutes and fifty-four seconds." He beamed and tapped the crystal face. When he rose and turned away, loosening his tie, the hidden camera memorialized his triumphant grin.

"You egg-sucking coyote! You were timing me to see how fast you could get me to flashpoint?"

"No, I was checking to see how long I could stifle that smart mouth of yours." He chuckled as he pulled his tie free and draped it over the corner of the armoire. "That was good, baby. You're a natural for domination games."

She kicked off her panties and stomped after him, smacking him between the shoulder blades with her open palms as she screeched, "You three-toed buzzard!"

He whirled, grabbed both arms, and in a blur had her on her back, pinioned on the brocade comforter, skirt hiked, his knees astride her hips. Strong hands subdued her wrists at her sides. He leaned in slowly, eyes seductive. Mouth wide, he kissed her tenderly, tantalizing her until she began to moan and writhe beneath him. Then he suddenly rolled off, flopped flat onto his back, and grinned up at the ceiling, unbuttoning his shirt. "Did I ever tell you I was on the Harvard wrestling team?"

She thunked his arm with her fist; the camera was angled at her exposed crotch. "Did you come here to brag about your athletic prowess?" she asked, her voice filled with insincere exasperation. He knew she liked his playfulness—the fact that sex with him was anything but a serious, predictable ritual.

"No. I came here so you could suck my cock." He reached both feet into the air and pulled off his socks.

"After that little game, I just might bite it off." She straddled him, leaning over his chest, tasting his furry nipples with the tip of her tongue.

In her living room, she could almost feel the hair tickle her chin, could almost smell his exciting muskiness.

"Then what? Keep it in your nightstand? You know, baby, a piston's only as good as the engine that drives it." He smirked as he unbuckled his belt and separated his fly.

"You've got a dick like a King Ranch fence post."

He chuckled. "Why don't you pretend to be a Texas tornado and suck my big ole fencepost as if it were sunk in cement?"

Catherine watched herself slowly, tantalizingly work her way down to his erect penis, taking the head in her mouth, fingers fondling his balls.

"Yeah, baby."

In her living room, Catherine closed her eyes and covered her face with both hands. She thought about other people. Strangers. Or worse yet, colleagues, friends—people who knew her—seeing her like this. Guard down. Completely exposed. Her stomach roiled. She was embarrassed by her lack of inhibitions, ashamed to have been captured this way.

"Oooh, yeah."

Who had done this? Who filmed them? Who invaded the privacy of her sanctuary? Recorded her most intimate moments? And what did he plan to do with the tapes?

"Come up here."

Something in her brain began to boil. She did an emotional hundred-and-eighty-degrees. Shame fueled defiance. Violation stoked anger. "How *dare* you," she snarled at whomever had perpetrated this low-tech invasion of her private life.

"I want to feel your wet cunt squeeze my cock."

Catherine opened her eyes and stared at the screen. She was spell-bound. Seeing herself in a way she could have never imagined. She was embarrassed. Surprised. Aroused? She couldn't sort her feelings.

Still fully clothed, breasts jutting from her open dress, she slid him inside her. He guided her hips as she slowly moved up and down. She moaned. Her breath quickened, each exhalation audible.

She grabbed the remote and jabbed "stop." The screen flashed to fuzz. She pressed rewind, dammed her emotions, and concentrated on the facts. The stakes had changed. The killer wasn't stopping at Stephen's murder but was now sending a powerful message that Catherine was also a target. Flaunting that he—or she?—had power over Catherine.

"Enjoy the score while you're ahead, peckerwood," Catherine whispered to her anonymous tormentor as she pressed "play," "because the A-team's just getting off the bus..."

She watched the tape again; this time studying it for camera angle, microphone placement—anything she could learn that would help her nail this ratbag.

Chapter Four: Friday

The lobby was dark except for the solitary spotlight that lit the ETC logo. The quiet was eerie, even though Catherine was accustomed to being there before anyone else arrived to start the business day. But that was before she was stripped of every sense of privacy. Now, she imagined unknown eyes watching her at all times.

Catherine pushed aside paranoia and concentrated on her mission: check out the ETC FedEx log. Last night she'd phoned the FedEx automated package-tracking system and learned that they had picked up the package at a drop box rather than at ETC's headquarters, as was the standard. The one that contained the video—the one left at her apartment door—wasn't logged into their system. That meant FedEx hadn't handled it at all. Catherine deduced it had been delivered by whoever stole the billing labels.

In her dark office, the familiarity—the shadowy shapes of the furniture, even the smell of recycled air–fostered predictability; but there was no time to relax into it. She retrieved a large key ring hidden in Aida's cubicle and marched through the murky illumination supplied by green "exit" signs. Inside the mailroom, with lights ablaze, she passed rows of neatly labeled cubbyholes and went directly to the long work counters that filled the back wall. In the left corner was the FedEx station. The logbooks. She pulled a folded Post-it from her pocket.

"Seven eight five seven four four three," she read aloud from the Post-it, repeat the first three digits as she flipped through the binder, index finger trailing down the column when she neared the sequence.

She had to track all the way back to August—eight months ago—to find that series. The bill numbers, the one on the envelope sent to

Stephen and the one containing the video, were marked "VOID." No one claimed responsibility for using them; no notation of where they'd gone. Just "VOID."

The next two numbers in the sequence were logged the same way, in the same handwriting. That surprised her. She quickly scanned log pages and saw there were very few VOIDs—and no other multi-label groups.

Someone had pilfered four ETC FedEx bills? Two were accounted for; two were not. Two more opportunities for deliveries that appeared to originate from ETC?

Who had taken them? She couldn't imagine ETC personnel were responsible. She thumbed her memory for disgruntled employees; nothing significant came to mind. How easy would it be for someone outside the company to come into the mailroom and appropriate FedEx forms?

"What are you doing?"

Catherine jumped, clutched at her jacket.

"Jesus, Sam!" Her heart pounded in her throat. "Are your CPR skills current?"

"Sorry, Catherine. I half expected you to be that reporter—that Jerry Woodstock." Fluorescent glare turned his ruddy skin the hue of a seasick sailor. His khaki topcoat was buttoned top to bottom and the collar was hiked as though he were expecting high wind. His brown leather briefcase weighed down his left hand; extra-large Tully's coffee container splayed the fingers of his right. Indignation flared. "That guy sneaked into our employee kitchen yesterday. Set up shop—started asking questions about you as if he were exercising some God-given right."

"Hope you dumped him off the roof before he had a chance to pack his 'chute."

"We called Security." He eyed her suspiciously. "I thought you were on a leave of absence."

"My name is still in the annual report. Why are you here at five forty in the morning?"

"I'm running the business. Remember?" He dropped his briefcase to the tile floor and began to unbutton his coat. "What are you looking for?"

"A missing FedEx bill."

He grimaced. "Things are always disappearing from this mail room."

"Really?" She picked up the cue; perhaps there was a pattern that would lead to the FedEx thief. "Like what?"

"Staplers," he said with great exasperation. "I buy more staplers for this mailroom than I buy for the company as a whole. What can they do with so many staplers?"

"Good thing we're not in the cattle business..." She pronounced it "bidness." "You'd go crazy keeping track of all those straws in all those bales of hay."

He ignored her. "And pencils."

"Basic cost of doing business, Sam." Catherine shoved the FedEx log into its slot on the shelf.

Sam gave a tight nano-grin. "What's happening with your... situation?"

"I've made about as much progress as a one-legged turtle on an uphill climb," Catherine responded as she slid by him, headed for the lunchroom. The thick scent of his herbal hair tonic settled like oil on her tongue.

He grabbed up his attaché and followed. "I thought you turned in your keys?"

They had discussed the merit of that possibility when they met yesterday. Sam suggested it would create more authentic distance between Catherine and ETC than just announcing she was on sabbatical. At first, she went along. Reluctantly. But when it came time to actually drop them on Aida's desk, she demurred.

"Gee, Sam," Catherine said conversationally as she flipped on lights, "are you hankering to put your brand on my spread?" She knew he coveted the CEO role.

"I'm trying to protect this company," he responded, voice huffy. Defensive. "You're the primary shareholder. You should be grateful I care so much."

"If you're worried about your stock losing value," she said as she opened and closed kitchen cupboards, "call my broker. He'll take it off your hands."

She located a three-gallon coffee thermos stashed under the sink, grabbed it, and slammed the cabinet door.

"Where are you going with that? That's company property."

She held her arms to her side and flipped off a quirky smile. "Wanna frisk me to see if I boosted any staplers." She pushed past Sam into the hallway.

She turned on him, fashioned her thumb and forefinger into a gun. "ETC is always my first priority. Linda Gordie is running the project teams when Joel's away, and you know how good she is. Things will run so smooth you'll think you're ridin' in a brand new Cadillac with four new tires."

"I heard they're—"

"They're tracking their hours. You'll be able to charge-back their time to me personally and I will reimburse the company."

"This will have to be brought up at the Board of Directors meeting." He was petulant. A four-year-old threatening to tell Mom.

She eyed him thoughtfully as two ideas fought for priority: No director on any corporate board would get involved in something as trivial as the charge-back of an employee's hours; and secondly, the next ETC Board of Directors meeting was scheduled for June, four months away, by which time any issue around charge-back would be completely moot. Sam's comment made sense only if a meeting were scheduled for the near future. Perhaps, a secret meeting? One that would be necessary if Sam decided to initiate some action against Catherine that required their buy-in?

Surely not, she thought; but anger and betrayal prematurely coursed her veins.

"When's the meeting?" she asked. Voice soft. Eyes cold.

Sam's pale skin blossomed as if blood vessels had spontaneously released their cargo. His eyes traveled as if expecting to find the answer printed on the walls behind her. He shrugged. "May? June? Aida would know."

He was lying.

As she turned for the door, Catherine singsonged, "Don't piss on my boot, Sam, and tell me it's raining."

She prayed he didn't think himself clever enough to make a power play for her company. She would never let him have it.

A half moon and a dozen stars languished behind a milky scrim of gossamer clouds. A breeze ruffled and murmured as Catherine waited for Wilson at Cala Foods on Geary Street. His midnight blue Porsche Boxter circled through the empty lot right on schedule.

136

Every time Catherine saw him climb out of that car she wanted to launch her fist into the air and cheer, "Yes!" She felt maternal pride for Wilson's accomplishments. Not bad for a twenty-two-year-old kid who was on probation for "unlawful entry" when she hired him to heft hardware three years ago.

Chocolate skin and signature black attire—this time turtleneck and jeans—turned him into an agile shadow crossing to her Rover. One gold earring, shaved scalp, and a fold of something tucked under his arm were the only things that bounced light.

He greeted her with, "Nobody stirring but the Highway Patrol," as he climbed into the passenger seat.

"We could be in trouble. I've got six dozen donuts in the back of my truck."

Last night when she met Joel and Wilson at Lil's, she voiced her suspicions that Stephen's murder might have been witnessed by one of the many vagrants who roam the coastal area. She told them about the bungie-corded grocery cart outside the gate of Stephen's property and of her plan—newly minted—for an early-morning outing to meet the local "residents." She figured donuts would be a good lure.

Catherine nodded toward two CD cases Wilson cradled in his massive hand. "Got anything foot-stompin'? I feel like I've been incarcerated in the bowels of a dirge."

"Then we better hang with the Dixie Chicks. *Don Giovanni* doesn't have many laugh lines." He inserted the disc.

Wilson was familiar with every opera singer who had performed in the twentieth century; Catherine suspected all of his Dixie Chick exposure had taken place in her presence.

The Chicks crooned "Wide Open Spaces" as she cruised west on Geary, meeting the occasional pre-dawn commuter. Wilson unfolded a sheaf of paper too small to be the *Chronicle* and folded back pages. "I know this news gig ain't your thang," he mugged, "but we thought you ought to know about this one." He held up the pages; streetlights scanned them like an open-face Xerox machine.

"This isn't giving me a good feeling," Catherine responded.

Wilson flicked on the overhead light and read: "*Secrets of the Guardian of Privacy.*" After a pause. "Want more?"

Acid flamed the lining of her stomach. "Cliff's Notes version."

"It's Jerry Woodstock. That guy from—"

"I know who he is," Catherine cut him off. "Is he spinning his yarn about Korean children smuggled in for illicit sex?" She hoped the story Wilson was about to preview was as fictitious as that.

"It's about your past. Where you grew up. Your divorces... Chloe... He talks about your... that thing where you used the Personal Image Consultant." Wilson sounded embarrassed. As if he were discussing her monthly cycle.

Catherine chuckled. Relieved. "He should hire one himself. His hair looks like it was hacked with an electric pencil sharpener. So that's the big exposé? My makeover?"

Wilson shrugged. "Joel thought you'd want to know—says the guy's after you."

She could feel his awkwardness. "Eh, he suffers from a paparazzi complex. I'm his Princess Di. Classic bottom-feeder aspirations."

"Good thing you don't have skeletons in your closet," Wilson said.

"Yeah," Catherine replied. "Good thing I'm not human."

The road curved south in front of Cliff House where it became the Great Highway that fronts the Pacific Ocean. Catherine scanned the murky, indistinguishable mass of sky and coastline. Short segments of pale breakers rose up in plateaus, crashed down, thinned to a silvery line, and vanished into the sand. A string of fishing boats—ablaze with high beam headlights—formed their own watery interstate some distance from the shore.

Catherine drove until she reached the turn-off for Stephen's beachfront property.

"The grocery cart was somewhere along here," Catherine said to Wilson as the Rover crunched slowly down the trail toward the gate to the property. Bright headlights turned patchy fog into a ripped curtain.

They scrutinized the brush on both sides of the path. No cart. Couldn't be that easy.

With a sigh, she backtracked a mile up the Great Highway and turned into the first beachside parking lot.

Beige seawall separated the highway, the adjacent parking lots, and the broad cement sidewalks from the stretch of sand that gave way to the surging tide. Three joggers, one with Golden Retriever trailing, pounded the wide walkway in front of the seawall. Half a dozen camped homeless were beginning to stir, rummaging through their shopping carts or shuffling along stacked like ragged pack mules.

Catherine squinted into the shadows, looking for the cart with the mound of bungie-strapped black garbage bags. Not there.

She nosed the Rover against the curb, facing the ocean beyond. Morning had brightened creating lines of demarcation where sky met water and water washed sand. The lapping tide licked the charred remains of a fire pit.

A tattered man pawed through a trash barrel at the edge of the asphalt. Catherine called, "Hey! Want some hot coffee?"

He tossed her a look of disgust and bent deeper into the can, stretching onto tiptoes.

"Want a donut?" She opened the back of the vehicle.

"I don't believe in God," he crowed in a rough cigarettes-and-whiskey voice. "I ain't gonna go to no church—ain't gonna listen to no sermon." He freed the contents of a wadded paper bag.

Marlboro Man. Maverick to the core. "You're on your own with the bible-banging," she called. "Best I can do is coffee and donuts."

She set up a small folding table and laid out a dozen pastries and a handful of rough paper napkins. She poured coffee from the three-gallon thermos she'd borrowed from the ETC kitchen.

Gray and white seagulls flapped and soared on arced wings, squawking loudly, anxiously diving to get a closer look at the booty of the donut boxes. A golden sun was poised to breach the eastern horizon.

The population that visited her little breakfast site looked—and smelled—like refugees en route from a third-world country. She and Wilson took turns asking each newcomer if he or she knew anything about the murder that had occurred "behind the Big Gate," as one of their first visitors referenced the Forsster property. And they inquired about the owner of the shopping cart that was loaded with bungie-strapped garbage bags.

"That would prob'ly be Sick Dick you're lookin' for," a man in a scarred blue greatcoat, previously a silent participant, said to Wilson; then he stuffed his mouth with three-quarters of a jelly donut. "He wraps all his shit in garbage bag after garbage bag." The man's words were bogged in the donut that he worked in wide, slow ruminations. "One time I told him I didn't think he had nothin' in there but jes' more garbage bags." He snorted a companionable laugh.

Wilson smiled and nodded. He lifted the donut box and extended it arm's length, letting the man come to him. The man pointed back and forth with a dirt-encrusted forefinger, the motion of skimming words on a page. He pulled out an apple fritter.

Catherine inched closer. The man's hand trembled when he raised the styrofoam cup to his lips; but, in this group, it would have been an anomaly if it hadn't.

He chomped the fritter and glanced at Wilson. He talked and chewed at the same time. "Stays mostly down by the Big Gate, Sick Dick. Me, personally, I think it's dumb to be way off down there. No food close by... nobody to help ya out with gettin' any. But he don't like people, Sick Dick." Big swallow followed by a gulp of coffee. "Says his name's Richard, but I call him Sick Dick."

"Where does he go when he leaves that area—by the Big Gate," Catherine asked as she came up behind the man.

He wheeled and gawked at her, wild eyed. Mouth clamped into a tight line. Hand released styrofoam cup; milky brown coffee splattered worn black boots. He tossed the remains of his pastry as if it were a live grenade, turned, and limped stiffly across the asphalt.

"Wait," Catherine called and started after him. He wheeled into a crouch, arms spread wide, positioned to catch an invisible barrel. His eyes were vacant—except for the fear. He flicked his hand and light glinted off the edge of a long, thin blade.

Wilson caught Catherine's arm and dragged her backward. He held out his left hand like a priest conferring a blessing.

"It's okay, bro," he said gently. "Glad you stopped for coffee."

Some kind of lucidity flickered in the man's eyes.

"Go ahead on," Wilson continued to soothe. "You're safe here."

The man's face softened, but then he looked at Catherine and anxiety returned. He hesitated, and then started backing up. When he was fifty feet away, he whirled and scrambled out the south end of the parking lot, disappearing over a sand dune.

Catherine turned to Wilson, palms up in exasperation. "Most men don't react to me that way until the third date." Catherine was frustrated to have lost her only lead. "I think we're huntin' with the wrong bait. Put out word that I've got a case of Jack Daniels for any cowboy who helps me round up Sick Dick." She muttered under her breath, "If there is such a clown in this rodeo."

Coffee and donuts gone, Catherine and Wilson packed up the thermos and the folding table, and drove back to the Porsche. On the way, she asked him to visit the Diablo Community College campus where the Forsster family's nanny attended classes the day before a tidbit he'd unearthed.

"You'll be less conspicuous on a college campus than I will." She outlined the info he should try to learn from the nanny and he drove away. Catherine backtracked to the beach and re-parked the Rover at the south end of the lot where she'd spent the morning hosting the homeless.

She studied the Xerox photo—the one Maureen O'Malley had acquired—of Stephen following her down the trail on the day he was killed. She wanted to pinpoint the photographer's location; see if maybe he left behind something that might identify him. And she wanted to continue her search for the owner of the garbage bag–laden grocery cart; but she *didn't* want to chance another encounter with the police.

She jogged a mile down the beach to a grass-covered promontory that nudged into the ocean. The Forsster/Hallison property line was at the top of that ridge. She picked her way through ice plants and other low-growing vegetation that hunkered against the hillside. When she reached the fence line, she located a spot where strips of weathered wood had rotted and fallen loose from the heavy wire. She peered through the hole, across the basin of land, comparing the angle to the beach photo. A fuzzy dark border on the left of the shot suggested it was taken from this side of the fence, catching a wooden slat at the edge of the shutter.

A shock of dune grass was captured in the top right corner of the photo; she used it to get her bearings, moving slowly along the fence line, evaluating different locations until she found a ragged, six-inch hole where the wire was ripped loose and a chunk of slat was missing. She compared the shape to the shadow at the left edge of the photo. This was the place. The photographer had stood here.

Surveying the ground, she looked for anything the snoop might have left behind on Monday—empty film box, cigarette butts? There was nothing... but a growing sense that she was being observed.

She visually combed the surrounding vegetation looking for signs of humanity. At least a dozen eight-feet-tall pampas bushes dotted the dune. Lots of places to hide.

On her side of the fence, the plateau was narrow and fell away at a sharp angle. Catherine sidestepped down the slope, tennis shoes skidding on small rocks and crumbs of seashells. With the toe of her sneaker, she poked through trash hidden near the shadowy roots of dwarfed shrubs. The wind whipped a willowy pampas bush that grew five feet from the trail. Catherine inched down the hill and peered in at the clumpy roots.

A brightly colored plastic sack was impaled on a rotted stalk, just out of reach in the quiet eye of the blowing blades. She squatted to get a better look and her attention caught on something on the other side of the roots. Something that snapped with the blowing leaves. Something black and shiny.

She cinched the hood of her sweatshirt into a tight circle around her face, pulled down the sleeves to cover her fingers, and crawled under the slashing fronds on the backside of the pampas grass. Blades hacked at flannel as she tugged a garbage bag clear of the vegetation. It was heavy. The top was wound with a faded yellow-and-blue bungie cord.

Her pulse quickened. She unlooped the cord.

Still on her knees, she heard rocks grating behind her. She whirled. Bright sun haloed a wind-flapped human figure that loomed less than a foot away, facial features obscured by the glare.

Her eyes crossed on the tip of the gun barrel held steady six inches from her nose. Left grip was inscribed with *SF*.

Stephen's Colt .45.

Half her mind screamed *grab the gun!* The other half knew she could be shot dead. She raised her sun-blinded gaze, squinting again to see the face.

A baggy sleeve-draped arm came out slowly and a protruding fingertip pointed at the garbage bag.

"That's mine." The voice was gruff and raspy. Like Maureen O'Malley's.

Catherine sensed a swing of motion and instinctively ducked, but sharp pain ripped above her left ear. Rocks and sand pillowed her right cheek as she tumbled to the ground. She rolled to her back, dazed by the blow.

The apparition bent and snatched the garbage bag. Catherine tried to focus—fought for details, but black throbbing murkiness blanked out the hazy form and she lost track of time. Prolonged retching brought her conscious and to her knees. When the heaving stopped,

Catherine frantically scanned the horizon. The man was gone. No one was in sight.

She gingerly probed the side of her head. Swollen. Smear of blood. She rose unsteadily. Looked for him again. He had vanished. She studied the closest pampas bush, wanting to find him. Too stupid, she decided. What would she do if he were there?

Come back later, she told herself. When she was prepared for an encounter. Cautiously, she inched her way down the hillside, sitting to rest each time she felt bile rise up her esophagus. Still dizzy and unsettled, it took forty-five minutes to get back to her car. She slid behind the wheel and fought the urge to sleep. She knew she needed help.

She wrestled with her cell phone as she weaved north on the Great Highway.

"I'm on my way to your house," she said when Maureen O'Malley answered.

"Bring bullets," O'Malley said and broke the connection.

"I found the gun," Catherine said as she pushed past O'Malley, stumbling against the walls of the narrow entry hall. In the family room the blaring radio threatened to cleave her head in two. She turned it down four notches.

"You look like fucking shit."

"Stephen's gun. I found it," Catherine said as she rolled onto a barstool by the kitchen counter. She felt light-headed. Dizzy.

Lie down. Sleep. No.

"So, let me see it."

Catherine slid off the stool and paced, or, more accurate to her current condition, she ambled. Fought to maintain balance. "The homeless guy has it. He whacked me with it." She pointed to her temple. "Right here."

"I'll make some tea." O'Malley said as she wheeled into the kitchen.

"Tea. Good."

O'Malley filled the kettle and put it on the electric burner. Catherine described her encounter.

"You've probably got a fucking concussion. You should get your head examined."

"I'm not gonna spend the day in the ER polishing the seat of some cracked plastic chair. I just want to pump some caffeine into my veins and then I'm going back to the beach to look for the gun. Or, the guy who's got it. I'm going to stay there until I find it." She punctuated her declaration by pounding her right fist limply into her left palm.

O'Malley dropped two tea bags into two cups. "You're the wrong man for the job."

"Hey! You've never seen *me* behind the wheel of a pink pickup truck." Catherine said indignantly. "He surprised me, that's all. Next time, I'll drop a loop on him."

"Okay, so lemme get this straight," O'Malley said, as she poured boiling water into the mugs. "You've got a homicide dick working nights and weekends to convince the D.A. to charge you with murder, but you're going to spend the day kicking back at the fucking beach?"

"Did I say I was gonna pack a bikini?"

"So what?" O'Malley snapped. "So what if you find the fucking gun?"

"Well, then Hiller—"

"Hiller my ass. You know what Hiller's doing while you're out Easter egg hunting? He's hammering out a fucking jury-convincing case against you; but you—the self-appointed Girl Scout in charge of solving this fucking murder—you haven't done a fucking thing to come up with the identity of the actual fucking killer."

O'Malley clamped her jaw and shoved a steaming teacup in Catherine's direction. Catherine pursed her lips; stared at O'Malley. "You know, I've figured out the more times you say 'fuck' in one sentence, the more irritated you are."

"Yeah, well use your super-impressive powers of observation to interview Rina Gold. And your next potential suspect. And the one after that."

"You left out 'fucking'," Catherine said. She sipped the hot tea; it scalded her tongue. "Wait a minute. How do you know about Rina Gold?"

O'Malley pointed a stiff index finger at Catherine. "Your job is to rattle some fucking cages. Send your brawny fucking man-servant to do the heavy lifting with the homeless freaks."

It didn't seem the right time to take issue with "man-servant" or "freaks." "Wilson has a criminal record," Catherine said firmly. "I'm not going to set him up as a target on Hiller's shooting range. Forget Wilson. What about Rina Gold?"

"Just the fuck tell Wilson that Forsster had a gun. It disappeared. You've discovered who has it and you want it. If he locates it, he should turn it over to you right away. Don't tell him you fingered the fucking heat and your prints may be on it. The less he knows the less chance he'll bob up as an accessory. And pay attention to this, Calabretta: If your *team*," sarcasm emphasized the word, "isn't quali-fied to do their job, you'd better get a new fucking team that won't hobble you because *you*, Pollyanna, don't have one extra goddamned minute to flit around chattin' it up with bums at the beach."

Catherine glared at O'Malley. After a long pause she said. "How do you know about Rina Gold?"

O'Malley downed half a cup of tea. "I'm gonna tell you a fucking bedtime story," she rasped. "Once upon a time, I was working the Eddie Phuong takedown. Eddie Phuong was a recently deceased Tenderloin candyman. Musta burned somebody in a drug buy 'cause he shows up gutted in a dumpster off Ninth. I'm looking for the cutter. So I'm sitting on O'Farrell one afternoon staking a place that belongs to the scag of this snitch that owes me some buzz; but the snitch doesn't show up like he's supposed to. Anyway, the scag lives above Hong's Domestic Agency. Hong's is a front for the game."

Catherine was trying to follow O'Malley's unique vocabulary, but she must have looked confused because O'Malley clarified.

"Prostitution. In Hong's case, high-end stuff. No pun intended. Anyway, while I'm scopin', this Rolls pulls up in front of Hong's and I'm thinking maybe it's my snitch getting delivered by his punk friends. Except this is a classy Rolls—no gold wheels, no spoiler on the back. So I run the plates and guess who it belongs to? Rina Gold. While I'm checking it out, these two baby-pros—a boy and a girl, Korean, couldn't have been more than twelve years old—come out of Hong's and climb into the backseat of the Rolls. And away it goes.

"About half an hour after the Rolls fetches *les enfants*," O'Malley continued, "I ring up the Tiburon blues and ask them to do a drive-by of the divine Ms. Gold's crib. Guess what they found? Your favorite stallion's ride parked in the driveway beside the Rolls."

Tea backed up in Catherine's throat. "Oh, my God," Catherine whispered, nausea coiling her stomach. "Asian children involved in illicit sex. Just like Jerry Woodstock said."

The thought sickened her. She wanted to scream. Wanted to puke. Wanted to scrub herself in disinfectant. But after her initial reaction, she didn't doubt it was true. Stephen had an unbridled sexual imagination. He often wove tales of one of his favorite fantasies: A mature woman introducing a young boy—or a young girl—to the pleasures of the flesh. She shuddered. She'd assumed he was projecting—that it was another of his mental games. She'd never imagined he manifested that fantasy in the real world. She realized now that she'd been naive. She shook her head and closed her eyes, disgust growing.

"I heard Rina was obsessed with Stephen—that she wanted him to marry her." Catherine recited what Joel had learned from Nikki, the blonde at Over the Counter. "She publicly threatened him about six months ago in a bar Stephen frequented. Several people heard it. She swore she would tell his wife and ruin his marriage one way or the other. Then she apparently backed off." Catherine shrugged. "Maybe he threatened to expose her connection to Hong's?"

"Possible."

"Maybe that pissed her off and she decided to kill him."

"See? Now you have something to work on while your gopher spends the day at the fucking beach tracking down smelly dudes with pop guns."

Her name was Jillya Shanahan and she'd come from Ireland on an F-1 visa—a student visa—just four months ago. Wilson found out about her because Stephen Forsster had co-signed for a MasterCard in Jillya's name.

Jillya Shanahan was nanny to the two Forsster children. She lived with the family full-time, but took day classes at Diablo Community College while her wards attended their respective private schools. Wilson hadn't had to do anything elaborate, and not much that was illegal, to build this digital picture of her; he just accessed various little-known databases.

Catherine wanted to know where Lili Forsster was when her husband was killed, and she assumed Jillya would be a good source for that information.

Registration showed Jillya was scheduled for computer lab from ten until noon on Fridays. As Wilson pulled into the parking lot at Diablo, he wondered if Jillya would be on campus today. Or, if she had been called away by duties involving the grieving Forsster family.

The lab was a secured facility—had an electronic card scanner at the entry. That made Wilson smile. He piggybacked in behind another student whose badge opened the door.

The room was bustling. Every computer terminal was in use and four students hung out along the wall, waiting for machines.

Wilson scoped out the room and immediately recognized Jillya from her visa application photo. Black curly hair. Wide blue eyes. Pert little nose. Sassy-looking. She was sitting at a terminal in the far corner, alternately scowling at the monitor and grimacing over the code sheets that lay beside the keyboard. She typed a few keys, then looked back at the screen. She clenched both fists, pressed them to her temples, and spread her lips in an expression that looked like a silent scream through clenched teeth.

Intense. Wilson doubted she'd be lured by an invitation for coffee.

He scanned the layout of the suite. The lab assistant's area was in the near corner, walled off from the rest of the room by a chest-high—or, in Wilson's case—a waist-high countertop. It was unoccupied. Wilson strolled over and dropped his backpack on the desk beside the control terminal, which was already logged-in. He studied the menu then accessed the log times for each of the sixty terminals. Jillya had been on the system for two consecutive sessions, the latest already forty-two minutes long.

He picked up his bag and went to stand behind her, inches from the back of her chair. She didn't look up. He bent his six-five frame until his lips were close to her ear. "You cheated," he said.

"Bugger off." She pounded more keys.

"Can't do two sessions," he said. "People are waiting."

She leapt out of her chair, fists clenched at her side. "If you get me kicked off this machine," she hissed in a thick Irish brogue, "I'll slice up your balls and feed them to the bleeding IRA for breakfast."

To Wilson, it sounded like, "Awl sleece oop yur bols 'n fid 'em ta th bleedin' eeiray fer brickfist." It took him a moment to translate.

"Can't take meat products through Customs," he said.

She glared through her black eyebrows and hissed breath through her nostrils, clearly not amused. She dropped into the chair and typed a few keys. Wilson saw her hit "enter"; then the screen froze and flashed the message: "Program aborted."

She hunched over, elbows on the desktop, forehead cradled in the curl of her fists. Her yellow sweater-covered shoulders jerked as if she were laughing. Or sobbing.

After a moment, she swiped a hand across her eyes and looked again at the screen. She pressed a dozen keys and lines of code scrolled up the monitor.

From over her shoulder, Wilson quickly scanned the program. C++. A good foundation. Not exactly state of the art.

He pointed to the screen. "Here's the problem."

"Leev me the fook alone," she snapped, but she corrected the code he'd identified.

In an instant the screen started flashing the results of her program. Her, "Hmmm," sounded like satisfaction.

She swatted a few more keys, printed her results, then logged off. She stacked her texts and notebooks, grabbed her denim jacket off the back of the chair, and whirled away.

"All yours," she said and she started out of the lab.

"And my balls? Are they mine too?" Wilson asked.

She didn't acknowledge him so he followed her, thinking he'd probably already blown it, but he wanted to be able to tell Catherine that he tried. *Really* tried.

Jillya pushed through a double door and marched down the sidewalk, wild hair and gauzy gray skirt flouncing behind as she struggled into her jacket, shifting books from one arm to the other. She took off across the landscaped campus.

"Can I buy you a coffee?" He knew when he heard his own words that they were not gonna fly.

"I'm a lesbian," she tossed over her shoulder.

Wilson raced in front of her on the tree-lined asphalt path and walked backwards, watching her face, refusing to let her pass. "So we'll drink it black. No wussy cream and sugar."

He gave her his most winning smile and thought she might return it; instead her face crumpled and she started to cry. She whirled away from him and plopped onto a wooden bench just off the walkway. She tossed her books beside her and hunched over, elbows on knees, fists curled and pressed to her eyes.

Wilson was completely surprised; he didn't know what to do. She sobbed for a good three minutes while he stood shifting awkwardly from one foot to the other, listening to chirping birds, trying to shrink from the curious, condemning glances of passing students. He rested his backpack on the bench, then picked it up again, afraid he was invading her personal space.

Maybe she was grieving Mr. Forsster.

"I het this fookin' country," she said.

"You hate it?" He wanted to confirm his translation. "Why?"

"I het all you bleedin' horny American men." She looked at him with weepy disdain. "Don't your women ever put out?" She ripped a tissue from her bag and scrubbed it across her nose.

Wilson felt embarrassment crawl his cheeks. "Wrong guy," he said and started down the sidewalk. "That ain't my gig."

He'd just have to tell Catherine that he'd failed—that he wasn't any good at this investigating stuff. She could send Joel. He related better to women.

"Wait!"

Wilson kept walking. This female seemed moments away from going postal.

"Please, stop. Here I am, layin' on a bruiser when you were just being nice."

He could tell from her voice that she was close behind him. He slowed, turned to face her.

"I don't have even one friend in this bleedin' country." She sniffled and tears welled in her red-rimmed eyes. "I guess that's no surprise to you."

Wilson watched her fumble for a tissue; then he held out his hand. "Wilson Ramsey," he said.

"Jillya Shanahan." She shook his hand tentatively and looked pathetically into his eyes. "You want to go for a pint?"

He studied her, trying to decide if she were sane. "Okay," he said.

"But one condition," she said and tightened her arms around the stack of books. "You can't ask me any questions about my employer. I'm bleedin' tired of everybody badgerin' me for gossip."

Catherine watched Laura's plane from New York taxi slowly to gate 41, feeling fairly certain Laura wouldn't be too happy to see Catherine and her Rover in place of the car-and-driver she was expecting. And that awareness made Catherine consider her friendship with Laura Tyler Jackson.

They'd met three years ago at a WATT—Women at the Top—conference for women executives. Laura ran her own ad agency and ETC was looking for someone to design new marketing materials. ETC hired Laura's firm. During the process of developing the campaign, Laura invited Catherine to a couple of social events: a client cocktail party and the opening of an art exhibition sponsored by Laura's agency.

Newly separated from Nicolas, Catherine was acutely aware of how solitary her existence had become. Even as an adolescent, she'd had virtually no friends—thought it would be torture to hang out with a gaggle of girls, painting their toenails, gossiping about their enemies, and giggling over their escapades with boys. As a woman flying solo, she decided it would be good to cultivate some female friendships—especially since the idea was so far outside her comfort zone.

She invited Laura for dinner, and over the course of the next year, they got together socially at least once a month. Two entrepreneurs discussing business problems, sipping martinis, and, inevitably, Laura sharing anecdotes about the trials of being single while Catherine mused about her failed marriage and her vow of celibacy.

"I'm sticking to computers. They follow an exacting pattern of logic and they never stomp on your heart," Catherine said one night as they sipped cocktails in the Redwood Room of the Clift Hotel after seeing *A Streetcar Named Desire* at the theater down the street. "A relationship dies—as they all must—and you end up with the self-esteem of a hairball puked up by a scabby, feral cat."

"Are you kidding? Men are easy," Laura argued. "You just gently take hold of their little pee pees and lead them wherever you want them to go."

Catherine asked, "Who should be more insulted by your philosophy: men... or women?"

Laura shrugged, sipping her martini. "I just go with what works."

"Intelligent, successful women with many varied interests," Catherine remembered grousing, "but what do we end up talking about? The opposite sex."

"Or sex, period." Laura mused. "It's the most interesting game in town."

"I have more fun tweezing my ankles."

"You've obviously been playing with little-leaguers. You need a mentor—a coach." She smiled mischievously. "And I know just the man for the job."

That man turned out to be the inimitable Stephen Forsster.

Now, as Catherine watched the airplane pull to the jetway, she pondered Laura's determination to distance herself from Stephen. Catherine had assumed Stephen and Laura were good friends. But then, everything changed when Laura started dating Ben Admire.

The jetway door opened; Catherine inhaled jet fuel and momentarily felt absurd holding the "Tyler Jackson" sign she'd lettered with a bold, black marker—her attempt to interject humor after the strain of their last phone conversation.

Laura was the first passenger through the door, but Catherine almost didn't recognize her. Gone was her mass of long sandy curls; her hair was cropped short and straight, and dyed sable. Very New York. Very chic. Full-length Black Diamond mink flowing open over red Escada two-piece suit confirmed it was Laura.

Catherine smiled and waggled the "Tyler Jackson" sign.

Laura looked as if she had been caught in a customs' sting operation. She glanced over her shoulder and seemed to consider trying to fight the outward flow of travelers to get back on the plane. Irritation flared, but Catherine twanged, "Don't you look like you just stepped out of a Madison Avenue picture window."

"Where's my driver?" Laura asked. She stopped. Scanned the gate area.

"I'm auditioning for a new career."

"I told you, Catherine, I can't be associated with this." Her voice was a hoarse whisper, her expression unfriendly. "If the press picks up anything..."

Laura turned her back on Catherine and started down the concourse. Catherine shoved the "Tyler Jackson" sign in the closest trash bin and took off after the woman. "I need your help," she said, anger bubbling to the surface. "You introduced me to Stephen—"

Laura wheeled around so quickly Catherine almost crashed into her. "Are you saying it's my fault you got yourself into this mess?"

"You knew Stephen a lot longer—and a lot better—than I did." Her voice was tight.

"I didn't know him *that* well. Look, Catherine." Laura clutched Catherine's jacket lapel and pulled them both out of the flow of passengers heading for Baggage Claim. Her voice took on a note of pleading. "If the press connects me to Stephen Forsster, Ben will drop me like a hot rock. He'll have to. He does his first re-election rally in two weeks and he can't be fending off scandal, imagined or real."

"Laura, they're trying to hang a murder charge on me."

Laura's expression softened to empathetic dismay. "I don't know how I can help you, honey—except to confess to it myself."

"I only know how to say this in English: I need information."

"Well, I can't stand here in this very public place with you. I'll call you tonight and try to answer all your questions. I promise."

She pushed off from the wall and walked briskly in the direction of Baggage Claim.

"Your limo was cancelled," Catherine called disgustedly.

"I'll take a taxi," Laura tossed over her shoulder and never broke stride as she hit the top of the escalator.

Sheltered by twenty-feet tall palm trees, feeling cranky about being dismissed by people she needed to talk to, Catherine paced back and forth on Rina Gold's small front porch. She had a headache—considered the possibility of concussion. Too bad if it was.

The red lacquered door had closed on her twice: the first time when she told the pink-uniformed maid she wanted to see Rina Gold; the second when the maid returned to say, in her heavy Japanese accent, Ms. Gold "is not take visitor."

Catherine half expected that reception, so she instructed the maid to, "Tell Ms. Gold I know about Hong's." She thought she saw a reaction in the maid's stoic demeanor.

Yellow narcissus bloomed in giant marble urns at either corner of the porch, weighting the cool air with its sweet fragrance; otherwise, this property irritated her. Very L.A. with its rows of palm trees, its acres of curving concrete driveway, and black wrought-iron spiked fence separating the grounds from the narrow, winding Belvedere Street.

Joel's research indicated Rina was originally from Southern California; that she was the only child of the late Hubert Gold, a banking scion who had been ambassador to some small country—Madagascar or somewhere—under Ronald Reagan.

The door opened and the maid said, "This way."

Catherine followed her through a marble foyer and down a hallway, past the step-down entrance to a living room with sleek rose sofas and nothing but glass along the wide, back wall. They paused at a closed door. The maid tapped once and motioned Catherine inside a candlelit room. Steamy eucalyptus and lilac assaulted Catherine's nostrils. Japanese chimes ponged soporiferously; somewhere, water trickled over river stones.

"Have a seat. Until I'm done." The voice was drowsy. It came from the woman lying face down on a massage table in the middle of the room. A blonde Adonis-type in a navy blue muscle shirt stood at the head of the table, eyes closed, posture trance-like, thumbs pressing into the deeply tanned flesh of the woman's lean shoulders.

"I said I *knew* about Hong's," Catherine said testily. "I didn't say Hong's sent me here to do your bidding."

The woman slowly swiveled her head in Catherine's direction. The room was too dim for unimpeded eye contact.

"Okay, Hans," she said.

Hans, Catherine thought. A woman like Rina Gold would never have a masseur named Jim... or Fred.

Hans scrubbed his meaty fingers on a white hand towel, picked up a gym bag, and exited the room quietly, arms held at his side like an Olympic weight lifter flexing for the crowd.

Rina Gold reached toward a small table and the row of blackout shades slowly hummed upward, morphing the back wall into a blinding blaze of sunlight, Golden Gate Bridge, and a panoramic view of the Sausalito hills looming across the harbor. The adjacent wall housed an assortment of chrome barbells.

"So you're one of Stephen's other women," Rina said.

"Yep, a woman. Decades past puberty," Catherine quipped acerbically before she leashed her attitude and refocused on sucking up in order to get the info she'd come for.

Rina stretched languorously on the table and rose like a sleepy cat. She was completely nude and her silhouette, back-lit by the windows, was as perfect as any ever drawn by the hand of man. She sauntered to a brass valet, bronzed skin glistening of oil.

"I wonder what he saw in you," Rina said as she pulled a white terrycloth robe over perfectly shaped breasts, perfectly waxed pubic patch. Catherine had to admit: at that moment she wondered the same thing. Such flawless female flesh daunted her.

"You were always his favorite," Catherine fawned. "The rest of us were just... stand-ins."

Rina reclined on a chaise lounge and the robe separated, exposing shapely calves and half of one well-toned thigh. She tossed her long strawberry curls and reached for a glass of Evian that awaited her on a near table. Triumph twinkled in her eyes.

"How would you know that? Stephen never talked about his conquests." Rina emptied the glass.

"Maybe not to you, but he always challenged me to be more... imaginative. 'Like my favorite,' he would say. And one day he slipped up and said, 'Like Rina.'"

She preened. Flattered. Hungry to hear more of the crap Catherine was shoveling.

"I'm surprised Stephen told you about Hong's," Rina said as she replaced the empty glass on the table. "He didn't usually kiss and tell."

"Stephen didn't tell me. I got it from a cop."

"A cop?" She sat straighter on the chaise and Catherine scored satisfaction at finally having gotten the woman's attention.

"Yeah. One who was speculating that Stephen might have threatened to blow the whistle on Hong's and implicate you."

No reaction. No flinch. No shift of the eyes. Wrong guess? Catherine continued anyway. "That you might have been worried about that... and maybe did something to make more than his dick turn stiff."

Rina smiled seductively. "If I'd wanted to kill Stephen, I would have done it while he was tied spread eagle on a bed at the Ritz. I would have used very sharp surgical instruments. Lots of blood. It would have been oh so much more personal than a gunshot to the head."

Somebody really nasty had hard-wired this woman's motherboard.

"I hope your alibi is as well-conceived as your fantasy."

"I hadn't seen Stephen for at least six months," she said dismissively; then stopped. "But you didn't come here to warn me about the cops."

"I told you about the cops because I thought perhaps we could exchange information," she said. "You know, since we're both members of a sort of... elite club. Masterminded by the late, great, three-legged man."

Rina smirked and lowered her feet to the floor. "You flatter yourself to think you're in the same class as I." She poured fresh Evian.

Catherine fought to staunch her repugnance. "Well, it's true I didn't help Stephen consummate his fantasies of deflowering adolescents."

"Oh, he liked them much younger than adolescence," Rina said, and smiled mischievously above the rim of the glass.

Catherine couldn't maintain the charade—could no longer pretend she was here as a cohort. Her lip curled in disgust. "I'd say a prayer for you, but I doubt God would recognize your name," she said.

"Mary Magdalene speaks." Rina sipped placidly.

"You threatened to tell Stephen's wife that he'd been fucking you. How did he stop you from doing that?"

"He didn't stop me; I changed my mind."

"Did he threaten to expose your penchant for having sex with children?"

"Children aren't sexless creatures. They have sexual desires, too." Her smile was mean. "Think back to when you were a sparkly preening little girl."

"Is that what fucked you up? Someone taking advantage of your childish innocence?"

"Don't give me the blushing virgin routine. I knew Stephen Forsster for a very long time and I never knew him to be fond of the missionary position. So what's your specialty? Are you the librarian-type who begs to take it up the ass? Or did you gang bang his friends?" She smiled knowingly. "Now, *that* was a favorite fantasy of Stephen's."

"Where were you on Monday night when Stephen was killed?"

"My whereabouts is a matter of public record." Rina sneered. "As is your fling with our favorite sexual deviant."

Disgusted by this whole exchange and certain she was wasting her time trying to finesse a confession from this bimbo, Catherine strode across the room and grabbed the doorknob. "If you killed him, I'll come after you like Santa Ana went after the Alamo."

"Ooooow, that sounds like a fun game," Rina smirked. "Why don't you drop by tomorrow night and we can play it with a few of my favorite friends." She winked provocatively. "The dress code is black leather."

Catherine slammed the car door, convinced she'd have to be boiled in bleach before she would ever feel clean again. Perhaps Joel could abrade her "aura" with one of those smudge thingies.

Perverts. Hong's and their prepubescent prostitutes. She shuddered in disgust. Her proximity to Stephen Forsster made her a part of it. She wanted to wretch. He was abhorrent. How could she have not known? How could she have? She scrubbed her hands through her hair and downshifted her anger. Her repulsion.

Who was she to cast the first stone? She laid her head on the steering wheel. Exhausted by her unqualified attempt at playing God. Leave that to the evangelists. And the politicians.

She steered the Rover into the narrow street. A young African American teenager stood in the driveway of the estate next door, less than ten feet from the road, aiming a water hose at a shiny black Audi.

The boy glared at Catherine, memorizing her car as she drove past. His body language was hostile. Territorial. Catherine was surprised until she realized what she'd witnessed was the moon-eyed glare of a jealous adolescent protecting his turf... and Catherine deduced Rina Gold had seduced her young neighbor.

Catherine clamped her jaw. Whether or not the seduction of a child violated the laws of God, it sure as hell violated the laws of man. And murder violated both. Rina Gold was due for a day of reckoning.

Nikki, the blonde at Over the Counter, had confided to Joel her knowledge of the business competition between Stephen Forsster and Buzz Benson, basically the same information Catherine had gotten from George Hallison. But Nikki also told Joel that everyone suspected Stephen, who had mastered the art of euphemism in order to brag about his sexual conquests without directly admitting any indiscretions, had developed more than a passing interest in Buzz's wife, Angelina. And, in his own inimitable way, Nikki said, Stephen had driven Buzz to more than one public display of jealous rage.

Catherine had learned Benson's address and phone number in Kentfield, a wealthy Marin County community, from the illegal background check Stephen had run on Buzz. As Catherine headed north over the Golden Gate Bridge and exited at Sir Francis Drake Boulevard, she dialed the Benson's home phone and a woman answered.

"Is this Macy's?" Catherine asked.

"You've got the wrong number," the woman responded in a timid southern drawl.

Catherine apologized and hung up. Someone was at home at the Benson residence.

When she pulled in front of the house five minutes later, she was relieved to see the property was open to the street. No gates. No security systems to navigate.

She walked up the winding sidewalk that divided a broad expanse of green lawn. It looked as if it had been groomed for croquet—if one were good enough to drive wooden balls around four branching magnolia trees that undoubtedly canopied the yard in summer. Chest-high rose bushes, pruned for winter, separated the lawn from the wide veranda with its two-story white pillars. It was a scaled-down replica of a southern plantation mansion. Tara, right out of *Gone With the Wind*. Catherine would bet her favorite Stetson that "Buzz" also came packaged with a southern drawl.

Her finger on the bell button commenced chimes bonging the first twelve notes of "Dixie." Catherine rolled her eyes, then realized a security camera to the left, at the top corner of the double doors, recorded her reaction. Anger flushed her cheeks. She was tired of starring in unauthorized videos. She squinted at a metal logo tag attached to the unit and read, *Personal Security Systems, San Rafael, CA.*

Catherine gritted her teeth and waited a full minute. She hated to hear the notes again, but punched the bell anyway. When the chimes died, the house was silent.

Five minutes ago, someone had answered the phone. Catherine decided to check out the garage to see if there was a car parked inside.

She followed the driveway to the rear. All three garage doors were pulled closed; no windows, even on the sides. As Catherine reversed her path, a chainsaw roar commenced nearby. From behind the house? Perhaps Scarlet O'Hara was out back overseeing the plantation slaves.

Catherine called out, "Hi, y'all. Anybody home?" as she rounded the corner to the back yard. They oughta love that here in Dixie Land West. She followed the noise toward a twenty-by-twenty greenhouse in the far corner of the property.

A blonde, ponytailed female wielded an electric pruner on the shrubs growing up the tan cinderblock wall that enclosed the periphery of the property. The scent of freesia emanated from white and yellow blossoms that stood in orderly, well-tended rows in the greenhouse.

The woman shaved off leaves and twigs that fluttered to the grass at her feet. She was so small, Catherine wasn't sure if she was adult or teen. She was wearing a yellow, sleeveless sweatshirt over faded, baggy jeans. Her smooth skin glistened with perspiration; smears of dirt tattooed her lean, muscular biceps.

She flicked off the pruners and, after a moment of shocking silence, birds protested raucously.

"Excuse me," Catherine said, from fifteen feet away.

The woman whirled, pruners held out defensively, fear flaring in the aquamarine eyes that were distorted behind clear, workman's goggles.

"What do you want?" the woman asked in a terrified whisper.

Catherine noted smudges of dirt on her cheek and wondered fleetingly how the grime had worked its way inside the goggles, circumscribing the woman's left eye.

"I'm Catherine Cala–"

"I know who you are," the woman cut her off. She ripped off the goggles and Catherine realized it wasn't dirt that smudged the woman's eye and cheekbone. The flesh was swollen and bruised, the blue iris surrounded by red hemorrhage.

"Jesus. Who did that?"

"Please leave!" The woman's tiny voice matched her stature; but she was genuinely frantic. She glanced up to the roof of the greenhouse and Catherine saw a camera lens tucked under the eave. The woman shoved the pruning shears onto a tabletop just inside the greenhouse and took off at a lope across the lawn.

"Wait!" Catherine followed. "I want to ask you some questions about Stephen Forsster."

"You're going to get me killed." The words were barely audible as she pushed into the house and slid shut the patio door.

The lock clicked into place. Catherine stood staring through the glass at the woman inside.

"Pleeeeaaase," the woman mouthed, agony on her face, tears in her eyes.

Out of the corner of her eye Catherine saw the *Personal Security Systems* metal logo tag on a camera lens that was aimed at the back door, directed at the exact spot where she stood.

She stared at the woman for a moment, then shrugged for effect and turned and walked away.

Angelina Benson. No doubt about it. And what a misnomer for the *Personal Security System*. It was an incarceration system.

Catherine didn't look back as she climbed into her car and drove away. There was no doubt in her mind that Angelina Benson was very afraid. And Catherine was elated that she had identified her first solid murder suspect: macho wife-beater Buzz Benson.

"I'm beginning to think you're taking advantage of me," O'Malley rasped when she opened the door for Catherine.

"Hell, I'm bringing you gifts!" Catherine said as she moved into the family room. She rummaged in her handbag and pulled out a bent Butterfinger that looked as though it had been purchased at a fire sale. She held forth her offering. O'Malley eyed it glumly then wheeled to the kitchen.

On her way back to the city, Catherine had detoured to San Rafael to check out the Personal Security Systems store. A sign on the door said, "Gone fishin'. Check back tomorrow." Feeling frustrated, she decided it was a good time to confer with Maureen.

"You're getting pretty casual about seeking my counsel, but I don't remember hearing you say the words, 'I. Agree. To. Your. Terms, Maureen.'"

"You know I can't do this without you," Catherine said.

"The warden," O'Malley nodded her head toward the upstairs flat, "called my brother in Hawaii and told him I'm associating with a known criminal. He subsequently called me and said when he returns from his holiday with the lovely British cunt he's married to, he's going to file a restraining order to keep you from coming here." She sagged in her chair. "He gets back on Friday. Bring bullets on Thursday."

"Maureen..."

"That cock-sucking judge will do anything Thomas asks."

"Why don't you fight back?"

"There's only one thing I want," she whispered vehemently, fires of anguish blazing in her eyes. "Don't you fucking *get it*?"

Catherine lowered her head and stared at her hands folded in her lap.

"You'll be incarcerated, too, just like I am," O'Malley continued, emotion shaking her words. "But for you, there's a possibility of parole—or the fucking governor might pardon you. There's at least a remote chance that someday you will *walk* out of there."

She snatched up a mug and flung it against the far wall, black tea tracing a trail in the air before it splattered across the rug and the unpainted pine coffee table.

"That's something I'll *never* do."

Catherine sighed. "Maureen, I can't—"

"Yes! You *will*." O'Malley spoke through gritted teeth and jabbed her index finger forcefully at Catherine. "I'm helping you and you *will* help me."

Catherine rubbed fingertips across her forehead and knew she most definitely could not do what the woman demanded. It would be the same as pulling the trigger herself.

She rose and marched to the kitchen and pulled off a handful of paper towels. She mopped up tea and retrieved the mug, which had thudded and dropped unbroken to the carpet. She stuffed the wet towels into the metal kitchen trashcan and smelled urine and feces emanating from the wad of soiled diaper that lay just under the lid. She knew she couldn't possibly understand the emotions that ruled O'Malley's determination to die.

"What did you learn today?" O'Malley asked quietly, calm having returned to her demeanor.

Catherine returned to the barstool and perched on the edge. "Maureen..." she began.

"Just answer the fucking question," O'Malley said. "This is a put-one-foot-in-front-of-the-other process."

Catherine sighed, "First, I should tell you that I got a surprise package."

She told O'Malley about the FedEx that had been waiting at her door last night. She also apologized for not mentioning it when she was there ten hours earlier, but blamed the whack on the head for giving her a flash of amnesia.

Maureen asked few questions about the content of the video but was more interested in the technical aspect: What was the camera angle, did the lens seem to move, was the audio clear, was there any doubt it was Catherine and Stephen?

Catherine had reviewed the tape several times last night, evaluating those exact aspects. She was pleased she could answer all of Maureen's questions.

"There had to be separate microphones in order to pick up sound that well," O'Malley said.

"Yeah. I thought the same thing."

"Someone did a very thorough fucking job of bugging your apartment."

"I don't think Stephen could have set that up. Besides, how would it benefit him?"

"If he'd done it without your knowledge, it would have been for blackmail."

"I'm not a very good candidate for that."

"What about the displaced CEO? George Hallison? He seems to have a real hard-on for Forsster. Plus he had a lot to gain."

Catherine hated that thought but she wrestled with it again. "I suppose he could have hired someone."

"It doesn't feel like a professional job. A pro wouldn't send you a copy of the client's evidence," O'Malley said. "This feels more like a taunt. Like something personal." O'Malley sneered. "Whoever it is, you better hope he doesn't put you on the fucking Internet."

"Oh, I wish he would," Catherine said with grim determination. "I'd bag his ass in a New York minute." Catherine changed the subject and told O'Malley about the four voided ETC FedEx billing labels, two of which had come into Catherine's possession.

"Expect more deliveries," O'Malley said.

"Who's doing this?" Catherine asked rhetorically. "And why?"

"You wanna be a junior fucking detective, there's only two words in your job description: Find out."

"Right." She described her visit with Rina Gold, summed up with, "If that encounter had been a fall harvest, I'd be one bankrupt farmer. I've got Joel Hodges—he's a computer guru who works for me—I've got him doing a news search to see if he can '*find out*' where Rina was when Stephen was killed. She said it was 'public information.' If that's true, we'll track it down.

"I also met my friend Laura at the airport, but it was a bad time for her." Catherine didn't tell O'Malley how betrayed she felt by Laura's behavior. "She's going to give me background info on Stephen tonight."

Then she told Maureen about her brief encounter with Angelina Benson. "She knows something. But she won't talk to me."

"Then you'll have to fucking make her."

"What am I supposed to do? Tie her in a chair and shine a bright light in her eyes? I'm not an L.A. cop, for chrissakes."

"It's called 'manipulation.' Lie. Deceive her. Threaten her."

"She's so beaten down already. And so afraid."

"That's a good time to take advantage of her."

"I was never good at drowning kittens," she said sarcastically.

"Are you trying to solve a crime or earn a fucking Girl Scout badge honor? This is a murder investigation. Do whatever you have to do to get the information you need."

"You didn't see her. She's so... so vulnerable."

"Ahhh. It's a posthumous badge for bravery. You're going to walk to the electric chair, head high, proud you didn't inconvenience anyone. Is that the glory you're holding out for?"

"God, you're relentless," Catherine said, angry at this continual badgering.

"I don't believe in God."

"You don't believe—"

The door buzzer meeped twice and Catherine jumped.

O'Malley closed her eyes and gritted her teeth. "Someday you'll know what it's like to be in prison and," she pointed at the door as if cueing a grand entrance, "have a fucking full-time, cunt-faced warden."

The buzzer gave an elongated meep and O'Malley slashed palms up and down on the wheels of the chair, driving toward the front door. "What the fuck do you want, dick breath?" she screeched as she threw open the door.

"Is that any way to greet an old friend?" The voice came from the dark outside the porch gate. A voice that haunted Catherine's recent dreams. Her blood went cold and her heart pounded into overdrive.

"Well, if it isn't the ghost of Christmas past," O'Malley said.

"You gonna invite me to join your little tea party?" Inspector Hiller asked. "Or am I interrupting your private time with the criminal element?"

Catherine rose and stepped behind the barstool. The gate clicked open. O'Malley said, "Are you here to clear your conscience?"

"You've been stealing police files in order to help a suspected felon," he said as he came into the light of the family room. He smiled knowingly at Catherine. She stood her ground.

"Yeah," O'Malley said as she wheeled into the kitchen and parked herself under the glow of the fluorescent light. "I sneaked up three flights of stairs just this afternoon and went through your case book, you fucking hairball."

Hiller stood at the end of the bar, positioning himself, Catherine thought, as if he felt a need to watch them simultaneously. The stench of stale nicotine tickled Catherine's nostrils.

"Did you hear that your good friend, Rosalind del Rio, was fired today?" Hiller asked O'Malley. "Twenty-one years of loyal public service and she does something stupid that costs her her pension."

"What, Harry?" O'Malley asked calmly, but Catherine saw a spark of emotion—perhaps fear, perhaps anger—flash in her eyes. "Was she wearing the wrong lipstick? Leave the wrong color lip print on your big hairy ass, you cocksucker."

Hiller's mouth curled. "I believe I'm the only one in this room to whom that description doesn't apply." He looked back and forth between the two women, his eyes coming to rest on O'Malley. "But, of course your infamous cock-sucking days are a thing of the past, Maureen, because you'll never find a guy desperate enough to want it from an ugly macho broad with a dead useless twat."

Color crawled into O'Malley's cheeks. Catherine watched her struggle for self-control. Catherine silently calculated how much jail time she'd have to do if she crashed the barstool over Hiller's head.

"No matter what IA says, Harry, you and I will always know those were your rounds lodged in my spine."

"If that were true, Mo, I would have done a better job. And then you wouldn't need the felon." Hiller turned his gaze to Catherine. "Did she tell you all the ways she's tried to kill herself? How many people she's asked to bring her rounds so she can die like a *real* cop with a bullet out the back of her head?"

Catherine didn't respond. He continued.

"Is she just gonna load the gun, Maureen, or did you recruit her because she's got experience firing into a live torso at close range?"

Catherine spoke through clenched teeth. "You wanna be careful when you piss on an electric fence, Inspector Hiller."

"Whoa, you're spunky when you're not locked in a jail cell. And isn't it nice we could get together like this... get to know each other a little better."

"You're following me," Catherine said, her eyes full of anger.

"Oh, no. *I'm* not," he said and lifted his right foot to the barstool where Catherine had been sitting. "Tell her how understaffed we are, Maureen." He raised his pant cuff and exposed an ankle holster. It contained a snub-nose .38. Police-issue of yesteryear.

He removed the gun from its leather case and opened the chamber. Catherine shifted her eyes to O'Malley. She was staring at the gun like an addict watching a needle hover over a cook spoon.

"Tell her how we oftentimes don't have the manpower to do our own stakeouts so we rely on volunteerism by concerned citizens to help us keep track of our prime suspects," Hiller said and spun the cylinder, checking it with one squinted eye. He glanced at Catherine. "Somebody out there in volunteer-land thinks you're worth keeping an eye on."

He snapped the chamber closed, took out a handkerchief, and wiped the gun clean. He dangled it by its brown plastic handle. "Unregistered. Fully loaded."

He carefully placed the gun on the yellow formica countertop as if it were a fragile prize. O'Malley's eyes followed it—never left it. Hiller turned and walked toward the front door.

"Send me a postcard from the Pearly Gates," he said and closed the door behind him.

The loaded gun lay on the bar between them. Neither woman was more than five feet from it. Catherine moved first.

"Noooo!" O'Malley screamed and lunged.

Catherine beat her by nanoseconds. She snatched the weapon off the counter, heart pounding erratically.

"You can't do this!" O'Malley's rasp turned guttural and tears streamed down her face.

"Maureen."

"That's mine! Give it to me!" She pressed fists to temples, eyes squinched tight, and sobs wracking bony shoulders.

Catherine could feel every ounce of agony that tortured the woman's soul, and she felt unsure—selfish—for stealing away the one thing Maureen O'Malley wanted for her life: the opportunity to end it.

O'Malley sobbed and rocked back and forth, stretching the constraints of the wheelchair seatbelt, resignation pressing her into an upright fetal form.

"Okay," Catherine said as if quieting a child. "Okay, Maureen. Shhhh." Catherine sat on the barstool, clutched the gun to her breast, whispering, "Shhh, shhhh," until the sobbing diminished.

Catherine took a deep breath and swallowed hard. "Okay, Maureen. I promise. I will help you." The burden of her promise brought tears to Catherine's own eyes. "I will help you. But not yet." She had to stop and swallow again before the words would come. "Please understand, Maureen. I need your help. I need you."

Chapter Five: Saturday

Floating out of a deep sleep Catherine became aware of a weight pressing heavily on the edge of the bed. Before she could react, Garbo's wet tongue swiped her face.

"Oh, Garbo," she groaned and felt the bed come alive with the rhythm of Garbo's stubby tail. "You're as predictable as warts on a frog's butt."

Catherine knew without opening her eyes that Garbo had belly-crawled onto the edge of the mattress, and that it was exactly seven o'clock. Any morning Catherine's alarm didn't go off by seven, Garbo's internal clock kicked into gear.

Catherine was too exhausted to mirror Garbo's enthusiasm for the new day. She'd worked late into the night reviewing all the digital information compiled by Wilson and Joel, mapping it, making notes on the voids she needed to fill. Organizing her thoughts; outlining a plan. Once she'd finished, she felt some small relief; she was prepared to move forward. But she was also frustrated. She had only four potential suspects: Rina Gold, Buzz Benson, Lili Forsster, and, reluctantly, George Hallison.

Joel was researching the potential enemies Catherine had learned about from George Hallison. Her objective: clear those names off her list or turn them into actual suspects.

With her new game plan, Catherine had a busy day ahead but she knew she would be more productive on five hours sleep instead of the measly four she'd managed to wrack up so far. The only obstacle to that one-more-hour goal was seventy pounds of optimistic Weimaraner.

"Not now, Garbo." Catherine said. "Go lie down."

Immediately the bed jerked as Garbo leapt to the floor and raced to the hall. Catherine heard paper swishing as the dog rummaged the basket that stored the week's unread magazines—and her black leather leash. Catherine burrowed into the warmth of the down comforter, muffling the thud of Garbo's feet and the jangle of the leash clasp. She groaned when the leash clunked to the floor; she knew she would find it lying on the white carpet next to her slippers.

"Garbo! I'm serious." She tried to sound tough. Clint Eastwood making his point with a bad guy.

The closet door squeaked—nosed open. Rustling. The thud of Catherine's sneakers hitting the floor. Strategically placed, she knew without looking, next to the leash. She couldn't stop the smile that spread her lips.

"No, Garbo! We're going to sleep in." She could hear the busy dog. "I'm tired," she whined.

More thuds. Little ones. Like dress shoes. Garbo could displace the entire contents of the closet floor in less than sixty seconds.

"Garbo," she pleaded. "Can't we go at eight, today? Why must we always go at seven?"

A large thud caused Catherine to raise her head and peer over the edge of the bed. Garbo loomed proudly over a brown leather hiking boot, tail wagging ferociously.

"Garbo, I mean it!" she spoke sharply. "Go lie down!"

The dog tucked her tail and dropped to her haunches, head hung low. She slowly walked her front paws out until she was flat on the rug.

Catherine pulled a pillow over her head to block out sad, amber eyes.

Twenty minutes later, they were getting out of Catherine's Rover at the Presidio beach. Low clouds hung heavy and gray, obscuring the orange towers of the Golden Gate Bridge. Wind whipped the terrain, dragging along tendrils of fishy-smelling fog and blasting sand through the chilled air. Breakers undulated, swelled, and crashed, hurling foamy water high up on the shore. Foghorns bleated imperatively. A lone pelican battled the wind and dove into the choppy waters. With few exceptions, the miles of beach were unoccupied.

Oblivious to the elements, Garbo alternately stalked and chased the roosted seabirds, snooped at the soggy debris that littered the sand, and sprinted through the racing waves. Occasionally, she would pause to scan the coastline behind, making certain her mistress was still following, as they headed toward the dark timber pier that stretched into the bay.

Catherine trudged through loose sand, head hunched into the wool scarf that flapped against her neck, arms folded protectively around the cellophane-wrapped white roses that would be her final tribute to Stephen. She squinted her eyes against the slicing wind and glanced at her watch. In just four hours, his funeral would begin and Stephen Forsster's life would be officially concluded.

Garbo led the way down the familiar wooden pier; Catherine slumped onto an unsheltered plank bench. She pulled her navy knit hat low around her ears and idly watched a lone fisherman cast his line into the choppy leaden waters. Cellophane snapped and crinkled against the roses. Catherine contemplated mortality. Stephen's. Maureen O'Malley's. Her own.

She tried to imagine how Stephen's family must feel at that moment. His widow. His two fatherless children. Eating a solemn breakfast. Dressing in black.

Guilt consumed her. She was, after all, only one of the many women whose bed Stephen had rumpled; but Lili Forsster didn't know that. She probably thought Catherine was the source of all her problems. Catherine contemplated unintended consequences.

After a while, she untied the white satin ribbon and folded the cellophane into her pocket. She moved to the corner of the pier and released one white rose into dark, restless waters. The tide greedily claimed it and chaperoned it toward the Golden Gate. The open sea. She dropped the next and watched it bob away. When the last one disappeared from sight, Catherine wiped her eyes and retraced her steps to land.

Garbo charged past, spraying Catherine with flying sand, pausing momentarily to stalk a seagull before ecstatically dashing down the beach. Catherine dropped onto a huge, half-buried log, legs drawn up, arms wrapped around shins, chin cradled on knees. She had work to do she needed to stay focused on finding a killer—but she felt she owed Stephen a moment of silent contemplation. She hadn't been in love with him, didn't even think she could claim they were friends. But there was no question she felt... well, *something*, for him. Sadness swelled her heart as she mentally revisited the trail of their relationship.

For almost a year, she and Stephen had been together once or twice each week, strictly for sex. He called it recreational athletics. Catherine regarded it as her last chance—a liaison equivalent to "Warren Beatty plays 'slip the dog a bone' with a grateful Janet Reno."

Catherine had suspected men were from Mars long before some Ph.D. wrote a book about it. And sexual intimacy—forget it. Her personal experience told her fornication was like playing the slots in Vegas; you keep plugging those coins, feeling your pulse dart with eager anticipation when a two-dollar hit starts plinking those eight piddly quarters into the tray, knowing in your gut there's gotta be a bigger pay-off. And although she thought sexual ecstasy was as likely as hitting the million-dollar jackpot, her body still ignited at the thought of sliding between satin sheets with a sexy, testosterone-fueled member of the opposite sex.

Stephen, on the other hand, considered himself a sexual connoisseur; claimed the secret of his success was his inherent ability to discover anything and everything that would inflame a woman in ways she'd never imagined. Six sessions with him convinced Catherine that it wasn't just his ego talking.

But talk he did. More than any other man Catherine had been with. He asked personal questions. *Do you like it when I touch you here? Do you ever come more than once? How often do you masturbate?* On their second meeting, he insisted Catherine tell him about the first time she'd had sex.

"Geez, are you publishing a case study?" she asked with a flush. She made jokes. Changed the subject. Wasn't going to tell him about the rainy May afternoon when, at age fifteen, she'd lost both her virginity and her only friend at Lyndon B. Johnson High School: her calculus teacher, stern, bookish Mr. Madsen. She'd never told anyone. Was embarrassed to remember how, afterward—spine bruised by the wooden desktop, mind numbed by her surprise at the act just concluded—she'd tugged down the hem of her brown wool skirt and covertly glanced to see if Mr. Madsen looked pleased—like when she aced the calculus quiz everyone else failed. Or how he'd averted his eyes and handed her his scarlet streaked handkerchief. "You're bleeding," he'd said, barely getting the words out before he turned and walked stoically from the room.

Personal history quiz successfully evaded, Catherine took full advantage of Stephen's tutorial skills.

The first half-dozen times he was scheduled to occupy her bed, Catherine waited for him, heart pounding. She alternately paced and sat lotus style, trying to calm her mind and regulate her respiration; she finally gave up and tossed back a couple shots of Patrone Silver. Stephen teased her about the Tequila—about her anxiety. But he was patient and she persisted toward her goal like a grimly determined rodeoer who remounts the bull that threw her and stomped her ribs. She masked apprehension in glib colloquialisms and, with no romantic fantasies of love everlasting and no fears of being judged or rejected, she slowly opened to Stephen. She learned what made her satisfied, learned what excited him. It was all titillating, erotic—the best she could imagine.

And then the emptiness set in. Three months ago, she had decided to end it. But before she could break the news to Stephen, he suggested an entirely different scenario.

"You've come a long way, baby; now it's time you became my love slave," he'd said on their last afternoon together. "Submit unquestioningly to all my whims. Maybe spend a little time with some of my friends."

As he said it, he lightly trailed his index finger down her stomach, tickling exposed flesh and raising goose bumps. The words had conviction, but his tone belied the foregone conclusion he was fishing with an empty hook. It wasn't the first time he'd suggested group sex.

Catherine smiled, rolled atop him, straddling his muscular thighs, giddy that, at last, she could banter with him instead of scurrying into an emotional cave like a bat fleeing the dawn.

"Every cowgirl knows it's dangerous to invite more than one stud horse inside the corral." She nuzzled his neck; his black curls tickled her cheek. He smelled musky. Like sex.

"Okay." He grinned mischievously and attempted to mimic her drawl. "We'll stick to studettes. I know a little redheaded filly who would just eat you up—and I'd love to watch her do it."

Catherine laughed aloud. "Don't ever use that phony accent in the Lone Star State, sugar britches. They consider it a felony to impersonate a Texan."

"I could call her." His eyes sparkled with anticipation. "Bet she could be here in twenty minutes."

"Fold up your cell phone, cowboy." She eyed him wistfully. "This rodeo's packing its tent... and you just had your last ride."

"Uh oh." Stephen's blue eyes turned serious. He locked his fingers around her wrists and studied her intently. "I warned you not to fall in love with me."

She giggled and rolled off him. "Too bad I can't buy you for what you're worth... and sell you for what you *think* you're worth," she said as she padded to the bathroom.

He followed. "Is that it? Are you getting too emotionally involved?"

"Recalibrate your sights, honey, 'cause you're a good twenty feet off the target." She turned to the mirror and brushed out tangles.

Now that she'd figured out the sex thing, she wanted more. She wanted a man who warmed her heart and touched her soul. Even if Stephen weren't married to someone else—even if he didn't consider it his righteous responsibility to share his virtuosic sexual talents with as many willing females as possible—he would never be that man.

"You've been real good for me, honey," she told him as they both stood naked in front of her bathroom mirror for the last time. She genuinely appreciated all he'd taught her and knew she would miss him. "Want me to recommend you to my friends?" she asked playfully as she returned to the bedroom and reached for her bra.

"Oooh," Stephen said, eyes twinkling brightly. "You could give me to your daughter."

"Careful there, sweet thang," Catherine cooed, "I'm proficient with a gelding knife."

It annoyed her to field yet another comment about Chloe, whose picture on Catherine's nightstand had gotten Stephen's attention early on. She acknowledged that she might be overly protective of her nineteen-year-old daughter, but Stephen's innuendoes made Catherine glad Chloe was far away at university in Paris; and they also reaffirmed her decision to end the relationship. Stephen's sexual suggestions had recently begun to push the outer limits of her bell curve. She might have come a long way, but she would never be, "Debbie Does Dallas."

"It's okay if you've met someone else." He stepped into chocolate wool slacks. "We can still see each other. I'm willing to share."

"You're awfully generous when you're picking flowers from someone else's garden." She yanked the zipper on her skirt.

He hadn't let her go easily. She thought it was the salesman in him; she knew he had no emotional attachment to her. He debated with her until they both left her apartment on that last afternoon, and he called several times afterward—when he had a few free hours—to make sure she hadn't changed her mind. And then she hadn't heard from him again. Until Monday. When he received the FedEx from ETC.

Catherine pulled the whistle from her jacket pocket and rose from the beached log. She stared out at the gray ocean. In just a few hours the self-described sexual connoisseur would be officially committed to history.

At the trill of the dog whistle Garbo's head jerked in Catherine's direction. Catherine waved her arms in a summoning motion and turned toward the Rover, still thinking of Stephen.

It had been so different with him. He had a slow, gentle touch. A tender, sensitive mouth. And he explored her. He was uninhibited. He was playful. Everything about him was the exact opposite of Nicolas.

As she toweled the wet Garbo, she relived that afternoon when she'd sprawled languid amidst wrinkled sheets and confessed to Stephen, "Sex with my ex-husband was like going to a formal dinner with a stern parent. There were a prescribed number of courses. You had to use the appropriate utensils at the appropriate time. Napkin in lap—don't eat with your hands. Sit up straight. Don't say anything indecorous to the host..."

Catherine's cell phone rang and jolted her from her reverie. She tossed Garbo's towel to the floorboard and pulled the phone from her pocket, grinning when she saw Nicolas's name displayed on the tiny screen.

"Well, hello, Nicolas," she grinned. "I was just thinking of you."

"I'm trying to be sensitive to your current dilemma, Catherine," he said without preamble, "but my practice is being impacted because of my relationship with you. How much longer do you expect this notoriety to continue?"

"Give up alimony and the relationship is *finito*," Catherine said gleefully as she climbed into the car and turned the key in the ignition.

"My attorney says I can file for damages since this publicity is hindering my ability to earn income."

"Income. Wow. You've expanded your vocabulary." She pulled out of the parking lot and headed for Lombard Street. Garbo curled on the seat, eyes drowsy.

"I expected your usual sarcasm, Catherine, but I thought I would try to be conciliatory since we'll likely have to suffer each other's presence today."

"Am I scheduled to be where free food is served?" she asked rhetorically, irritation rising around glee. Nicolas's usual ploy—lay out a teaser that requires the listener to ask a question if she wants to know what he's talking about—was another of his infamous forms of manipulation. A power thing. In recent phone calls, she had simply hung up when he went into that mode, but she had a bad feeling about this one. She nibbled the bait.

"Well, I assume you'll go to your lover's funeral..."

It took her a minute—incredulity slowed her brain from leaping to the obvious conclusion. "*You* are going to Stephen Forsster's funeral? What? Are you drumming up grief counseling business? How perverted."

"It seems 'perverted' is a term with which you've recently become intimately familiar."

She could hear the triumph in his voice.

"Actually," he continued, "I'm a friend of Lili Forsster's."

"...a friend of...?" Dumbfounded.

"Um hmm." He left it hanging, forcing her to ask if she wanted to know more.

"Well, then. Have a great time," she said through clenched teeth and flipped the phone closed.

"Fuckhead!" she screamed and pounded the wheel. Garbo whipped her head up, eyes dazed but alarmed. "How the hell does *Nicolas* know Lili Forsster?" She gnawed her lip as she drove. The coincidence was more than she could overlook. Phone open again, she dialed Joel Hodges's cell.

"I've got another research project for you," she said. "I just talked to Nicolas and he claims to be a friend of Lili Forsster's."

"Nicolas has no friends."

"Don't say that in front of his chia pets."

"He knows the wife... now that's an interesting little coincidence."

"My thought exactly. Pull data—everything you can find, *legally*. Pay attention, Joel: public databases only. No illegal mining of my ex-husband's personal data."

"You're sooo prissy. A butterfly fart draws more attention than I do when I'm slipping in and out of those systems."

"You're right. It's not about getting caught, it's about integrity. Let us always be so trustworthy and above reproach that ETC clients would shoot dice with us over the phone. When can you work on this?" Catherine asked as she turned onto Union Street and headed east.

"You sure take the fun out of being a hacker. I'm at Tati's ballet class for twenty more minutes. She'll take a nap after lunch, so I can work on it then." Catherine heard him take a long drag on his cigarette. She could almost smell the smoke through the phone.

"How is little Tati?" Catherine crooned. "Is she over her cold?"

"I probably should have kept her home today, but it's the last rehearsal before the big recital next Sunday, so here we are, nine four-year-olds tippy-toeing all over the place. Miss Tilly would have an easier job if she were herding cats. And by the way, Tati asked me for the ninetieth time this morning if Auntie Catherine reallyreallyreally will come see her dance next week."

Catherine smiled. "Even if I have to bust out of jail, I'll be there." She wheeled the Rover around the cars double-parked in front of Union Street boutiques. "How's your other research coming along?"

"You'll be very interested in what I learned," he said. "I confirmed Rina Gold's alibi. She was at a dinner party given by Mrs. Godwin Duffy at the Ritz Carlton, in honor of Count Wisznewski, some obscure royalty from Poland."

"Poland doesn't have royalty."

"Yeah, the society column said something about him reclaiming some old family title or some piffle like that. But you know, if Mrs. Duffy says he's a count and wants to throw a soiree for him, what society matron has the clout to challenge her? Anyway, I found a write-up and photos in two papers—the *Examiner* and the *IJ*," he said.

"The *Independent Journal?* Why would they be interested in a San Francisco event? They're Marin County."

"Because the ever-lovely Ms. Gold, who is a resident of their fair land, was the arranged date for the phony count."

"Damn," Catherine said as she pulled into her garage. "So we're sure she couldn't have shot Stephen?"

"I didn't say that. In fact, I think there's a good chance she left the party and came back later."

"She was shuffling her men in some kind of dating shell game?"

"I emailed you a file. When can you get to a computer?"

"I'll be in my garage in thirty seconds," she said as she clunked across the Hyde Street cable car tracks.

"Go take a look and call me back," he said and the phone went dead.

When Catherine redialed Joel she said, "I'm looking at your email. Can one of these be a newspaper file photo? She's wearing two different outfits."

"Right," Joel said. "That lovely little black Versace dress—I saw it in the Versace store on Post Street. Five thousand dollars and it only came in size four," his voice was rife with envy. "There aren't three women in the world who would look as good in that dress as Rina Gold."

Catherine had seen her naked. She wasn't about to disagree.

"But that white pants thing is strictly Ross Dress for Less. I'm sure it's not a haute couture designer because I've never seen that—"

"Skip the Paris runway commentary," Catherine interrupted. "We need to confirm that these two photographs were taken at the same event." She pressed *print* on her keyboard.

"Well, both shots have the count and Mrs. Duffy, and *they* didn't change *their* costumes."

Catherine studied the pictures, still warm on the page. "It increases the probability, but it still isn't one hundred percent."

"Yeah, and if I know anything at all about you I know that ninety-nine point seven percent probability isn't precise enough for you." Catherine smiled and imagined him waggling his finger at her. "I've already called the *Examiner* and managed to reach Jim Rosensweig—that's the Versace dress. He said he was at the dinner early—around six—because he covered an AIDS benefit starting at seven. I haven't been able to contact the Marin photographer, but I'm counting on the fact that she'll say her shot was taken later in the evening."

"Which could mean little Miss Shagbag left the dinner party and, for some reason, came back wearing different clothes," Catherine said. "So she *could* have been with Stephen."

"If she got blood on the Versace," Joel admonished, "she should be convicted under the 'special circumstances' law."

Catherine called Wilson Ramsey's cell phone at 9:30. Wilson was on "donut patrol," scouting the homeless who preferred to sleep with the sound of the ocean rather than curled in one of the locked gateways of commerce in the Financial District. His update was brief. He hadn't learned any additional information about the man who was, *perhaps*, named Richard, aka Sick Dick, who *perhaps* hung out near the property called the Big Gate. They agreed Wilson should abort this session and go back later in the day.

At eleven Wilson was scheduled to meet Jillya Shanahan, the Forsster's nanny, at St. Peter's and St. Paul's Cathedral in North Beach. Jillya had asked Wilson to accompany her to Stephen Forsster's funeral. In the interim, Catherine needed Wilson's assistance with one more little project. She asked him to pick her up at her apartment.

While she waited, Catherine dug through old boxes looking for a recent photo of Nicolas. A couple of years ago, Nicolas announced he was thinking about writing a book—some child psychology tome. "Thinking about" was what Nicolas did best. Catherine had responded to that idea with, "Plowing a field involves more than just turning it over in your mind." Undeterred, Nicolas had put together a press kit so he would be ready for the interview requests that would undoubtedly pour in. Catherine located one of the five-by-seven professional photos he'd had prepared.

Staring at the black-and-white image made her sad. What had happened to the Nicolas she'd fallen in love with? Or was it, as Nicolas claimed, she who had changed so drastically?

Nicolas was her first "romantic interest" after she divorced Rusty, fled Texas, and accepted a job at Boeing Aircraft in Seattle, working in their Information Systems department. It was probably the worst time in Catherine's life, and she'd been terrified—terrified she wouldn't be good enough at the programming work Boeing had recruited her to do; terrified she would fail as a single parent; terrified she would spend the rest of her life alone and unloved as her recently abandoned husband had predicted.

When Chloe—at that time a tenderhearted six-year-old—started having nightmares, Catherine believed her worst fears were coming to fruition. Nothing she did helped Chloe's dreams or her quiet, sad moods. Catherine decided to seek professional help. A new friend at Boeing, another single mother, had been taking her son to a psychologist at a children's clinic and told Catherine she thought the doctor was really good. When Catherine tried to get an appointment with the woman, the office manager informed Catherine the doctor wasn't taking new patients and gave Catherine the names of three Ph.D.s who might be available. Nicolas Calabretta was on the list.

Catherine checked him out after she made the appointment. His Ph.D. was from Columbia; he had published papers about children who experienced learning problems subsequent to a personal trauma such as divorce or death in the family. He was in Seattle working on a research project with Dr. Stroud, a respected pediatrician whose books on child-rearing had helped Catherine solidify her own parenting techniques. She joyously thanked the gods for watching out for her and Chloe–for leading them to Dr. Nicolas Calabretta.

Putting aside the bitterness of the ensuing marriage and divorce, Nicolas had been good for Chloe. Soon after she'd begun seeing him, Chloe's nightmares stopped, her appetite improved, and her interest in her schoolwork rekindled. She made friends at her new school and, within a couple of months, her adjustment seemed complete. To this day, Catherine was grateful to Nicolas for what he had accomplished with her child. Catherine still believed that, at that time in his career, Nicolas was doing good work with his young patients.

When he invited Catherine for coffee, she'd been surprised, flattered that he found her interesting. Attractive? Probably not. Nicolas was, after all, the god who'd saved her child.

What better way to a young mother's heart, she thought as she rode down the elevator to meet Wilson in front of her building. Nicolas and Catherine were married before Chloe's eighth birthday; divorced before her seventeenth.

Strains of Pavarotti singing *Nessun Dorma* reached Catherine before she opened the door of Wilson's blue Porsche. Catherine slid into the bucket seat and handed Wilson the photo of Nicolas.

He studied it for a moment.

"Meet my ex-husband. Nicolas Calabretta."

"You getting back together?" Wilson turned off the CD.

"He may show up at the funeral. He claims to be a friend of Lili Forsster's, but I'm finding it difficult to put down cash for that piece of swamp land. See if you can find out his connection to the family."

"I'll check it out."

"Also..." She handed him an eight-by-ten manila envelope. "Photos of potential suspects."

In the wee hours, Catherine had done a web search and found pictures of people she considered pertinent to the investigation. Lili

Forsster. Rina Gold. Buzz and Angelina Benson. George Hallison. Stephen Forsster, himself.

"I'd like you to show these to merchants along the Great Highway and on Sloat Boulevard—the ones closest to the Big Gate. Maybe one of these people put in an appearance around the time Stephen was rousting St. Peter at the Pearly Gates. You up for this?"

Wilson nodded. "That's it?"

"I need to rent a vehicle. Can you help with the logistics?"

"Sure."

Wilson steered the Porsche down Union, crossed the Hyde Street cable car tracks with a clank, and turned left onto Van Ness Boulevard. Catherine watched in her rear view mirror. No one followed.

At the corner of Van Ness and California, Wilson went into the Budget Rental Car office to pick up the brown panel van Catherine had reserved in his name. Inspector Hiller's comments last night had kept her mind stirring.

...I'm not following you... we rely on the volunteerism of concerned citizens...

Maybe it was O'Malley's caretaker who had informed Hiller of Catherine's whereabouts; maybe someone was actually tailing her. In either case, she'd decided precautions were in order.

Catherine drove the Porsche north on Van Ness. The sky was cobalt blue; the bay shimmered with the white sails of a hundred boats. Lots of tourists milled around on the sidewalks. She parked the car in a garage adjacent to Ghiradelli and slipped inside the Square. She grabbed an *au lait* and an orange/currant scone at Starbucks and went back to the Porsche to wait for Wilson. Twenty minutes later, he circled through the lot in a nondescript brown panel van. Catherine studied the drivers in the cars that filed behind him. They all seemed focused on finding a parking spot rather than on watching Wilson.

"Stay with Jillya for as long as seems appropriate," Catherine instructed, jangling the keys to the van as Wilson climbed behind the wheel of the Porsche. "She could be a good source of information."

Wilson thrummed out of the garage as Catherine studied the shoppers who sauntered by. By the time she reached her apartment, she decided she hadn't been followed.

Buzz and Angelina Benson's Kentfield house glared stark white against a bright winter sky; deeply shadowed conifers ringed the quarter acre.

The stately two-story columns and the wide, grandiose veranda were out of synch with the neighboring California architecture.

Catherine parked the brown panel van at the curb. She grabbed a clipboard off the seat and bounced to the street. She retucked her fudge-brown work shirt into fudge-brown chinos; pulled her brown baseball cap low until it snuggled the top of the mirrored sunglasses that tinged her world blue. At the rear of the vehicle, she removed a cardboard carton upon which she'd plastered a UPS label addressed to Buzz Benson. She marched up the sidewalk, whistling a response to gleeful songbirds that were enjoying the unseasonably warm morning. The clean, light air smelled fertile, as if all of nature were preparing to burst into sweet blossoms.

Two upstairs windows were open. Sheer white curtains luffed in the breeze.

Catherine rang the bell and grimaced through the chimed rendition of "Dixie." She cradled the box in her left arm and held the clipboard ready in her right hand. She angled away from the camera lens that guarded the front porch, hoping the chocolate uniform—rented from a costume shop on Post Street—would fool Buzz Benson and his prying security system. Buzz, himself, was attending Stephen Forsster's funeral, as confirmed by Wilson fifteen minutes ago.

When there was no response to the bell, Catherine gritted her teeth and rang it again, listening intently to the silence that followed the chimes.

Without warning, Angelina opened the door. Her eyes were red-rimmed; a wad of tissue clutched in her left hand. Her sad, distracted gaze sought no target. Even with a hemorrhaged eye and bruised cheek, she radiated a Charlize Theron kind of delicate beauty.

"Delivery for Mr. Benson. Sign here," Catherine said and held out the clipboard. She suspected the "security system" recorded audio as well as video.

Angelina moved slowly. Dreamlike. She took the clipboard Catherine offered and stood, pen poised, forehead wrinkling into confusion as she read the message at the top of the page: *I have to talk to you about Stephen Forsster. Meet me in ten minutes at the Ripe Fig coffee shop at Kentfield Square.*

Angelina looked up, eyes wild. Fearful. She squinted to see behind the reflective blue lenses; Catherine flipped them down just long enough for the woman to confirm her identity. Eyes dilated, Angelina shook her head no and shoved the clipboard at Catherine.

Foot wedged firmly against door, Catherine juggled the box and awkwardly flipped back the first sheet, exposing a second. "Sorry. Wrong page," she said. "Sign on this one." She offered the clipboard to the woman.

Angelina pushed it away but stared at the words: *I talk to YOU... or I talk to BUZZ.*

Her eyes flitted to the security camera, then back to Catherine's face. She shook her head again. "Wrong address," she whispered; then more firmly. "That package doesn't belong here." She shoved the door. Catherine removed her foot; the door slammed with the crack of a gunshot.

She shrugged for the benefit of the camera and marched back down the sidewalk. She was surprised Angelina had rebuffed her—would have bet her favorite Garth Brooks album the woman was too afraid of her husband to take a chance on Catherine talking to him.

Box returned to the back of the van, Catherine slid behind the wheel and drove away. She circled the block and parked four doors up from the Benson's house, waiting to see if Angelina might have second thoughts and go to the café for a face-to-face.

Ten minutes later, a white BMW convertible rolled down the Benson's driveway and paused at the curb. The navy canvas top blocked the bright sun and left the driver in shadow. Dark sunglasses hid the middle band of the woman's face, but when she looked both ways before pulling into the street, Catherine was sure the profile belonged to Angelina.

Catherine followed her through the subdivision, but instead of going to the Ripe Fig coffee shop where Catherine had asked to meet, Angelina headed east and turned into a strip mall parking lot. Catherine quickly found a spot and tailed her into Towne Kids Toy Store.

Angelina gave a startled squeak when Catherine came along side. Nervous fingers gathered the collar of her shirt. "I don't have anything to say to you," she whispered vehemently and darted into the next aisle.

She gave off the energy of a cowering dog—one that expected to be whipped. She turned her back on Catherine and picked up a miniature baseball glove.

"For Kyle? Or Roddy?" Catherine asked, naming Buzz's two sons by a previous marriage. "They both have birthdays coming up next week."

Angelina blanched white. "How do you know about them?" she asked in a soft Georgia drawl.

"Honey, I know more intimate details about your life than your mother and the IRS combined."

"Please go away," Angelina pleaded, pretending to examine the stitching on the tan leather glove. Catherine noted Angelina had covered her bruises with concealer. Professionally. As if she had a lot of experience with a make-up sponge.

"Look, I don't like being a bully. I don't like threatening to rat you out to your husband. Clearly you already have enough problems. But my life is on the line. I need to ask you some questions about Stephen."

Angelina picked up a baseball and pounded it into the pocket of the glove three times.

"There's a Starbucks three doors down. Let me buy you a coffee. I'll tell you what I heard about your relationship with Stephen, I'll ask the things I need to know, and then I'll leave you alone."

"I'm on a tight schedule." Angelina strode down the aisle and stopped at the greeting card section. "Buzz expects me to be home in half an hour."

"Buzz is at Stephen's funeral," Catherine said.

Angelina fingered cards that said, "Happy Birthday, son," and finally settled on one that said, *Happy Birthday, 4-year-old!*

"Oh, I see," Catherine said, thinking of the network of cameras that no doubt monitored Angelina's comings and goings. "Even when he's away, Buzz has you on a short leash."

"He worries about me if I'm gone too long," she said indignantly and stepped into the cashier's line.

"Right," Catherine said. "Fine, Angelina. We'll do this your way... but don't say I didn't try to be fair." She cleared her throat and raised her voice. "How many times did you fuck Stephen?"

The cashier and two women customers turned. Aghast. Angelina squeaked, dropped the gift items to the floor and began shoving through the female bodies that blocked her path. Catherine pursued; she could hear the woman weeping.

"Go away!" She fled across the parking lot, mindless of two cars that skidded their tires to avoid throwing her over their hoods.

Catherine followed more cautiously. "We *are* going to have this conversation, Angelina. If I have to, I'll camp out on your front porch. I'll talk to Buzz when he gets home. Your choice," she said as the woman reached her BMW, beep-opened the door, and slammed herself inside.

Hunched over the steering wheel, her sobs were audible through the closed windows. Catherine crossed her arms over her chest and stood at the left front fender so Angelina would know she was still there. After about five minutes, Angelina reached into her handbag, removed a wad of tissues, blew her nose and dried her aquamarine eyes. She leaned across the console and opened the passenger door. Catherine moved around the car and slid into the seat.

Tears had washed away the pancake makeup; bruises glowered on Angelina's delicate peach skin. Catherine waited silently.

"He asked about my flowers," she said, her voice tiny, hoarse with emotion. "He came one Saturday when Buzz was golfing. I was out back in my greenhouse. At first he said he was there to see Buzz. But then, when I told him Buzz wasn't at home, he stayed... and talked to me." She wiped her nose and watched out the front windshield as a shopper loaded grocery bags into a Jeep Cherokee. "I never meant for it to happen."

"Did Buzz find out because of the security cameras?"

She shook her head no. "We didn't have cameras then."

Catherine nodded. "What happened with Stephen?"

Angelina turned away, but Catherine could see her chin trembling. She clutched the steering wheel and took a deep breath.

"I told him about the irises I grafted. They're a breed I developed on my own." A tentative pride crept through the words. "He stood close to me while I showed him. He asked questions like he was really interested. He touched my arm. His hands were soft."

She sounded like a child who had never known tenderness.

"Before he left, he... he kissed me." Her eyes reflected guilty sadness. "On the lips."

She looked down at the tissue and confettied the dry edges. "He came back the next week. Buzz was out of town."

Two tears tracked down her pale cheeks. "I didn't plan it—didn't even want it to happen—but he was so... nice." She looked out the window. "He was so..." For the first time, she made eye contact with Catherine. "It felt like he... cared about me."

Catherine nodded and let the silence act as a salve to Angelina's grief. Finally, she asked, "How many times did you see him?"

"Seven." Her voice was barely a whisper; she didn't have to calculate—would have memorized every detail. She looked like a prisoner resigned to execution.

"When was the first time?"

"July eleventh."

"And the last time?"

"December twelfth." She took another Kleenex from her purse. Hurt... confusion suffused her eyes.

"Did he tell you he wasn't going to see you anymore?"

She studied her palms in her lap; shook her head no.

"Did he say anything that made you think it might be your last time?"

She tore a strip from the tissue. "He asked me if Buzz suspected anything. I told him Buzz always suspected something... but nothing specific—not about him. He told me he thought someone was following him."

Catherine straightened. "Did he say why he thought that?"

She shrugged. "He said he kept seeing this same guy—when he left his office, coming out of the bank, when he got out of his car at his country club..."

"Did he describe the man?"

"No." She sniffed and blew her nose.

"Did Stephen come to your house... for you to be together?" Catherine wondered about the timing of the camera installation. Wondered if the inside of the house was "secured" as well.

"We met." Her cheeks blotched rosy. "At different... places."

"In the city?"

"No. I couldn't be gone that long."

"Where?"

"Just..." Another tissue. More confetti. "...hotels."

"And Buzz found out?"

"No!" Her eyes saucered, one blue iris shot through with red hemorrhage.

"Then why did he hit you?" Catherine asked and half expected the woman to say, "which time?" But, she didn't.

"He was in a bar that he goes to after work sometimes and someone made a joke. About me and Stephen. He came home and asked me... about it. I told him he was wrong, that the only times I'd seen Stephen were when we were at those Christmas parties the last two years and when we went to Stephen's farm for a barbecue last summer. Buzz didn't believe me. Buzz never believes..."

She stared out the window, vision tuned to inner thoughts.

"When did this happen?"

She shrugged as if it didn't matter sifted the small mound of white fluff in her lap.

The bruises were at least a week old.

"Where was Buzz on Monday night?"

Angelina swallowed hard. "With me. He was at home with me," she said. "He came home at four–like he always does and worked in his office for a while. We had dinner at six thirty and watched TV until nine. Then we went to bed. Buzz gets up at four because he likes to work out before he goes to the office so we always go to bed early." She ended the recitation and held fluttering eye contact with Catherine.

"What did you eat for dinner?" Catherine asked.

"He had stuffed pork chops with mashed potatoes and green beans; I had a salad."

Catherine nodded. People are best with minute details when they're delivering a well-rehearsed lie.

"How often does he hit you?"

"I deserved what I got," defiance returned to Angelina's voice. "I cheated on my husband. My wonderful, thoughtful, generous husband. Even if he'd beat me to death, I woulda deserved it."

Catherine climbed out of the BMW, but leaned in the door so her words could be heard. "Wake up and smell the grits burnin', Angelina. This isn't about punishment, it's about control. No court hands down the death penalty for adultery." Her eyes locked with Angelina's. "Buzz isn't a judge and he's not a God-sanctioned executioner. Neither yours... nor Stephen's."

Catherine steered the van into a Chevron station, grabbed a gym bag off the floor, and hiked into the gasoline-scented women's room where she ripped off the fake UPS uniform and pulled on jeans and a black v-neck sweater.

Angelina had begun her relationship with Stephen in July; Catherine was also spending time with him then. The new "smoke detector" had been installed in Catherine's apartment in July. Coincidence? Buzz could have hired someone to follow Stephen—either because of jealous suspicions about his wife... or perhaps he thought it would give a bounce to his business if Stephen were occupied battling charges of philandering. And, if Buzz discovered Stephen was doing the deed with Catherine, he might have had her apartment bugged so he could blackmail Stephen. No matter what, if Buzz believed Stephen was diddling Angelina in his spare time, he would undoubtedly believe himself justified in terminating, once and for all, the possibility of future liaisons.

Catherine took a left off of Fourth Street in San Rafael and located the Personal Security Systems camera shop. Adjoining a gun store. Uh huh. Very convenient for the "spectate... then perforate" model of varmint disposal.

Since Buzz Benson was obviously a platinum customer, she planned to trade on his good name and tell them she was a friend who wanted to set up a security system of her own. If the gods were particularly generous, she might learn that Buzz was the buyer of the equipment that had been installed in her apartment; if they were mildly cooperative, she hoped to at least find out how that particular system worked.

The store was cold inside—perfect for stashing poached game—and it smelled of gun oil. Catherine ambled over to one of the showcases where she saw lots of different cameras and recorders; many gadgets whose purpose she didn't know. Another case held a collection of binoculars. She bent to examine them through the glass. When she straightened, a middle-aged hard-body in a red Polo shirt and new Wrangler jeans was standing on the other side of the counter. His nametag read, "Bob–Manager."

"Catherine Calabretta. Guardian of privacy," he said. "Gonna switch sides and start doing covert ops?" He finger-combed a long swath of frizzy brown hair over the top of his leathery scalp.

Shit. She hated this newfound notoriety. She started to flip off a caustic comment about the nature of his business, but decided it best not to alienate him.

"Who rigged my apartment with a hidden video camera and filmed me without my permission?"

Bob made a clucking in his cheek and shook his head. "That's illegal. I wouldn't know anything about that." Pride and deceit glimmered in his hard hazel eyes.

"Right. So let's talk hypothetically. What kind of video system would an illegal operation like that require?"

She explained about the smoke detector unit and described the mechanics of the porn video and how it was shot from a stable camera position, no lens movement, and with a slightly distorted image that suggested a modified fish-eye.

Bob interrupted. "Was it filming your bed?"

"Noooo." She smiled with phony coyness. "It was shooting the altar where I say my evening prayers."

He grinned knowingly, revealing the need for orthodontia and some industrial-strength dental floss.

"The system picked up voices in a different room than the one the camera filmed."

"Probably separate audio transmitter bugs that record continuously—maybe hidden in the phone so they pick up both sides of a phone conversation, as well as all sound in the room," he said. Was he trying to impress her? She was weak-kneed with the growing awareness of how exhaustive the invasion had been.

"Best thing would be to let me review the film. That way I could spec it out better." The vulgar leer looked natural on his face.

She smiled provocatively. "Bobby-boy, you strike me as the kind of guy whose had to shave his palms since puberty. Skip the strip-tease and tell me about the technology."

Bob flushed; his mouth went thin. He reeled off questions about the lighting in the room, the quality of the image and the size and location of the smoke detector unit. He asked when her apartment building had been constructed and whether or not there was a ceiling light in her closet.

When she'd answered all his questions, he began to lay components on a wooden counter next to the glass case. The last piece he brought out was a smoke detector cover that looked exactly like the one that had hung over her closet door. She blew air through tight lips then shook her head in disgust.

"Camera unit," he said and pointed a stubby finger at a two-by-three-inch black box with a quarter-inch lens. "Transmitter." This box was bigger—probably six by ten. "Power connector." The power supply trailed a thick cable with a converter plug on the end. "Connector cables." One red, one black—like the ones that connected her CD player to the amplifier. "And," he pointed to the plastic smoke detector cover, "the shield."

Bob surmised the peeper mounted the camera unit above the closet doorjamb, inside the walls, and then put the transmitter unit behind the ceiling, close to the closet light.

"He probably tapped the ceiling light power supply. The only thing you would have seen was the fake smoke detector cover, so you wouldn't suspect an intrusion."

Catherine pointed to the camera unit. "Where's the tape?"

He picked up the transmitter. "This sends the image to a receiver at a different location. Probably set up with a monitor and VCR just like your basic home unit."

"You mean someone watched me from a different location?"

"Probably another apartment in your building—or maybe across the street. Could even be transmitting to a car, but that's dicier—not as reliable."

"How does the... peeper," she used his term, "turn the camera on and off?"

"It transmits all the time. Twenty-four hours a day."

She wanted to tell Bob she knew the fricking definition of "all the time," but she ground her jaw instead, dumbfounded by the magnitude of the intrusion.

"Somebody bought this system from you back in July. Who was it?"

Bob shook his head and clucked his tongue. "Don't share customer lists." He shrugged. "Besides, I'm not the only source."

"Who's the other source?"

"Lots of 'em." He grinned as if he considered himself clever. "Ever been on the 'net?"

"Funny," she quipped. And then she negotiated for him to come and do a sweep to clear her home of the intrusive electronics. She intended to be bug-free by sundown.

Wilson Ramsey was squeezed into a small slatted chair, forearm propped on a scarred, basketball-size wooden table adjacent to the bar at Leprechaun's Luck. An unfamiliar Irish jig energized the lads and lasses. They danced, sloshed beer, and shouted out lyrics over the strength of the jukebox, drowning out the strains of an Irish fiddle.

Jillya Shanahan was facing off on her fourth Guinness and her Irish brogue was getting more and more difficult to decipher. She hadn't yet said much that Catherine would find useful, but had plenty to say about the media people who tried to pry information from her.

"Fookin' vultures. They just want ta use me."

Wilson felt guilty. He liked this woman. She was spunky—would likely throw a nasty left jab if she discovered *his* primary goal.

At the funeral, he'd been able to question her about some of the mourners. He'd learned that Nicolas Calabretta did pro bono psychological counseling at a shelter called Children's Haven.

"That place for ditched kids," Jillya explained. "Or kids that get beat up or molested. It's Mrs. Forsster's pet project. She spends a lot of time raisin' money and doing speeches and workin' with the kids. She used to be a teacher."

They were standing in the back of the church, air redolent with the fragrance of white lilies and the expensive perfumes of the subdued mourners who filed by.

"The missus is pretty pissed at him right now," Jillya continued as they both watched Lili Forsster accept kisses from Nicolas, one on each cheek, and then turn away to greet one of the legions of women in black. "He was supposed to give a speech at some big important benefit this week but he was really late. Ran out of gas on the bridge or something. Didn't get there until eight thirty when he was supposed to speak at seven. Embarrassed her."

Wilson thought about Stephen Forsster being killed on Monday night and wondered when, this week, Lili Forsster would have had her attention on fundraising. He asked Jillya. She confirmed that it was the night Forsster was killed.

"When she got home, she went bonkers. She said first Dr. Calabretta no-showed for his speech, and then her husband didn't come home like he'd promised. She went into the kitchen and downed a couple Brandies. Prob'ly a good thing, 'cause then the coppers came and told her about Mr. F."

After the funeral, Wilson offered to drop Jillya at a friend's apartment where she was spending the weekend. She accepted his invitation with the condition that he first went with her to the pub on Geary Street, "fer a pint er two."

After her first beer, Jillya got very friendly, resting her hand on his thigh, touching his face. He liked it... but he wasn't getting much 411 for Catherine.

Three ales made Jillya homesick for Ireland; the fourth made her mournful for her former boyfriend. Above the strains of *Danny Boy*, she lamented how she'd caught him naked with her best friend on the sofa in the work shed the day before she left Kilkenny.

"He started cryin' like a babe, blubberin' he only did it because he was so sad fer me leavin'." She propped her forehead on the heel of her palm, then angled it and gave Wilson an unfocused glower. "You men are all alike," she slurred.

Wilson pushed back his chair. "Time to go," he said and lifted her under her armpits. She caught her balance and tried to twist away from him. He guided her through the crowd and out a front door that looked as though it had been an unwilling referee in too many drunken brawls.

Jillya had already given Wilson the Sunset address of her friend's apartment. He aimed the Porsche down Geary Street to thirty-sixth Avenue and turned south while she curled up in the passenger seat and continued her rant against the opposite sex.

"Men have only one goal in life. I know where you zip your brains. This wasn't my first job as a nanny, ya know, and it wasn't the first time I've been chased around the bed by the lord of the manor."

"Mr. Forsster? He macked on you?"

"If that means propositioned, then 'mack' was his royal title," she smirked and looked as if she might throw up.

"You gonna be sick?"

"Only if I keep talkin' about Mr. F. Nice car." She seemed to notice it for the first time. "You dealin'?"

"Want me to pull over?"

"I can hold my liquor." Her breath smelled like sour beer.

"Okay. Let's talk about something else." He rolled down the window to get her some air. He did *not* want her tossing her cookies in his car. "You like your computer classes?"

"Hate 'em."

Her head lolled. Wilson wanted her awake so she could tell him if she was going to be sick.

"Yo! Jillya!"

"Huh?" She rose up and looked at him.

"You hate computers? Why you taking the classes?"

"Fallback."

"Fallback from what?"

"Me Da thinks I'll never make it as a photojournalist—that's what I really want to be—so he made me promise on me Ma's grave that I would learn computers." She hiccuped. "My cousin, Eoin, he took computer classes and he got a good job working for an American company in Belfast."

She twisted around in her seat and tucked her knees against her chest, cheek resting against the window. Her skin would leave a moisture smear on the glass but at least she hadn't puked.

"Photojournalist," Wilson said. "I took a class on film development. Once."

"You're not going to offer to tour me through yer darkroom, are ya?" She raised her head and scowled at him with droopy eyelids.

"Don't have a darkroom," Wilson said as he pulled to a stop in front of the address she had given him. It was a yellow stucco two-story flanked on either side by one tan and one orange replica. The houses stood shoulder-to-shoulder, no more than eight feet apart.

"Neither did Mr. Forsster, but that didn't stop him from offerin'," she said and tried to unfasten her seatbelt. "I told him I didn't believe him..."

Wilson let her continue the struggle with the belt in order to keep her talking.

"...But he laughed and said he'd be glad to shoot some nudes of me... and..." She whacked the belt lock. "Ouch! Bollocks!" She jerked on the strap that crossed her chest. "Let me out!"

Wilson pressed the seatbelt lock and the belt retracted freely. Jillya grabbed her duffle bag off the floor and reached for the door handle. Wilson wrapped his fingers around her wrist.

"Shoot some nudes and... what?"

"And then we could develop them together. In his darkroom." She snarled. "Fookin' pig. All you men are fookin' rapist pigs."

She shoved open the car door, promptly tripped on the curb, and fell on her ass. "I het this country," she said and began to yowl. "I het all you fookin' macho male pigs..." She sat on a tuft of scraggly, dried weeds. Big tears coursed down her cheeks.

Wilson circled the car and helped her to her feet.

"...tekin' advantage of us lonely... immigrants... women."

He followed her as she stumbled up the sidewalk that bisected a brown, shaggy front lawn and crossed to the side of the house.

"Don't think I'm so pissed that you can tek advantage o' me," she tossed over her shoulder as she sniffled and wiped her nose on her leather-encased forearm. She took the narrow walkway, stumbling and slow-motion ricocheting off the walls. At the back of the house, she fumbled a key from her pocket, carefully aimed it into the lock of the sliding glass door, stepped over the track, and tossed her duffle bag in the corner.

She turned to Wilson and her cold fingers grasped his hand. He tried to gently extricate himself, but she held on.

"Will you take me to the beach tomorrow?" she asked and started to lean backward, still holding his fingers.

He watched her eyes, which had a new, sober flicker in them. He didn't answer.

"Will you be my friend?" she asked and leaned harder. Tugging.

He ducked to avoid the doorframe as he stepped into the one-room apartment. To the left there was a compact kitchen with miniature stove and refrigerator and a two-foot wide counter piled with dirty dishes. The scent of fried bacon produced a hungry growl in his gut.

Behind Jillya, a futon was folded out from the wall; it was littered with a variety of lacy, satiny-looking laundry. She used his own momentum to pull him forward as she retreated until the back of her knees hit the edge of the bed.

"...My only friend?"

She angled backward and he followed until she hit the mattress, flat of her back. He broke his fall with his elbows and supported his weight so he didn't crush her.

"I need a friend," she whispered.

Both hands moved across his scalp and pulled his face to hers. She kissed his mouth. He tried to raise himself off her, but she locked her arms around his neck and ran her tongue between his teeth. She tasted like beer. She kissed him for about seven seconds before he felt her hands begin to relax on the back of his head. In another five, her fingertips slid down his cheeks and her arms splayed across the bed-spread. She began to snore softly.

He rose off the bed and blew hot breath in a low whistle, glad Jillya wasn't awake to witness the bulge that was pressing uncomfortably against his fly. He liked this chick. Didn't want to validate her claim that all men were rapist pigs. He hoped when she was sober, she would still want him to take her to the beach.

Catherine headed for the shower, sweaty from a four-mile jog with Garbo. Two hours earlier, she'd talked to Wilson. He'd clarified the relationship between Nicolas and Lili Forsster and conveyed Stephen's comments to Jillya about a personal dark room.

Wilson also added, "Your homegirl was at the funeral, too. That Laura chick."

"She's as unpredictable as the trajectory of a hurricane," Catherine said, thinking how Laura had insisted on having no association to Stephen.

"She was with the flesh–presser–the senator. He talked to Forsster's mother. Before. And at the end."

"Makes sense they would know each other," she mused.

Catherine had signed off after Wilson confirmed he was on his way to the beach to "Look for the homeless gun-toting dude. Check out the stores. Show those pictures around."

Catherine had her fingers crossed that the photos of Lili Forsster, Rina Gold, Buzz and Angelina Benson, George Hallison, and Stephen Forsster would produce some lead she could pursue. Maureen O'Malley had told Catherine the police identified no additional tire tracks, other than those made by Stephen's Mercedes on the dirt-and-gravel road into the property. Catherine and Maureen speculated the killer probably left the property on foot, the way Catherine had. And, that he–or she–may have parked a car close by; or perhaps had visited a nearby business to summon a taxi. Catherine knew it was a long shot, but she had to know if any local shopkeeper recalled one of those individuals patronizing their establishment on the day Stephen was killed.

As the shower warmed up, Catherine's phone rang. Joel.

He'd dug up an article in the Marin *IJ* about Lili's fundraiser last Monday night for Children's Haven. It confirmed what Catherine had learned from Wilson: Dr. Nicolas Calabretta was very late for his speaking engagement and left Mrs. Forsster to improvise while her guests waited expectantly over white chocolate mousse and cappuccinos.

"Are you really blown away?" Joel asked. "Isn't this just the most amazing fluke–Dr. Nic extremely tardy for a well-publicized event at the same time someone drilled new buttonholes into your lover's pecs?"

"If someone got killed every time Nicolas failed to keep a commitment, human beings would be facing extinction."

"I don't think you can ignore this coincidence."

"I can ignore it for two reasons: First and foremost, Nicolas can't stand the sight of blood. He grew a beard because he passed out or puked every time he nicked himself shaving. And let me tell you, there was a lot of blood when Stephen was killed."

"Didn't you tell me they found barf near the scene of the crime?"

"Nicolas had nothing to gain by killing Stephen. I can't imagine how he would even know about my relationship with him."

"Maybe *he* hired the detective. Maybe he wanted to humiliate you."

"I'm sure he would enjoy that; but not at the expense of losing his alimony. And that's exactly what will happen if I have to spend all my financial resources defending myself in a trial—and especially if I go to jail."

"I don't know..."

"Nicolas is an asshole but he doesn't have the guts to be an honest-to-goodness bad guy. Believe me: I'd be the first to go after him if I thought there was the remotest chance."

"I still think you need to look at the possibility..."

"I'll look at it," Catherine said. "But I'm not going to let it derail me." She grimaced. "As they say down home: A smart ass just don't fit in a saddle."

The electronic sweep of Catherine's apartment turned up only one audio bug, which was found in the kitchen telephone's handset. Nothing more. She'd sealed it in a plastic sandwich bag and tossed it in the back of her freezer where it could do no harm. She hadn't yet decided if it would be worth trying to track down its purchaser.

When Bob the Security guy was sweeping the north-facing wall of her bedroom, he'd peered out her eighth-floor bay windows and pointed down to a row of three-story red buildings across the street. "That would be an ideal location for your peeper to set up," he said. "Even though they're a lot lower than you, shouldn't be a problem receiving transmissions from here."

Catherine nodded noncommittally. That was exactly what she'd been thinking when she bought the high-powered binoculars—camouflage paint and all—from his surveillance emporium.

After dusk, Catherine and Garbo completed a walk-around, examining the targeted structures from street level and taking a slow jaunt down the alley that backed them. There were four identical buildings, all with two apartments side-by-side on each of the three floors—a total of twenty-four units in the complex.

Tenants accessed their apartments through their building's common front door, or through individual back doors with wooden stairs that led down to a small, fenced communal backyard that abutted the alley.

By 9:55, Catherine was back in her own apartment, lamps extinguished and a cushy armchair pulled to the window in her dark living room. A pale glow from the streetlights far below drew rheumy circles on the ceiling. The light tower on Alcatraz Island flashed in a regulated tempo. A cruise ship, pristine white upper decks glaring festively, sailed under the Golden Gate Bridge, heading for open sea. The clang of a cable car bell drifted up from Hyde Street.

As she read "Diet Pepsi" on the label of a plastic bottle sitting on the coffee table in an apartment across the street, Catherine decided Bob's claim about these glasses, "You could count the curlies on a elk's ass at a hundred yards," had been accurate.

Catherine planned to watch these apartments until she identified the one where the peeper had been ensconced—or until she ruled out those locations altogether.

As she began her surveillance, a man walked into the living room of apartment 2-4—her code for building two, apartment four—picked up the remote, changed the television to channel 2, and started watching the ten o'clock news. Catherine marveled that he had no concern that someone might watch him through his second-story window; but then, she might have felt the same way... until five days ago.

In the next half hour, she observed normal activity in seven other apartments and marked a "u" for "unlikely" on those units of her hand-drawn sketch of the complex.

Just before 11:30, Garbo, who was curled by Catherine's chair, raised her head and growled deep in her chest a nanosecond before the doorbell rang.

195

Annoyed that someone had skirted lobby security system and come directly to her door, Catherine peeked through the peephole and saw a woman with cropped, sable hair. It took her a moment to realize it was Laura Tyler Jackson.

Anger flared. Laura had a lot of nerve showing up here after ignoring Catherine's voicemail messages for the past two days. Catherine inhaled deeply, attempting to wick off anger before she flipped the deadbolt, jerked the door wide, and crossed her arms over her chest.

"I've been a selfish bitch. I've been a terrible friend," Laura said. "I'm really sorry. I'm here to ask your forgiveness—and to give you whatever help I can." She carried a bouquet of yellow calla lilies interspersed with brown cattails.

Catherine pursed her lips and grudgingly invited Laura in.

Mink tickled Catherine's wrist as Laura breezed into the apartment. She smelled of Chanel No. 5.

"I've been inconsiderate and self-absorbed," Laura continued the self-flagellation. "This time, I've even surprised myself with my selfishness." She whisked to the living room and turned to Catherine. "Why are all the lights off?" She handed off the lilies to Catherine and ignored Garbo's happy greeting.

"I'm contemplating the dark night of my soul... in the dark," Catherine said and went to the kitchen where she found a crystal vase and filled it with water.

"Am I to understand you're investigating this murder yourself?" Laura asked, her pale hazel eyes full of concern as Catherine arranged the flowers.

Catherine breezed by Laura's questions with, "Want some tea?"

"I'd rather have cognac." Laura tossed her fur over a kitchen chair. "It's been a really ghastly day. I went to Stephen's funeral." She neatened the tuck of her pale pink cashmere sweater into the waist of her navy wool slacks.

Catherine turned on the fire under the kettle and took a snifter from the cabinet. "I thought you didn't want to be linked to Stephen."

"Ben was a friend of Stephen's grandfather."

Catherine poured a shot of Courvoisier. Laura leaned against the edge of the kitchen table and crossed her right ankle over her left.

"How convenient. You got to say goodbye to your good... close friend, and Ben still doesn't know you were intimate with the bush dog." She handed the glass to Laura.

"Is that what Stephen said? That we were intimate?"

"He wouldn't tell me," Catherine answered as she put a teabag in a mug.

"But you asked..." Laura's eyes were mischievous above the rim of the snifter. "You wanted to find out if you were getting sloppy seconds... or if you were going to be compared to me...?"

Catherine felt heat rise up her cheeks. She crossed her arms over her chest. Anger and embarrassment crinkled her left eye. Her voice carried the full load of her indignation. "I'd guess he blew by 'seconds' around the time he was ten."

"Well I'm glad he didn't mislead you into thinking he'd had sex with me."

"You know... I'm having a really hard time following this." Catherine poured steaming water into her mug. "If you never had sex with him, how could you tell me he was a great lay, or a fantasy fuck, or whatever the hell you called him?"

Laura sighed. "Stephen tried to seduce me for years, but I wasn't interested in him because he was available only for sex. I like to be able to be seen in public with the man I'm fucking." She smiled. "But that didn't stop him from telling me about some of his escapades. I think it was his way of convincing me I was missing something special by not getting involved with him..." She shrugged. "Anyway, I figured from the stories he told that he probably was pretty hot."

"So you did me a big favor and gave him to me."

"I always believe in sharing with my friends. So shoot me."

Laura tossed down the last of her cognac. Catherine handed her the bottle and she poured a healthy shot.

"Which is what I came here for tonight. To share with you some things I know that might help you." She took a swallow and studied Catherine over the rim of the glass. She pulled out a kitchen chair.

Catherine sipped tea then put the cup on the kitchen counter. She crossed her arms over her chest.

"Do you want my help, or not?"

"I've practically begged for your assistance for three days. Why the sudden change of heart?"

"I've already told you: I realized I was being a lousy friend."

"Ummm," Catherine said.

"And, speaking of being a friend... have you told anyone that I introduced you to Stephen?"

"I've answered that question for you more times than a gold-rush whore spread her legs on a Saturday night."

"So you haven't brought up my name at all, in relation to him?"

"I thought you came here to help *me*—not to cover your own ass."

"I *am* here to help you." She swirled cognac; watched it coat the snifter. "It's just that it's very different when you're involved with a public figure. I mean, I really have to be careful that I'm not tied in any way to anything tawdry." She sipped. "Ben's campaign manager doesn't like me. He's already had my background investigated, the little pencil-dick." She swirled some more, watching amber liquid travel the sides of the crystal. "He didn't even have the courtesy to tell me. I found out when my trust fund manager called me." She looked up and made eye contact with Catherine. "That's why I have to know."

Catherine pursed her lips and nodded her head. "I haven't mentioned your name at all, Laura. Not to anyone."

"Thanks," Laura murmured. She perched on the kitchen chair, rolled the snifter between palms. "So. When Stephen was in college, he took some courses in photography and film development. He said it was because he heard they were taking pictures of naked models." Her mouth tugged into a wry grin. "Typical Stephen." She sipped cognac. "Anyway, when he started messing around on his wife, he told me that he only got involved with women on whom he could get an 'insurance policy.' I questioned him about that—at first I thought he meant life insurance. Then I realized what he really meant was insurance that the woman wouldn't tell his wife about his philandering. Odd as it sounds, he really did love Lili and he didn't want to create problems with his marriage."

Catherine pulled out a chair and sat across the table from Laura.

"The women on whom he could get 'insurance' were primarily married women. Apparently he took pictures of them in compromising situations, developed them in his own dark room, and kept them in case they ever threatened him in any way."

"So there *is* a dark room somewhere." Catherine leaned in over her teacup.

"You knew about that?"

"I heard about the possibility from someone we questioned, but didn't know for sure. Where is it?" she asked, feeling excitement replace her irritation.

"I don't know, but I know it's not at his home. I think Stephen may have kept an apartment somewhere."

"Did you ever go there?"

"No. I'm not even sure about it, but some things he said led me to believe it's likely that he had a secret crash pad."

"He owns an apartment building," Catherine said, "but I checked it out and don't think he was shacking up there." She scrunched her brow. "Why did these women let him take compromising pictures?"

"They didn't know."

"How could—"

"He had this little camera. It fit in his palm. He showed me once. He said it had autowind, but it didn't make any noise at all. He took my picture and he was right: it was completely silent. So, apparently he was able to take pictures without anyone being the wiser."

"How could he take pictures while he was having sex with someone with a camera that he held in his palm?"

"Oh, he didn't include himself in the pictures. That would have created evidence that would work against him. He just took pictures of the women..."

"How incriminating can that be?"

"...sometimes with other... people. Maybe with his friends. Did he ever ask you to do it with his friends?"

Catherine felt her cheeks color again. "I'm not a group-grope kind of gal."

Laura held up both palms. "I don't know for sure. That's just what I deduced."

"Did he ever take videos?"

"I don't think so. I only saw the one little camera. Why do you ask?"

Catherine told Laura about the videos taken in her bedroom.

"You're kidding. Someone filmed you here? In your own home? Without your knowledge?"

"So it appears. I think Stephen was being followed."

"Or you were," Laura said. "After all, it happened in your apartment."

"Yeah, but I'm not very good blackmail material."

"Well I can assure you Stephen would never knowingly allow himself to be filmed in a compromising position. You've got to figure out who filmed you."

"No, shit." Catherine mentally switched gears as Laura drained the snifter and refilled. "Did Stephen ever talk about his enemies? Anyone who had a reason to want him dead?"

"Buzz Benson. When I heard Stephen had been shot, I immediately thought of Buzz Benson." Laura recapped two of the things Catherine already knew: the business rivalry between Buzz and Stephen and the rumored relationship between Stephen and Angelina Benson.

"Also, there was this woman—Rita somebody. I think she was into some kinky stuff. Minors, maybe."

"Rina Gold."

"Sounds right. She made a big play for him last year... wanted him to leave his wife, threatened to tell Lili about their affair. I think they had been carrying on for quite some time. Anyway, whatever he did to back her off really got her pissed. He said Rina was the closest he'd ever come to having Lili find out."

"How do you know that?"

Laura grinned. "Since he couldn't fuck me, he talked to me. Like a sister, I guess."

Catherine sipped her tea and contemplated Laura's information.

"Well," Laura said as she shoved back her chair, "I think if you find the apartment, you'll find the insurance policies... and maybe pictures of a lot of people who wanted him dead."

She reached for her fur. Catherine rose from her chair.

"I'm going to help you in every way I can." Laura put her arm around Catherine and gave her a quick hug. "I just have to do it inconspicuously."

Chapter Six: Sunday

The glare hit Catherine's face. She twisted to elude it; awoke when her wrist cracked the lamp table.

"Uhhh," she groaned and rubbed her eyes. She was curled in the same living room chair from which she'd monitored the apartments across the street. Binoculars lay on the carpet six inches from the ottoman; The annotated diagram had floated to the floor, eighteen inches beyond the foot stool.

Her left leg was numb, beginning to needle and prickle, and her neck muscles were stiff and spasmed. She stood carefully, pressing foot to carpet, anxious to hobble to the bathroom and relieve the strain on her bladder. Garbo came out of the bedroom, stretching long sleek legs, yawning wide, eyes still sleepy.

"What happened to you, slacker? You're acting like my other daughter—the one who used to sneak out and go drinking with her friends," Catherine said as she limped into the kitchen and shoveled kibble into Garbo's bowl. "Next thing you know I'll have to take away your phone privileges."

Garbo wagged her tail happily, but her snout was planted in her breakfast.

Catherine hobbled down the hall to the bathroom. As she lowered herself to the toilet seat, sweats tugged down around knees, her new, unlisted phone rang. She swore audibly then tottered back and yanked up the receiver.

"Mom?"

The one title that instantaneously overwhelmed her with a mix of emotions: Responsibility for the trusting young life she had influenced and molded; guilt for not having done a better job; gratitude to the gods for giving her such a special person to love in a way she would love no other.

But now, Chloe stretched the title into a two-syllable indictment. *Ma-ahm?*

And Catherine knew Chloe had heard.

"Hi, honey, I was just telling Garbo about your rebellious teenage years." She kept her voice level. "What a nice surprise. It's not our day."

Two years ago, when Chloe departed for Paris to begin her university education, she and Catherine agreed to talk every other Sunday. With few exceptions, they had kept that schedule. They had spoken last week; Catherine had hoped to have this mess cleared up before their next conversation.

"Is it true what this says?" Chloe's voice was rife with anguish. She read aloud, "*Computer industry executive Catherine Calabretta was detained and questioned about the murder of Stephen Forsster, San Francisco investment banker and philanthropist...*"

Catherine listened around the words, hearing the disbelief and fear in Chloe's voice.

Chloe concluded with, "This was in the Thursday *New York Times.*"

"Was it written by that guy who interviewed Elvis at the WalMart last week?"

"Mom!" Two syllables again. Distress instead of indictment.

Catherine spoke evenly. She explained it was all a mistake and was delicate around the details of her relationship with Stephen.

"I don't care if you screwed him," her nineteen-year-old daughter proclaimed. "I live in France, remember? Everybody has sex with everybody else. But murder? How could they think you killed him?"

Catherine bagged her instinct to be glib; again she gave as little information as necessary, listening to the tenor of Chloe's questions and monitoring the change in her emotions. When she heard the right level, she switched the conversation to reassurances. It wasn't a big deal... the police had asked a few questions but quickly realized they had the wrong person..."It was an adventure for a middle-aged broad like me whose biggest crime is occasional jay-walking."

"You always say stuff like that just to protect me," Chloe said. "I'm an adult now, Mom. I don't need protecting."

"Cut me some slack, Chloe. Here I am, peacefully at home on a Sunday morning. Do I sound like I'm weeping in terror?"

"You wouldn't weep if they sawed off your arm without anesthetic." Sarcasm confirmed Chloe was calmer, although still uncertain.

"What did you do today," Catherine asked, checking the clock. It was after four in Paris.

Chloe reluctantly changed the subject and was telling Catherine about her day of rollerblading in Bois de Boulogne Park when someone began banging on Catherine's front door.

Garbo raced from the kitchen and planted herself in the hallway, barking and growling. Catherine used the hubbub as an excuse to say goodbye to Chloe, with a promise to call if anything else happened with the Forsster case. She headed for the door, feeling guilty for her deceit but figuring if things really went south, Chloe would find out soon enough. Why worry her in the interim?

The banging intensified. "Open up, Ms. Calabretta."

Hiller. *Shit!*

Garbo lunged at the door; Catherine's heart slammed against her ribs.

Oh, God. They were here to arrest her! She couldn't let that happen! She would refuse to let them in!

"We have a search warrant, Ms. Calabretta."

A search warrant? They'd already been through this place like boll weevils through a cotton crop. What could they be looking for now? She thought of the FedExes—the video.

She grabbed Garbo's collar. "Stand down!" she whispered fiercely. The dog hesitated, then lowered to her haunches and growled low in her chest.

"Just a minute," Catherine called. She dashed into her office, spun the dial on the safe. Locked. Video and FedEx were as secure as they were ever going to be. She snatched up the cell phone and punched in Jordan Lawrence's number with trembling fingers. She barreled over the answering service greeting, fiercely whispered her name and that she had an emergency.

"Mr. Lawrence isn't available. Can I take a message—he can call you within four hours."

"You get him on the goddamned phone!" she hissed.

Hesitation. "Please hold."

More pounding. "Ms. Calabretta?..."

Garbo growled louder.

"I'm getting dressed!" Catherine didn't have any trouble sounding put out.

"You've got one minute to open the door." Hiller must have known she had no avenue of escape. He sounded confident... and bored. "After that, we take it off the hinges."

"Come on, come on," she whispered into the phone as she stroked the agitated dog.

"Go ahead Mr. Lawrence," the answering service said.

"Catherine? What's going on?" His voice was gravelly, full of sleep.

"Hiller's here." Words tumbled. "He says he has a search warrant. Does he mean that? Or is he here to arrest me?" She heard bed sheets rustle.

"What does it say?" He sounded fully alert now.

"I don't know. I haven't let him in yet. I was afraid he wouldn't let me call you."

"Keep me on the line and open the door."

No, no, no! She didn't want to!

"Ten... nine... eight..." Hiller began a countdown.

"It'll be all right, Catherine," Lawrence's voice soothed.

"Okay, Jordan." She barely squeaked out the words.

She locked the distressed Garbo in the bedroom and forced air into her constricted chest.

"...five... four... three..."

She flicked off the door chain, flipped the deadbolt, and glued a haughty expression on her face.

"...two..."

"I hope my neighbors file a disturbance complaint against you, Inspector Hiller," she said as the door swung wide.

"Got a search warrant, Ms. Calabretta."

He held it out. She snatched it from his hand, studied it, then raised the phone to her ear.

"It is indeed a search warrant, Jordan," she said into the phone, trying to mask her relief, emphasizing Jordan's name so Hiller would know she was represented in this exercise.

"It's a warrant for DNA," Hiller said, again sounding bored with the whole procedure. "We're going to take you to the station and a State of California criminalist is going to take hair and blood samples."

Catherine fought for self-control. "For what purpose?" she asked.

"I don't have to answer that question..." Hiller leaned in and raised his voice in the direction of the phone. "...do I, Mr. Lawrence?" He straightened and looked weary. "Get your coat."

"Is the warrant signed?" Jordan Lawrence asked through the phone. "Look on the last page."

Catherine flipped paper. "It appears to be."

"Judge Smolian," Hiller said, again aiming his comment at the phone. "Get your coat," he repeated to Catherine.

She kept up the pretense of irritation. "Does it say here that I have to wear a coat?"

"It's forty degrees outside. Wouldn't want to put a chill on that toasty warm heart of yours." He turned to a female officer who stood quietly in the hall and nodded in Catherine's direction. "Let's go," he said.

The woman stepped forward, positioning herself to manhandle Catherine.

"You have to go with them, Catherine, or they'll cuff you and take you in."

Catherine flashed back on her night in the jail cell. Her heart beat so hard it shook her whole body. She feared if it sustained its pace she would have a heart attack. "How long..."

"Tell Hiller you insist on having your attorney present for the sample collection—that's your right. I'm on my way now," Jordan said. His voice softened. "This won't take long. We'll be sitting in Starbucks sipping lattes by ten."

Jordan disconnected. Catherine forced a defiant glare. "You're walking yourself to death in a revolving door, Inspector."

As she went to the coat closet, she dialed Wilson. "Can you walk Garbo? Now?" she asked without preamble, grabbing a jacket off a hook.

"You up against it?" he asked, his baritone voice gruff with sleep.

"Got cops at my door and a dog that needs to pee." She picked up her wallet.

"Get your head right, Ms. C.," he advised. "I'm down with Garbo."

Hiller's generic brown unmarked was parked in front of a black-and-white. An officer stood at attention and opened the back door when they emerged from Catherine's building. The back seat smelled of stale urine and sour body odor. It took all her self-discipline to climb into the police car—to curb her desire to bolt down the street.

At the station, they put her in a tiny, airless interrogation room and closed the door. She paced the full eight feet of floor space for exactly twenty-seven and a half minutes before Jordan Lawrence arrived.

"About time," she snapped. "I'm as tranquil as a barn cat getting blow-dried for a beauty pageant. What's Hiller's game?"

"I don't know and it doesn't matter. They've got a valid warrant; we have to let them take DNA samples."

"Why now? Why not before?"

"They probably found something, some new potential evidence, and they want to link you to it. I've got a call in to the D.A., but, historically, he's unresponsive on Sunday mornings."

Two officers led her through a maze of hallways to a small, sterile room that looked like a medical mini-lab. She sat in a plastic-and-wood student's desk; a diminutive Japanese man in a white lab coat meticulously plucked hair from her scalp and sealed it in a clear, plastic envelope that resembled a Ziplock bag.

Jordan asked questions about the equipment and procedures the man was using.

Catherine followed instructions to flex her fist as the tech tied a tourniquet around her biceps and probed the tender fold of her arm with his latex-encased index finger. He unsheathed a needle. She closed her eyes before the prick.

Was Hiller going to let her leave? Or would he be skulking in the hall, handcuffs ready.

Adhesive tape secured cotton to the puncture; Jordan immediately opened the door and said, "Let's go."

Hiller was waiting in the anteroom. "As always, counselor, the San Francisco Police Department appreciates your genial cooperation," Hiller said and turned to Catherine. "I believe you dropped this." He handed her a folded strip of brown paper.

Whatever it was, she was certain it wasn't hers. Cautiously, she unfolded it. It was a bumper sticker in white with navy blue letters, a rattlesnake coiled on the left introducing the words *Don't Mess with Texas.* She raised her eyes to meet Hiller's gaze. He smiled and winked. Mocking. He turned and sauntered down the hall.

"He's saying he's gonna take you down," Wilson said when Catherine relayed the bumper sticker story. They were standing in her kitchen, Sunday *Chronicle* stacked on the table and the fragrance of freshly brewed French roast coiling the air.

"My interpretation exactly," Catherine said, stroking the anxious Garbo. "I think this dog is developing abandonment anxieties."

"She picks up your play."

Catherine nodded glumly.

Wilson refolded the pages of the Sports section then studied her quietly. "Lay tight. We gonna handle your business... so your business don't handle you." He roughed Garbo's ears and headed for the door, tapping the phone pouch clipped to his black jeans. "I'm on cell."

The front door closed behind him. Catherine sank into a chair feeling defeated and spiritless. So much to do, so many impossible tasks. Find a killer. Exonerate herself.

Get a grip. Get a grip.

She allowed herself the luxury of a five-minute shower and had just slipped into clean sweats when her cell phone rang.

"Have you had your double espresso and the fucking morning news?"

She stumped into her office and pinned *Don't Mess with Texas* to the top of the dartboard as she said, "All I've had is Hiller over-easy." She picked up a handful of darts and told O'Malley about the DNA samples as she peppered the bumper sticker.

"Yeah. Bad news," O'Malley wheezed. "They found your blue rain-coat."

Catherine's fingers stuttered; the dart hit the wall and dropped to the rug. "How'd you learn about that? I thought Hiller fired your friend who was shuttling information."

"I don't ask my friends to do things that would cost them their fucking pensions."

Catherine knew she'd never learn the identity of O'Malley's sources. "So that's why Hiller came with a warrant for my DNA this morning?"

"Nah. He probably had that planned before they found the coat."

"Why?" Catherine laid the last two darts on the desk. "Why not do the DNA thing when he had me in jail?"

"Did it rattle you? Him banging on your fucking door? He's intim-idating you. Wants you to know he's going to stay in your face and not back off. That's how you get a perp to panic." O'Malley paused before she continued. "The coat makes the clock tick louder. You gotta pick up the pace—go balls to the wall. But first, did you read the fucking newspaper? Your ex-husband is doing a little domestic violence to your already battered reputation."

"He's a piss ant. I'm not going to waste my time reading his palaver," Catherine said, lip curled with irritation.

"Good attitude, except I think we probably racked up FedEx number three. Claims you sent him a fucking tape... or, from his commentary, I'd say it's a tape of you fucking. Claims he turned it over to Hiller."

"I hope the two of them found it instructive". Indignation flamed her face. "The suspense of this is better than *Survivor*. 'Who's going to get envelope number four?'"

"My guess is, you won't have to wait long to find out. Ciao." The phone went dead.

Catherine dropped the handset onto its base and accidentally caught her sleeve on the edge of a red plastic file box that housed a hundred or so business cards. The box crashed to the floor, spewing its cargo–including alphabet separators–across one granite-colored carpet.

"Shit!" She punted the box with the toe of her tennis shoe. It cracked when it whacked the wall. "Shit, shit, shit!"

She stormed to the kitchen and snatched the newspaper off the table. Someone had stolen her blue raincoat and planted it for Hiller to find. Someone had sent a very intimate video to her ex-husband. Who the hell was doing this?

The Sports section was on top; The front section buried in the middle. It didn't take long to find the article: "*Guardian of Privacy or Exhibitionist?*" by Jerry Woodstock, in conversation with Nicolas Calabretta, Ph.D.

"Two vultures singing a duet..."

It started with, *While Dr. Calabretta was reticent to discuss his ex-wife...* and it read like the transcript of a typical conversation with Nicolas: generalized psychobabble to camouflage personal accusations. For titillation, he tossed out "hyperactive libido," "classic symptoms of exhibitionism," and wrapped up with "sexual perversion."

Catherine wadded the newspaper and crammed it into the trash. Then she marched to her office, minced over the spilled business cards arrayed across the floor, and dialed Nicolas's number.

Answering machine. Of course.

"Nicolas, I know you're there—even over the phone. I can sniff you out like fresh dog shit in a rose garden. Pick up the phone or I'm going to talk until your machine runs out of tape. Then you won't get all those messages from all those reporters you're hoping will call for follow-up interviews. I know you, Nicolas: you're eating up this publicity like maggots on a fresh cadaver." One beat of silence. "Nicolas!"

The line opened.

"You are so hostile, dear," he said, coolly. "Have you considered anger management therapy?"

"I didn't send a tape and you know it. You'd better retract everything you said."

"That's strange," he fawned innocence. "It came in a FedEx envelope from ETC. Do you still work there?"

Touché. If she'd asked directly about the FedEx, he wouldn't have told her. She changed tones to learn if it was a copy of the tape that had been left at her door. "Okay, you caught me. So what do you think?" she asked seductively. "Does it work for you as a training film?"

"Film? You must have your tapes confused. This one is audio. Are you sending out videos, too? I feel cheated."

Catherine was speechless. *Audio*? "What are you talking about? What's on the tape?"

"Words, dear. Check Webster's for a more detailed definition of 'audio.'"

A click sounded and the line went dead.

An audiotape? What the... Would the peeper have reduced the video to audio only? That didn't make sense. She thought of the audio bugs. She'd never had phone sex with Stephen, but they'd made use of multiple rooms of her apartment. Why would the peeper bother with an audio picked up from the living room or the office when he had full-color video shot in the bedroom? It didn't compute.

Catherine scrubbed her fingers through her hair and paced, overwhelmed by the endless possibilities. She squatted and raked the spilled business cards into a heap.

Nicolas claimed to have passed the tape on to Hiller, but Catherine was sure he'd made a copy. Maybe she should break into his house and steal it.

She reached for the last dozen cards. A flash of gold caught her eye. The gold and blue logo of San Francisco Financial Services. Stephen's business card.

She pulled it out of the pile–didn't remember having it. She pondered it and turned it over in her hand. On the back, written in blue ink, were the letters "R L"; below them, there was a sequence of numbers that appeared to be a phone number: 34 6–19 01.

Now she remembered. She'd found the card one day after Stephen spent the afternoon at her apartment.

He'd delivered his motto, "Even an Olympian rests between events," with a smile and a wink as he headed to her desk to call his office. That day, he'd fielded some crisis. He had sworn loudly then taken his billfold from the slacks that hung on the corner of her armoire.

He'd planted a quick kiss on her lax mouth, flopped her limp hand to her pubic patch, and said, "Amuse yourself. I'll be back in five minutes." His mischievous, seductive smile dissipated as he strode from the room, pulling a fold of paper from his wallet.

Sometime after he'd gone, Catherine was at her desk and noticed the card tucked under the edge of the phone. Because of the writing on back, she'd kept it, intending to return it to Stephen. How had it ended up in her card file? No matter. Here it was, a lifeless reminder of her former *inamorato*.

She dialed the phone number written on the back of the card. After two rings, the phone was answered by a thin, quavering male voice.

"I'm calling for Stephen Forsster." She left it open to interpretation. Calling on his behalf? Calling to talk to him?

"Don't you read the papers? He's dead," croaked a raw, wavery voice. Old.

"Was he... a friend of yours?"

"How could he be a friend? I never met him."

"Did you talk to him on the phone?" she asked, intentionally slowing the pace of her words.

"Why would I do that?"

"I was sure this was his phone number. Have you had it for very long?"

"I remember exactly when I got it. I was seventy at the time. That was fourteen years ago. Maybe he had it before that."

"Ummm..." She studied the card. "Are your initials 'RL'?"

"ZJ. For Zachary Jennings." He wheezed. "Hey! Are you one of those phone sex girls?"

She almost laughed aloud. "Not in this lifetime, Mr. Jennings."

"'Cause if you are..."

"I'll call back if I make a career change."

Catherine hung up and stared at the blue digits. Maybe it was a different area code. Or maybe it wasn't a phone number at all. She stuffed the card into her jeans pocket and turned from the desk. Garbo sat at attention, leash clutched between jaws, tail quivering tentatively.

Catherine laughed and shook her head, which Garbo translated as an affirmative response.

"Garbo, you're as predictable as ice in the Arctic." Next on Catherine's list was to talk to Joel but she didn't want to use her own phone for this call. There was a pay phone at the park. Might as well kill two birds with one stone.

It was a typical February Sunday in the park: Leisurely strolling dog owners and a lawn spread with picnicking families. Blue skies, a warm breeze. Where else but San Francisco? Catherine kept Garbo under tight voice command so the dog wouldn't wander from blanket to blanket, Hoovering picnic leftovers, and mopping the messy faces of small children—neither action generally welcomed by protective mothers.

At the phone booth, Catherine called Joel.

"Are you Okay, sweetie? Wilson told me about the DNA thing. I meditated and envisioned you surrounded by protective white light—I hope you're taking massive doses of vitamin C. And smudge yourself. White sage is best. It will clear away those awful criminal justice system energy vibes. I was going to wait another hour before I checked on you—give you time to recoup."

"See how fast that 'white light' thing works?"

He ignored her sarcasm; she told him about the business card with the phone number and asked him to search the myriad other area codes to see what he could find.

"One other thing," she said. She swallowed hard and hated herself for what she was about to do. "I want to look at some bank accounts."

There was a moment of pregnant silence. "Oopsie. Excuse me for saying so, but it sounds as though Catherine the Unsullied might be proposing a black hat hack."

"We're just going to count the eggs under the hen—not pack them in a crate and sneak off with them."

"Wow! I bet Kevin Mitnick wouldn't have gotten four years in Sing Sing if he'd copped that plea."

"Don't rub it in. This is hard for me."

He sobered. "Yeah. I bet it is."

She outlined the illegal records search she wanted to do. They agreed to meet later that evening.

"What's next on your list, girlfriend?"

"I'm on my way to spend quality time with the Pee Wee team mascot."

Catherine called Wilson and asked him to accompany her. She explained her mission as they crossed the Golden Gate Bridge. When he parked his Porsche across the street from Rina Gold's Belvedere estate, Catherine stalked up the semicircular drive while Wilson waited in his fancy ride, hoping to draw out the glowering teenager who lived next door. Chat him up.

An ocean breeze buffeted the tops of the palms. Catherine punched the bell and braced herself. When the door opened, she shouldered past the pink-uniformed maid.

"Rustle up Rina," she ordered.

The maid protested in Japanese-accented English; flapped her arms as though shooing chickens. Catherine sidestepped further into the foyer.

"Lady, I'm feeling about as mean as a pitbull on a gunpowder diet," she growled, not certain if the woman understood. "Don't fuck with me!"

She got that. She scuttled down the hallway in the direction of the massage room.

Catherine stepped into the sunken living room and fought a sense of vertigo. The house was cantilevered over the hillside and the Golden Gate Bridge loomed through an expanse of glass.

Rina sauntered in majestically, rose satin dressing gown trailing on white carpet, strawberry curls loose down the middle of her back, flowery perfume wafting.

"Miyako is calling the police," she said in her low, cultured voice. "They're exceedingly efficient here in Belevedere." She sank casually into the corner of a plush, silvery sofa, raised her feet to the cushions, and arranged folds of satin to frame her tan legs. "They should be here in less than five minutes." Her jaw was set, but her golden eyes projected boredom.

"Oh, good," Catherine said and plucked a white envelope from her jacket pocket. "Maybe they'll give you a Public Service Award for these birthday parties you throw for underprivileged children." Catherine removed six snapshots from the envelope and fanned them with her fingertips, careful to show Rina only the white backs. She stopped and eyed Rina quizzically. "I mean, I'm assuming these are birthday parties... since you and the kids are all wearing your birthday suits."

Color drained from Rina's face. "Where did you get those?" she hissed.

Bingo. A good bluff so far.

"At Stephen's apartment. In the darkroom. You wanna chitchat while we wait for the cops? Or you want to deal?"

Rina rose from the sofa and advanced slowly, eyes narrowed. "Give me those."

Catherine shoved the photos back into the envelope and stuffed it in her pocket. "When I found these, I figured out Stephen threatened to show the pictures... so you murdered him."

"I was at a dinner party Monday night. I've already told you that." She circled once.

"Yeah, you arrived wearing five ounces of black silk that barely covered your tits and ass. You vamoosed for a while and returned in a pantsuit that could have come out of Rosie O'Donnell's closet. I think you got blood on your dress when you shot Stephen; then you stopped at that secondhand store on Sloat Boulevard—the shopkeeper gave a tentative ID on your picture—you picked up new duds and went back to the dinner to create a not-too-believable alibi."

Icy indignation dripped off her words. "I don't shop at secondhand stores."

Catherine smiled. "Good squeal, honey, but it won't call the hogs to the trough."

Rina calculated; Catherine could see it in her eyes. "Okay, I did leave for a while." She crossed her arms in a practiced manner, pushing her breasts into perfect cleavage. "I went to a friend's apartment. A couple of blocks from the hotel."

"With the fake Polish count?"

"No." Rina hesitated; Catherine waited. "With the valet. Who parked my car."

Catherine pointed an index finger. "Hold on. You're telling me that in the middle of this big to-do at which you were clearly center stage—photographers trailing you with their tongues hanging over their lens caps—that you want me to believe you left to get laid? By the hired help?"

Rina shrugged. "He looked like Antonio Banderas."

Catherine dropped her chin and stared with sarcastic disbelief. "So. You spent what? Some 40 minutes with your legs wrapped around some buffed valet? 'Antonio'"?

"Right."

"What about the dress? He drew his sword and Zorro-ed it off?"

Rina's eyes narrowed. "Let me see those pictures. How did you find the apartment?"

"Stephen took me there."

"No he didn't. He never took anyone there."

"How would I know about the darkroom if I haven't been to the apartment?"

"Just like the rest of us: He told you when he thought he needed to exert control."

Catherine heard a car pull into the circular drive. Rina's eyes darted toward the front door and she dropped all pretenses, speaking through clenched teeth. "How much do you want?"

Chimes bonged soporiferously; a police radio squawked on the other side of the door.

"I'm going to find 'Antonio,'" Catherine said over her shoulder as she headed toward the exit. "If he doesn't verify that he was with you and that he took you straight back to the hotel after your little sport-fuck, I'm going to give the pictures to the homicide investigators."

"He didn't go back to the hotel," Rina hissed.

Catherine turned and raised her eyebrows questioningly.

Rina shrugged nonchalantly. "I patted him on the ass and gave him cab fare."

"Cab fare? Is that what you call it when money changes hands? How much 'cab fare?' Enough to taxi to L.A.?"

Catherine opened the front door and smiled at the two men who stood there. "Hello, officers. Either of you qualified to hear confessions?"

Rina Gold laughed with false gaiety and greeted them by name.

Catherine could feel their eyes on her back as she strode to Wilson's Porsche.

"The neighbor kid never showed," Wilson said. "You clear with the man?"

The Porsche thrummed down the narrow mountain road.

"Cops are no problem. Kid is no problem—we don't need to involve him." Catherine said as she returned the white envelope of photographs to the glovebox. "Nice shots of your Mom, by the way. Where were y'all, Mendocino?"

He nodded silent assent.

Catherine stared ahead, unseeing. "I don't think she killed Stephen," she murmured. She sighed, frustrated to have hit a dead end but ready to move to the next target.

She directed Wilson to the Benson house in Kentfield to try to shake loose Buzz's alibi. She planned to confront Angelina–to say she'd interviewed the Benson's neighbors and one of them saw Buzz come home after six on Monday, instead of the four o' clock arrival Angelina promoted.

They cruised slowly up the street, past the house. A white Mercedes was parked in the driveway, trunk open and golf bag leaning against it. Catherine slid down in the seat and peered above the window ledge. They U-turned six doors up and cruised back by. Buzz Benson—Catherine recognized him from shots she'd pulled off the Net—threw the bag in the trunk and slammed the lid then stomped to the driver's side and yanked open the door.

Wilson turned right at the corner and pulled to the curb a hundred feet from the stop sign. In the side mirror, Catherine watched Benson's Mercedes race through the intersection, barely braking at the corner. Wilson waited a full minute, wheeled another U-turn and parked across the street from the plantation-style house.

"If he comes back," Catherine said as she got out of the car, "blast your horn."

She pulled on a baseball cap, marched to the front porch, and rang the bell. She gritted her teeth while the "Dixie" chimes played, but she avoided a face-to-face encounter with the *Personal Security System* camera.

She listened for pruning noises from the back yard but heard only the lazy chirp of birds.

Catherine rounded the house and jerked to a stop. Greenhouse walls glittered like crystalline spiderwebs. The twisted shaft of a golf club lay on the grass among chunks of glass. The greenhouse door hung lopsided, dangling from one hinge.

"Angelina!" Catherine loped across the manicured lawn–peered over smashed clay pots and thrashed flower stalks; squatted and scanned the dirt-strewn floor. She spied a heap of powder blue fabric... an arm draped over a fern. "Oh, Angelina..." Her voice was hoarse with fear as she scrambled beneath a hanging plexiglas pane and crawled under a wood potting table to reach the woman.

Angelina lay on her back, one hip rolled up against a bench leg. Her face was blood-streaked; eyes swollen closed. She was lifeless, but for the ragged rise and fall of her chest.

Catherine backed out of the shed, all the while yelling for Wilson. He sprinted around the garage.

"Phone! Give me your phone!"

He handed it off like a relay runner passing the torch.

"She's been beaten," Catherine said as she punched out 911 with trembling fingers. "I'm afraid to move her. Her head's at a funny angle–neck may be broken."

Wilson crawled into the greenhouse, carefully clearing a path to the injured woman.

"We need an ambulance," she shouted to the 911 dispatcher and gave the address.

The dispatcher asked Catherine's identity.

"Just send the goddamned ambulance before this woman croaks!" She clicked off the phone, suddenly aware of her own vulnerability. Here she was at the site of what might soon be yet another homicide. But what else could she do? Let Angelina die?

"She's in shock," Wilson said. "Get a blanket."

"Right." Catherine ran for the house. The slider was unlocked. She raced through the family room and up the stairs looking for a bed-room. The first door revealed an office–bookshelves, a desk with a computer. She did a double take at the sight of a photo–one of several items pinned to a corkboard. She stopped in her tracks and stared, slack-jawed. Stephen and Catherine. Naked. In Catherine's bed.

Holy shit! She dragged herself away—forced herself to move on. Find a blanket.

The next room appeared to be a guest room. Small... tidy. Floral bedspread, handmade quilt folded across the foot of the bed.

Catherine grabbed the quilt and found another in the cedar chest. She plunged back down the stairs and across the yard.

She shoved the quilts to Wilson. "What else do you need?"

"The hand of God," he said. Wilson previously worked with paramedics; she trusted his judgment. "Pulse is weak. Probably bleeding internally. Nothing we can do—just wait."

Catherine imagined the police car that was, at that moment, racing toward them. "I'll be right back," she said and scuttled out of the greenhouse.

Tennis shoes flew up the stairs to Buzz Benson's office; to the bulletin board. There were four items impaled on soft cork. The grainy, color photograph was similar to the ones sent to Stephen in the FedEx, but this one wasn't cropped to protect Catherine's identity. And Stephen was X-ed out with red marker.

Catherine snatched the photo, pushpin flipping free, clicking as it bounced across the hardwood floor. Quickly, she grabbed the other three items: a yellowing photo of Stephen and his wife at a symphony benefit; a newspaper article headlined "Gregg/Admire Bill Regulates Investment Firm Profit;" and a word-processed list of names. She folded them and shoved the wad down the back of her jeans, pointy corners poking bare flesh. She ripped off her sweatshirt and used it to glove her fingers. She opened and slammed desk drawers looking for more photos, for videotapes—for anything that might be related to Stephen. Nothing. One drawer contained a library of porn films. All appeared to be commercial; none appeared to be homemade.

A siren blasted half a block away. Tires squealed, an engine roared.

Catherine spotted a file cabinet in the closet; she yanked the drawers. Locked.

Voices rose from the driveway; a police radio squawked. More sirens.

She pulled on her sweatshirt, snatched another blanket from the cedar chest, and raced down the stairs. She crossed the den just as a policeman slid back the screen door.

"She's in the greenhouse," Catherine said and pushed by, loping across the lawn.

A second officer stood at the corner of the greenhouse, legs parted, left hand resting on the butt of his holstered gun. "Are you the woman who called it in?"

"I am."

Two firemen trundled a gurney toward the greenhouse. A paramedic was inside, bent over Angelina. Wilson's head was visible around the edge of the gaping door.

"We didn't move anything after we found her," Catherine said. "We saw her husband pulling out of the driveway as we were coming up the street."

The policeman's eyes were evaluative but otherwise expressionless. Once again, Catherine felt her heart go into overdrive. She had visions of being detained in yet another jail cell.

The police kept them for almost two hours, asking questions long after the ambulance raced Angelina toward Marin General. More officers arrived. A technician took pictures and dusted for prints.

Catherine was terrified they would search her and find the things from Buzz's bulletin board. But they didn't.

From Wilson's Porsche, Catherine called Marin General trying to get a report on Angelina. Even when she lied and said she was Angelina's sister, the only thing they would say was that Angelina was in surgery. Catherine clicked off the phone and shook her head.

"They're gonna force me to hack their system just to get an update on Angelina."

They cleared the Rainbow Tunnel and cruised to the north end of the Golden Gate Bridge. Salt air tousled her hair.

Shifting tacks, Catherine said, "I think someone is following me." She stared at the San Francisco skyline, resplendent in the distance. "Also, I need an exit strategy in case the police come for me again."

"Not good to run from the man," Wilson said, and his smooth brow furrowed.

"Tell that to the calf that's about to be loaded into the slaughter-house delivery truck." She stretched, arms high, massive bridge cables flashing by, wind whipping her sleeves. "So here's the plan."

She told Wilson she was going to hang onto the brown van he'd rented for her and gave him instructions for renting three more vehicles. Nondescript cars. "Vehicles like middle-aged women," she said. "Ones that can sit at a curb, move down a street, and no one will notice them." She asked him to park them in her neighborhood, suggested specific locations.

"Also..." She swallowed hard and rubbed her forehead. "I wonder if you would take Garbo. Until this is over." Loneliness, like an anchor, attached to Catherine's heart.

Wilson frowned. Silent.

"I need to be mobile—not have to worry about her."

Wilson nodded. They agreed he would pick up Garbo later that day and that he would take Catherine's Rover. Wilson was fond of Garbo but Catherine understood it wasn't cool to have Garbo's nose prints smeared across the Boxter's windows.

They reviewed the other part of Wilson's plan: Show the collection of suspects' photos to more beachside merchants then have another go at finding the gun-toting vagrant.

At her apartment, Catherine dialed George Hallison's personal phone numbers—all three of them—and left messages at each location.

"I need to ask you about some things I found. Would you please call me at your earliest convenience? I'm on my way out with Garbo—back soon, then home for a couple of hours." She made no assumption that he'd kept her phone number; she left it with each message.

She fed Garbo and hiked up the hill to the park. By the time they returned, there was a message on her phone. Her heartbeat quickened when she heard Hallison's resonant bass.

"I'm in the city tonight. Come to my place at seven thirty. I've ordered Chinese to be delivered at eight."

What was that—a summons? A dinner invitation? Some kind of conciliatory gesture? Half her brain screamed, *screw him!* The other half wished for the opportunity.

"Don't even start," she said aloud.

She studied her image in the bathroom mirror and chided herself to not go to any special trouble while she meticulously refreshed her makeup and brushed her hair. Basic good grooming, she justified. She stood in front of her closet, flipping through different outfits, mentally arguing that there was nothing wrong with the jeans she was wearing. Well, Okay; they were a little dirty from the greenhouse experience. She settled on a long charcoal wool skirt with a slit up the back, red cashmere sweater that fit nicely, but didn't show cleavage, a pair of tall Cole Haan boots.

She checked her appearance as she grabbed a black pea coat and red leather gloves.

She shuffled through the items she'd taken from Benson's bulletin board. She left behind the photo of herself and Stephen naked in her bed and put the other three articles in her purse. She checked the mirror again, draped a pale gray scarf over the coat, and left the apartment.

In the car she admitted she was nervous about being in Hallison's sensual, masculine presence... but she wasn't going to tolerate any of his chauvinistic, judgmental crap.

Forget about it. Stephen's death had voided out romantic possibilities with Hallison. Now her only mission was to find a murderer. *And remember,* she chided herself, *George Hallison benefited from Stephen's death.*

She parked in the driveway and told Roger, the doorman, she was there to see Mr. Hallison.

"Unless you're delivering Chinese food, you must be Ms. Calabretta," he joked.

She rode in the elevator, fidgeting her gloves. Hallison was waiting at the door of his penthouse flat. She mentally battled the chemical reaction that seared her loins. God, the man was sexy... and she liked his style. Tonight he wore pleated brown silk slacks and a taupe pullover sweater that emphasized muscular shoulders.

"Thank you for seeing me," she said, determined to maintain a business-like demeanor.

"Anything to help find the killer of my nemesis."

Sarcasm. Great start.

He closed the door and took her coat. Hung it in the entryway closet and announced he was having a Sapphire martini. Offered to pour one for her. She accepted.

She paced across forty feet of ash floor to the windows that formed the north and west walls of the room. The dramatically lit Palace of Fine Arts glowed to the west; the Bay looked like black velvet. Across the water, Sausalito twinkled like a fairyland.

Oscar Peterson played softly in the background; ice clinked in the martini pitcher. Soft lamps cast overlapping moons on the vaulted ceilings. Inset spotlights etched three modern sculptures displayed strategically in the open space. Atop the baby grand, a soaring arrangement of cherry blossoms perfumed the room.

"I'm following up on the leads you gave me," she said as she took the proffered martini, steadied it with both hands, and sipped. She angled toward the piano and fitted herself against its black lacquer curve.

Hallison sank onto an eggshell suede sofa and raised his feet to the low tansu that served as a coffee table. He crossed his ankles and contemplated Catherine.

"What happened with my computer system?"

She gave a quick rundown of Joel and Wilson's work. No virus, no logic bomb, it was all a hoax. She answered his questions.

His voice grew wry as he switched tacks. "Stephen must have been ecstatic when he learned you and I had met."

"Let's just lay this out, Hal. You asked my friend, Laura Tyler Jackson, to introduce us, but you've subsequently decided Stephen and I were plotting against you?"

"I don't believe in coincidences."

"Two things you should know. First, Stephen and I never talked about our private lives; and secondly, I had broken off my liaison with Stephen before I knew you—I talked to him only once after you and I met." She stopped short of admitting she had been with Stephen on the day he was murdered.

"The media thinks otherwise."

"The media sells sensationalism. My life story, reported without distortion, is about as exciting as a peewee football game." She moved to the tansu, put her martini glass on a coaster. "I didn't even know the two of you knew each other."

"Everyone on both coasts knows Stephen and I had a business relationship."

"Well I didn't notice your names tattooed on each other's dicks, if that's what you mean. Let's turn this around. Someone bugged my apartment and videotaped me with Stephen, presumably so they could blackmail him."

"And?"

"Blackmail isn't always for extortion of money. Sometimes it's a hammer—to control someone... their actions."

He squinted at her. "You're suggesting I'm the bad guy in this scenario?" He shook his head and looked away. "Now you've ventured into the absurd."

"It's no more absurd than Stephen and I plotting against you so I could... what?" She paced the length of the sofa. "Now that I think about it, what motive could Stephen have had?"

Hal dropped his chin and studied her through thick, black eyebrows. "He couldn't get to me in business anymore, so he devised a way to get to me personally."

"And knowing me would 'get to you?'"

His smile was bitter. "It was really nice... the few times we were together." He swirled the last of his martini and drained the glass. "Does it feel particularly good to you now?"

A sour knot grew in the pit of Catherine's stomach. "Listen." She sighed and perched on the edge of the sofa, not sure what to say next. Hallison watched with frosty blue eyes.

"I told you the first time we were... together... that I'd had sex with exactly three men in my life—four including you. In this day and age, that practically qualifies me as the Virgin Mary. Don't you think I'm incredulous that, of the four men I've been with, *two* of you had... bad blood between you?"

He smirked, rose from the sofa, and poured himself another martini. He leaned his hips against the wet bar and crossed one ankle over the other. "You balled a married man for over a year... and you're still trying to maintain your virgin act?"

Catherine straightened her spine and glared. "It's amazing," she said. "No matter how hard I try to think of a clever retort, the only words that leap to mind are, *fuck you!*"

She bounded off the sofa and strode to the entryway to retrieve her handbag from the pedestal table. "I'll ask my questions and be on my way," she said over her shoulder.

A phone rang softly in the distance. She heard Hallison's low voice, words indistinguishable. She yanked the folded pages from her purse and whirled toward the living room. She gave a small yelp of surprise as she bounced off Hallison's chest. His hands clutched her biceps, steadying her.

"Dinner is on the way up," he said, gazing down into her eyes. She couldn't help it, her heart throttled into overdrive. He hesitated. He released her and opened the tall ash door. A uniformed chauffeur crossed from the elevator and hesitated when he saw Catherine.

"I'll take it, Ernesto." He took the two white bags, closed the door, and headed out of the foyer. "I want to eat while it's hot," he said over his shoulder.

"Just answer my questions," she said tightly, "and I'll be on my way." When he disappeared down the hallway, she felt she had no option but to follow him to the kitchen.

He put the bags on the center island. Copper and aluminum pans, various stirrers, strainers, and other paraphernalia hung from the pot rack a couple of inches above his head. He started unpacking white cartons. She smelled sweet and sour; smelled lobster sauce as she smoothed the folded pages on the cold marble countertop.

"These are the things I want to ask you about," she said, tone icy enough to frost the steaming rice. "I think they're related to Stephen. They might mean something to you."

She peeled off the top sheet, held it for him to see. He glanced at it as he folded a paper shopping bag. He put the bag on the counter, found reading glasses in a drawer, and took the list in his hand. He studied it for a moment.

"This has something to do with Buzz Benson," he said over the top of the glasses.

"How did you know?" Surprise took the sting out of her voice.

He handed back the page, took two plates from a cabinet beside the Sub-zero.

"Those people are our high-net-worth clients." He spooned rice. "Accounts Stephen managed personally."

Savory smells caressed Catherine's stomach; she couldn't remember when she'd last eaten. She restrained her impulse to tell him she wasn't joining his little feast.

"As you know Buzz works for Morgan Phillips. He blew into town two and a half years ago and made it his mission to strip away as many of our premier customers as he could. His first year he took two of our best clients. Last year he took eight." He opened another carton. Steam escaped so thick with the smell of lobster Catherine could taste it on her tongue.

He pointed the serving spoon at the list. "He's taken five accounts since the beginning of the year—three this week, after Stephen died. Buzz Benson is the bane of our existence." He ladled chunks of lobster and creamy sauce onto the rice.

"What about this?" Catherine asked and held out the newspaper photo of Stephen and his wife, Lili, at the symphony benefit. "Any special significance?"

Hallison angled his head up, peered through his glasses. He shrugged and closed the lobster carton. "They went to lots of charity events. Benefits." He pulled in another white box and raised the top. "I don't know of any significance attached to that particular event." He stopped and looked thoughtful. "Except I do recall hearing that Buzz was pursuing a spot on the Symphony Board—of which Lili Forsster is a member."

"And this article?" she held up the newspaper clipping headlined "Gregg/Admire Bill Regulates Investment Firm Profits."

Hallison's mouth tightened into a grimace. "Now you're into a whole different arena. Let's eat in the library. There's a fire." He picked up the two food-laden plates, napkins, and silverware and asked her to bring the wine. She complied.

He deposited the plates on the glass-top coffee table six feet from the marble hearth.

They settled on tapestried floor—cushions facing the flickering fire, backs resting against the buttery leather of the room's only sofa; then Catherine directed the conversation back to the newspaper article. "What other area does this open up?"

Between bites, Hallison talked about the proposed law that had been introduced by two senators. "I couldn't believe Ben did this. He's been a friend for years and I thought he was more in tune with what this kind of change would do to the industry."

"Which is?..." The lobster was sweet, the sauce creamy and warm.

"It essentially limits brokerage firm profit margins," Hallison said. He voiced his opinion—and that of most industry watchers—that the bill would do for the financial services industry what managed care had done for medicine.

"Why would anyone do something so stupid?" Catherine asked.

"To garner votes. It's an election year—it's an underdog bill. Nowadays, more and more middle-income families are investing in the market, but they've been naïve—they thought they could get rich quick. Some of them have lost their entire savings—even their homes. This is the government's way of trying to protect them from their own ignorance."

Catherine couldn't see how this specifically applied to Buzz and Stephen's relationship so she asked.

"It doesn't." He wiped his mouth and waved his napkin toward the article where it lay on the red Oriental rug. "Go into the office of anyone in our industry and you'll find something on the Gregg/Admire lying around. But I think Stephen was taking it personally because Ben Admire was a longtime friend of his grandfather's. I heard in last week's meeting of the SFFS Operating Committee that Stephen had announced he was using his personal influence with Senator Admire to get him to change his mind."

Catherine moved the last of the rice and lobster sauce around her plate, pondering the possibility that Stephen had tried to leverage Laura Tyler Jackson's connection to the senator. She made a mental note to follow-up.

"I asked your assistant for a copy of Stephen's appointment calendar. His cell phone records. She promised to get back to me, but I haven't heard anything."

"She told me." He raised his eyebrows. "You're the computer whiz. If you're tired of waiting, why don't you just hack the files?"

She ignored the acid that had returned to his voice. "For the same reason people in the money-business don't print their own twenties."

"Ah. Business ethics at play in the domain of murder... and infidelity."

She let the criticism go unacknowledged.

He stared at the smoldering fire. "Come to the office tomorrow at five. I'll ask Betsy to have those records available for you."

He put his napkin on the coffee table and drained the last sip of wine from his glass. Catherine glanced at her watch, aware of the pinch of time constraints. She was due at Joel's in ten minutes. If she got up and walked out right now, she would still be ten minutes late.

She felt his gaze and turned to him. "I have to go," she said.

"Why Stephen Forsster?" There was the merest flash of vulnerability in his blue eyes.

She wiped her mouth and put her napkin beside her plate. She rolled up on one knee, hiked her skirt, and straddled his lap. She rested her forearms against the well of his shoulders and floated her fingers through his silky hair. Inhaled the herbal tang of his shampoo, the clean scent of his skin. His mouth was close to hers. She looked into his eyes.

He didn't push her away, but he didn't move toward her, as he always had before.

"Because he was a sexual connoisseur," she said. "He knew women's bodies better than women know their own. I needed him to teach me." She turned her head and stared out the French doors. The top of the Transamerica Pyramid glowed in the distance. "Stephen was a low-risk, no-involvement sexual experiment."

She returned her gaze to meet Hallison's. The vulnerability was back. She stroked the silky silver that gleamed at his temples. Felt the unbending rigidity of his body.

"If I'm honest, Hal, I have to say I owe Stephen," she said. "For how he opened me–helped me lose my inhibitions. For what he taught me about my own body–my own sexuality."

She put her hands behind his head and pulled it forward slightly. His palms remained flat on the floor as her lips softly brushed his forehead. She looked into his eyes again.

"But he didn't touch my heart," she said, her voice tender with the sorrow that ached in her chest. "He didn't make me... soft inside." She trailed fingertips lightly down his cheek. "Like you did," she whispered.

She rose from the floor. Got her coat. And left his apartment.

When she pulled in front of Joel's house in St. Francis Woods, she was surprised to see a bright yellow Volkswagen parked in the driveway. It was the new model–the huggable one. Wilson's Porsche was an ominous shadow behind it.

Catherine rang the bell and heard the pound of miniature feet. The doorknob rattled, then a tiny voice asked, "Who is it?"

"Hi, Tati. It's Auntie Catherine."

The knob rattled in earnest as Tati yanked the door open. Joel was standing five feet behind. Tati locked her arms around Catherine's knees.

"Auntie Catherine, Auntie Catherine, did you see my new sunshine car?" Tati gurgled childish enthusiasm.

Catherine lifted the little girl, enveloped her small, lithe frame; inhaled the Johnson & Johnson Baby Shampoo. Tati's wide gray eyes glimmered with happiness and excitement.

"It's a little huggie car that got painted by the King of Sunshine and when you sit inside, it wraps its arms around you and makes you giggle. Can we go sit in it, Unca Joel; can we please, so Auntie Catherine can see how it makes you giggle? Please, please."

"It's past your bedtime, Tati."

She wriggled for release until her feet hit the floor; then she latched onto Joel's knees. "I know, I know, but can we pleeeeease, just this one time?" She looked up at him imploringly.

He crossed his arms and tried to look stern. "Well," he said. "It's damp outside. Go get your rain boots."

She tore across the wooden floor, pajama-clad feet thudding like pistons. "You're going to love it, Auntie Catherine..." The child prattled enthusiastically, her chatter never ceasing, even when her words were indistinguishable from the back of the house where she'd apparently gone to fetch her boots.

Joel brushed tears with the backs of both hands.

"Have you seen her this excited since Brenda died? I mean, my God, we saw that car on the street yesterday—we were driving home from ballet lessons—and she just started giggling. I was so shocked I nearly ran off the road. It's the first happy noise the child has made in eight months."

"So you have a new car..."

"Of *course* I have a new car. It's a good thing she only wanted *one* or I'd probably have a whole freaking fleet of them lined up in the driveway. And I fall supplicant before the gods that she hasn't yet decided she wants to *sleep* with the thing or I'd be trying to figure out how to get it up the blessed staircase."

"A yellow Volkswagen." Catherine glanced out the door where the car gleamed in the dark. Tati chattered away from the other end of the house. She smiled. "You're probably the only queen in town who's driving one of those."

"Yeah. The dark blue German mafia car is locked in the garage. I can't yet bear to part with it." He looked wistful. "I don't feel much like a queen anymore." He brushed his eyes again. "Children change you."

"You're not going hetero, are you?" He snorted. "Some things even children can't change." He frowned. "How are you, by the way? You look like you need to have your aura purified."

Thoughts flashed to Hallison and she wanted to weep. Instead, she sighed and lapsed into a slow, heavy twang. "Honey, I feel like I been ate by a coyote and shit over a cliff."

Joel nodded knowingly. "Ah, yes: it must be love." He looked over his shoulder toward the hammer of little footsteps. "Here comes trouble. I'll put her to bed when you finish the car tour. Wilson's in the office." He thumbed toward a room behind the staircase. "We're working on some things."

Tati came galloping out of the dining room, stuffing an arm into a tiny pink parka. "Will you zip me, Auntie Catherine?"

Catherine squatted. "Sure, sweetheart." She reached for the zipper and glanced up at Joel. "We'll talk about bank records after the tour."

He waved dismissively. "I know what you're looking for. We've already got most of it."

Catherine scowled. "You weren't supposed to start until I got here."

"Go look at the car." He bent from the hips, put his face two inches from the little girl's. "And hurry up! It's past your bedtime."

She giggled, stretched on tiptoes, and gave him a wet smack at the corner of his mouth. Then she turned and raced out the door, chattering away.

Joel rolled his eyes as once again they filled with tears. "What did I ever do to deserve her," he said, his voice trembling.

Catherine followed the little girl.

"See, Auntie Catherine, I can open the door all by myself." She pulled it wide.

"Unca Joel says I can sit in this seat when the car is in the driveway, but when we're driving I have to ride in my seat in the back. I told him I'm too old to ride in a little-kid seat, but he says I have to until I weigh at least forty pounds and I only weigh thirty-seven pounds now and he says that I only have to get fifty more pounds until I don't have to ride in it anymore. How long will that be Auntie Catherine, until I get fifty more pounds?"

Catherine smiled at the exaggerations of parenthood—recalled how she used to tell Chloe she couldn't go on her first date until she was forty. "Probably when you're five, honey."

Tati prattled non-stop, pointing out the yellow silk daisy that graced the dashboard, demonstrating how to turn on and off all the lights, the radio, and the blinkers.

As the child played, Catherine remembered Chloe at age four and missed the days when she could wrap Chloe in her arms the way she had Tati. Missed the smell of that child—the softness of her shimmering curls. She thought of Brenda, Joel's sister... Tati's mother, who would never again be a part of her daughter's life. Catherine knew she was blessed to have shared all of the wonders of Chloe's childhood, and vice versa. Would Tati fully recover from the feeling she'd been abandoned by her mother? Did any child ever recover?

"I bet my Mommie has a sunshine car. In heaven. Do you think so Auntie Catherine?"

Catherine stroked her hair. "I'll bet she does, darling."

Tati yawned a wide, slow yawn. She insisted on kissing the car's "face" before Catherine carried her into the house.

"I already had my story. Unca John read it to me when he was here for dinner, but could you tuck me in Auntie Catherine? Pleeeeeease?"

"Of course, sweetheart."

Tati made the rounds, hugging Unca Joel and Unca Wilson. Catherine carried her up the stairs, pulled the covers tight around her, smoothed her hair away from her face, and kissed her soft cheek.

Downstairs Catherine pushed through the sliding door of Joel's office. The acrid smell of recently smoked cigarettes burned her nostrils, involuntarily crinkling her nose.

"Geez. You're gonna have to run a jet engine in here to defug this place."

Joel fanned toward an open window as if he could instantaneously clear the room of its long-accumulated stench. "Is she sleeping?"

"To the sounds of Barney singing a lullaby." Catherine angled a chair across coils of cable and sat beside a wide, equipment-laden table. The collection had grown since the last time she'd visited. The room looked like a parts depot.

"You got to get that child some real music," Wilson said. "Von Stade. Pavarotti. He's got a kids' album." Wilson propped one hip on the "L" of the desk and drummed a pencil on the desktop. "I'll bring it for her. Next time I come."

"Isn't she wonderful," Joel said. "When we went to buy the Volkswagen, I let her pick exactly the one she wanted..."

"That explains the yellow," Wilson said.

"I mean when I saw her so happy, so giggly after months of somber introspection, from a four-year-old child, no less—" He shook his head and raised his palms helplessly. "I just welled."

"Welled?" Wilson ceased his drumming, pencil poised mid-beat.

"Yes." Joel glared at Wilson and nodded defensively. "My eyes welled with tears."

"Welled?"

"That's what I said. Welled."

"Dude! Inject some testosterone." Wilson drummed the eraser on his black jeans.

"You heteros have no imagination."

Joel lifted pages off the printer and handed them to Catherine. "Here's a little something to keep you occupied while I finish my research project."

Catherine glanced at the pages. Anger and frustration crackled. "Damn it, Joel, I told you not to do anything illegal. You were supposed to guide *me*." She didn't want Joel—or Wilson—busted for a crime she'd initiated.

He rolled his eyes and typed more keys. "Sit down and give me two more minutes. You're unbalancing my energies." He squinted at the screen as code scrolled by. "And they call this a firewall," he snorted. "You should tell Biz Dev this bank is prime for a cyber-security sales pitch."

"Why bother? Once they figure out you've back-doored them, they'll come to us. Probably with a lawsuit, of course, instead of as a client..."

"Hey." He swiveled toward her, hands up like a traffic cop. "I'm not some script kiddie who's out to make headlines on CNN. I'm like, the king of stealth. Think of this computer system as a gnat. I just crawled up its butt and removed today's lunch from its stomach but it won't even suspect I've been there until tomorrow morning when it wonders why it doesn't feel the urge to poop."

Wilson scowled. "Don't ever use that analogy to describe the work I do."

Catherine shook her head and studied the pages in her hand.

What Joel had found was a bank account that was used solely by Stephen—not shared with his wife—and that had limited activity. Monthly account statements were sent to a post office box. Eighteen months of records revealed checks written to only five different entities, including monthly checks dated the first of each month, payable to Preston Property Management Company.

The name leapt off the page. PPMC was the company that managed the building Stephen owned.

Another series of checks were written to Ahn Mai Nguyen on the first of each month, always in the amount of one hundred dollars.

Monthly checks to PG&E. Six checks to Folsom Photographic—two in the four-figure range. Dark room supplies?

Catherine now believed she had evidence of the apartment—perhaps the rumored darkroom. And she hoped those would bring her closer to finding Stephen's killer. But this doing-something-wrong-to-try-to-make-something-right dismayed her.

She pushed the thought aside, afraid she would give up the fight if she got too far into the ethics.

They finished the bank data review; then Wilson downloaded the details of his afternoon. He'd talked to two more merchants in the area of the beach property. Neither recognized any of the people in the photos he'd shown. He'd also combed the beach parking lots and searched the area around the Forsster beach property in a vain attempt to find the vagrant known as Sick Dick.

More dead ends.

She told Joel and Wilson about yesterday's trip to the Personal Security Store.

"Want me to hack their client database?" Joel asked.

"Absolutely not," Catherine said, voice and emotions rising in a way he couldn't mistake. "We're already so far over the line, we're in the next county."

"What's the big deal," Joel said, thoroughly disgusted. "We reviewed the bank records of some dead guy. Want me to channel his spirit and tell him we're sorry?"

At 12:30, Catherine, dressed all in black, quietly slid open the window in her dark home office and clicked the stopwatch to begin timing. She bent through the opening and stepped out onto the metal fire escape. Instead of going down, she climbed up. She crossed the roof in a low crouch, grasped the hooked handles of the ladder on the opposite side of the building, and began an adrenaline-fueled descent. Swift-moving black tennis shoes quietly alighted each rung. The ladder was concealed in an inset, exposing her to the windows she passed—all dark at this hour—but not to the street below, where someone might note her flight.

Seven floors down, she dropped to the concrete apron at the side of the building, adjacent to the outer door of the garbage room. She clicked the watch and angled it toward a streetlight. One minute and six seconds. Not bad for the fourth attempt. She'd shaved more than four minutes off the first run.

The master key in her jeans pocket opened the trash room door, as well as all other generic locks in the building. Catherine had pilfered the key from the management office desk after her first dry run when she realized she could find herself trapped beside the building if she didn't have unlimited access to all external doors and gates.

Back inside, she returned to her apartment by zigzagging between two stairwells, crossing from one to the other at each floor.

As she moved, she mentally reviewed the locations of the three cars Wilson had rented and stashed on various streets close to her building: a white Ford Taurus parked a block down on Union Street; a beige Chevrolet around the corner on Leavenworth; a blue Pontiac on Hyde, half a block from the curvy part of Lombard Street. If she had to make a quick exit from her building, she had access to wheels, no matter which direction she fled.

In her apartment, Catherine checked voicemail and returned a midnight call to Laura Tyler Jackson.

"I'm consumed by guilt," Laura said. "Tell me what's going on. I want to *do* something—help you in some way."

Catherine wanted to be happy Laura was once again being supportive—a true friend. But she couldn't dismiss the nagging suspicion something was wrong with this picture. That Laura wasn't being completely honest... that there was something too coincidental about the Stephen/Laura/Senator Admire connection. But she didn't yet have any evidence to strengthen her nagging doubts so she gave Laura a sketchy update on some of the day's events, never mentioning the bank records.

Laura pressed to meet and to get actively involved in the investigation. Catherine demurred. But, at Laura's insistence, she agreed to talk the next day.

In her dark living room, Catherine settled into the cushy armchair she'd positioned in front of the windows. The room was silent. Too silent. Garbo was with Wilson. A weighty void filled her absence.

Through the binoculars, most of the apartments across the way were dark. Catherine watched for over an hour, concentrating on apartment 4-4 across the street.

That apartment had been dark last night, as it was tonight. But tonight, the window shades were up and she could see what appeared to be a back wall filled with electronic equipment—six red dot-lights and four pale green LED lights glowed like a beacon. Each of the LEDs displayed the time. One was a minute faster than the other two; the one that had caught her attention blinked on and off as if it had recently been unplugged.

That apartment was the perfect place to receive transmissions from a camera hidden in her bedroom. She'd eliminated all of the other apartments. This was the place.

Of course, she had no guarantee the perpetrator had been in *any* of those apartments; he could have worked from a car... or from a closet in her own building. But in her gut, she believed this was not the apartment of some innocent bystander with an electronics fetish; it was where her stalker had holed up. She had to risk checking it out.

"Tomorrow night," she whispered. "I'll confirm it tomorrow night."

Chapter Seven: Monday

A phone call to Marin General confirmed Angelina Benson was in stable condition; her unspecified surgery apparently had been successful.

Catherine asked for a prognosis—asked how long Angelina would be in the hospital, when she would be able to receive visitors—and got indefinite responses on all counts. But the nurse was guardedly optimistic. A good sign. Catherine prayed Angelina's spirit would prove as durable as her mortal form.

After a brief check-in with Aida, Catherine tried to reach Sam to see if Nicolas's weekend interview had stirred up new client problems. His secretary said he was in a meeting with a client. Catherine left a voicemail.

Next on her list: get the address of the apartment for which Stephen had written monthly rent checks. She dialed Preston Property Management. Her ruse—that she was personal assistant to the late Stephen Forsster and she needed a copy of the contract for the apartment he'd rented in order to facilitate wrapping up Mr. Forsster's affairs—didn't impress the receptionist. Nor the supervisor to whom she was transferred.

"We have no legal access to the property," Mrs. Ellis said, "until Mr. Forsster's March rent is past due, or until we receive official notification from his next of kin to release the apartment."

"We're not asking for access. The keys were found in Mr. Forsster's briefcase, so we have access," she lied. "What we need is the address, because, unfortunately, Mr. Forsster's file copy of the lease is a poor-quality fax. The address is illegible."

Mrs. Ellis was clearly an unflinching protector of personal privacy—Catherine's kind of gal. She referred Catherine to the PPMC attorneys for further assistance.

Catherine blew air through tight lips and moved to the next task: locate Ahn Mai Nguyen. A quick scan of the white pages turned up a hundred Nguyens, None of them Ahn Mai. An online search garnered the same results.

Next: Folsom Photographic. Another recipient of Forsster checks. Catherine's call was answer by a recording; the store didn't open until ten o' clock. She decided to go there in person—maybe encounter a non-confrontational sales clerk who would give in to Catherine's persistent questioning just to be rid of her.

She took the rented Chevrolet and found street parking half a block from the store. A lucky omen, she decided. Street parking in San Francisco was harder to come by than gold had been for the forty-niners who'd mined the hills a hundred and fifty years before.

An electronic meep notified the proprietor when Catherine pushed through the door. The acrid smell of chemicals tickled her nose. The diminutive man behind the cash register clicked orange price stickers onto aluminum cans. He grinned a white, buck-toothed grin that emphasized the darkness of his skin and eyes. Vietnamese, Catherine thought; and when he asked if he could help, his strong accent confirmed his nationality.

Catherine smiled benignly as she walked to the counter. She slumped her shoulders in an attempt to match his height.

"I'm Joyce Byrd," she said and held out her hand. He shook it hesitantly.

"Sam Wen," he said. "I'm Sam Wen."

"Stephen Forsster was a customer of Folsom Photographic. Did you know Mr. Forsster?"

The man shook his head sadly. "He killed."

After mumbled acknowledgment, Catherine continued. "I was his business manager. We found a note in his files that indicated he owed you money. I'm here to settle his debt."

She'd heard somewhere the best con started with the perception that dollars might be about to change hands.

"Mr. Forsster, he don't owe money." Mr. Wen frowned. Confused. "He good customer. He pay cash 'n' carry." He nodded his head up and down continuously as he spoke. "I build his darkroom. He buy he supplies from me," he said proudly.

Catherine smiled solemnly. "I didn't know you had such a long relationship. Which darkroom did you build? The one at his house in Danville?"

Wilson had reported the nanny saying there was no darkroom at the Forsster home, so it was a good bet Mr. Wen knew the location of the mystery apartment.

"Danville? Danville?" He looked confused. "No, no, no. He live San Francisco." His eyes narrowed in suspicion. "You know Mr. Forsster?"

"He has several residences," she said confidently. "You built it at one of his apartments in San Francisco?"

"Yeah, yeah."

"Which one?"

He shrugged several times and shook his head no. Eyes cast about as if he'd suddenly lost command of the language.

"Did you deliver supplies to more than one place for Mr. Forsster?"

He squinted. "I don't deliver. He pick up."

Half-dozen more questions. Catherine learned Mr. Wen had built the darkroom more than five years ago. Nothing more. If he remembered the exact location of the apartment, he wasn't confessing it to her.

Frustrated with no other avenue to pursue, she thanked him and headed for the exit. So much for lucky parking place omens. Door half open, she paused and turned back to the man.

"Sam Wen?"

He raised his head from his orange-sticker job. "Yeah?"

"Do you spell Wen, N-g-u-y-e-n?"

"Yeah?"

Catherine held her breath. "Is Ahn Mai here?"

"Sure, sure." Bobbing again, he turned toward the back of the store, called loudly, "Ahn Mai! Ahn Mai!"

A female voice responded and there was a lengthy exchange in Vietnamese before a petite, self-conscious woman emerged from a door in the back corner of the store.

"This my sister. This Ahn Mai," Sam Nguyen said as the woman sidled up next to him, looking as though she were trying to shrink into her beige turtleneck. She smiled nervously, eyes studying the countertop she'd taken shelter behind. Catherine approached, trying to mimic the woman's meekness when she said hello.

Vanished were fleeting thoughts of Stephen having traded money for sexual favors with this woman. "Did you get your check from Mr. Forsster on the first of this month?" Catherine asked, voice soft. Non-confrontational.

Ahn Mai nodded. Catherine waited, allowing the silence to nurture a growing tension. The woman drew an invisible pattern on the countertop with the tip of her finger.

"You want her clean again?" the brother asked anxiously.

The cleaning woman. Someone familiar with darkrooms. Of course.

"How often did you clean?" Catherine had to repeat and rephrase the question before the combined translation skills of the brother and sister resulted in an answer.

It was the brother who spoke. "Two time. She clean third and twenty. Every time was third and twenty."

"The third and the twentieth of each month?"

"Yeah, but not much to clean except in darkroom. She say he messy in darkroom; but not many laundry, not many dishy. You want her give back money?"

"No, no," Catherine reassured. "Was Mr. Forsster there at the apartment when she cleaned?" Catherine asked the brother, allowing Ahn Mai to feel invisible.

"No, no, he not there," Sam Nguyen responded.

Catherine's heartbeat ratcheted up a notch. "Does she still have the key?"

They both looked confused.

"The key she used to open the door to his apartment."

Another exchange and they both nodded. "Yes. She have key."

"Could I see it, please?" Catherine asked.

The next exchange was longer. "Mr. Forsster give key to Ahn Mai. No one can have key but Mr. Forsster."

Catherine was ready for that one. "How about the police? Would you give the key to a police officer?"

Sam Nguyen shrugged. "Sure, sure. We give to police."

Catherine raced home and exchanged the Chevrolet for the fake UPS van she'd parked on Greenwich Street. It sported a shiny new parking ticket. She didn't care. As she drove west, she called Wilson and Joel, and arranged for both to meet her at Maureen O'Malley's house.

O'Malley greeted her with the usual, "What the fuck are you doing here? You're supposed to call first."

"I bought bullets. They're in my car," she said as she pushed into the dark, narrow hallway. The house smelled of chicken soup.

O'Malley paused, hand on the doorknob, and peered outside.

"In my other car," Catherine said. "You don't get them until the investigation is finished, but I want you to know I'm committed. I've bought them."

"What brand?" O'Malley asked suspiciously.

"I don't remember. They're in an orange box."

"Thirty-eight caliber?"

"Right."

Catherine stalked to the radio and hiked the volume. Twanging, weepy guitars reverberated off the walls. She leaned close to O'Malley's ear.

"Is your caretaker at home?" she asked and raised her eyes toward the ceiling.

"She's fucking always at home," O'Malley rasped, eyeing Catherine suspiciously.

"Okay, listen." Catherine squatted beside the chair. "It's time for you to earn your pay. I need your help."

"So this is what the bullet foreplay was about? This must be fucking huge," she sneered.

"Do you still have your badge? Your inspector's shield?"

"Yeah," she snorted. "I'm gonna wear it on my fucking bathrobe when I paint my brains on the ceiling. Tell my brother I want it buried with me in my casket."

Catherine explained about Ahn Mai Nguyen and told O'Malley about the key to Stephen's apartment—that the Nguyen's had agreed to give the key to a cop.

"So you're gonna add 'impersonating a police officer' to your list of crimes?"

Catherine held her palms up. "What's to impersonate? You're the real deal, Inspector O'Malley."

She squinted at Catherine. "No fucking way."

"Listen. This one little bull ride can make or break my entire rodeo career. I have to have that key. And you have to get it for me."

"What part of 'no fucking way' do I need to translate into Shitkicker?"

"You want bullets?"

"Fuck your bullets. You can't even get me out of the fucking house. The fucking cunt upstairs has the only fucking key to the wheelchair gate and she doesn't unlock it unless my fucking brother tells her to. You wanna call him up? Ask his permission?"

"I can get you out."

"Not unless you can pick a lock. Besides which, if I go out that door," she tapped her chest, "I set off the Med-Alert."

"I'll override the system," Catherine said.

"Then what? Tie my fucking chair to the back of your car and drag my ass down the street with the cunt upstairs chasing after us?"

"You know, O'Malley, you're a real pessimist—the kind of woman who'd marry Robert Redford and be disappointed if he didn't mow the lawn." Catherine walked to the sink and filled the tea kettle. "You put all your attention on the problems. You've got to start focusing on solutions."

"Fuck you and your solutions. My fucking brother is itching for me to do something that will convince that prickless judge to commit me to a fucking retard farm. He threatens me all the time."

The doorbell rang.

"Of course he threatens you, Mo," Catherine said and formed her thumb and forefinger into a gun she snapped at Maureen. "An empty bucket always makes the most noise."

Catherine pivoted and went to open the door for Joel and Wilson.

"I don't fucking wear makeup, bitch-boy." O'Malley raised her arms as if she were warding off a tire iron.

"You're not wracking up any positive karma with this juvenile name-calling, Inspector O'Malley. And a tiny bit of blusher is not exactly greasepaint," Joel said. He daintily held a large cosmetic brush in one hand, a compact in the other, waiting for his subject to calm herself.

Wilson stood at the end of the hallway, appearing prepared to evacuate the premises. Catherine crossed arms over chest, giving Joel more time, hoping she wouldn't have to intervene.

"And you can stick those fucking scissors and combs up your dilated asshole. I don't care how limp your wrists are, you're not getting near my hair."

"A butcher with a meat cleaver could improve that 'do of yours. What are you afraid of?"

"Life. In a fucking insane asylum." She glared at him. "Get out of my house, queenie."

Joel put his hands on his hips and glared at O'Malley. "You're the most obnoxious female cunt I've ever met."

"And I bet *you've* met every kind there is... other than female..."

Joel squinted at her. "If you give me any more lip, I'm going to have the big guy here," he nodded in Wilson's direction, "hold you down while I scrub you like a struggling toddler."

Catherine thought Wilson actually blanched; he definitely inched toward the door.

"What the fuck does a flaming fruit fly like you know about struggling toddlers?"

Joel had his back to Catherine, so she couldn't see his face, but she heard the wretchedness in his voice and saw O'Malley sober when he said, "More than you'll ever imagine, even if you live longer than God." Then he changed to all business. "Now. Here's what we're going to do..."

Catherine glared at O'Malley with cold determination. O'Malley slumped in the chair and stopped resisting Joel's ministrations.

Catherine and Wilson went down the hall to check out the *Med-Alert* home security system that was linked to the smoke detector and fire alarm, as well as the chest-band that tracked O'Malley's temperature and heart rate.

During a previous visit O'Malley had explained that the system continually monitored her condition and transmitted data to a home-care health company. If the chest monitor couldn't detect Maureen's normal pulse, the system would send out an alert that brought paramedics in fire engines roaring to the house. O'Malley said the first day after her brother won the court order to connect her, she had intentionally summoned the fire department five times. The judge told her if she set off another false alarm, he would consider her mentally unstable and would confine her to a "care facility." O'Malley was convinced he meant a mental institution.

Joel had analyzed the system and reported the computer would be easier to tame than O'Malley's wild graying mane.

"Okay, let's compromise a computer system," Joel said as he came into the bedroom.

Catherine returned to the living room.

"You can't do this to me," O'Malley rasped, voice desperate. "The fucking warden will see me—she'll call my brother."

Catherine was shocked by O'Malley's appearance. Her hair was pulled into a neat bun. Cheeks sported the barest stroke of pink; miniscule amounts of mascara darkened lashes around ice-blue eyes. The woman was actually pretty.

"It's Okay." Catherine soothed. "We're going to sneak you out through the garage."

"Yeah, like I have this much fucking foot traffic through my house every day. You think she hasn't noticed you're here? You think she isn't watching?"

"She's glued to her soaps," Catherine dismissed. She had to have that key, and O'Malley was the one who could get it.

O'Malley dropped her head; stared at the floor. Catherine paced and waited for word on the computer system.

"You're going to make me do this, aren't you?"

Catherine spoke firmly. "Maureen, I'm asking you to get a key. That's all. You, on the other hand, are asking me to load a .38 caliber police special to help you punch a skylight in your attic."

O'Malley glared, turned her face away. She sat quietly for two minutes before she spoke again. "I can't go in smelly sweats." Her voice a quiet rasp. "We have to change my clothes."

Catherine waved her off. "It doesn't really matter what you wear. All they'll care about is the badge—and that your picture ID matches your face."

Pain flashed in O'Malley's eyes. Her voice was tight. "You don't represent the shield dressed like a fucking panhandler," she said.

"Okay. Sorry." Catherine held up her hands in surrender. "No problem. You can change."

"You don't fucking get it, do you? I *can't* fucking change my own clothes. You'll have to do it *for* me."

Catherine couldn't catalog the roil of emotions that shadowed O'Malley's face.

"We do it on the bed?" Wilson asked from behind Catherine. She turned to see him watching O'Malley. "With a sheet?"

No response.

"That's how we did it with my grandmomma."

O'Malley hung her head and stared at her lap; then she pushed off down the hall to her bedroom. Wilson lifted her onto the bed. She looked as if she were going to cry.

Wilson draped a sheet over Maureen's lower body, and then instructed Catherine. Tug off the sweats, wrestle on wool slacks—pants that had been tailored for buffed muscles. Wilson helped with the lifting. They redraped the sheet and changed her shirt. O'Malley lay flat. Limp. Staring at the ceiling.

Joel appeared, said he was ready to test the system bypass. Maureen heaved an exhalation that sounded like a suppressed sob. Eyes closed.

Joel and Wilson disappeared, calling out instructions from the office. Catherine held her breath, unhooked the black band.

"Houston, we have lift-off," Joel crowed from across the hall.

"See there, Mo. That was about as smooth as sunset in Utopia."

O'Malley buttoned her shirt over the excess fabric of her white cotton bra, tucked the tail into the loose waistband. Wilson resettled her in the wheelchair.

"Sweetie, you look just great!" Joel crooned. "Isn't it amazing what magic one can work with a few brush strokes and some clean duds? You gotta check this out—see for yourself." He angled a closet door mirror.

O'Malley turned away.

Maureen's chair was too wide to fit through the kitchen door that exited to the garage. Wilson carried her across the threshold; Joel collapsed the chair and wrangled it into the brown rental van Catherine had backed inside. Wilson hefted O'Malley in place.

Joel said his goodbyes; Catherine pulled out of the garage and headed downtown.

Catherine double-parked in front of Folsom Photographic and Wilson lifted O'Malley to the sidewalk. She straightened her shoulders, sitting a bit higher in the chair. Wilson opened the door to the shop and Maureen tried to roll across the molding, but the wheels caught. When she tried to back up to free herself, she snagged the foot rests on the doorjamb. The chair lodged. Maureen slumped again, radiating hopelessness. Wilson guided her through the opening.

Catherine circled the block. On the fourth pass, Wilson and O'Malley were waiting on the sidewalk. Inside the van, Wilson handed Catherine the keyring containing three keys. A tag on the ring was labeled with a street address. She wanted to whoop with glee. Finally, she was getting somewhere.

They rode in silence until they turned down O'Malley's street and saw the garage door open.

"She knows I'm gone." O'Malley sounded as if she'd been officially sentenced.

Catherine pulled into the driveway and noted the caretaker's front door stood open inside the wrought-iron gate. Guilt twanged at her. She had known, in the depths of her consciousness, they couldn't sneak O'Malley out of the house undetected.

Wilson lifted O'Malley from the van as the caretaker came screeching out the kitchen door.

"I called your brother." She sailed into the driveway, skirt of her old-fashioned housedress winging behind, cropped gray hair flapping. She was a hell-fire evangelist bent on eternal damnation. "He's flying home from Hawaii—coming in tonight. He's going to call the judge."

O'Malley's face was unreadable, eyes directed toward her palms in her lap. The woman bent down, face in O'Malley's line of vision. "Did you hear me, Maureen? I'm sick of you."

Wilson interjected himself between the two women. The caretaker shrieked, "Don't you touch me! I'll call the cops on you!"

"Back off," he said quietly, the threat unmistakable.

She faltered. Wilson pushed the chair toward the kitchen door.

"What did you people do to the monitor system?" She stomped alongside the chair.

Wilson ignored her. She whirled to Catherine and glared with squinty eyes. "I saw you on the news." She clenched her jaw and looked self-righteous. Smug. "I told her brother about you. That's why he's coming in. Gonna go to court tomorrow. We know you're a killer."

Wilson lifted O'Malley through the kitchen door; Catherine met the caretaker eye to eye.

"Then you'll want to run along upstairs and update your will," she said, voice deadly soft.

The woman stepped back, mouth and eyes wide with surprise and uncertainty.

Catherine folded the chair, slid it into the kitchen, and closed the door.

"That's it for you, Maureen," the woman's words penetrated the wooden door. She banged it twice. "You're the worst invalid I ever looked after."

Wilson disappeared toward the back of the house and returned with the monitor belt. "Let's reconnect you, Inspector O'Malley," he said. Maureen's pose was catatonic. Wilson silently handed the belt to Catherine and headed down the hall.

Catherine unbuttoned Maureen's shirt and worked the belt around her chest. "Is that right?" she asked when she thought she had it properly arranged.

O'Malley didn't respond.

"It's on," Catherine called to Wilson. She went to the kitchen, filled the tea kettle, and put it on the stove. As her fingers reached for the knob, O'Malley said, "Don't."

Catherine turned. O'Malley was staring at her.

"I thought you might like some tea."

"Get out."

Catherine hesitated. "Maureen, I can—"

"Get out."

Wilson came down the hallway and made eye contact with Catherine.

"Maureen, I..."

O'Malley turned away.

Catherine scrubbed a hand over her forehead and through her hair. She picked up her purse and followed Wilson out of the house. Tears stung as she walked down the drive. What had she done? For God sakes, what had she become?

She leaned her head against the van door and closed her eyes, consumed with the guilt of having callously put O'Malley in this untenable position. How could she have been so insensitive—so self-absorbed?

"I'm with you," Wilson said quietly.

Catherine sighed, shifted thoughts, and closeted her regrets for examination at a later time.

"No." She pulled open the van door and turned to Wilson. She understood he was offering to go to Stephen's apartment. "I really appreciate your help," she said, "but this flock of pigeons is due to crap on my head any time now. This one I do on my own."

"Somebody's got to watch your number. Tip you if the cops show."

She shook her head. "Go back to the office. Help Joel on the BankNet project."

He hesitated, and then nodded. "Tonight I'm hangin' at the beach. Flash the photos." He stalked to his Porsche parked at the curb, turned and leaned a forearm on the dark roof. "Her bro's been hammering to get her against the ropes," he said. "It's not your load if he does."

Tears renewed their threat. Catherine clenched her jaw and nodded in resignation; but she didn't agree with him. It *was* her load.

In the van, driving through the warm sunshine, Catherine obsessed about how to make this up to Maureen. How to assuage her own guilt. When she cemented an idea, she gave a grim, "Yes!" then forced her thoughts to the task ahead: A visit to Stephen's secret crashpad.

The address was just off Lake Street, in a cul-de-sac that backed to the edge of the Presidio. The park-side of the four-story beige structure faced a rock wall that separated it from a stand of ancient eucalyptus and evergreen trees. Arched windows fronted the grove. Fire escape ladders angled down the walls. Probably twenty to twenty-five units inside. Yellow package-delivery stickers stuck above brass mailboxes confirmed there was no onsite manager to receive deliveries... or intercept visitors.

Catherine parked a block away, removed a briefcase-style tool kit, straightened her navy wool blazer over starched white shirt, and shoved latex gloves into her jeans pockets. She approached the building like a tenant returning home and quickly slid the largest of the three keys into the front door lock.

Muted bird songs filtered into the quiet lobby. Fresh paint and floor wax perfumed the air. Their was an old-fashioned elevator to the right; carpeted stairs to the left. On the second floor landing, she caught a whiff of Downy fabric softener.

Apartment 201 was adjacent to the elevator, park-side. She pressed her ear to the door listening for movement inside. She knocked quietly. No response. Heart hammering, she pulled on the latex gloves and tried various keys until the knob lock and deadbolt clicked free, noting that, curiously, one key seemed to fit neither of the locks. She eased the door open with a gentle squeak.

Catherine stepped into a short, carpeted hallway. She closed the door, flipped the deadbolt, and stood perfectly still.

"Hello?" she called softly, then tiptoed into the spacious living room.

The shades were drawn, the room gloomy. A milky couch faced a wall of pale bookshelves and cupboards; shadow shape of a television in the middle, books on three of the shelves. Sofa table with a black-shaded lamp. Glass-top coffee table in front of the sofa; ladderback chair in the corner, edging one of the tall, arched windows.

A door to the right revealed a small dining nook—no table, no chairs—with a chest-high, white-tiled bar that separated it from a tiny kitchen. The refrigerator cycled on.

Catherine crossed the thick-pile carpet, treading close to the base-boards, and raised the nearest window shade. Cheery sunlight flooded the room.

A vacuum cleaner had recently raked velvet swaths in the russet carpet; feet had subsequently trampled trails that bisected the room. Opposite the windows, between the entry and a hallway that veered to the right, two doors split a short wall. The one to the right was open and exposed a pedestal sink and the front lip of a toilet. The one to the left, closest to the entry hall, was closed; a brass deadbolt bounced a beam of sunlight. The lock-mate for the unused third key?

Catherine deposited her briefcase on the coffee table, skirted the trail of shoe prints, and followed it down the hallway into a large, shadowy bedroom. Again, she edged the perimeter of the carpet and rolled up the window shade. Sunlight fell across a maroon patterned futon; a second ladderback chair and a stack of three large pillows were propped against the wall. There was a bathroom on the right side of the bedroom door; a walk-in closet on the left. Inside, a bare ceiling bulb illuminated a large red and black safe, the words "Fort Knox" stamped in gold across the front. *Yes!* What better place for "insurance policies?"

Seven white, glossy cartons, shoebox size, were stacked on the shelf above. No clothes. No shoes. Just the boxes and the safe.

Heart beating, she opened the first box. Empty. Same for the next. All of them. She grimaced and restacked the boxes on the shelf.

The safe stood six feet tall, four feet wide. A black combination lock was embedded above a three-pronged spinner handle that looked like the captain's wheel on a boat. It spun freely—did not engage the locking mechanism. This baby was built to take its secrets to the grave.

Catherine moved on. A white Polo terrycloth robe hung on the back of the bathroom door. Two bath towels, and two hand towels, two washcloths were stacked neatly on the middle shelf of the linen closet; ivory sheets and two pillows on top.

She flipped on the hall light and studied the dark pile runner until she located one complete shoe print. It was long and wide. Masculine, with a distinctive tread. Like a hiking boot or a tennis shoe. Stephen's?

Ahn Mai said she always cleaned on the third and the twentieth; Stephen had been killed on Monday, February 3. If Ahn Mai cleaned in the morning, this might be Stephen's print. If she cleaned in the afternoon, it was unlikely Stephen would have been here after. Catherine made a mental note to ask Ahn Mai, sidestepped the print, and retrieved her briefcase from the living room. She removed a piece of white paper and a pair of wire-cutters—the closest thing she had to scissors. When she found that the eleven-inch paper wasn't long enough to cover the shoe print, she stapled two pages together with her miniature tool kit stapler. She made a rough outline and cut the paper to the shape of the sole. She trimmed it until it was exact, then sketched the tread pattern onto the cast as best she could. When she was satisfied, she put the paper in her briefcase and returned to the living room.

The third key fit the deadbolt of the locked door.

She turned the knob and was greeted by the potent smell of chemicals and by slats of heavy black rubber that curtained the entrance. Excitement raced through her veins. She found a light switch, parted the center slats, and pushed into the small room. The space had once been a sizeable walk-in closet; now, photographic equipment, cabinets, and shelves covered all but a narrow center aisle. Water faucets hooked through raw plaster and arced over basins on the right. Cans of chemicals lined the shelves; boxes of paper stacked next to them. A countertop shredder and an empty trashcan completed the inventory.

No photographs. Catherine searched twice to make sure.

Frustrated, she returned to the living room and studied the bookshelves. They contained mostly hardbacks, with a sprinkling of paperbacks. Erotica and pornography. Some of them would be called art; others were just plain crude.

A 25-inch television was centered on the middle shelf; a boom box with CD player and dual tape deck to the left. Below were a VCR and a collection of porn films. Atop the VCR was an empty cardboard tape jacket. Catherine pushed the eject button. A tape slid from the VCR. No markings on the label.

She slid it back into the player and powered up the TV and the VCR. She held her breath and pressed *PLAY*. Screen fuzz was replaced by the image of a naked man and a naked woman, missionary position in a four-poster bed. She could see only body parts—the man's legs and buttocks, the woman's knees pulled wide, her hands stroking his back. No faces. But, it was Catherine's bedroom—Catherine's bed. She didn't have to read the credits to know the identity of the stars.

Fear fed anger. She shoved the tape into her briefcase, locked up, and vacated the premises.

Catherine checked her voicemail as she headed downtown. Hallison had left a message saying, "The plan has changed." He had Stephen's calendar and cell phone records as promised; but Catherine would have to meet him at his apartment at eight rather than picking them up at his office at five. His voice was cold. Hostile?

Fine. Maybe this was a good time to catch Ahn Mai Nguyen. Catherine altered her course.

Traffic was at a standstill on Van Ness; the parking gods had clocked out for the day. She found a spot four blocks away, dashed along dirty sidewalks, pushed through the door of Folsom Photographic at five minutes before five, and called out to Sam Nguyen.

He appeared through the door marked *Employees Only*, stopped, and frowned at her.

Catherine jangled Stephen's apartment keys so he could see them and said, "I'm helping the police with their investigation. I need to ask Ahn Mai about the last time she cleaned Mr. Forsster's apartment."

He crossed his arms over his chest and spread his legs in an aggressive stance. "You the woman killed Mr. Forsster," he said. "They arrest you."

"Police in all countries make mistakes." She gave him a few beats to digest that thought before she continued. "I'm working with Inspector O'Malley—the one who came here this morning. Inspector O'Malley is interviewing a potential suspect right now, so she sent me to ask Ahn Mai these very important questions."

"How we know that honest?"

"Because I went inside Mr. Forsster's apartment with the inspector after she picked up the keys from Ahn Mai. Would she have let me do that if I were a suspect in her case?"

Catherine was amazed—appalled—at how easily the lies rolled off her tongue.

He stared a moment longer, then called out for Ahn Mai. Catherine learned the woman had cleaned the apartment between four and six in the afternoon on the day Stephen was killed; the footprints in the hall didn't belong to Stephen. A quick visual confirmed that neither Ahn Mai nor her brother could have left the print she'd copied, unless they'd been flopping around in shoes twice as big as their own feet.

Catherine asked if anyone else had been in the apartment with Ahn Mai.

Her eyes widened with fear. "No! No, no, no."

Catherine asked if there had been a tape in the VCR, its cardboard jacket on top of the machine. After a native-language dialogue between brother and sister, Ahn Mai blushed a deep rust and said Mr. Forsster kept movies in a cabinet; she didn't know any specifics about the one in the machine.

What about the safe in the bedroom closet?

The woman claimed to have never seen it open, had no idea what it guarded.

Catherine asked if Stephen ever left photos in the darkroom; learned that he was messy with the chemicals and trays, but the paper was either blank or shredded to confetti-size.

He'd never been in the apartment when Ahn Mai cleaned and she'd never seen any other person—or any sign of another person—in those rooms.

That might be, Catherine thought, but someone had been in Stephen's apartment after he was killed. She was sure of it. Someone had planted the incriminating videotape, and that someone had a rather large foot. A man-sized foot.

"He ain't here no more."

A bulletproof window separated Wilson from the stout, bushy-bearded, Chevron attendant. Fog, drifting off the ocean like a slow-moving train, swirled and evaporated under bright fluorescent lights.

"He works Monday nights," Wilson said. "He's supposed to be here."

"Got canned." The man pushed a lever that extended a metal drawer. "Step aside and let this guy pay for his gas."

After a few minutes of verbal jousting, Wilson learned that Lonnie, the pump-jockey who had been on duty the night Forsster was plugged, had gotten fired for coming to work drunk. His replacement was unwilling to answer Wilson's questions—Where's his crib? How about a phone number?—but finally divulged that Lonnie like to chill at "a kicker dive about a mile up the Great Highway."

Five minutes later, Wilson fishtailed the Boxter into a gravel lot under a bright sign that read "Dusty's." Blue and red neon bled together in the fog, creating a purple shroud. Wilson parked at the back, angling away from the dozen-or-so other vehicles. Mostly pickup trucks. Not his usual gig.

He grabbed the manila envelope off the floorboard and hiked to the door.

Paint cracked and curled off warped siding; moldings hung loose or were MIA. A twangy female and a pack of whiny fiddles sang out in the night air. Definitely not his usual gig. Wilson gripped the doorknob and pushed inside.

A massive wood bar filled the back wall; a solitary chandelier—deer antlers interspersed with nicotine-stained lampshades—brightened the middle of the room and cast shadows deep around the periphery. Red votive candles lit silver-dollar-sized formica tables and rickety wooden chairs. A dingy tile dance floor featured a man and a woman swaying a slow, upright, dress rehearsal of the moves they were destined to perform later, horizontal and naked.

Five barstools were occupied, as were several tables. Most of the men wore cowboy hats; the four women wore jeans and boots and sported haystack hairdos. A dozen or so anesthetized Caucasian faces turned to stare at Wilson. The bartender, who was drawing a beer, eyed him above the foamy glass.

Wilson ambled to a vacant stool, ordered a Heineken, and glanced casually around the room. His chest relaxed; everyone seemed to have lost interest in him.

He studied the drinkers as best he could in the muted light, looking for someone who matched the description of Lonnie.

One of the bar-leaners pushed off his stool and stumbled a circuitous route to the jukebox. Scruffy blonde hair poked out from under a dark-colored baseball cap. Plaid shirt and baggy jeans hung on his

251

assless frame. He dropped coins into the machine, punched a couple of buttons, and then pounded the sides until the female twanger went jerky.

"Hey! Hey! Lonnie!" The bartender hurled a damp towel; hit the man on the back of the head, knocking off his baseball cap.

"It ate my quarter, man," the blonde guy whined as he scooped his cap and the towel.

"How many times do I have to tell you, I'll give you another freakin' quarter. Just don't total my player."

Lonnie stumbled back to his stool, argued with the bartender about how many quarters he was due, concluded his negotiations, and selected a few more tunes. Back at the bar, he stood beside his stool, hunkered over a shot glass, rocking from side to side—perhaps in time to the music—on one booted foot, the other boot balanced on the wooden foot rail.

Wilson picked up his beer and the manila envelope, left a dollar tip where his glass had been, pulled out a stool next to the man, and put his beer on the scarred wooden counter.

"How's it hanging, Lonnie."

The man hummed tunelessly under his breath. Didn't acknowledge Wilson or alter the rhythm of his movements. After a minute, Wilson tried again. "What's happening, man?"

Lonnie hunkered deeper over the shot glass and mumbled, "I ain't interested in having your big black dick stuck up my lily white ass."

"How 'bout your girlfriend, honkey? She interested in some black action?"

Lonnie lurched back, blinked wide, trying to focus his eyes. "Teresa? You're fucking Teresa?" he whined.

"I ain't hoochin' anybody you know, bro. I just want to ask you some questions."

A drunken reevaluation. "You the man?"

"Do I look like the man?" This dude seemed too dim to cough up much buzz.

Lonnie repositioned one boot on the foot rail, the bar supporting his upper body. "Then I'm busy." He resumed the tuneless humming.

Wilson tucked a twenty-dollar bill under the edge of his own beer mug. "Maybe I could buy a few minutes of your valuable time. Get you to look at some pictures. Tell me if any of these upstanding citizens visited your former place of employment last Monday night."

Lonnie's eyes roved to the money, then to Wilson's face. Scrawny fingers walked across the bar, scooped up the twenty, and slipped it into the pocket of his baggy jeans.

"You just sealed the deal, man," Wilson pulled out the photos. "You get squirrelly on me, we gonna play periscope with that shot glass and your lily white ass."

Wilson took another twenty from his pocket, ordered a new shot-and-a-beer for Lonnie, then nodded toward a table in the center of the room. Wilson rotated a rickety chair and straddled it, the back pressed against his abs. Lonnie settled in and angled the photos into the flicker of the candle, shuffled through, and restacked the pile.

"This guy came in on Monday. 'Bout six thirty." he said. "He was, like, my first customer after I clocked in. Had a real shitty attitude. You can always tell how the shift is gonna go by the first few customers—it's like there's some Lord of the Cosmos that sets the attitude of the day and everybody just follows along. This guy..." He pointed to the photo. "...He was like the Darth Vader of bad moods."

Wilson eyed him drolly. "So far, dude, I ain't gettin' down with the *Star Wars* bullshit."

"He drives one of those little Mercedes convertibles. Black. Or dark green, right?"

Wilson shrugged noncommittally.

"Typical rich dick in a big-ass hurry. Like he had a ticking bomb stuck up his butt and if he stood at my window too long, it would explode." Lonnie flicked the edge of the photo in time to some country singer wailing about the woman who took off with his pickup truck and his *dawg*. "Credit card machine wouldn't read the stripe on his card. Had to ask him for it twice. That really cooked his lunch. Squealed his tires when he pulled out."

"You remember his name? On the credit card?

"Nah," he shrugged.

"Station keeps copies?"

"Only for a day. Then they get sent to some accounting department or something."

"So, what I'm hearing is, you just jerked my chain for five minutes and now I'm supposed to leave with a smile on my face?"

Lonnie shrugged again; then he brightened. "I can tell you his license plate number."

"I'm all ears," Wilson said skeptically.

Lonnie shook his head and grinned drunkenly. "3761"

"Dealer tag?"

"No. It had letters. I just don't remember them." He squinted at the tabletop and wrote invisible numbers with the tip of his index finger. "Three... letter, letter, letter... seven-six-one." Lonnie grinned drunkenly. "Last four digits of my SSN, man."

"Hmm." Wilson slid the photos back in the manila envelope with only a glance at George Hallison's stoic image. Wilson was glad he was going to be able to deliver some real-time 411 for Catherine... but was also glad she wasn't the type to plug the snitch.

Catherine swung the rented blue Pontiac into the passenger circle in front of George Hallison's building, confused, and scared, by Wilson's new information.

Was George Hallison a murderer? This latest "coincidence" made it difficult to think otherwise. But then, she thought to herself, many people said the same about the "coincidences" that linked her to Stephen on the day he was killed. Shouldn't she give Hallison the same benefit of the doubt she was claiming for herself?

First things first. She was here to pick up Stephen's cell phone records and his calendar—items, which might help her figure out what was really going on. And Wilson was on alert—had wanted to come here with her. But instead, Catherine had insisted he hang tight, prepared to call the cops if she got into trouble; so she felt relatively safe.

When she strode into the lobby, Roger, the concierge, covered the phone with his hand and said, "Mr. Hallison just arrived and is still in the elevator. Do you mind waiting until he phones down?"

"No problem," she chirped as she breezed by the reception desk and slipped through the door that separated the lobby from the garage. "I just need to grab..." the door slammed and she aborted her phony explanation, racing down the row of fine luxury automobiles to Hallison's Mercedes, quickly checking the numbers on the back plate.

Shit.

"Ma'am!" Roger protested as he barged after her. "Guests are not allowed in here without their host."

She shrugged and gave a lame smile. "I lost an earring in George's car." She flipped the door handle. "Should have known it would be locked." She shrugged and followed him back to the elevator.

When she reached the penthouse, Hallison was standing in his doorway, loosening his tie, charcoal suit jacket open over starched blue shirt.

"Roger's sending some wine up from the loading dock," he said, tone aloof. "Come with me."

She followed but kept her distance.

In the kitchen, a phone jingled softly. Hallison opened the door of a large, walk-in storage room, picked up a yellow handset, and said, "Okay," then hung up the phone and crossed to an elevator door in the back wall of the pantry. He punched numbers into a keypad: one, one, zero, four; "enter."

Catherine rolled her eyes. He might be a murderer, but he didn't have much of a thief mentality using his birth date as the security system password.

The elevator door parted on a stack of crates. No person. Just boxes.

"You were at the Forsster beach property the night Stephen was killed."

Hallison hefted two boxes into the pantry then glanced up to make eye contact. "No, I wasn't. I did, however, buy gas at the Chevron station that's two miles away."

"Isn't that an odd fluke," Catherine said sarcastically, watching him drag in the other six cartons.

"The Queen of Coincidence is asking me for justification?" He re-keyed numbers on the pad; the elevator doors closed as he exited the pantry.

"You were angry with Stephen because he was ruining the business you worked so hard to build," Catherine said as she followed him down the hall toward the rear of the apartment.

"That's true," he said over his shoulder, "but fortunately operating committees and boards of directors are the ones who terminate CEOs who indulge in fiduciary irresponsibility. Otherwise, there would be a significant number of dead assholes buried under Wall Street."

Hallison turned into his library and pulled out the middle drawer of his desk. Catherine watched carefully as he removed a stack of small papers and extended them to her.

"Gas receipts," he said. "I expected someone to ask me about this. However," he gave a wry grimace, "I expected it to be the police, not you."

She stepped into the room and hesitantly took the pile. He watched, jaw rigid, as she flipped through the miniature pages. They all had the same imprint on the top left; they were all from the Chevron near the beach property.

She scanned the dates. The one from last Monday was on top; the others were in reverse chronological order, dating back nineteen months. There were seven of them.

"Creatures of habit," Hallison said. He came around the desk and sat one hip on the edge. "I go to an angel's club meeting in Mountain View the first Monday of every month."

Catherine had recently been invited to join an angel's club—a group of investors that privately financed worthwhile entrepreneurial endeavors that weren't large enough to get the attention of the professional venture capital firms. It was easy to imagine Hallison involved with such an organization.

"I almost always come back by way of the Great Highway and have dinner with my uncle. He lives in a retirement home not far from the beach."

She flapped the receipts against her palm contemplatively. "I didn't know you had an uncle in the city."

He heaved a sigh and studied the carpet at his feet. His voice held a weariness when his eyes met hers. "There are a lot of things we didn't have a chance to learn about each other, Catherine."

Hallison reached behind him, retrieved a large manila envelope from the desk.

"Here are the phone records... Stephen's calendar." He held out the envelope and she took it. "And, this..." he reached behind again, "I'll return to you."

He extended a FedEx envelope. Her heart went into overdrive.

"Oh, no," she whispered. She couldn't make her hand reach for it. Her voice was hoarse. "You got this today?"

"Oh, yeah."

She slowly raised her arm and took the blue and orange envelope in trembling fingers. The last of the missing labels. It was addressed to George Hallison in care of SFFS.

Heat raced her cheeks. Hallison's sad eyes confirmed it was a tape; and he had watched it.

She wanted to weep. Instead, she pressed her lips into a tight line and turned to leave.

"I don't understand why you sent that to me, Catherine."

The hurt in his words stopped her.

"And you probably won't believe that I didn't," she said quietly and left the apartment.

Catherine threw her things into the Pontiac and screeched out of the circular drive. She drove a block away and found a parking space. She pulled in, killed the motor, and laid her forehead on the steering wheel. Half a dozen tears squeezed through closed lids.

Who was doing this? Who was trying to destroy her life? For the first time, she seriously considered that she, instead of Stephen, was the real object of this whole campaign. But why?

She pushed emotions away and forced her mind to be analytical. She hefted the FedEx and realized it wasn't bulky enough to hold a videotape. She parted the cardboard flaps and peered inside. An audiotape?

She took a tissue from her purse and gingerly removed the tape. There was no label—no identifying marks of any kind. She stared at it, puzzled. Nicolas claimed to have received an audiotape. Was this a replica?

Dome light aglow, she located the tape player in the Pontiac dashboard. She popped the tape inside, pressed play, and switched off the light. Static in the background, then Stephen's voice clear and recognizable.

"Put in "Hotel California." I've got a special treat for you today, baby."

Background noise—street traffic—melded with his, "Voila!"

"What? We're gonna smoke pot and pretend we're surly teenie-boppers?"

Sitting in the Pontiac, concealed in shadows cast by the corner streetlight, Catherine knew when this tape was made. It was the first time Stephen had taken her to the beach property—the only time she'd been there, until the day of his murder.

She heard the *flick, flick* of a lighter and felt embarrassed knowing what was coming; knowing George Hallison—and probably Nicolas—had been privy to such an intimate encounter.

In the Pontiac, parked a block from George Hallison's penthouse, audio cued the visuals in Catherine's memory.

It had been one of the last warm, blue days of Indian summer. The Mercedes's soft leather seat embraced her. The beach landscape flashed like an out-of-sync movie projector. Sun warmed her hair; wind through the open sunroof ruffled it. Saltwater mingled with the scent of Stephen's aftershave.

For a minute or two there was only the Eagles singing "Desperado" and an occasional fit of coughing as her lungs rebelled. She remembered thinking she'd never been crazy about grass, but maybe it would be different with Stephen. Everything else certainly was. Then she heard, "That's all you get. I want you highly sensitized and receptive, not unconscious. We're about to have a very unique experience."

Stephen's hand slid under her skirt. Fingers trailed up her thigh, electrified the bare flesh above the tops of her stockings. "Ohhh," she moaned. "I am definitely stoned."

She burst into a fit of giggles as she watched a puppy cartwheel over itself as it loped down the beach.

"Yep," Stephen said. "You're stoned."

They turned off the highway, followed a gravel trail through a secured wrought-iron gate, and stopped at the crest of a grassy knoll. A tall dune sheltered them on the left; the Pacific Ocean stretched into forever on the right. No other person or vehicle was in sight. "What is this place?" she asked.

"Property my family owns." He changed the CD. "We're going to expand your horizons, and this is the perfect place to do it." He kissed her slowly. She was consumed by the desire to crawl atop him, feel him slide inside her. She reached for his zipper.

"Nope." He took her hand and grinned with boyish enthusiasm. "Today, we're going to do a little fantasy. A mind fuck."

A smile played at her lips. "Your cock's really big, sweetcheeks, but no matter where you stick it, it'll never reach my mind." She laughed until she choked.

When she stopped giggling, he said, "It's like a wet dream... except you're awake."

"Can't we just *do* it?" she whined. "I really want you bad."

"You're going to have to concentrate."

"I can concentrate." Defensive.

"Good. Because we're going to do this until you come."

He reclined her seat until she was lying almost flat. "Close your eyes and follow the sound of my voice."

"I'm not into this guided meditation shtick. Can't we just take off our clothes?" She started giggling again.

"Next time, you only get two hits. Close your eyes and be still. Or I'm going to go walk the beach and leave you here to entertain yourself." Stephen's hand slid inside her blouse. Fingers tweaked her nipple and cancelled all desire for comedy.

Stephen shifted closer, kissed her cheek, lightly brushed her lips. Fingertips trailed her throat, across her silk blouse, lightly teasing her breasts. Nipples stiffened. His mouth teased upward from the hollow of her throat, tickling her jawbone. He kissed her, tongue probing. Drums and bass from the Eagles's "King of Hollywood" accompanied his hypnotic voice.

"I picked you up at the office on a gorgeous sunny day just like today. We drove down the coast to spend the night in Carmel. Smoked a joint in the car. You're very excited because we're going to have a little sexual adventure. You don't yet know what it is, but because we're far from home, you're feeling very uninhibited. Very free. You want to try things you wouldn't normally do."

The music pulsed rhythmically. Stephen stroked her hair; fingers tickled her earlobe.

"We check into the hotel and you want to make love. I touch your breasts..." fingers through silk. "...And I stroke your thighs." Skirt slid upward. "But I won't make love to you. I tell you I'm in total control and that I want you so aroused you'll be on the verge of orgasm all evening."

Stephen caressed her arms, lightly brushed her breasts.

"You with me so far, Cat?"

"Um hmmmm."

Insistent bass filled the car.

"You brought a short, black dress—high neck and long sleeves. Very elegant. Very sexy. I tell you to put it on with a skimpy black lace bra and garter belt and black stockings. No panties. Feel the silky stockings as they slide up your legs..." Hand grazed her ankle, moving slowly up her calf to her thigh. "...Soft dress against your skin as I zip the back. Put on black suede heels and walk across the room. You're very beautiful... and you're highly aroused.

"We take a few hits, leave the room and go to dinner. As we walk to the restaurant, you're very conscious of your bare pussy under your tight skirt."

Silk skirt swished, tickling thighs. Stephen's hand gently parted her knees. Her pulse quickened.

"We go to an intimate little restaurant adjacent to the hotel. Men watch as you walk by. They know you're hot—you can see it in their eyes.

"While we eat, I keep my hand under your skirt." Fingertips circled her left knee, trailed up her inner thigh. She moaned. Felt her panties moisten.

"We finish dinner and go into the bar where there's a small dance floor. There's one empty stool beside a very handsome, well-dressed man. He's there by himself and I noticed him watching you all during dinner. I guide you to the barstool. I stand between you and this man. We order drinks and I begin kissing you..."

His tongue probed her eager mouth.

"He can see my hand up your dress... stroking the inside of your thigh."

Actions mimicked words. She could barely breathe.

"I've pushed your skirt up so he can see your black garters... your bare pussy. Feel the air on your sweet, wet cunt. You know he's watching you... and you are hot.

"He leaves the bar and heads to the men's room. I follow. He's standing at the urinal. His dick is so hard, he can't pee. He says, 'That is some sexy woman you're with.'

"I ask if he'd like to fuck you while I watch. He's surprised; but he's very interested. I tell him you'll go along if he seduces you.

"He comes back and tells you I had to make a phone call. He pulls his stool close. Facing you. One knee between your legs."

Hand parted her knees.

"He tells you his name is David... he says you're the most exciting woman he's ever met."

The provocative beat of "Those Shoes" began in the background as Stephen continued.

"He asks you to dance. The music stimulates you even more. You are completely uninhibited... and you are highly aroused. You desperately want to feel his hard cock moving inside you. He pulls you close, puts his hands on your ass. Your hips sway back and forth...

your arms around his neck... you rub your pussy against his rock-hard erection."

Stephen's hand pressed her pubic bone.

"Do you feel him, Cat?"

Catherine's breath was ragged. She moaned.

"That's right, sweet baby. He feels soooo good. I'm back at the bar—you see me watching you. That excites you even more. He's holding you tight against him and he whispers he has a suite upstairs. He wants to take you up there and fuck you. His prick is making you so hot you're on the verge of orgasm. Feel it, sweet baby?"

"Touch me," Catherine said.

"You're wet to your knees. You come to me, put your arms around me, kiss me deep and long. You say, 'Let's go to David's room.'"

"The three of us get in the elevator and David starts kissing you. He puts his hand between your legs and presses hard. He sticks two fingers inside your cunt and your hips begin a slow thrust. I move up tight behind you and you can feel my hard dick against your ass. Feel it, Cat?"

The music reverberated in the enclosed space, creating its own intensity. Catherine's legs were spread. She was breathing hard. Stephen's fingers teased her thighs, her breasts, and the hollow of her throat.

"We get to his room and David backs you against the wall. He pulls your skirt over your hips. You unzip his pants and rub his rigid cock between your legs. You're ready to come. Feel it?"

Stephen's fingers were like raw electricity as they traced her inner thighs. So close. So close.

"I watch you as I take off my clothes. My own dick is so hard I can barely get my shorts over it. I kiss you as I unzip your dress while David takes off his own clothes. You beg me to put my cock inside you; but I tell you to wait for David. That we're both going to fuck you.

"Step out of your shoes. I'm behind you, pulling your dress off your shoulders. Feel it slide down your hips? I kiss the back of your neck. David kneels in front of you. He puts his mouth between your legs. Feel it, Cat. Feel his tongue on your clit."

"Touch me," Catherine moaned, hips gyrating slowly.

"Now he stands up and slides his cock inside you while I hold you from behind. Feel his huge prick fill you? Taking his time... moving in... moving out."

"Pleeease. Put your fingers inside me, Stephen."

"Feel it in your mind, Cat. I know you can feel him. Moving. Lifting you off the floor."

She laid her hand between her legs; Stephen grabbed her wrist.

"See it in your imagination... feel him fucking you, sweet baby. You're close. You're so close. We want you to come, Cat. We both want you to come. Again and again. We've got all night with you. Think what we're going to do to you. All night, sweet baby. We're going to be with you all night."

Her breath caught, she moaned. Stephen pressed his hand between her legs. She squeezed with her thighs and rocked her hips in extended release.

The tape reversed with a click, snapped Catherine back to real-time in the Pontiac. She ran fingers through hair. Listened to the white noise that was Side B.

Catherine ejected the tape, cataloged a roil of emotions. Arousal... embarrassment... rage.

Who was this creep who had followed her with hidden cameras and microphones, perpetrating a privacy rape that couldn't have been more complete if she'd stuffed a speculum and a web-cam up her twat? And what about Hallison and Nicolas! What were they thinking? Were they thinking at all? Did they believe she'd tired of being the guardian of privacy and reinvented herself into an amateur porn star? Fools!

How could she ever again have uninhibited sex without wondering if she were inadvertently starring in someone's unauthorized recording? The whole point of her involvement with Stephen had been to get past her self-conscious feelings of inadequacy. Feelings born with Rusty—husband number one, king of the sixty-second erection, who'd convinced an eighteen-year-old Catherine she "wasn't doing it right" when she moved and made noise—and nurtured by Nicolas with his casually cold comments about her "undesirable body" ...her "slutty enthusiasm" ...She'd never wanted to feel that vulnerable again.

She scrubbed her fingertips across her forehead.

Forget it. Not going there. No matter what she'd learned about Stephen, he had been good for her. He'd tutored her like a pro at an exclusive golf club. And with him, she'd grown to like the game. She wasn't going to let some pervert—or a judgmental George Hallison—take that away from her.

Move on. She had a job to do.

Why had she suddenly become the target of Stephen's murderer? She would almost welcome a blackmail note, some instructions for re-purchasing her privacy. But, no, this was personal. Someone was out to bring her down.

She wasn't going to let him.

At ten P.M., Catherine pulled up to the valet at Garibaldi's restaurant on Presidio. Through the front window, she saw Wilson inside, waiting at the bar, an imposing presence in black blazer over black turtleneck and black slacks.

"How's Garbo?" Catherine asked wistfully when she reached his side. She really missed her dog.

He slid off his stool; offered it to her. "Did a beach run today. She's cool," Wilson said. "Inspector O'Malley?"

"She won't answer her phone," Catherine responded as the host seated them at a window table. "I drove by her house a few minutes ago. All the lights were on in the caretaker's unit, but O'Malley's place was completely dark. There's a Volvo in the driveway. Probably belongs to her brother."

"Got bad news," Wilson said.

Catherine held her breath.

"Hung at the beach tonight. Rapped with some of the regulars. Cops put out the buzz that they're looking for a missing murder weapon. They're gonna roll a thousand big ones for it."

"A reward?" She panicked. "Did you counter?"

"Took liberties with two thousand of your George Washingtons. Everybody's looking for Sick Dick. Not just the usual beach crowd. Downtown street dudes, even some losers who usually hang in Marin. Everybody wants to play show-me-the-money."

Catherine ran her fingers through her hair, knowing time was running out.

The sunshine car—Joel's yellow VW—pulled up to the valet. Joel tossed his keys, took two hurried drags on a cigarette, dropped it in the gutter, ground it with his toe, and dashed into the restaurant.

"Sorry I'm late," Joel said. "Tati gave me unmitigated poo-poo because I wouldn't bring her to see her Auntie Catherine and her Unca Wilson." He turned to the waiter. They had a three-minute conversation about the Pinots-by-the-glass before he finally selected one.

"How was it with Hallison?" Wilson asked. "I told Joel about the pump-jockey from the gas station."

"Yeah, and I want to see those pictures you're showing around town," Joel said. "Whom are you asking about?"

Wilson pulled the photos from a leather satchel and handed them to Joel. He studied them while Catherine told them about the receipts Hallison had produced; about the alleged angel's club meeting in Mountainview followed by dinner with the geriatric uncle. Tomorrow she would try to verify his alibi. And she told them about the audio-tape.

"It may be a duplicate of the one Nicolas received," she said.

"Was it triple X-rated?" Joel's eyes were wide, his whisper conspiratorial. "Did Hallison listen to it? What does he think of you after hearing—"

"Are we conducting a murder investigation or writing a gossip column?"

"Ummm." Joel rolled his eyes. Went back to the stack of photos, shuffled to the one of Rina Gold. He stared and tsk-tsked. "This woman is a monument to the wonders of plastic surgery."

"She's been cut?" Wilson asked.

"Oh, boy child, look how tight those tits are." He held up the photo and flicked his fingers at the deep vee of cleavage. "If she jumped up and down, they'd pull her face off."

Joel shuffled to the photo of Buzz Benson. "This FedEx envelope thing really bothers me," he said. "I've been giving it a lot of thought and—you know, someone really has it in for you, Catherine. And that someone obviously has access to ETC's mail room, so I've been thinking... what do you think about Sam?"

"Pious Sam? Are you kidding—that guy was raised on prunes and proverbs. He wouldn't do the crime because he wouldn't want to do the Hail Marys."

"No, really. Think about this. He could have seen you leaving with Stephen—or heard you on the phone with him and gotten suspicious. He has the means to hire a private dick that could wire your apartment. That's opportunity. And if you go to jail and get ejected from ETC, it's like he wins the lottery. That's motive."

"I'm not going to be ejected from ETC–I *am* ETC. And Sam–as greedy and manipulative as he may be–did not follow me to the beach, shoot Stephen three times, and frame me for murder just so he could take control of my company."

"Okay. Then maybe he tried to blackmail Stephen into doing something to oust you and Stephen said no and then Sam decided he had to knock off Stephen so you wouldn't find out." He raised both hands and both eyebrows. "I'm just saying..."

"And why did he send the tape to George Hallison?"

"To embarrass the hell out of you."

"Have you ever thought about writing for daytime TV?"

"I'm just bringing something to your attention that I think is worth considering. But, fine. If you're going to be testy and condescending, I'll just drop it."

"I didn't mean to be testy," she apologized.

"Well, no offense, kitten," he stage-whispered in a confidential tone, "but you act like someone who's thong got lost up her butt about six weeks ago."

She sighed in resignation. No doubt he was right.

The waiter interrupted to take their food order.

"So, girlfriend, are you thinking you're going to see Hallison when this is over–socially, I mean?"

"What is it with you? Have you got the Liz Smith gene?" She changed the subject. "I went to Stephen's apartment this afternoon."

She told them about the safe, about the footprint in the carpet, about there being nothing of note in the darkroom. She was about to relate her end-of-day visit with Ahn Mai when her cell phone rang. She scowled. She'd changed cell phones again just yesterday and very few people had the new number.

Laura's cheery voice chirped, "Hi, sweetie. I'm on my way home from a fundraiser and I've remembered some things that might be helpful to you. Where are you?"

After a brief exchange, Catherine flipped her phone shut and said, "Laura Tyler Jackson is coming here. She has some information about Stephen."

"I never trust a person who finds it necessary to use three names," Joel snipped. "Is Tyler her middle name, or does she have another name that is so poufy she's embarrassed to use it? Like Estelle. Or Dorinda." He shook his head. "Tyler Jackson. I mean, it's not even a hyphenated married name that she invented because she didn't want to give up her identity and become known as her husband's appendage like that thing some women go through. And what is she going to do if she *does* marry that power-monger politico that she's got her sights set on and her hooks sunk into—change her name to Laura Estelle Dorinda Tyler Jackson-Admire? She'll sound like one of those Spanish nobility types who are so proud of having trackable paternity they feel obliged to include every ancestral name shift of the past two hundred years."

"Whoa, dude! You need a cigarette break?"

"Why does she have to come here? I just don't like her."

"You don't even know her."

"Yes! I do!" Joel shook out his napkin and dabbed his lips. "We hated each other when her agency developed the ETC promotional campaign last fall. Remember? Her ego is as vast as the wide-open plains of George W's brain cavity. She always wore those short, tight little skirts and low-cut blouses with push-up bras, like some Marilyn Monroe throwback. And she carries a *six thousand dollar* Hermes handbag." He tsk-tsked. "Gauche and completely tasteless." He slathered butter on a hunk of sourdough. "Personally, I think she's about as deep as the milk in Tati's cereal bowl."

"You're jealous," Wilson grinned. "You're a Laura-Tyler-Jackson wannabe."

"Joel, she's my friend. She counseled me through my divorce. She spent hours listening to me process the trauma of my life. She was sensitive and caring. And supportive."

"And she got a half-million dollar ad campaign from your company. How much does that work out to by the hour for relationship counseling? About a hundred times more than a shrink would have charged to listen to you download your issues about that sartorially splendid eunuch whose mission in life was to corrupt your hard drive and disable your logic algorithms."

"Joel." He was giving her a headache.

"I'm just saying..."

Catherine turned to Wilson. "I don't want Laura to know we found Stephen's apartment."

"See! I'm not the only one who doesn't trust her," Joel interjected through a mouthful of bread.

"It's not about trusting her: it's about implicating you. I don't want anyone to know you hacked into bank records, and I don't want anyone to know that O'Malley presented herself as an active-duty homicide inspector in order to confiscate the key from the cleaning lady. The fewer people who share that knowledge, the better."

Catherine rose from her chair as Laura breezed through the door. "Hi, honey."

Wilson stood, said hello. Joel gave her a syrupy smile. Laura remembered them—especially Joel—from the ETC ad campaign project.

Laura shrugged out of her mink; she loaded it and her handbag on a vacant chair.

"Nice purse," Joel said. "Loehmann's?"

Laura gave him a condescending smile. "It's a Kelly."

"Is it?" he asked innocently. "With so many knock-offs on the market, it's just so hard to be sure."

Laura turned to Catherine. "How did your little Peeping Tom project go?" she asked.

The waiter delivered food—a platter of grilled vegetables for Wilson, steaming pasta with cream sauce for Joel, Caesar salad for Catherine. Laura ordered a glass of champagne. When the waiter departed, Catherine explained Laura had dropped by her place on the first night Catherine observed the apartments across the street.

"Were you able to offer any tips on voyeurism?" Joel asked.

Catherine tossed him a dirty glare and turned to Laura. "I've narrowed it down to one apartment." Catherine described the stack of green LED lights. "There's no name on the mailbox and I've knocked on the door several times, but no one answered. I'm going to check it out... later."

"Let me do it for you." Laura stiffened her spine and looked determined. "If the killer is there, he would recognize you. I'm an unknown."

"No, no," Catherine shook her head.

"What if the killer answers, Catherine? I insist on going with you."

"Good idea." Joel pointed a fork of dripping noodles. "You could distract him with a search of his jockeys while Catherine looks for the incriminating goods."

"I don't expect a face-to-face encounter—no one has been there at night. I think he may have gone underground since the murder."

"You're going at night?" Laura's eyes widen. "You're not going to break into this stalker's apartment?"

"That would be illegal," Catherine responded innocently.

"Hey, toots," Joel talked around a mouthful of hot pasta. "This is a murder investigation. Ya gotta do what ya gotta do."

Catherine held up both hands. "Let's stop talking about this."

"But, Catherine. You could go to jail."

"Duh-uh," Joel said.

"Tell me about Stephen," Catherine said.

"Fine. Shut me out." Laura raised her eyebrows, cleared her throat, sipped water, and changed gears. "Here's what I came to tell you. A couple of years ago, George Hallison supposedly hired a private investigator who took photos of Stephen... things like Stephen going into a hotel, kissing some friend... pretty innocuous stuff, I seem to recall. That was before Hallison left the company—before his wife got sick." She shrugged and sipped her wine.

"What did he do with the photos?" Catherine asked, feeling a new wave of depression.

"Well, there was this big rivalry between them and Hallison said Stephen's behavior was a liability to SFFS, that he was unfit to run the company."

"And because of that you think George Hallison killed Stephen?"

Laura shrugged again. "He certainly had a lot to gain... You should review Stephen's calendar—his phone records. Maybe he and Hallison had been in contact."

"Interesting you should mention that," Catherine said and reached for her bag. "I have Stephen's cell records. Joel? Can you trace these tomorrow?"

"Sure," he said. "But I can't get to them until after noon—unless I cancel several meetings. Want me to have someone else check them out?"

"Let me help," Laura said. "You just want to know who Stephen called, right? We have a system at the office that we use to reconcile our phone bills. I can run these through that system—identify every number on here."

"I can have them done by eleven," Joel said.

Laura wrapped her fingers around the exposed end of the envelope. "I feel bad that I didn't help you sooner, Catherine. I'm trying to make up for that but you keep shutting me out."

"Probably by ten, ten-fifteen," Joel said.

"I'm beginning to think you don't trust me," Laura said.

"Of course I do." Catherine handed the records to Laura.

"I'll have the info by nine," Laura said and cast a slow glance at Joel. "What else?"

"Catherine's checking out all of Stephen's family... his friends." Joel said to Laura. "You seem to have known Stephen a long time."

"Casually, yes."

"So where were you on Monday night when he was killed?"

Catherine ground her jaw, but Laura smiled demurely.

"I'm accustomed to you gay boys envying me, Joel, honey, but, as wonderful as you may think I am, even I couldn't shoot someone from thirty-five thousand feet. I was on a four o'clock flight to the Big Apple." She rose, smiled mischievously at Joel, and stage-whispered, "I've had about enough of you..."

She gave Catherine a quick kiss on the cheek, shrugged into her mink, and said, "I'll call you in the morning."

When Laura was gone, Catherine glared at Joel. "You went after her like conventioneers at a free buffet."

"I can't believe you're taking her at her word. If anyone could pull a trigger three times and worry about nothing more than chipping her nail polish on the safety release, it would be your little Miss three-names."

Catherine pressed her mouth in a firm line and made a decision. "Laura checked in at American Airlines at two forty-five on Monday for a three forty flight to New York. The gate agent verified her ID; the boarding pass scanner confirmed she boarded the airplane, and the actual passenger-count matched expectations. She occupied seat 3B; the airplane left gate 46 at 4:05 P.M." She studied Joel quietly. "Any other questions?"

"Wow. Did you hack those records all by yourself?"

"I called a friend who's a VP at American. He checked it out for me. Legally."

"Fine. Whatever you say." Joel flipped his hand dismissively. "But she still irritates me."

Wilson grinned at Joel. "You covet the purse, dude."

Joel wadded his linen napkin and threw it at Wilson.

"Forget about it," Wilson said. "Doesn't go with your new sunshine car."

Catherine dressed in sweats, black from head to toe, and mentally psyched herself to break into the apartment across the street. She pulled on black leather gloves; shoved latex ones into a pocket. She drew the line at wearing a ski mask. She left her building through a back utility door; let herself out a locked back gate. She crossed Filbert Street and walked to the corner. It was 12:15. Most windows were dark.

Wilson and Joel had argued she shouldn't do this alone. She'd declined their offers to accompany; the group-participation crime spree was over.

Hyde Street was jammed with parked vehicles—a good thing. Gave her more cover. It was quiet—virtually no traffic; only the continuous buzz of the underground cables that pulled the Hyde Street cable cars up and down the hills.

Catherine did a slow reconnaissance of the neighborhood before heading toward the alley that was her ultimate destination. A dryer vent spewed Snuggle fabric softener; a Duraflame log smelled of smoldering wax and sawdust. Two men and a woman stood a block away at the entrance to the curvy part of Lombard Street. Camera flashed. Ubiquitous twenty-four-hour tourists.

No one was else around. She approached the alley; sensed movement to the left, but before she could react, strong arms wrapped her torso and a bare palm clamped her mouth. Dogs at the other end of the alley began to bark and growl. She struggled but was forcibly dragged behind a brick wall.

A soft whisper against her ear. "Lay dead, Ms. C. There's a man and two Rottweilers down there."

She twitched against Wilson's grasp; he immediately released his hold.

"Jesus Christ," she hissed, lightheaded with adrenaline overload.

He shrugged and looked sheepish. "Rottweilers can bring down a water buffalo."

"Can't remember the last time I was mistaken for one of those," Catherine whispered. "I told you not to come here."

Wilson made a show of checking his watch in the glow of the streetlight. Tapped the dial twice. "Not on your payroll. Don't take your orders."

Catherine ground her jaw. Now what? Abort the mission? She needed to get inside that apartment. Needed to do it now. Before Hiller came to haul her away.

"Wilson. You're fucking up my plan."

"Just going to back you up. Make sure you don't get yourself into some mess."

"You're not carrying a gun, are you?" she asked.

"Packing heat gets you burned but good."

The dogs barked again. They were further away. No more time to argue with Wilson.

They picked stealthily through the alley. Silently opened the back gate of the building she'd labeled "number four" of the three-story, four-building complex.

"You gonna jimmy the lock?"

"That's my plan," she said and hefted a small canvas tool bag. She didn't feel confident with locks that were seriously designed to keep people out; she was best with the kinds found on bathroom doors and file cabinets.

"If that crack goes bust?"

"The top half of the door is glass. I have a hammer."

They headed up three flights of stairs to a six-by-six landing. Weathered wood creaked under foot.

Catherine exchanged black leather gloves for pliable latex ones and noted Wilson's bare hands. "I didn't bring an extra pair," she said.

"Bad scene if we get busted."

"Not as bad as a trail of fingerprints."

"I'm here to get your back. Not gonna lay no dabs."

She fished out a pinlight and examined the locks. Doorknob keyhole; one deadbolt. She fanned the beam across the kitchen window to the right. It sat crooked in its frame. Catherine quickly removed the screen, wedged a screwdriver under the edge, and heaved. One pop, like a book dropped to a wood floor, and she shoved the window up enough to reach the dead bolt. She quickly discovered her arms were too short to grab the doorknob.

Wilson tapped her on the shoulder, flashed a white hanky, and reached inside. The door opened six inches; stopped at the end of a chain. He flipped it free and moved out of her way. She closed the window and replaced the screen; whispered to Wilson to stay put.

Inside, standing motionless, all senses tuned into the dark environment, she pushed the door shut, but not to the point of latching.

A vapor light in the alley cast patches of fluorescence and shadow across the ceiling; a stove light illuminated a corner of the small kitchen. A clock ticked in another room. The place had the chemical smell of six-week-old lemons; the human smell of bed sheets that hadn't been intimate with soap and water for at least six months.

She flicked on the pinlight and tiptoed to the door that lead to the rest of the apartment. The clock ticked louder. She took one step into the hall. Behind her, bright light flared and held. A voice from the alley below yelled, "Police! Don't move!"

Catherine whirled. Lunged toward the back door. Spotlights raked a glare across the ceiling, lighting the kitchen so bright Catherine could read the dials on the stove. The night vibrated with static from a police radio. A male voice, still a couple of flights below, commanded, "Hands in full view. Back away from the door."

Wilson stared stoically through the window. He raised his hands to ear-height; held eye contact with Catherine. Imperceptibly shook his head no.

"Turn around," the voice commanded. Boots thundered up the wooden stairs.

"Go," Wilson mouthed.

Adrenaline clogged Catherine's heart, nausea curled her stomach. Her first instinct was to fling herself out the door—insist Wilson was an innocent bystander, demand they release him. But that wouldn't save either of them.

"Turn around. Now!" The voice was impatient. From the yard, a dog barked and growled.

Wilson slowly pivoted to face his pursuers; Catherine's brain kicked into gear. She dropped to her knees and dragged her tool bag off the counter. Gently she pushed the door until the catch clicked shut and snaked her arm up the frame where the door chain hung at window height. Careful to keep her sleeve out of range of the intrusive spotlights, she flicked the chain into place and secured the deadbolt. The police would have nothing on Wilson. He was just some unlucky guy standing on a wooden stoop.

She reached for the button lock—might as well make the case airtight. The lock mechanism slid free of the knob. Shocked, she fumbled it through her fingers, caught it before it hit the floor. Holy shit! A beam from the spotlight pierced the half-inch hole in the doorknob. Catherine ducked. She shoved the locking mechanism back into the knob, hands shaking uncontrollably; heart pounding to the point of blackout.

"Hands on top of your head." The voice was closer now—half a flight from the landing.

Catherine slung the tool bag over her shoulder and duck-walked across the kitchen floor and into the short hallway. She closed the door that separated the kitchen from the rest of the unit, flipped on the pinlight, and scanned the dark corridor. Dull light glowed through uncurtained windows at the front of the apartment. She darted in that direction, but on her way, checked out a bedroom—mattress on bare floor, striped sheets in a tumble, closet empty—and the bathroom—wadded towel on sink, barren medicine chest.

The living room was unfurnished except for a scarred wooden desk pulled under the eastern-most window and a wooden chair shoved into the knee space. An eighteen-inch metal tripod was mounted on the end of the desk closest to the window. A small black box filled the space between the three legs; on top was a black gadget that looked like a remote control. It was pointed outward. Aimed at Catherine's apartment windows.

Bingo!

She quickly inspected the black box. Two cables exited the back, dropped off the desktop, and snaked across the bare wooden floor to the bookshelves at the backside of the room. There, shoved against the wall, were the LED-flashing electronics. She brandished the pinlight and counted three VCRs, a large and a small television, a reel-to-reel tape deck, and some other pieces she couldn't readily identify.

Voices reverberated from the back landing. Footfalls pounded.

Catherine raked the shelves and the cabinets below looking for videotapes. Found none.

She flashed her light back to the tripod and its small black box. Wanted to classify the device. She leaned close and passed the beam around the base, looking for an identifier. Glare bounced off a metal tag. *Personal Security Systems.*

"Buzz Benson, you shit-on-a-stick," she whispered.

The back door rattled. Fists banged.

Catherine panned the rest of the room. Walls were bare, no other furniture, no place to hide things. Returned to the desk. It had one drawer. Inside, a single manila file folder lay flat. She scooped it out, shoved it inside her black leather jacket. It was cold against her tee shirt.

She careened to the front door. Peered through the peephole. Nothing moved within the fisheye view. She pressed ear to door, listening for sounds of occupancy. Nothing. She stepped into the carpeted hallway, heart thrumming loudly, and pulled the locked door closed with a click.

As she hit the landing below, she heard a female voice from the building's entry hall.

"Go back inside, ma'am. We're just checking on one of your neighbors."

Catherine whirled. Scampered back up, taking the stairs two at a time.

At the front of the building, twelve feet from the peeper's apartment door, a window opened onto a fire escape. She flipped the lock, raised the glass, and slid onto the ladder inset. She closed the window and turned to get her bearings. A delivery truck clanked across the cable car tracks on Hyde Street as a terrifying sense of vertigo almost convinced her to go back inside and take her chances with the cops. Red and blue lights strobed from the top of a police car double-parked directly below.

She looked right. Looked left. Building four ended twenty feet away, and there was nothing but empty space beyond its roofline. A small lip of roof, to the right, traversed the four almost-connected buildings. She climbed onto the ledge and leaned against the roof tiles, gritty pebbles denting her palms through the latex gloves. She inched away from the exit window, made the curve, and stepped across the three-inch gap that delineated the end of building four, the beginning of building three.

She dropped into the well of the fire-ladder as a car roared up Hyde. She crouched in the shadows of the eave, peered down, and saw a brown unmarked plant skid-tracks as it cornered onto Filbert. Brakes screeched, the engine died. Her heart pounded faster. The car was exactly like the one Inspector Hiller drove. A police radio squawked. A man leapt from the car and took off around the corner heading, presumably, for the alley where Wilson was entrapped.

Catherine climbed quickly over the railing and started down two flights of fire escape. Ragged bolts bit the flesh of her palms. One latex glove snagged and unfurled across her hand. She ripped it off her fingers and crammed it into her pocket.

At the bottom of the second-floor ladder, she stepped onto a two-by-three platform. The ladder to the street was the accordioned, extendable kind. She figured that puppy would squeal like a stuck hog.

A cable car bell clanged on Hyde Street. Catherine swung through the metal space, clutching the floor of the landing until she was fully extended. She dropped the six feet to the sidewalk, landing with knees bent, the toolbag whacking her right shin. She dashed up the street, cable car clanging closer. If it were northbound, it would be of no help to her.

She hit Hyde; saw the cable car rolling south, mere yards from the intersection. Over her shoulder, the front door to building four swung open and a uniformed officer stepped onto the sidewalk. She felt his eyes on her. He took off at a dead run, calling frantically into his radio.

Catherine darted across the street just behind the cable car, hooked a quick left, and caught it from the backside. She didn't think the cop had seen her. She crouched on the outer ledge of the car, surprising three tourists and the cable car operator.

"Hey, lady," he scolded. "You're not supposed to get on when the trolley is in motion."

"I won't do it again. Scout's honor," she said as the car clanked down the hill. She watched over her shoulder. The cops didn't reappear. She climbed through to the other side of the car; jumped off as the car cruised through the intersection of Hyde and Union.

"Hey!" the cable car conductor yelled.

She race-walked up Union Street, barely hesitated, then sprinted toward her sleeping building and up seven flights of stairs.

She was breathless by the time she reached her apartment but heard the elevator chugging as she stepped inside her door. She began stripping in the hall and was nude by the time she reached the bedroom. She flung the leather jacket on a hook inside the closet and buried the black sweats in the bottom of the hamper. She grabbed her tool bag and the manila folder that she'd lifted from the desk drawer and raced to her office. She stashed both in the safe.

Someone banged on her door. She snatched a nightgown from the dresser drawer. Flung back her comforter and wallowed for two seconds between the sheets as the banging intensified. She tousled her hair then grabbed a robe on her way to the door.

She didn't bother to look through the peephole; just popped the chain and opened wide. It did her heart good that Inspector Hiller looked surprised.

"Your dog didn't bark," he noted.

"You get promoted to Animal Control?"

Chapter Eight: Tuesday

At 7:15, Catherine bolted awake, immediately alert to the fact that the anticipated phone call from Wilson hadn't yet terminated her fitful three-and-a-half hour nap.

She dialed Jordan Lawrence's number; the answering service put her on hold. She slipped from under warm covers, slid feet into sheepskin slippers, and trekked to her office, cell phone pressed to her ear. She picked up a handful of darts and nailed a few bull's-eyes as she mentally reviewed last night's debacle.

Hiller had been chagrined to find her home.

"You're breathing as if you just ran a mile, Ms. Calabretta," he said.

"I was in the throes of orgasm, Inspector."

He deadpanned. "A solo performance, I presume."

"Like I always say, if you can hoof-it at your own pace, why ride a slow, smelly bus that may break down before it gets you to the top of the hill."

He gave her a dead expression. "Are you going to ask me in?"

"Have you got an invitation signed by a judge?"

He smirked. "Next visit." He asked where she'd been that evening; she declined to answer. He told her they'd arrested one of her employees, Wilson James Ramsey, at an apartment building across the street. Hiller said he was disappointed they hadn't caught her with Wilson.

She feigned shock about Wilson, commended Hiller on his sensitivity and thanked him for letting her know one of her key personnel required legal representation. She closed the door and immediately phoned Jordan Lawrence—woke him yet again. He assured her Wilson would be released before sunrise. Apparently he'd misrepresented the facts.

Just as she impaled the last "s" in the *Don't Mess with Texas* bumper sticker, Lawrence came on the line, voice miffed.

"Hiller's a horse's ass," he said by way of explanation. "He's taking his sweet time signing the Authorization to Release. They've got no case. Wilson had a note in his pocket that said to meet 'J'—just an initial—at midnight, at the address where they picked him up."

Catherine already knew about the note. Under pressure at two A.M., Joel had confessed Wilson's plan to keep himself and Catherine out of trouble in the event they got caught on the property.

"Claims to have been there to meet some guy he knows casually. He wasn't wearing gloves, yet they didn't find his fingerprints anywhere. The door was bolted and chained, but the locking mechanism had been pounded out of the doorknob—cops found it on the kitchen floor. They suggested Wilson was in the process of committing an unlawful entry, but there's no evidence to support that."

"How did that lock thing get broken?"

"Don't know. Apparently it actually does look like someone tried to break in."

"I've been thinking about this Jordan. How did the cops... ummm, find Wilson there? I mean, it sounds as if he had just arrived... to see this 'J' person, and they showed up immediately. What alerted them he was there?"

"They got an anonymous tip."

"Anonymous? So it couldn't have been one of the neighbors or 911 would have ID'd the caller."

"Definitely anonymous."

Jordan signed off leaving Catherine to consider other anonymous tips: the one that had alerted police to Stephen's dead body in his car at the beach; the one that had alerted Hiller to Catherine's meetings with O'Malley. In spite of last night's precautions, someone had apparently followed her. She shivered in the warm room. Who was this ubiquitous stalker?

The phone interrupted her thoughts. Joel anxiously asked about Wilson. Catherine downloaded her conversation with Lawrence and finally asked about Garbo, who Joel had retrieved from Wilson's apartment at around three A.M.

"She's in little girl heaven," Joel said, affection warming his voice, "and my favorite toddler thinks the fairies blessed her with a special delivery. Garbo slept beside Tati's bed. She was there when Tati woke up this morning, and they haven't been separated by more than six inches since the day began—except when I took Garbo to the park for twenty minutes, which Tati allowed me to do only because I explained if Garbo didn't go outside and poop, she would get a big yucky tummy ache."

Catherine smiled. "Can you keep her for a day or two?"

"Oh, the problem isn't the *keeping* her. John is going to take her for a run this afternoon and I had to promise Tati that Garbo would ride to school with us in the Sunshine car and that Garbo would be waiting in the Sunshine car when I come to pick her up from school. So *keeping* the dog isn't the problem; however, sending her home will completely disrupt the tranquility of my domestic life."

They commiserated for a moment. Catherine wrapped up with, "I'll be on cell. Call if you hear from Wilson before I do."

Catherine headed for the shower, turned the tap to hot, stripped, and was about to step through the shower door when her cell phone rang. It was Aida.

"Robert Bradley is trying to reach you," Aida said. "He says it's urgent. I told him I would try to track you down and have you get back to him ASAP."

"Okay," Catherine said, puzzling why her favorite director on the ETC board would be so anxious to talk to her. A lump of anxiety grew in her throat as she took Robert Bradley's number and told Aida she would check in later in the day.

She covered her face with both hands and massaged her temples and her brow. Foreboding swelled like open seas in a heavy gale.

She paced in her living room as she dialed Robert Bradley's number.

He answered on the second ring. As ETC's first board member, he and Catherine shared a very collegial relationship; but today, his tone was tense. Reserved.

"I feel personally obligated to tell you Sam has called a special Board meeting for this morning."

She hesitated, caught off guard. "I wasn't aware of that." Anger pulsed her temples.

"Right. You weren't. It's a closed meeting, the purpose of which is to strip you of your position within the firm."

A gut-punch. "*Strip me?* He can't do that." Her knees trembled. She dropped to the sofa. "ETC is *mine*." Her voice was raw. "I started it—it's grown because of my professional reputation. Who does he think he is? He has no right."

"Ah, but Catherine, he does."

Silence. She wanted to throw up. Wanted to scream.

"This publicity... your legal problems... have begun to impact ETC."

"According to Sam, no doubt." She failed at keeping anger out of her voice.

"But it makes sense, Catherine. He's got escalating client issues. He thinks the Board must intervene or ETC's viability will be irreparably damaged."

Catherine forced bile down her throat. "Do you think that's true, Robert?"

He hesitated. "I think we have to listen to the facts as Sam presents them this morning. It's the job of the Board—"

"Then you have to listen to my facts, too," she interrupted as she leapt to her feet. "When is the meeting? I'll put everything aside. I'll be there."

"Catherine, don't make me sorry I called you."

"I won't make you sorry! Just tell me when and where to show up."

"You're not invited, Catherine."

Anger kicked in. "How could I not be invited to a meeting that directly impacts my company? The company I built from nothing!"

"Catherine," he spoke sharply. "This is a business. This isn't your child."

"Oh, you're wrong there, Robert. ETC *is* my child—and I won't give it up. I'll fight this so hard Rocky will seem like a baby doll in a pink frilly dress." Her voice broke.

His tone softened. "I know how important this is to you. That's why I called."

The line was quiet. Catherine struggled for composure. When she was able to speak she asked, "What can I do, Robert?" Defeat overwhelmed her. Did he hear it in her voice?

"Sit tight. Do what you can to clean up the... personal problems."

She could only nod.

"I don't know what action the Board will take today, Catherine, but remember: Nothing is permanent. You'll see your way clear of this. I believe in you."

She nodded again, squeaked out a goodbye. She ran for the shower, yanked the water to hot, and sobbed in the stinging spray.

She didn't remember washing, but her hair and skin felt clean; and by the time she stepped out of the shower she was in a rage.

Fingers trembled as she dialed Sam's number. Gloria, his assistant, was guarded. She claimed to be uncertain of Sam's whereabouts. Catherine disconnected and called Aida; told her to find Sam and tell him to call immediately.

She paced while she dressed. Four minutes later her cell phone rang.

"You motherfucker!" she screamed. "You will not get away with this."

Silence.

"Hello?" She pulled the phone away from her ear, checked the green "on" light. Put the phone back.

"Mom?"

"Oh, Chloe." She sighed. Exhaustion and depression sucked at minute physical reserves.

"What's going on, Mom?" Alarmed.

"Nothing, honey."

"Nothing, bullshit!"

"Don't use foul language—"

"Then don't blow smoke up my skirt. Who were you expecting on the phone? Who's the 'motherfucker?'"

How to get out of this one? A version of the truth was, no doubt, the best avenue. "Sam. He and I are having a little difference of opinion over something he's trying to do with the business."

"Yeah, Mom, it sounds like just a little something—like maybe he wants to store the paperclips in the left-hand drawer instead of the right-hand one? When are you going to stop treating me like a six-year-old dweeb? I'm an adult. I'm your daughter. You think I know nothing about you—about your business?

"It's not that."

"Can the bullshit, Mom. I called to tell you I've got a flight out of Paris tomorrow morning. I'm coming home and I'm going to help you through whatever mess you're in, whether you want my help or not."

"Chloe, please—" Catherine's voice broke.

"Skip the Mary Poppins pitch. It's Air France flight seventeen and it arrives at three-twelve. Pick me up at the airport or don't; either way I'll see you tomorrow afternoon."

As the line clicked dead, Catherine fought the urge to dissolve into tears.

Catherine left her apartment at quarter to nine, picked up the beige Chevrolet on a side street, and drove to Stephen's apartment to keep an appointment with a locksmith. On the way she called Aida. Nothing from Sam. Aida said he hadn't come to the office; no one had heard from him.

"The chickenshit," she murmured as she dialed Maureen O'Malley. Still no answer.

Next, she called Joel's cell phone, asked if he'd heard from Wilson.

"It's only been an hour, honey. Your hotshot attorney said they might keep him the full twenty-four, right? You gotta let this go. He's a big boy. They can't do anything to him."

She clicked off and dialed into phonemail. There was one message, time-stamped 6:45 A.M. She immediately recognized George Hallison's voice.

"I'm running for asshole of the year. With your vote and my own, I'm fairly assured I'll win the election. I was hoping you'd host my victory party." Hesitation. "Sometime during my sleepless night I wrestled my bruised ego to the ground and acknowledged I haven't done much to give you the benefit of the doubt—like why *would* you send me that tape?" A sigh. Change of tone. "I'm in back-to-back meetings all day. Should be home by seven. I dusted off an '82 Lynch Bages that I'd like to decant for you. Can we at least clear the air?"

An '82 Lynch Bages, eh? Be still my boot-stompin' heart. Nothing wrong with clean air... but... She'd have to think about this one.

She spied a parking spot on Lake Street then quickly made her way to Stephen's apartment. Inside was dark. Quiet. Yesterday, she'd used a broom from the pantry to rake the plush, rust carpet to a smooth plane. With the pinlight from her satchel, she checked the dark pile. A jumble of footprints. She stood in place, studied them. They led to and from the entry.

She straddled them, her own western-style work boots edging the baseboards, and rocked side-to-side down the hall, squatting to examine the pattern from the perimeter of the living room. The intruder had walked to the bookshelves, continued down the hall toward the bedroom.

A generic videotape jacket lay on top of the television. She crossed the room, careful to dodge the shoe indentations. She popped the tape from the player. Recognized the brand.

Footprints down the hallway led into the walk-in closet, to the safe. Did the intruder have access to it?

Moving back down the hall, she looked for a clean shoe print and found one in front of the coffee table. She knelt quickly and traced the outline onto two stapled-together pages from her satchel. She duplicated the tread pattern as best she could, thinking how last night's illegal tour of the stalker-apartment had unearthed recording equipment from Buzz Benson's favorite spy shop; and a manila folder containing half-a-dozen photos of Stephen chatting up Buzz's wife. Two photos were shot in front of the Benson house; the other four outside two different Marin hotels. That mode six really compelling reasons to try to connect this tread print to Buzz Benson's shoe wardrobe.

The intercom brrrupped just as she finished the drawing. She confirmed it was the locksmith and buzzed him in the front door.

Joel had referred this guy. Catherine had fabricated a story about apartment sitting for a friend and having lost the code to the safe and needing to get some papers from it and could he come take a look and perhaps unlock it for her.

The round, balding guy who greeted her at the door looked as though he'd been around the block enough times to have seen it all. Wasn't very chatty, which suited Catherine fine; but, as he studied the safe, he asked again how she'd come to lose the combination.

She reprised her lie, resisting the temptation to embellish the original version.

In less than two minutes he gave her the bad news: "The only way you're going to get into this safe is to contact the manufacturer, prove ownership, and have them send out a locksmith who will use special X-ray equipment to read the settings and give you access."

He stressed the part about "proving ownership" four times.

Ninety dollars later he was gone and Catherine was grinding her jaw, arms crossed over her chest, giving him five minutes to clear the neighborhood. Rather than just tap her foot impatiently, she decided to check out the new video. She powered up the television and VCR, shoved the tape into the deck, and pressed play. Fifteen seconds confirmed this was simply a new version of a very old subject. She ejected the tape and stormed out of the apartment, heading for a costume shop on Clement Street. Frustrated. Irritated. She was itching for hand-to-hand combat.

Catherine braked at a red light and heard the cell phone ringing.

"How was your illegal entry thing last night?" Laura's voice came through the headset.

"You have a vivid imagination, sweetie. I spent the night snuggled in my bed dreaming of sugar plum fairies."

"Sounds like a video-feed from your friend Joel," she cooed.

"I promise not to tell him you said so. Find anything useful in the phone record search?"

"If there's something here, it doesn't leap out at me," Laura said. "There are seven numbers I can't ID the owners of. I thought you could take a look—see if you have a different read. Want me to fax it or email it?"

"Any calls to or from Buzz Benson?" Catherine asked as she turned onto Clement Street.

"Not for a number that's listed to him. Why? Is he your guy?"

"Maybe. Would you fax it to my home office, please?"

"Did you find something during that thing you didn't do last night that makes you suspect Buzz?"

"If I'd done that thing, I might have found something. Plus I've got a shoe print I'd like to connect to him."

"Shoe print? From the murder scene?"

"No. From carpet pile." Oops. Catherine realized she hadn't told Laura about finding Stephen's apartment.

"Something you found last night?"

Having sneaked behind Laura's back to verify her alibi, that she was on an airplane at the time Stephen was killed, Catherine felt guilty for not trusting her friend. Wasn't that, after all, the basis of friendship? Trust?

Time to come clean. She gave an overview without revealing the bank records's hack that had opened this avenue.

"You *found* Stephen's apartment?" Surprise. "And you didn't *tell* me?"

Hurt feelings: another hurdle to learn to navigate if Catherine intended to cultivate relationships with girlfriends. One of those emotion-things Catherine had previously avoided by limiting her primary relationships to hardware and software.

She squirmed. "I've been so busy... I guess I forgot to mention it."

"Forgot? Did you also forget to tell me you found Stephen's dark-room? His 'insurance' cache? Photos? Videos? Other things as trivial as our friendship?"

"Okay, Laura, I'm sorry. The truth is, I've already implicated too many innocent people by involving them in things they shouldn't have done and sharing knowledge they would be better off not having. I simply didn't want to do the same to you."

"I see." Voice stiff. "So you've involved *other* friends, I assume those are the innocent people you refer to, but were so considerate of my well being that you kept me at arms length in this critical chapter of your life? Well, I appreciate your concern and sensitivity, Catherine."

"Laura, please don't take this personally. Please, let's just put it aside until I wake up from this nightmare. Then I can concentrate on being a better friend."

A moment of silence. Catherine continued. "We'll go to dinner—just the two of us. We haven't done that in a long time."

"Well." Conciliatory. "I'm one to talk. Putting my relationship with Ben before our friendship when this thing first started. I should probably still be apologizing to you."

Catherine sighed. Relieved.

"So, do tell. Where is this apartment? What did you find?"

Catherine relayed details. The location. The darkroom with its blank photo stock, paper shredder, and cans of chemicals. The safe with the lock she couldn't open. She even recounted the exercise with the locksmith. Then described the two homemade videos.

"Someone has access. Maybe the murderer stole Stephen's keys after he killed him."

Silence.

"Hello?"

"You're sure the shoe prints aren't Stephen's?" Laura asked.

Catherine described her carpet-raking experiment.

"Very clever, honey." Breath blown into *whew*. "Who would have guessed you'd be so good at this detective thing."

"Hey, it's easy. Like picking fly shit out of black pepper."

A chuckle—forced, maybe, but back to being friends. "Now what?"

"Buzz Benson. I want to confirm he had both motive and opportunity," she responded as she parallel-parked half a block from the costume shop. "Gotta go. I'll try to call you tonight."

"Wait! I'm offering to help—is that the best we can do?" Laura said, exasperation creeping back. "Can't we at least meet later today?"

"Laura, honey, my schedule's about as predictable as the lottery numbers."

Laura argued; Catherine acquiesced. They tentatively agreed to meet at Garibaldi's at nine. Catherine hoped she wouldn't be in jail by then.

Catherine maintained a slow, thoughtful stride as she entered Marin General Hospital. Her rented black robe swayed around rented rubber-soled Rockports. Rented fake Bible clutched in left hand; crucifix hanging from long, silver neck-chain.

People noticed her. Some looked away quickly as if they'd just remembered they were two-years past due for confession; others smiled and said, "Hello, Sister."

She responded with a simple "Hello," and her best imitation of a beatific smile. A "bless you my child," routine would probably get her busted.

At Reception she asked for Angelina Benson's room number. The woman behind the desk—a "senior volunteer" in a pink-and-white-striped uniform—tediously two-fingered a computer keyboard, then nervously raked blue hair.

"Ohhh, I'm so sorry, Sister, so very, very sorry. But Mrs. Benson isn't receiving visitors."

Catherine placed both hands on the white formica countertop and leaned in to create a sense of heavenly intimacy as she attempted to get a look at the monitor.

"I can't give out her room number." Eyes darted heavenward, perhaps seeking absolution from the Almighty for the rejection she'd just bestowed on one of His chosen.

"I understand, my child," Catherine said benevolently. "I wouldn't ask you to do anything to compromise your duties to the hospital... or to Mrs. Benson."

Catherine turned away, right hand nudging a plexiglas business card caddy displayed on the counter. It toppled backward, contents spilling into the alarmed senior's lap and onto the floor.

"Now it's my turn to apologize," Catherine clucked as she rounded the desk and stooped by the septuagenarian's chair, scanning the monitor while they gathered the splay of cards.

On the sixth floor, the critical-patient unit where Angelina Benson was housed, Catherine cruised past the nurse's station, glad for the staffing shortage created by managed care: There was no one around to question her.

She found Angelina's door and pushed quietly through. Shades were drawn, the room in shadows. It smelled of antiseptic. To Catherine's relief, Angelina was alone.

The hospital bed folded Angelina's body upright. Her face was bandaged, her jaw wired. Left arm, in a blue canvas sling, lay heavily on her frail chest. Rage filled Catherine's own healthy torso and nurtured a desire to see Buzz Benson locked in a cellblock with a dozen hands-on abusers of his own genre.

No matter what O'Malley had counseled—"take advantage when she's down... do anything to get the info you need"—some actions were simply too reprehensible. Taking advantage of this child-woman would be one of them.

Angelina gasped shallowly, eyelids fluttering. Catherine was embarrassed by her own audacity; there was good reason for the moratorium on visitors. She turned to leave.

As she reached for the door handle, a small, breathy voice said, "Don't go."

Catherine turned.

"I need to pray..." Angelina said. Her tone carried sad resignation, like someone whose loving God has stopped smiling down on her.

"...For someone else."

Catherine removed the phony headgear and skirted Angelina's bed. She laid her hand lightly on the woman's pale arm. Tears pricked her own eyelids.

"I'm sorry, Angelina," she whispered. "It's only me. Catherine Calabretta."

The woman struggled for a full breath. "Then my prayer... has been answered."

Both eyes were purple-green, circumscribed with yellow, the color of the Texas sky in tornado weather. Angelina Benson looked like a survivor of Mother Nature's most violent windstorm.

She spoke haltingly. Softly. Breath gurgling in her chest. Monitors blipped tracking her vital signs. Catherine didn't have the medical knowledge to decipher them, but no display altered its rhythm in any drastic manner.

"He wasn't at home on Monday night," Angelina said with great effort. Paused to inhale. "I lied."

With the fervor of a penitent giving last confession, Angelina insisted on telling her story.

She didn't know where Buzz had been on the night Stephen was murdered—didn't know if he had, in fact, killed his rival. But two weeks earlier, he'd hung the picture of Catherine and Stephen on his home-office bulletin board. He'd ranted to Angelina that none of Forsster's women meant anything to him—they were all just his whores; and then he beat the crap out of Angelina. A couple of nights later, she caught Buzz watching a video. She blushed when she said, "It was you... with Stephen."

She told Catherine that Buzz had stashed the film and some still shots in a file cabinet. "I'll tell you how... to get into my house. You can get them." She laboriously recited the alarm code, explained the locking mechanism. Catherine was familiar with the type.

"I need to go when Buzz won't be there," Catherine said. "When's the best time?"

"Anytime. Buzz is in jail. I pressed charges." Tears settled in the corners of her eyes; defiance curled the corners of her mouth.

"Good for you, Angelina. Good for you."

Angelina reached up, touched her uninjured hand to Catherine's sleeve. "They told me. You saved... my life." Her eyes were dull with pain. She reached for the intravenous narcotics pump. Pressed the switch and closed her eyes.

Catherine stood a moment in the shadows, watching lines of pain soften on Angelina's face. She exited the hospital and crossed the parking lot already ripping off the nun's costume. It was inhibiting her ability to plan her next crime.

Catherine tossed the black garments into the backseat, rolled down her jeans cuffs, changed Rockports for work boots, and climbed into the Chevrolet. She called Jordan Lawrence to verify that Buzz Benson was indeed in jail and asked him to find out when Benson had been picked up. Lawrence hung up with the promise to check it out and call back.

She drove toward the Benson's home in Kentwood. If Benson had been picked up prior to four o'clock yesterday—when she'd raked smooth the carpet in Stephen's crash pad—he couldn't have left fresh footprints in the pile. She was just turning onto Benson's street when her cell phone rang.

"He was in lock-up in San Rafael. Picked up outside a Kentwood restaurant last night at seven-eighteen; appeared before a judge and posted bail about twenty minutes ago."

Shit.

She did a quick drive-by and found no reason to abandon her plan; she parked two doors away, slid latex gloves on her hands, and rummaged in the trunk until she found the tire iron. On the front porch, she stared boldly into the eye of the security camera, punched the doorbell, and hooked the tire iron over the camera's metal support strut. To the first twelve notes of "Dixie," she yanked until the unit dangled from its black cables; then she whacked it five times in her best imitation of Barry Bonds. The lens shattered; the metal casing caved.

The doorknob housed a combination-lock system. It responded readily to the numbers Catherine entered. A red light on the foyer alarm panel blinked a warning. She called, "Hello?" as she tapped in the alarm code. The light switched to green.

She dashed up the stairs, mentally allotting herself five minutes inside the house.

First to Benson's office. Angelina had said the video was in the bottom drawer of a file cabinet in the closet. Catherine leaned the tire iron against the side of the desk, snatched a key from the center drawer, and slid back the closet door. She popped the lock and squatted in front of the file cabinet. Immediately she found the tape. It was lying on top of a Colt .45.

Catherine stared at the gun. It was similar to Stephen's, minus his initials. She lifted it carefully. Smelled gun oil. She ejected the magazine. Fully loaded. She shoved the clip into the front pocket of her jeans. She checked the safety then tucked the gun into her waistband. She rifled through three plain brown envelopes until she found the snapshots; then slammed the drawer closed.

From the other end of the house, the garage door grated open. Her heart leapt in panic. She locked the file cabinet, removed the key, and tossed it into the desk drawer.

Down the hall, she zipped into the master suite and threw open closet doors until she found Buzz's wardrobe. She glanced at the floor, then grabbed one Nike, one Reebok and one hiking boot. Let the fucker ponder that. She shoved the door on the run and sprinted back down the corridor.

She took the stairs two at a time and heard the garage door grate close as she hit the foyer tile. She quietly opened the front door and waited until she heard a door open somewhere in the back part of the house. She scooted out the front and closed the door gently. She cut across the lawn, squeezed through a slit in the privacy hedge, and hit the sidewalk at a full-out run. She was in the car when she realized she'd left the tire iron leaning against Benson's antique desk.

"This is Robert Bradley," the voicemail message started. "I promised to call to give you the news—and I'll start by saying it won't be what you want to hear, Catherine. The Board met with Sam. He presented a very compelling case. In the end the Board voted to give Sam total control of ETC."

She dropped the phone into her lap. Pulled the Chevrolet to the curb. Fought nausea.

They couldn't have. They can't do this to ETC. They can't do this to me.

She picked up the phone with trembling hands. The system was asking what she wanted to do with the message—delete it, replay it, save it. None of those options were satisfactory: she wanted Robert to take it back, to tell her it was a bad joke. She pressed replay. Sat through the beginning again, confirming what she'd heard the first time.

"The vote was four to two."

He paused. She rolled her chin low to her chest, trying to release the knots that convulsed her shoulders.

"It's a temporary move, Catherine—one we can revisit at any time... and I will personally push to do that when you get your... private affairs straightened out. Please understand, this was not a joyful occasion. For any of us. We've believed in you from the beginning. But we must act responsibly to ensure the health of ETC.

"I'm sorry to be the one to deliver this news, Catherine, but we all agreed it would probably be best if you heard it from me." His tone changed to irritation. "Besides which, Sam is golfing with two members of the Board. Poor Sam needs to work off the stress of the morning. The other three members and I declined to join his little soiree."

He sighed through the receiver.

"I'm really sorry, Catherine. Please call me if you want to discuss this." He left his pager number.

There were two more messages in her queue but she couldn't listen to them. Not now. She turned off the phone and laid it on the seat. She crossed her arms over the top of the steering wheel and rested her forehead against them.

How had her life come to this? In one short week, she had lost so much. ETC. Chloe's confidence in her. Her personal privacy. She didn't even bother to add George Hallison to the list. So many important things... gone. She had lost them all.

Four of the Board had voted against her. She had to accept the significance of that. They now considered her a menace to ETC—not the architect of its future success.

She sat for five minutes, trying to reduce the roil in her mind, trying to wade through the emotions and devise some course of action. But she just felt numb; she had no clue what to do.

Finally, she dialed back into the voicemail system. Laura was trying to reach her. So was Joel.

"What the hell is going on, Catherine?" His voice screeched on the recording. "I got this message from Sam saying there are significant changes in the management structure of ETC and he wants me to join him for lunch at his golf club so he can get me on board before he announces the changes at a special staff meeting tomorrow morning. Excuse me? What does he mean, 'changes?'" Joel's voice tottered on the edge of hysteria. "If he wants to advise me of changes, he can tell my boss—that would be *you*—and my boss can pass them on to me. And what is this special meeting he's scheduled for tomorrow? Everyone's asking if they have to go. We don't understand what's going on and we don't know what to do. I need some information here, but I am not debasing myself by showing up at that WASPy, homophobic, *non-smoking,* frat house he calls a golf club just so he can deign to tell me! Catherine, call me! We need you!"

Rage exploded; her vision blurred and her pulse drummed in her ears. That impotent, furtive, underhanded coward! Convening a secret Board meeting to strip her of her power–and not even having the balls to tell her directly when he'd done the dirty deed. And then, going after her loyal staff.

She wrenched the ignition key and slammed the accelerator to the floor, laying six feet of rubber on the quiet Marin street. She was so angry her mind couldn't congeal a plan; but she knew where she was going.

The beige Chevrolet screeched to a stop between Lincolns, Mercedes, and Jaguars. Catherine stomped toward the stone clubhouse, past two liveried Rolls Royces and a group of frolicking bronze mermaids spewing water into a reflecting pool.

She'd been here only once before, when Sam invited her to lunch after he'd golfed with a potential ETC client. The restaurant was on the backside of the pro shop. Catherine marched through, tossing a Texas cheerleader smile at the testosterone-pumped caddy who lounged beside a display of plaid Calloway golf pants. He evaluated her like a bouncer at a New York nightclub. His slow grin confirmed she'd been certified USDA prime. She hip-swung past the fortress-style wooden door, into the cavernous restaurant.

"How y'all doin'?" She greeted the maitre 'd–made it syrupy. "I'm joining the Princeton party."

He head-to-toed her, pursed lips a silent condemnation of her ecru cableknit sweater, jeans, and brown western boots. He asked her name as he scanned a handwritten list on the podium.

"Joelle Hodges," she lied.

"Ms. Hodges..." He made eye contact. "I think we were expecting *Mister* Hodges." He raised his eyebrows. She fought the urge to grab the ends of his black bowtie and yank them until they cut off his air supply.

"You probably have me listed as 'Joel' instead of 'Joelle.'" She flicked her wrist dismissively. "Happens all the time. I hate to keep Mr. Princeton and the other princes waiting. Where are they?"

He gave her a haughty stare. "I read *BusinessWeek*, Ms. Calabretta. And the *Chronicle*." He paused to make sure it sank in. "Let me check to see if Mr. Princeton would like you to join his table..."

She ground her jaw and shrugged as any silly, presumptuous little woman should.

The commander summoned a manservant type and whispered in his ear. The lieutenant looked Catherine up and down. She gave him her most seductive eye batting. He nodded once and turned away, headed toward the stone mantle that framed a lazy, decorative fire on the far side of the room.

The restaurant was host to some sixty diners—at least three of them female. Elk, wild boar, and grizzly bear "trophies" decorated the stone wall above the mantle. Cigar smoke hung like smog over Los Angeles. The bar displayed bottle after fine bottle of imported, rare cognacs and brandies. To the right, tables flanked floor-to-ceiling windows that overlooked the city's most exclusive par four first hole. Manicured green lawn, flawless blue sky.

Catherine projected the waiter's course, spotted the crown of Sam's head above the back of a massive leather club chair. Fred Bailey and Donovan Haynes, Sam's two Ivy League cohorts, flanked Sam. A fourth chair—Joel's—sat empty between Fred and Donovan.

Anger rumbled through Catherine like steam in an over-fueled boiler. She took one step toward the table, but was dragged back by a strong hand on her arm.

She whirled, grabbed a mechanical pencil off the host stand, and stabbed the top of the fist that curled her biceps. The maitre 'd yowled quietly, undoubtedly conscious of annoying his royal clientele, and lurched backward, watching blood droplets seep around the metal that impaled his flesh.

Catherine dove across the room as the manservant leaned to deliver his message to Sam. Catherine grabbed a steak knife—it looked like a baby Bowie—from a four-inch slab of blood-rare carnage that steamed on a serving table.

Sam turned toward the entrance. Indignation, then fear, flickered when they made eye contact. He gritted his teeth, threw back his shoulders, and rose to his full five-eleven.

"Catherine, you weren't invited—"

She didn't even slow her pace as she planted her knee in his groin. He doubled over and backslid into the waiting embrace of the soft leather chair.

The manservant grabbed her arm. She flicked the knife a half inch from the tip of his nose. His eyes crossed as he took in the blade. He raised both hands to ear level and backed away.

Catherine whirled to Sam and locked her fingers in his thin, orange hair. She jerked his head back and laid the knife blade against his throat.

His eyes were cloudy with pain. She wedged her knee between his thighs; his hands dropped protectively to his lap and he mewled. Catherine stabilized his head against the corner of the leather chair-back. She didn't want to slit his throat accidentally. She lowered her lips to his right ear and spoke soothingly. Mother to child.

"This is like an old cowboy movie, Sam. Like when the black hat makes his move to take over the town and the white hat straps down his holster... and you know he's willing to die."

"The Board..." he rasped.

She yanked his hair, asked agreeably. "Did you ever know a black hat who didn't have a couple of drooling stooges backing him up?"

A tremor passed through him. "You'll be paid... for your shares," he whimpered.

"Oh, Sam, tsk, tsk. Is that what they taught you in B-school? Gallantly write a little check as token reparation for your rape and pillage?" She jerked his head; he made a strangling noise deep in his throat. "I came here to tell you one thing, Sam Princeton, and one thing only: You have lost this war. There will be no meeting of *my* employees tomorrow morning and there will be no transfer of power. You go back to your little office, pack up your little pencil box—your smiling family photos—and *get the fuck out.*" She yanked his hair again. "Now, before I go... Is there any part of that ultimatum I need to translate into Whartonese?"

"This wasn't personal, Catherine. It's a business decis—"

"Oh, very B-school, Sam. Here's a little lesson I learned at Cowlick U: Every. Fucking. Thing. In *life*. Is *personal.*"

"It's only a temporary move, Catherine..."

She couldn't believe it. The fucker wasn't going to give up! She jerked his head. A droplet of blood rolled to the end of the knife. She stared. Horrified.

"Catherine!" The familiar voice came from behind.

She glanced over her shoulder. Joel shoved across the room; Wilson followed, golf club positioned to tee off on someone's neck.

"Sweetie, it's okay," Joel singsonged. "Just let the dickhead go— he's not worth this. You're not a murderer. Don't convince all these nice gentlemen in this room that you are."

Joel put his hand on her arm. She slowly released Sam's hair and stepped back.

Sam looked as if he'd just shit his pants in relief. He put his hand to his throat. A speck of blood congealed on his fingers. Rosy indignation fueled his glare.

"I have witnesses, Catherine. You're a loose cannon. You'll never again have control of ETC." He looked triumphant.

She lunged for him. Wilson grabbed from behind, lifting her off the ground.

Joel put both hands on his hips and strutted his neck forward. "You can have ETC, you ass-wipe, because I resign—and Wilson resigns— and everyone on project team Alpha resigns, too. Nobody with any talent is going to work for a scum-sucker like you." Joel turned then minced toward the door. "So there!" he said over his shoulder.

Catherine relaxed her struggle. Wilson planted her feet on the floor as she observed, for the first time, uncertainty creep across the faces of the two Board members. She addressed them.

"Did Sam neglect to mention that I handpicked all 274 members of the tech team? And that I don't believe in non-competes—meaning they're all free agents?" She leaned over and tapped the table with her index finger, eyes moving from one face to the other. "You go forward with this stupid plan and the only other Board you'll ever serve on is the one for Sam's lemonade stand."

She straightened and started for the door, Wilson close behind.

"You bitch!" Sam squealed. "You'll be sorry!"

The steak knife was still in her hand. She whirled. Sidestepped Wilson. She brought the knife up quickly and let it fly. Its trajectory wasn't what she expected—didn't track as smoothly as her darts. The knife sliced to the left, impaled Sam's wingback chair two inches from his ear—a full four inches from her intended target.

Sam's mouth dropped; his eyes saucered. He blanched the color of new-fallen snow.

"Why, Sam, I bet your backside just puckered so tight it bit two pounds of stuffing out of the seat of your fancy club chair." Catherine winked and turned to the door.

Joel had stopped four feet away. A contingent of busboys and waiters were poised alongside like sharks teasing a bleeding swimmer. The maitre 'd blocked the exit.

Catherine pushed past Joel and provocatively hip-swung her way toward the tuxedoed man. "You gotta ask yourself, honey," she said when they were face-to-face, "is this the hill you want to die on?" She spoke so quietly only he could hear.

He smirked. "You and your army of one," he nodded toward Wilson, "are going to take us down?"

"Nooo," she cooed sweetly. "But I know a whole flock of bored litigators who'd love to take a swing at this bastion of snobbery and intolerance."

He ground his jaw, eyes saying he was uncertain of climbing into the ring to engage in legal sparring. He stepped aside. Joel plowed through the massive gate that divided the restaurant from the pro shop, Catherine and Wilson close behind. Wilson's midnight blue Porsche was illegally parked in the passenger-loading zone.

"You ride, Ms. C," Wilson said and faced off two busboys who were having a hard time giving up the game.

"Give me your keys," Joel said to Catherine.

She dragged them from her pocket and pointed. "Beige Chevrolet."

Catherine climbed into the passenger seat of the Porsche. Joel loped off across the parking lot. Wilson walked backwards to his side of the car, keeping the busboys at bay by his sheer physical presence. He slid behind the wheel, waited for Joel to get ahead, then laid rubber to the street.

Catherine leaned against the seatback and covered her eyes with her hands. Exhaustion and depression settled on her like granite.

"How could they do this?" Wilson murmured. "I mean... nobody is more important to ETC than you are."

"Yeah, well," she drawled as she massaged her temple, "when you get to thinkin' you're a person of influence, just try orderin' somebody else's dog around."

"How'd you find me?" she asked Wilson as she borrowed his cell phone and punched in Jordan Lawrence's number.

"Joel. He marked his voicemail 'return receipt'—he got 411'd when you picked up the message. You didn't call. We figured some jive would be goin' down."

When she got Lawrence on the line, she told him she expected to have assault charges filed against her.

He was droll. "Who would have predicted that you'd become a full-time job, Catherine?"

She described exactly what she'd done; he told her what to expect. And, sure enough, within five minutes of Wilson having dropped her at the fake UPS van that was parked a block from her apartment, a black-and-white pulled into the passenger zone in front of her building. Two officers got out and went to the security telephone. She watched Mrs. Dorsett open the door and let them in.

While the cops were inside, Catherine sat concealed in the cargo area of the van, watching the street and examining the contents of the brown envelope she'd found in Benson's home office. Of the two photos, one looked like the shots sent to Stephen in the FedEx envelope, except this one hadn't been cropped to protect her identity. The other was an innocuous still-shot of Stephen and Catherine coming out of her apartment lobby. She couldn't imagine why that would be valuable to anyone.

Ten minutes later Catherine watched both cops exit her building. As they drove away she dialed Maureen O'Malley's number and headed west in the van. The phone rang unanswered, further fueling Catherine's determination to find out what was going on at O'Malley's Sunset District residence. She turned onto O'Malley's street and noted the gray Volvo station wagon parked in the driveway. She swung in behind it, dropped from the van, and marched to the door. She rang the buzzer but got no response from inside.

All of Maureen's curtains were drawn. Not so upstairs. Catherine jabbed the buzzer for the caretaker's unit.

Feet thudded on the stairs and the door whipped open.

"I know who you are," a stout, red-haired man shouted at her. "Because of you my sister is on her way to Ridgemont Center. She's been mentally unstable since her accident. You've—"

"Shut the fuck up, asshole!" Catherine screamed and lunged at the wrought-iron gate. "If you cared about your sister you wouldn't cage her. Treat her like a mindless animal."

"You're a criminal—"

"You don't believe in innocent until proven guilty? What kind of fucking lawyer are you?"

"One with enough connections to save my sister from a criminal like you."

Catherine grabbed the metal with both fists and rattled the gate. "Let me in. I want to talk to her."

He raised his hand; in it, a cell phone. "In my religion, suicide is a mortal sin."

"Open this fucking gate," Catherine raged, pounding the bars until her hands hurt.

He punched numbers on his cell phone. She heard only three beeps.

"You chickenshit! How can you claim to care about Maureen when you—"

"I have a trespasser on my property," he spoke angrily into the phone. "Can you send someone to remove her? She's driving a brown van, license plate..." he angled around her and read off the number before Catherine could block his view. He flipped the phone closed. "I'll have a restraining order in place and every cop in this city looking for you before sunrise."

"Get in line, fuckhead." She shoved her boots between the metal, planting her feet on the bottom rim of the gate, rocking back and forth, straining the hinges. "Maureen!" she yelled.

He reached his right hand toward his back pocket, came out with a flash of silver. He grabbed her hand through the wrought-iron cur-licues. Catherine jumped backward, yanked hard to free herself. He dangled handcuffs and grinned maliciously. He'd meant to lock her to the fence until the police arrived!

He flicked open the lock and started through. She raised her boot and kung-fu'd the wrought iron. He yowled, barely jerking fingers free of slamming metal.

"You bitch! You fucking cunt!"

She calmly held up her index finger. "Hey, Judas; that one's going to cost you about five hundred 'Hail Marys.'"

She turned and sprinted back to the van and peeled rubber in front of Maureen's house. She glanced back over her shoulder and saw a split in the curtain of the downstairs living room. Maureen's sad eyes haunted her as she drove toward her apartment.

The sun was setting, the sky turning hazy purple as Catherine slowly circled the block looking for a police presence anywhere in her neighborhood. She parked the van on a side street, grabbed the Benson cache, and entered her building through the garbage room door. She paused at the top of the utility stairs, listening to tenants coming home from work. Keys rattled, mailbox doors squeaked open and clanked shut. The staircase smelled of stale garbage and Lysol. She climbed quietly.

Inside her apartment she stood perfectly still, sensing the environment beyond, detecting no foreign smells, nothing out of place. She missed Garbo—wished the dog were there to greet her, wished they could go to the park and play with the ragged green tennis ball.

She moved through the dark rooms like a cat burglar. In the bedroom she changed to a black tee and sweatshirt, black jeans and black leather tennis shoes. In her office, she turned on the halogen desk lamp, retrieved the two different shoe prints she'd copied from the carpet in Stephen's apartment, and compared them to the shoes she'd swiped from Buzz's closet. She could tell before the official measurement they weren't going to match; Buzz's shoes were a good two inches shorter than the prints.

It couldn't have been that easy, she thought with a sigh.

She gathered all the things she'd collected during her investigation: Laura's faxed copy of Stephen's phone records and the calendar that offered no meaningful information. The ETC FedEx envelope containing the photos that had been sent to Stephen. O'Malley's confiscated copies of crime scene shots. Pictures she'd retrieved from the apartment across the street; Buzz Benson's Colt .45 as well as the bulletin board items from his home office. Four videotapes–two from Stephen's apartment, one from Buzz's file cabinet, and the one that had been left at her door. One audiotape inside an ETC FedEx envelope addressed to George Hallison. The keys to Stephen's apartment.

She spread it all on the desk, lowered herself to the leather chair, and stared at the collection, willing it to talk to her. She studied photos, back and forth, looking for anything she might have previously missed. She reviewed her top four suspects.

Buzz Benson—Catherine couldn't rule him out just because the shoe prints didn't match. He knew, or at least suspected, that Stephen had bedded his wife; and he'd made her pay. Did he do the same to Stephen?

And what about George Hallison? She reviewed the service station receipts. They provided a very convenient alibi. Was his "asshole of the year" confession a ploy? After all, he'd gained a lot from Stephen's death.

But then, so had Lili Forsster. She no longer had to suffer the humiliation of a philandering husband, while at the same time, she'd become financially set for life.

Rina Gold slept easier with her pedophilic fantasies.

All of them benefited from Stephen's death. Who else had benefited?

Catherine rose from her chair and grabbed a fistful of darts. In the distance, floodlights blinked to life at the foot of Coit Tower.

What about Sam Princeton? He'd finally conquered the throne he'd coveted for so long. He certainly had access to the ETC FedEx labels...

Catherine fired off three bull's-eyes.

Joel had been the first to point out that Sam had motive—and even opportunity. Sam lived in Seacliff, less than three miles from the beachfront property where Stephen was killed.

Catherine raked her hands through her hair. She was letting her emotions override logic. She *wanted* Sam to be guilty because, if nothing else, he'd turned out to be a prick.

She returned to the desk and began once more to review the various photos. She noticed a tiny mark on the right edge of one of the Stephen/Angelina Benson shots. There were similar marks at the right border of each. Her pulse quickened. She overlaid the shot of herself hiking the beach trail, Stephen following behind. Same blemish on the right border.

She yanked open her tool bag and dug out a magnifying glass. She held a photo under the halogen glare and studied it with a 400 percent magnification. Under the lens, the blotch looked like a tiny capital "H" laid on its side. Her hands trembled as she dropped the photo on the desk and grabbed another—of her and Stephen exiting her apartment building—the one she'd found in the envelope she'd pilfered from Buzz Benson's file cabinet. She raked the right border with the magnifying glass. Tiny fallen "H" visible at the edge.

"You fucker," she whispered. She dashed into the bedroom, grabbed a nightstand snapshot of Chloe—the one taken at the beach when she was thirteen years old. She loosened the ceramic frame on her way back to the office Then pulled the photo away from the glass and laid it on the desk, under the halogen glare. With trembling fingers, she positioned the magnifying glass over the photo. There it was. On the right border, a blight on the bright blue sky.

That's what Nicolas had called it. A blight. He'd accused Chloe of scratching the lens when she borrowed the camera to take pictures of her friends on their trip to Sea World. He'd kept the camera—taken all of their "family" photos with it to remind Catherine of the injustice he'd suffered at the hands of her teenage daughter.

At the time he called her attention to it, Catherine scoffed at its insignificance. "Nicolas, honey, it's about as big as the little end of nothing, whittled to a point. No one but you would have ever noticed it."

"That's how you spoil her, Catherine. Whatever she does is all right with you. She's damaged my personal property and you don't even care. Don't ever again ask me to loan her something that is mine."

Big huff; small provocation. A common event with her ex-husband.

Nicolas was childish and petty—passive-aggressive and prone to immature tantrums; but murder? He'd actually fainted when Chloe, at age nine, fell off a skateboard and split her lip, drooling blood down her chin. How could a weenie like Nicolas kill in cold blood?

Even though Maureen had suggested Catherine investigate him, she'd never seriously considered Nicolas a possibility. What did he have to gain by killing Stephen? And framing Catherine? If she were incarcerated, his alimony would be jeopardized. She couldn't imagine Nicolas endangering his cash flow.

She raised the magnifying glass, once more studying the undeniable pattern. Knew for certain Nicolas had followed her. Photographed her. Captured Stephen with Angelina Benson.

Again, why?

The phone startled her. Maureen O'Malley's name and number flashed on Catherine's caller ID screen. She snatched the receiver.

"Maureen! Are you?..."

"Hiller found the pistol," O'Malley rasped. "Your prints are on the clip. He's coming to arrest you."

Catherine mewled, dropped the phone as if it had delivered an electric shock. She scooped the evidence off her desk and threw it into her canvas tool bag. She tossed Benson's Colt .45 on top of it all and yanked at the zipper, trembling fingers almost defeating her. She grabbed up the van keys and stuffed the keys to Stephen's apartment into her jeans pocket as she ran to the living room window. Below, the headlights of returning commuters lighted the street.

Pulling on a navy windbreaker she raced back through the office, grabbed the tool bag, and slammed the fire escape window up. From the landing, she reached inside, grabbed the cord, and dropped the mini-blinds over the opening. Quickly she lowered the window and climbed the twelve rungs to the top. She ducked low and sprinted across the black roof to the front retaining wall. Eight stories down, Hiller's brown unmarked car whipped into the passenger zone. Two patrol cars—flashing lights, no sirens—accelerated around the corner. Catherine darted to the side of the building, hooked the toolbag's straps over one shoulder and pulled leather gloves from her jacket pocket. The fire ladder was dark except at two floors where lights glared through uncovered windows.

At the bottom, she dropped to the ground and slipped through the back gate, headed toward Leavenworth. Red and blue lights flashed through the intersection behind her. She unlocked the door to the brown van and climbed behind the wheel. Quickly she cranked the engine and pulled away. She knew the cops already had the license number, but the other cars were in the wrong direction—too risky with so many cruisers crawling the neighborhood.

She turned right at Chestnut, headed west toward Pacific Heights. Her heart raced. She needed to ditch the van and find new wheels. And she needed to do it fast.

Catherine parked two blocks from George Hallison's building and slipped past the night guard with a "Hello, Roger. He's expecting me," as Roger juggled three bags being handed off by the driver of a Waiters-On-Wheels delivery van.

Hallison was opening the door and portable phone in hand, as she stepped out of the elevator. Obviously she hadn't put anything over on Roger: He'd recognized her.

"Was it me... or the '82 Lynch Bages that got you here early?" Hallison asked and stepped aside.

"I'm in trouble. I need a car."

He closed the door and followed her into the living room. The Golden Gate Bridge glowed across the expanse of black sky.

"I thought I was your top suspect."

"Not any more. My ex-husband did it."

He looked surprised. "Why?"

"That's what I need to find out next. Will you loan me a car?"

"Who's after you?"

"Snow White and the Seven Dwarfs." She followed him to the kitchen.

"You want the Mercedes or the Ferrari?" He lifted two key rings off a hook.

"Nothing in your basic Honda? A Toyota, perhaps?"

"My getaway car is out on a bank heist."

"Mercedes. May I use your bathroom?" she asked as she headed down the hall toward the guest bath.

She flipped the light switch and closed the door. She unzipped her tool kit and stuck Buzz Benson's .45 into her waistband. Bullets were in her jeans pocket; clip in the gun to make it appear loaded. She pulled out her collection of evidence, wrapped it in a folded towel, and crammed the towel into the back of the linen closet. She flushed the toilet and headed back to the kitchen.

Hallison stepped from the pantry and closed the door. He laid the portable phone on the cabinet. Blue eyes held hers. He sauntered across the ash floor; backed her against the countertop, rested palms on her shoulders.

"Sure would like to stay and rest my horse," she twanged as she toyed with the car key that lay on the marble work island, "but I have to go."

"You bring out the best... and the worst in me." He combed a lock of hair from her cheek with gentle fingers.

"That's progress. I usually get credit for only the worst."

He pulled her close, strong arms a refuge. She returned the embrace, laid her cheek to his chest. She wanted to stay there for a very long time.

"You should come equipped with a warning label. 'Strap down your crash harness. Hold on for the ride.'"

He tilted her chin, mouth tender on hers. Hands roamed under her jacket. Chemical reaction seeped through her limbs. She flattened against him. He kissed her slowly. Deeply. The gun poked her hipbone.

He spoke with his lips brushing hers. "I hope your new appendage doesn't shoot off one of mine."

She shifted to relieve the angle of the pistol. "Don't worry..." she wrapped her hands behind his head, locked her fingers in his silky hair, and drawled. "...A bullet wouldn't even dent that titanium thang of yours." She grinned and kissed him again.

Nerve endings ignited. She wanted to take an hour—half an hour—feel this man's naked body blanket her, move inside her, make her believe the world would be okay. He pulled her tee shirt free of her jeans, warm hands caressed bare back, erection pressed her abdomen. She moaned softly. He unhooked her bra, one hand fondled bare breasts. Her breath quickened. She pressed her pelvis to him, felt him grow harder.

His mouth was hungry on hers. She pushed back enough to work his belt buckle. Had just freed it when a pounding on his front door jolted them.

She frantically shoved him away. "Are you expecting someone?"

"Yeah, but I thought we'd have more time." He stepped to the wall by the pantry door, pressed the intercom button.

"Yes?" he asked tersely.

"Mr. Hallison? Police."

Hiller!

"Open the door, please. We'd—"

Catherine lunged and shoved Hallison from the intercom. It went silent.

"You son of a bitch!" She screamed, flashing back to Hallison coming out of the pantry, phone in hand. "You ratted me out!"

"What? I didn't—You're running from the *police?*"

He started toward her; she grabbed the gun from her waistband. Aimed it at his chest.

The pounding intensified. "Mr. Hallison?" Hiller's voice was barely audible from the penthouse elevator lobby.

"If the cops have a warrant for you... Roger has a police scanner—he listens to it when—"

Catherine blocked his words, whirled about the kitchen, mind struggling to congeal a plan. She couldn't go out the front door; fire escape was out of the question. She snatched up her tool bag and dove past Hallison into the pantry. She slammed the door shut, but he shoved through as she ticked off his birthday password on the freight elevator keypad.

The motor whirred to life.

"Take the elevator to the basement," Hallison said. He pulled her to him and quickly kissed the top of her head. "Don't go out the main exit—go out the back, out the loading dock."

The doors parted. Catherine leapt inside the car, slammed the "B" button, fearing she was riding into a trap.

The elevator descended in slow motion. She stuffed the gun into her waistband, loose bra straps tugged at both arms. Mind reeling, heart beating at warp speed, she hooked hooks, tucked in her tee shirt, straightened her sweatshirt and jacket.

The cage settled. Doors parted. She stepped cautiously into a dark room she hoped would lead to the outside world. She smelled gasoline and motor oil. Voices echoed off concrete. A crack of light outlined a door. She pulled it open two inches. The room brightened. Navy coveralls hung on a hook beside two large push brooms. She lifted the work garment, stepped into the legs, and quickly zipped it over her clothes, ignoring the smell of dust and body odor. She grabbed a baseball cap off a hook and wadded her hair underneath.

Through the door, she bent in half and darted around a row of expensive cars, heading in the direction she thought the loading dock would be. She heard rustling and a thud; she crawled around a corner and saw a stooped man loading flattened cardboard boxes onto a pushcart. He picked up the last piece and balanced it on the pile. She crossed the distance in three quiet steps and pressed the gun to the nape of his neck.

"Agghh!" He jumped. Both hands reflexively sprang into the air. He froze.

"No noise," she said.

He rattled something in Spanish.

"Shhh!" She tapped him on the shoulder; he slowly turned his head. Dull black hair framed brown weathered skin and dark frightened eyes. She motioned him toward the elevator room she'd just vacated and said, "Stay!" She closed him in. She hoped he understood.

She wheeled the pushcart down the ramp toward an old pickup truck. The cargo bed had tall, rickety wooden sides that fenced a tidy stack of cardboard.

The cab light flicked on. Door slammed; light extinguished. Cigarette smoke wafted on cool night air. Catherine was careful to stay hidden behind the load of flattened boxes. The driver spoke casually in Spanish as he hefted a stack from the cart and shoved it into the truck bed, filing it neatly between bales. He turned for another load, saw Catherine... and her gun. Eyes went white in a lined walnut face. She put a finger to her lips, motioned for him to keep loading.

He didn't move. Rattled off words that included "*Mi padre.*"

Catherine understood he was asking about the old man. "*No habla Espanol,*" she said, followed by, "*Su padre okay.*" Said it three times, each more intensely; thought he got the drift.

"Let's go. *Vamoose!*" He balked. Red and blue lights flashed past the end of the alley. She cocked the gun; the communications problem disappeared.

Now what? She needed a car. She considered booting the driver and rumbling off in his rickety truck, but talk about a high-profile target. She directed him, by hand signals, back to her neighborhood. The Pontiac was parked two blocks from her apartment. A uniformed police officer directed traffic in front of her building. She instructed the Mexican driver to pull to the curb half a block from the Pontiac. She jumped from the truck, dropped her toolbag to the sidewalk, ripped off the jumpsuit, and shoved it through the passenger window. She pulled two twenties from her pocket, waved them at him, and said, "No police!"

She sprinted toward Green Street and the rented blue Pontiac. She reached up under the rear wheel well on the passenger side and located the hidden keys. In less than twenty seconds, she was behind the wheel.

Hiller had Stephen's gun; Catherine's fingerprints were on it. She was a fugitive on the run so she complied with all speed limits as she crossed the Golden Gate Bridge and headed up 101 to Tiburon. Nicolas was the key to this; she was going to pay him a little visit.

She still couldn't believe Nicolas had murdered Stephen—shot him three times in cold blood; but he had definitely photographed her with Stephen. And Stephen with Angelina Benson. He was very likely the one who'd rigged her bedroom with a video camera. So if he didn't actually kill Stephen, maybe he had witnessed someone else pulling the trigger.

Shit! Was that it? Nicolas had been following *her*... and had inadvertently *witnessed* the murder? Excitement coursed her veins.

Had he also stolen her blue raincoat, the silver card case, and the latex glove with her prints inside it and planted them, along with the adulterous video, to lead Hiller to Catherine?

But, *why?* What would Nicolas gain from having Catherine incarcerated for murder? Was he *that* pissed about the divorce? Didn't make sense. Maybe he really *had* killed Stephen.

She exited the freeway on Tiburon Boulevard and turned into Nicolas's subdivision. She switchbacked up the mountainside, San Francisco skyline twinkling in the distance across the Bay.

She pulled to a stop fifty yards from Nicolas's driveway. His house was a sprawling dark shadow; she tried to recall the layout. The Pontiac engine ticked loudly in the frosty night air as she stepped from the car and quietly closed the door, tugging on black leather driving gloves, zipping her jacket against the cold. The scent of pine mingled with loamy peat and night-blooming Jasmine. A plump quarter moon hung crooked in the sky.

The streets were dark; no street lights. A neighbor three doors away rolled trashcans up his hillside drive into a brightly lit garage; the garage door trundled down. Catherine's pinlight illuminated Nicolas's asphalt driveway. Window slits on either side of the wide, black-lacquered door confirmed darkness inside, except for a green glow on the home security system keypad. She was surprised Nicolas-the-paranoid had gone out without arming the alarm.

She pressed the bell; chimes bonged. No response. Perfect. He'd never confess to witnessing a murder, or videotaping her in her own bedroom, so she'd just find her own proof. She opened her tool kit and fished out two thin metal shafts that she used to work the lock.

Inside the house, standing quietly, she heard a thermostat click on; warm air from a floor vent circulated around her socks. Mustiness hung in the air, as if he never opened the windows.

"Nicolas? Hello?"

No response. She fingered the gun tucked tight in her waistband.

She found his study at the end of the hall. Long desk on the right; bookshelves stacked to the ceiling on the left. Pinlight scanned the shelves. No videotapes.

On a ledge in the walk-in closet she spied a black curly wig and recalled the dog-walker's description of "the stove guy"; she kept the beam moving to two gray metal file cabinets that stood shoulder to shoulder. A quick inspection revealed patient files in the first cabinet;

the second, personal stuff. Mortgage files and credit card statements in the first drawer; and a folder with a lease contract for a storage unit at a place called U-Stor on Army Street in San Francisco. She memorized the unit number and decided her next priority was to get a look at its contents. The second drawer...

Catherine sensed a presence before a voice said, "If you move I'll shoot you."

Nicolas. Catherine felt both fear and relief: at least it wasn't Hiller.

A bright flashlight flicked to life and bounced wavering shadows off the closet walls.

"My, my Nicky. Is this a fantasy enactment from your shrink tool-kit? Kill off the ex and you'll feel better?"

"Turn around. Slowly."

She complied, squinted around the powerful beam. She couldn't separate his form from the inky darkness that surrounded him. "Where are the videotapes? Who killed Stephen?"

"You should have been arrested by now." His voice was tight. Testy.

"Why are you doing this, Nicolas?" She inched forward ever so slightly.

"Back up!"

She hesitated, retreated one step.

"All the way against the file cabinets."

She moved until metal pressed her spine.

"All this preening in the press... Guardian of privacy." His voice dripped with disdain.

She was surprised at his venom. "I never realized you were this angry about the divorce."

"Of course you didn't," he sneered. "You're so smug and self-absorbed—couldn't wait to dump me now that your bratty daughter is past her childhood traumas and you don't need me to minister to her any more."

The flashlight shifted and a reflection lit Nicolas's face. His dark eyes burned with hatred. Catherine wanted to rebut Nicolas's skewed perceptions, but her instinct for self-preservation kept her silent.

"Catherine the Great," he spat. "Darling of your industry. Posing for the cover of national magazines... raking in a hefty salary while I sit and await my monthly stipend." His tone changed to mockery. "How are you enjoying the limelight now, dear?"

"How long have you been following me?"

"Almost a year." He smirked with great satisfaction. "But not just you—your boy toy, too. I've gotten quite proficient with surveillance technology."

"And apparently at breaking and entering as well, since you found it so easy to get into my apartment. You didn't have any trouble boosting my blue raincoat and tan pashmina and planting it for Hiller to find."

He seemed unable to control the smug grin that split his face.

"You took Stephen's briefcase out of his car—found the keys to the apartment..."

"You always did underestimate my many talents, dear."

"This stupid scheme won't work, Nicolas. I'm going to trip you up."

"Ah, yes. Mistress of *my* universe. What are you going to do—divulge your suspicions?"

"You took the beach photos with your old Nikon. I can prove that."

"I believe the crime of import is murder, not photography. And you can't prove murder because I didn't commit it."

"But you know who did."

"Go quietly, Catherine. Let them arrest you. Your high-priced attorney will get you acquitted." A smirk in his voice. "But in the meantime, it kinda fucks up your precious ETC. And your relationship with the big-shot grape-farmer. By the way, did he like the audiotape? Should I send him some videos to entertain him while you're indisposed?"

The light beam bounced to the sidewall. Catherine lunged toward the opening. The light extinguished and she careened off the closet door at the same instant it slammed shut. A lock clicked. She tried the doorknob—rattled it.

"Let me out, you prick!"

"Such language from the world-famous guardian of privacy."

"You won't get away with this, Nicolas."

"Ex-wife in jail—maybe even on Death Row. Wow. Every man's wet dream."

"Kiss your alimony goodbye, asshole."

"Oh, yes. Your big hold over me. Well, you'd be surprised how financially self-sufficient I've become."

Movement. A chair squeak. Footfalls on carpet.

"Have a nice life, dear." His voice was distant. From the hall?

She pounded with her fists. "Nicolas! Open this door!"

Silence.

She groped the wall, found the light switch and clicked it on. A deadbolt stood between her and freedom.

"One more fucking lock," she snarled as she dug for the lock shims in her tool bag.

An ear-splitting, "Waaahhnn, waaahhnn, waaahhnn," pierced the night. Catherine jerked involuntarily and the tool kit spilled on the closet floor.

Shit! The burglar alarm! He had triggered the alarm so the cops would come!

The continuous "Waaahhnn" made her frantic. She had to get out of there!

She yanked the gun from her waistband, ejected the empty clip, dug three bullets from her pocket, and shoved them into the magazine with trembling fingers. She crouched in the corner and fired one shot directly into the deadbolt. The explosion concussed her eardrums and blew out the lightbulb. Smoke and cordite curled into her lungs. She kung-fu'd the door, flicked on the pinlight, scooped up her tool bag, and raced for the front door. The "Waaahhn, waaahhnn" barely penetrated the numbness in her ears.

The front door stood ajar; glass from the broken window crunched beneath her shoes.

Dickhead. He was making a career of framing her!

Headlights flashed on the street above. Catherine reversed through the kitchen and out the back door. She pounded across the deck, down wooden stairs, and thrashed through greenery to the back property line. The burglar alarm drowned out everything except a pack of neighborhood dogs that barked and howled from various locations.

She scaled a fence, snagged her palm on stiff wire, and darted between two houses to the street below. Headlights flared; a car engine gunned around a bend. Catherine stumbled backward and crouched between bushy ferns waiting for the car to speed by.

At the bottom of the hill, she watched lines of traffic flowing east and west on Tiburon Boulevard. A green and white Tiburon-bound bus slowed and signaled its intent to turn into the bus stop across the boulevard. Catherine waited for a break in traffic, dashed across the four lanes, and climbed on board just before the doors closed. She dug in her pocket and counted out correct change. Slouched low in a back seat, she realized that somewhere along the way she'd lost her tool bag.

In downtown Tiburon she slumped behind a dumpster for forty minutes until it was time to board a San Francisco–bound ferry. She bought a one-way ticket and took refuge in a smelly bathroom stall, subconsciously monitoring the thrum of giant diesel engines as she evaluated her options.

It was too risky to go to her neighborhood to pick up one of the rental vehicles. The cops were probably still watching George Hallison–maybe even Joel and Wilson, too; and who knew what was going on with Maureen O'Malley.

What about Laura? They'd agreed to meet at Garibaldi's at nine; the ferry would moor at the San Francisco Ferry Terminal at ten after nine.

Catherine reflexively patted her pockets, looking for her cell. Nada. There would be a pay phone on the dock. She checked her jeans for phone change; came up short. She dug in her jacket pocket, found three more quarters, a wad of tissues, and a crumpled business card. Paused when she saw the gold-crested logo of San Francisco Financial Service. Stephen's card.

Her brow creased. She tried to remember putting it in her jacket pocket. Turned it over and read the initials "R. L." and the phone number penned on the back. Recalled her efforts to locate the owner of that phone number—and that Joel's search had also been fruitless.

Maybe it wasn't a phone number.

"R, L", she whispered aloud. "Right. Left. Holy shit."

Catherine forced a saunter as she exited the boat, conscious of blending with the other passengers. She ducked into the first phone booth and dialed Laura's cell.

"If you get this message, meet me at Stephen's apartment," she hurriedly rattled off the address. "I think I know how to open his safe."

The taxi's headlights swept a row of parked cars as it turned onto Stephen's street. Catherine spotted Laura's Jag at the curb.

She paid the driver and climbed into the passenger seat of Laura's car.

"What's going–" Laura began, but Catherine cut her off.

"I'm so glad you're here. Hiller has a warrant for my arrest. He's got the gun that killed Stephen and my prints are on it—but never mind that. Nicolas witnessed the murder—he knows who did it and he framed me, the fucker. I was at his house two hours ago, but he got away."

"Stop! You're not making sense—I can't follow this."

Catherine slumped as she heaved an exhalation. "Sorry. I'm just so..." She opened the car door. "You wait here. I'm going to go try to open the safe. If Nicolas shows up, come warn me. I'll be in apartment 201."

Inside the building, Catherine took the stairs two at a time then quietly stalked the carpeted hallway and knocked softly on Stephen's door. No answer.

She turned the key in the deadbolt, but it wasn't locked. She frowned, certain she'd locked it when she left that morning. Maybe Nicolas had been here since then—maybe he was in there now. Or maybe Hiller found out about this crash pad. Her pulse ratcheted up.

She clicked the doorknob lock, stepped quickly inside. She stood perfectly still, holding her breath, leaning against the door, one hand still on the knob. Listening. Hearing only the buzz of the refrigerator motor.

Something smelled foul. Like a backed-up sewer. Like Garbo's occasional bouts of diarrhea. She breathed through her mouth to minimize the effect.

Window shades were drawn, emitting only the faintest glow from the streetlights outside. She moved stealthily to the living room. A dark shadow spread the floor near the park-side bay window. She squinted through the darkness; it didn't move. Listened for noises—sounds of breathing—of motion. A steady, barely perceptible hiss came from the left; the radio dial was illuminated, two pinpoint lights on the tape deck glowed bright red. Water dripped in the kitchen. She inched toward the table lamp, flicked it to low. Squeaked and suppressed the urge to scream.

The shadow was a torso... legs stretched beyond the sofa. Blood outlined a sprawled right arm and congealed in a pool beside curled fingers. She recognized the ring on the right hand.

"No, oh no," Catherine whispered, her heart beating so hard her vision blurred. She rounded the sofa to see the face.

Nicolas. Slack-jawed. Wide-eyed. Surprised for eternity.

"Nicolas," she whispered urgently; stooped and shoved her palm beneath his nose.

No breath. No rise and fall of his chest.

Oh, God. Tears threatened.

Then, panic set in. Here she was, having shed a trail of forensic evidence—shoeprints, hairs, fibers from her clothes next to the dead body of her ex-husband, in her late lover's secret crash pad.

She leapt up and lunged for the exit. Stopped with her hand on the knob.

This was her only chance to get at Stephen's safe. She hesitated only a moment; whirled and dashed to the bedroom.

The closet light glowed and a brown canvas tool bag lay open on the floor. A heavy mallet and a twelve-inch screwdriver were propped against the door of the red safe. Scratches marred the lock dial, but it responded freely when she twirled it.

With jittery fingers, she dug the business card out of her jeans pocket, studied the blue writing. "R L" on the top line; "3 46–19 01" underneath. Spun the dial again; stopped on 3. Twisted left to 46, right to 19, left to 1. Grasped the captain's wheel and pulled. No resistance—it didn't engage with the locking mechanism.

She ran one hand through her hair.

"Okay," she said and took a deep breath. She studied the card, pondered what she was missing. If she were writing the combination to her own safe, she would encrypt it in some way.

The "R" was directly over the 3 and the 46; the L over the 19 and 01. She tried again, this time starting with the 3 to the right, 19 to the left, 46 to the right and back to the 1. She took a deep breath and grabbed the handle. Resistance! Her heart hammered in her chest. She cranked hard, gears chugged against each other. The door swung heavily.

Yes!

Inside, were shelves—six of them. Each was stacked with white boxes. But, unlike the empty boxes on the closet shelf above, these were labeled with black marker. Some had names—she immediately spotted "Rina"; some had letters... like initials.

Her eyes gravitated to one box on the bottom shelf. Unmistakable initials. She squatted. With trembling hands, she slid it from the shelf, rested it on her thighs. Removed the lid. Stared.

Inside, a one-inch stack of photos. The first a naked woman. Face, half-hidden by a swirl of strawberry curl, contorted in ecstasy apparently generated by the two naked men who sandwiched her.

Catherine lifted the photo. Held it to the light. Heard a click from behind; didn't bother to turn.

"You're looking pretty sexy here, girlfriend," Catherine said sadly. "But if this got published on the cover of *The National Enquirer*, Senator Ben Admire wouldn't be able to get elected to sort letters at the U.S. Post Office."

"Drop it back in the box and put the top on," Laura instructed.

Catherine sifted the stack of photos, all equally incriminating, as she said, "This whole thing is about the Gregg/Admire legislation, isn't it? Stephen told his Operating Committee he had connections with the Senator. Everyone assumed it was because of the relationship between Admire and Stephen's late grandfather... but it was really you, wasn't it? He was blackmailing you to use your influence with Ben to get him to withdraw that bill." She covered the box, rose, and turned to her friend. Laura stood in a shooter's stance, a silenced .357 in silver relief against a navy sweatshirt. The gun was aimed at Catherine's chest.

Laura shook her head grimly. "Body count rising because of stupid political maneuvering."

Catherine felt a heavy sorrow more than fear. "I've always heard murder is like that potato chip commercial... you can't kill just one."

"Ben Admire is a good man. He does good work in this world. I couldn't let Stephen use illicit photos of me to taint Ben's legacy."

"Oh, please. That spin might play to a Geraldo audience, but let's be real: you were protecting your own self-interests. You robbed the nest, then realized you weren't going to enjoy the eggs 'cause you were about to be picking buckshot out of your ass."

"I hate those cutesy shitkicker homilies." Laura backed away from the closet door, wagged the gun to the right. "Go to the living room."

"What are you gonna do? Kill me, too? I'm your friend, Laura. Look me in the eye and tell me you can do this."

The hammer clicked back. Laura's eyes were as cold and steady as the big gun.

"Jesus," Catherine whispered. "You are—you're going to kill me."

Laura wagged the gun again. "Go."

Catherine moved cautiously; she knew she couldn't get to the pistol that was tucked in her waistband. Suddenly feared this story was going to have a really bad, irreversible conclusion.

"Nicolas stalked me," Catherine said, thinking she might create some diversion. Some moment of inattention that she could use to her advantage. "He inadvertently saw you shoot Stephen. Figured he would carry on the extortion game after Stephen was dead; but he wanted money, not your influence with the Senator; that's why he wasn't worried about the alimony."

In the living room Laura said, "Put the box on the table."

Catherine set the box beside the lamp.

"You broke into that apartment last night. You're the one who tampered with the lock. You're the one who called the cops when Wilson and I showed up."

"Turn around and take off your jacket."

"What did you find? Videotapes of you shooting Stephen?" Catherine unzipped the windbreaker, spread it slowly.

"I found out Nicolas was my blackmailer *du jour*." Her lips pulled tight in disgust. "First Stephen with his photos of my party girl days, then Nicolas with his video camera." She shook her head. "Where was it ever going to end?" She nodded toward Catherine's waist. "What's under your sweatshirt? Raise it slowly."

Catherine complied. Laura looked surprised when she saw Buzz Benson's gun tucked in Catherine's waistband.

Catherine slowly reached for the gun handle.

"You ready to feel your heart stop beating?"

Catherine stopped.

"Turn around." She motioned with the gun. "Keep your feet where they are, stretch your hands high over your head... lean your palms flat against the doorjamb."

Catherine was angled like half a pyramid, precariously balanced. The muzzle of Laura's gun pressed the base of Catherine's skull as Laura tugged the .45 free.

"You checked in for your four o' clock flight to New York. I confirmed the airline records."

"You hackers can't account for the human element. Lucky for me, the airline overbooked. Some schmoe who got bumped to a later flight offered me a hundred bucks to trade boarding passes. I didn't plan to kill Stephen—or even to see him that day. Everything just unfolded to a natural conclusion." Pressure relieved from Catherine's nape; she heard the .45's clip being ejected. "I'm surprised at you, Catherine; this gun's actually loaded." Clip clicked back into place. "Turn around."

Catherine faced her captor as Laura tucked Buzz's gun into the waistband of her sweats.

"You were talking to Stephen on the phone when I got into the car that afternoon. You arranged to meet him."

"He said he would give me the pictures. The fucker lied." She grimaced and nodded toward a blue nylon gym bag by the darkroom door. "Unzip that bag."

Catherine squatted. "How did you get Nicolas to meet you here?" She worked the zipper.

"That was a good one." She actually smiled. "He was really surprised when I called and announced I knew he was extorting me. He denied it, of course—thought he'd been so clever. I told him you'd led me to the apartment across the street and that I found photos of you and Stephen at the beach. That was the clincher. He said that didn't mean anything to him, so I asked if it meant more that 'N. Calabretta' was inked on a laundry tag on the sheets in the bedroom. I convinced him I would take him down as an accessory if I got nailed for Stephen's murder. I offered the greedy bastard five hundred thousand dollars, cash, for the video; and to sweeten the deal, I told him the only way to ensure we were both free was if I killed you, too." Her expression was wry, she wrinkled her nose. "I think he liked that idea."

Laura nodded toward the gym bag. "Take out the sweatband and the duct tape. And the rope."

"So he came here..." Catherine focused her peripheral vision on the electronics stacked on the shelf over Laura's left shoulder. The tuner and tape deck were both on. Couldn't be sure from the distance, but she thought the "record" light glowed red. Good old Nicolas.

"Quit screwing around! Get the stuff!"

The items were at the end of the bag—a coil of heavy brown rope on top, silver tape and black wristband tucked between the bag's edge and a folded white, silk blouse.

"Put both hands through the band. Use it like handcuffs."

Catherine rose, stood perfectly still, eyed Laura rebelliously.

Laura heaved a heavy sigh. "Okay, here's the deal. Let's save time and cut the redundancy. Assume the following applies to every instruction I give you." She spoke meticulously. "If you don't do what I say, I'm going to shoot you. Got it?"

Catherine laid the duct tape on the sofa table, slowly worked the tight black band over her hands. "What about the evidence against you? He must have tapes... photos..."

"I'm going to search his place as soon as I leave here."

"How are you going to tie up all the loose ends? Two more dead bodies might draw some attention, don't you think?"

"It's the natural conclusion to a love triangle. Having just murdered your ex-husband, you realize your only option is to commit suicide."

"I'm not going to kill myself, Laura."

"I never intended for you to be involved in this, Catherine—you have Nicolas to thank for that. But once you were implicated, I did everything I could to have you simply go to jail. I didn't want to have to kill you. But Nicolas..." She shrugged. "As you yourself have said, sometimes you just have to ride the horse in the direction it's already going." Laura motioned. "Go into the dining room."

Catherine turned, inched into the dark space, and stopped.

"Keep moving."

She complied. Heard Laura behind her; then the overhead light flashed on. Electronics component boxes were stacked under the window; one ladderback chair edged against the wall.

"Hold out your wrists, straight in front of you."

Laura laid the rope coil on the countertop, ripped loose a foot-long strip of duct tape. Angled closer to Catherine.

"Do you have any doubts about my willingness to pull this trigger?"

Catherine held Laura's gaze. Didn't answer. Extended her fists.

Laura moved in and, with her free hand, draped the duct tape over the sweatband. Wrapped it tight, firmly binding Catherine's wrists together.

"How many people commit suicide with their wrists bound?" Catherine asked.

"I'll cut you free. There'll be no evidence—no marks, no tape, residue."

"You've given this a lot of thought."

"Get the chair." She nodded toward the ladderback. "Put it in the middle of the room."

Catherine moved slowly. Deliberately.

Laura unwound the rope. It had already been fashioned into a noose.

"Are you expecting the Terminator to come and help you put that thing around my neck?" Catherine's voice was icy with hostility.

"The choice is yours: death by hanging... or by gunshot."

Catherine's mind raced. She had to buy time. "Fine," she said through clenched teeth.

Laura gave a semi-smile. "Move to the wall and face it."

Catherine did as instructed, heard Laura climb on the chair, heard rope threading through metal.

Laura dropped to the floor. Moved away.

"Up on the chair."

Catherine turned slowly. The noose dangled from the center of the ceiling. She hadn't previously noticed the ornate, wedding-cake moldings and the flourish of eggshell plaster blossoms that surrounded the old-fashioned, iron light fixture. She stared at it. Was certain it was strong enough to support her weight.

"Get up there!" Laura said, shifting weight to one foot then the other like a sprinter anxious to begin a race.

Catherine inched toward the chair, maintaining steely eye contact with Laura.

The eerie quiet was broken by a series of clicks, mechanical switching—the tape deck reversing. Laura whirled, swiveled the gun in the direction of the sound.

Catherine dropped her shoulders like a linebacker, lunged at Laura as the woman started to bring the gun back around. Catherine hit her at waist-height with adrenaline-fueled vengeance, sending Laura stumbling into the living room.

The gun fired with a loud sphut; a window shattered.

Catherine kept going—butted the woman as hard as she could. Laura's feet tangled and she began to topple. She extended her hands to brace her fall. The gun flew loose and bounced on the carpet, fired again, taking out plaster on the opposite wall. Laura hit the floor, wrist twisting with a stomach-turning snap. She howled in pain. Catherine's own momentum kept her toppling in Laura's direction. She tried to hurdle the woman's prone body, but her toe snagged and she felt herself freefalling. She cleared Laura's fallen form, landed on her chest with a neck-snapping whiplash, and rolled. She struggled to her feet. Stumbled back toward her nemesis.

Laura laid on her back, clutching her wrist, face so white it was translucent. She whimpered like a coyote caught in a trap.

Someone pounded the door. "Open up!"

Fear—anger—flared in Laura's eyes. With her uninjured hand, she grabbed for the Colt .45 wedged in her waistband.

"Nooooo!" Catherine screamed and dove toward Laura, bound hands outstretched and grasping. Laura tried to scramble away as she frantically tugged at the gun. Catherine dropped to her knees, smashed into Laura's abdomen, and grabbed for the pistol. Lost her balance, pitched on top of Laura. Gunshot concussed the room.

Catherine lay perfectly still. Sticky wetness saturate her shirtfront. She held her breath, waited for pain. None came.

Laura moaned. Catherine rolled off the woman and onto the carpet as the front door splintered open. Wilson's crouched figure cleared the doorway.

"Call an ambulance," Catherine rasped. "Laura's been shot."

Epilogue: Thursday

It had been a harrowing two days.

Laura was in stable condition under police guard at San Francisco General after surgery to remove a bullet from her abdomen. Senator Ben Admire had thrown his love-train into reverse so fast it took out all his political consultants who'd been riding in the caboose.

When the cops showed up on Tuesday night, Catherine had immediately surrendered. They took her in, booked her on the Country Club assault charges, put her in a cell, and waited for Hiller. Jordan Lawrence arrived and, when Hiller came to question her in the wee hours of Wednesday morning, Lawrence negotiated with every piece of info Catherine passed to Hiller. She told Hiller about the storage unit Nicolas kept on Army Street. According to Lawrence's subsequent report, Hiller found a library of videos shot in Catherine's bedroom and, more importantly, an audiotape and a half-dozen stills of Laura shooting Stephen. That, combined with the tape of the conversation between Laura and Catherine—the one that had reversed and startled Laura into shifting her focus away from Catherine for one fortunate moment—convinced Hiller he'd targeted the wrong woman.

Chloe had arrived from Paris on Wednesday afternoon. "Perfect timing, honey," Catherine said, as she hugged her daughter at the airport arrival gate. "The twilight-zone circus just packed up its big-top and skedaddled out of town. The only thing on our agenda for the next couple of days is to reintroduce you to the American way of life: shopping, hamburgers, and Mom's apple pie." After twenty-four hours of togetherness, Chloe headed off to visit her San Francisco friends.

Now, as wind whipped Catherine's hair and flapped the long scarf that wound her neck, the sight of Garbo romping down Ocean Beach, rousting seabirds and tussling playfully with other dogs, brought a smile to Catherine's lips. But she knew that wouldn't last: she had a commitment to keep. Catherine pulled the whistle from her vest pocket, summoned the dog, and headed for the Rover. With Garbo toweled down and curled on the back seat, Catherine drove toward Maureen O'Malley's house.

She'd confirmed earlier that morning that James Dunleavy, a partner in Beverly Rathman's law firm and himself a paraplegic confined to a wheelchair for life by a climbing accident seven years ago, had indeed visited O'Malley to outline the "options" in her brother's pursuit of conservatorship. According to James, he didn't know if he'd dented O'Malley's ennui.

No matter. Catherine still had to honor her promise.

At five fifteen, Catherine stood in Maureen's living room. O'Malley sat under the fluorescent lights in the middle of the kitchen, head dropped, studying hands that lay lax in her lap. Garbo sat stoically beside the wheelchair.

"You probably heard Nicolas is dead and they arrested Laura," Catherine said conversationally. "They found—"

Maureen raised one hand, palm open. Catherine stopped.

Silently, Catherine went into the garage, pulled out a ladder, climbed to the ceiling, and pushed through a trapdoor that opened onto a narrow crawl space. Inside she located Hiller's .38 that she'd stashed there after his surprise visit on Friday. She removed the weapon, opened the cylinder, and verified it was empty. In the kitchen, she placed the gun exactly where Hiller had put it six nights ago. She straddled a bar stool across the counter from Maureen and removed the orange box of bullets from her vest pocket. She passed it back and forth between her palms. Slowly. Feeling the weight of it.

"The first time we spoke you told me Jesus had come to you in a dream and told you that I was your angel of salvation." Catherine's nostrils stung. Tears welled.

O'Malley watched the orange box. Catherine wiped her nose on the back of a trembling hand.

"I'm not a religious person," Catherine continued. "I don't buy into the idea of some old bearded white guy sitting on a celestial throne marking my personal score card... but I do believe that we're guided and we're watched over by an all-knowing being. I believe that we come into each life to learn certain things... and that, along the way, we encounter the people who can help us with those lessons." Her voice dropped to a whisper. "I wish I knew for sure... that I'm doing the right thing."

She took a deep breath and straightened her spine. "James Dunleavy can help you. You don't have to live under your brother's control—or anyone else's. You can build a new life, Maureen... and the world will be a better place if you remain in it."

Catherine held up the orange box and Maureen's eyes gravitated to it, locked it in her steadfast gaze. "With every fiber of my being screaming not to do this, I'm honoring my commitment to you." She laid the bullets beside the gun.

Maureen inched toward the counter and stretched out her hand. She nestled the .38... and tenderly laid the gun in her lap. She reached for the box of bullets and, for the first time, made eye contact with Catherine. Face soft, eyes gentle. "You've been a good friend, Catherine," she said tenderly. "Now it's time for you to go."

Catherine nodded. She dug a tissue from her pocket, blotted her eyes, wiped her nose, and headed down the hall. Hand on doorknob; she glanced back over her shoulder. Garbo sat statuesque beside O'Malley.

"Garbo, come." Catherine quietly commanded.

O'Malley raised her hand, gently stroked the dog's head... down her neck. Once. Twice. Then rested her hand on the gun in her lap.

Garbo followed Catherine out the front door.